APROPOS JIMMY INKLING

APROPOS JIMMY INKLING

BRIAN MARLEY

grand **IOTA**

Published by
grand**IOTA**

2 Shoreline, St Margaret's Rd, St Leonards TN37 6FB
&
37 Downsway, North Woodingdean, Brighton BN2 6BD

www.grandiota.co.uk

First edition 2019
Copyright © Brian Marley, 2019. All rights reserved.

Typesetting & book design by Reality Street

ISBN: 978-1-874400-73-8

Nobody owns life, but anyone who can pick up a frying pan owns death.

– William S Burroughs –

sing late o'clock
news and hopes absent

– Tom Phillips –

For help along the way
my thanks to
Ken Edwards

This book
is for
Joanna Swann

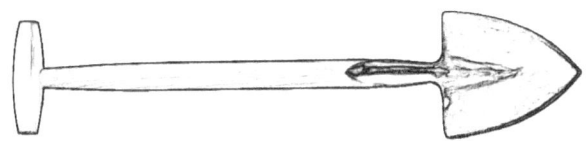

~~~: In the rotten heart of the criminal underworld, hidden from the prying eyes and ears of various law enforcement agencies, Jimmy Inkling is king. The man to go to if you want something done. The fixer's fixer.

CUSTOMER: Eh?

~~~: I know whereof I speak: in the many years I've known him he's done me favours galore, not all of which he expects to be repaid. In short, he's a sweetie. And versatile, a quick thinker, a game changer. Nothing fazes him.

CUSTOMER: Good to know. But why you're telling me this I have no idea.

~~~: Most recently he arranged something very much out of the ordinary: the vasectomy of one of my friend's daughter's unsuitable (to everyone but the daughter) boyfriend. I argued against death or castration, the radical solutions proposed by my friend, and Jimmy, on principle, agreed. All things considered, he's a principled fellow.

CUSTOMER: Is he indeed?

~~~: The friend – who shall remain nameless, he's a member of Parliament, it might affect his standing with the electorate – tried everything in his power to get his daughter to relinquish the ghastly youth. Chained her by her ankle

to her bed like a fairytale princess. Had her placed under heavy sedation in a grim lockdown facility for psychiatric patients near York. Sent her to a month-long lesbian induction workshop at Gels of Ramingining, the only internationally recognised finishing school for young ladies of wealth and distinction in Australia's largely uninhabited Northern Territory. No joy. Argument and bribery didn't work, either with the boyfriend or her, and enforced absence seemed to make the girl's heart grow – despite her hatred of platitudes and almost everything else, including, alas, her dear devoted dad – fonder.

What she was so stubbornly fond of was a gangly, ferret-faced youth, a long streak of piss and vinegar with chip-pan pallor and unfathomable sex appeal but

According to the daughter
on the telephone
her conversation accidentally overheard.

a colossal 'shaft of life'

Feeling broody
perhaps?

and a matching libido. He was inarticulate to a degree that suggested imbecility. Apparently he also deemed personal hygiene a bourgeois affectation.

'Glands are the source of the problem,' said my broken-hearted friend. 'If only we could remove all the glands, and while we're at it his liver and lights. Using something like a blunt spoon. Or perhaps a crowbar. Without anaesthetic or benefit of clergy.'

There speaks a loving father, a man worried sick, at the end of his tether, discharging his pent-up frustration like a squall of acid rain. Perfectly understandable. Were you in his shoes I suspect you'd feel the same way too.

CUSTOMER: You may well be right. Now, if you'll excuse me ...

~~~: The problem seemed insoluble, but Jimmy, quick off the blocks as always, suggested an alternative. 'Why not,' he said, 'give the boyfriend a surreptitious vasectomy, so that at least she, your friend's lovely daughter, his baby girl,

> Baby girl?
> At the last flick of the abacus beads
> she was all of twenty-two!

can't get pregnant. Not by him, anyway, the skunky stud.'

Late one night, in a West End drinking club, the boy was befriended by a couple of Jimmy's operatives, moonlighting medical students. They invited him over to their table and topped him up with hi-octane Belgian beer and a brace of whisky chasers. Hewing to the script provided by Jimmy, they claimed to be celebrating a spectacular once-in-a-thousand-lifetimes win at Haydock Park and Aintree on a doubled-up six-fold accumulator. That's right, *doubled* – whoever heard of such a thing?

> According to Srinivasa Ramanujan
> [or someone
> claiming to speak for him]
> the odds against
> this happening are so great they're
> impossible to comprehend
> and thinking
> incomprehensible thoughts
> can lead to
> headaches
> nausea
> anxiety
> and despair.
> Ramanujan's advice:
> Place simpler bets and
> whistle a happy tune.

CUSTOMER: Not me, that's for sure. Isn't anyone serving in
here?

~~~: They wanted, one of them said (as per the script), to share
some of the fruits of their outrageous good fortune. Share
it with just one other person, someone of honest mien,
suggestive of sound character, to whom they could safely
confide. Someone who'd join them in celebration but quietly, without drawing the attention of the vultures, rats,
cockroaches and vipers in human form that are always
worryingly near. They'd steal the very breath from your
mouth if they could, worthless to them though it is. As for
tomorrow ... well, it's another day, as all top-drawer
philosophers have been telling us since time immemorial,
and only an utter blockhead would gainsay their wisdom.
Tomorrow the whole world will know the epic scale of the
win. All hell will break loose. Life will never be the same
again, and aspects of it are bound to change for the
worse. It's inevitable. So while we can let's enjoy this
moment of reprieve, the heavenly calm before the apocalyptic shitstorm.

Having got that semi-plausible soliloquy out of the
way, celebrate they did. Soon he, the boyfriend, was para-
lytically drunk whereas miraculously they remained stone
cold sober. At closing time they waltzed him off the premises, one at either side, cupping his elbows to keep him
upright so he didn't spill, his legs swinging like pendu-
lums, toes barely skimming the floor.

What happened next must be left
to the reader's imagination
and/or
medical knowledge
assuming the reader is in
possession
of such things.

Just before dawn the boy regained consciousness, still reeling drunk, feeling like puke, dehydrated and aching all over, with a nagging/stabbing pain in the groin occasioned, he thought, by nothing more than a beer-swollen bladder. To his great relief and even greater surprise, nothing bad seemed to have happened: neither sexual assault nor vicious mugging. He staggered to his feet and pissed where he stood, with difficulty, against a large metal refuse bin that was accustomed to such indignities. The dried pool of blood in the crotch of his boxer shorts wasn't noticed until hours later, nor the ugly, inflamed keyhole wounds that looked like flea bites, little different from his other flea bites, just bigger.

To this day he probably has no idea that his sperm count is zero.

No future father he.

As Jimmy put it, with an unapologetic cackle: 'He's the Cockfosters of the procreative line.'

CUSTOMER: Hang on. Is that the same Jimmy Inkling who, at the tender age of nineteen, won the Victoria Cross for valour in QUOTE the face of imminent death, against insurmountable odds, under heavy machine gun and sniper fire UNQUOTE, who used the butt of his standard issue Enfield rifle like a cricket bat to send a German stick grenade caroming into the muzzle of a rapidly approaching Panzer tank, killing the crew and, in the nick of time, stopping the vehicle from crushing several of his comrades, one of whom, having lost an eye in the conflict and most of his wits, would later become a key advisor to Margaret Thatcher during her first term as Prime Minister?

~~~: The very same. You can read about that and Jimmy's many other World War Two exploits in a recently published omnibus edition entitled *Inkling Uncut* (books #2-4 in the Jimmy Inkling series), which consists of three highly acclaimed novels, classics of war literature, up

there with books by Heller and Wouk, that had, because of a copyright muddle, long been out of print. Their titles: *Fate Favours the Brave, Fountains of Blood*, and *Fighting Force Majeure.*

CUSTOMER: Is that also the Jimmy Inkling whose name was added to the 1943 Honours Board at Lord's Cricket Ground, although according to William Joyce, aka Lord Haw Haw, in one of the pro-Nazi anti-Semitic radio rants that got him hung as a traitor after the war, Inkling never played a satisfactory innings in his life?

~~~: That's him. Not much of a cricketer, he'd be the first to admit. The straight drive that sent the grenade soaring back from whence it came, or thereabouts, was a wild shot, a fluke.

CUSTOMER: It beggars belief.

~~~: How so?

CUSTOMER: The character of that brave, noble man and this ... this fiend. They're two different people, surely.

~~~: I can see why you might think that. But if you bear with me, I hope to persuade you otherwise.

CUSTOMER: Don't feel you have to, I'm really not fussed. In fact –

~~~: What manner of man is Jimmy Inkling? In a word, complex. As are we all, the male of the species. Apart, that is, from the likes of Mr Snipped Vas Deferens, the aforementioned boyfriend, an incestuously begotten son of an incestuously begotten son and, long way back, of Portuguese origin, one of Vasco da Gama's more distant relatives, a diseased bud on the spindliest twig of the family tree, not that he's aware of it.

Or
for that matter
who da Gama was.
So much for the benefit of
an expensive public
school education.

His complexity was evidenced only by the unnaturally large cluster of nerve endings in the glans of his penis, a bodily appendage he wields with the subtlety of a club.

CUSTOMER: I hate to nitpick, but don't you mean complicated rather than complex?

~~~: Certainly not! You don't know Jimmy Inkling like I do. In fact, apart from a few factoids gleaned from *Who's Who* or Wikipedia, you obviously know nothing about him.

CUSTOMER: Well that's where you're wrong. Couldn't be more wrong if you tried. A decade ago I was a contestant on *Mastermind*.

~~~: The television quiz show?

CUSTOMER: The very same. Specialist subject: The History of Inkling Inc., 1967-2007. After the first round I was flying high, no wrong answers and only one pass. It was my general knowledge that let me down, not the Inkling stuff.

~~~: Inkling Inc. is one thing, Jimmy Inkling quite another. I still contend you know nothing about him, nothing of real importance. We need to remedy that situation, and fast. Let me call my first witness.

CUSTOMER: Witness? I came in here on the not unreasonable assumption that this was a café. That's what's written on the sign outside, and there's nothing but café paraphernalia in here. The predominant smell is of coffee, not periwigs and dusty legal tomes. Look, on every table there's a laminated menu and a defanged rose in a glass flute. Over there, chalked on a blackboard, a list of lunchtime specials. Paper napkins in a stainless steel dispenser. Sugar in a bowl. This is definitely a café, not a courtroom.

~~~: It's whatever I say it is, according to need. Let me call my first witness.

CUSTOMER: Oh well. If you must I suppose you must.

Opening Session

~~~: Please state your name, age, present occupation and place of domicile.

FIRST WITNESS: Blenkinsopp with two peas, Rodney James Fulwell, known to friends as Rodders or Roddy and to the branch of the film industry in which I work as Hot Rod, for obvious reasons. I'd rather not state my age, it's bad for business. Occupations (yes, plural): male model and actor, currently resting and residing on a friend's sofa in Kew.

~~~: Tell us, Mr Blenkinsopp, what you know of Jimmy Inkling.

BLENKINSOPP: He did funny voices and performed magic tricks at the sixth birthday party of a boy I went to school with. His name escapes me. Bland or Blunt, something like that. Not a close friend, obviously. The school itself has since been demolished. Absolutely riddled with asbestos it was, and said to be cursed. It had a resident ghost: a maths teacher who hung herself in the headmaster's office, or perhaps his secretary's office, circa 1960, reason unknown. On stormy nights she'd occasionally be heard chanting the prime numbers from two to forty-seven, the age at which she topped herself, in a creaky old-crone voice. That's what I was told. I've no idea where she went after the school got pulled down. Into retirement, I suppose. An old ghosts' home, if such a thing exists.

~~~: And Mr Inkling?

BLENKINSOPP: What about him?

~~~: We'd like to know more. Much more, if possible. And please try to keep to the point, we haven't got all day.

BLENKINSOPP: No need to use that tone of voice, just because you offered to pay my return fare from Kew and promised refreshments, which, by the way, have yet to materialise. Not even a sip of water offered in all the time we've been here. Anyway, there's not much more to tell, is there?

~~~: I really wouldn't know. Perhaps you'd care to enlighten us.

BLENKINSOPP: There's that tone again. You really are a supercilious little shit, aren't you?

~~~: Mr Blenkinsopp ...

BLENKINSOPP: Don't you Mr Blenkinsopp me. We, your unhappy band of witnesses, have been waiting in that cold, dingy corridor, sitting on rock-hard benches, those of us who've managed to get a seat, since 8:00AM. You wafted in at 11:45 without a word of apology and immediately went out to lunch – stepping over the prone body of Mr Ancrum, who'd fainted from the stress of standing for so long – and didn't return for three hours. Three whole hours! – we timed you to the second. Since then we've had to undergo various humiliating procedures, including a full body cavity search that was filmed by a sniggering camera crew for some sleazy documentary or other and, one at a time, a Q&A session on a polygraph machine, while naked, the film crew still in attendance, to determine whether we're reliable or not, capable of saying a horse is a vegetable without the machine throwing a hissy fit. But mostly we've been hanging around, fully clothed, awaiting your summons. Waiting and gradually losing the will to live, those of us who had that to begin with. And now it's early evening, the light fading fast, day almost done, and the proceedings have only just got underway. You ought to be ashamed of yourself for treating us in such a cavalier fashion!

~~~: Perhaps we should have a short recess, to repair frayed tempers and calm frazzled nerves ...

BLENKINSOPP: Don't bother. What little I know of Jimmy Inkling can be boiled down to a single sentence. He's an extremely tall man with a terrible facial scar, an Old Testament beard, and he drew rabbits out of a hat, white ones.

~~~: And ...?

BLENKINSOPP: That's it.

~~~: What do you mean?

BLENKINSOPP: Just what I said: That's it. That's all I know. It's what I was told.

~~~: You mean ... you didn't attend the party in question, didn't actually see Mr Inkling yourself, in person?

BLENKINSOPP: Correct.

~~~: No further questions.

$$\ominus$$

CUSTOMER: My curiosity has rather got the better of me, though I sincerely wish it hadn't. How come you seem to know so much about that vasectomised boy, what he did, thought and felt?

~~~: I'm a psychic medium. In the pantheon of the gods, a minor one.

CUSTOMER: I see. But I'm still not entirely sure I understand. Are you a minor psychic medium or a minor god?

~~~: Both.

CUSTOMER: Ah.

⊖

~~~: The mediumship speaks for itself but knows when to hold its tongue. (Yes, I know the day on which you're going to die. No, I'm not going to tell you when that is, so don't ask.) Whereas my role as a deity requires explanation. No-one seems to know what gods are for nowadays, or what it is they do. The thunderbolt and lightning hurlers are a thing of the past. They're more myth than reality; a product of simpler times and primitive minds. Compared to those ancient gods my powers are meagre. If only my responsibilities were too.

My current portfolio consists of nine tasks, some of which have to be undertaken on a daily basis, several monthly, one or two seasonal. The tasks become more onerous year by year. Take a peek at my desk diary – crammed to the margins and beyond with small, spindly script detailing appointments, prompts and final reminders, more than I, or indeed any god, no matter how diligent, can cope with. It's the same for all of us: an occupational nightmare.

I was also, for nearly a decade, the god of Lifts & Escalators (Escalifts, in the vernacular; an inelegant word). But after a woman (a popular minor character in a low-budget soap opera) and her designer dog (maltipoo: a cross between a maltese and a poodle) were killed in a lift that plummeted from penthouse to basement, unchecked by the failsafe mechanism, I was reprimanded by the Council of Elders and Escalifts was removed from my portfolio.

An altogether nasty business, the lift thing, I'm sure you agree. But the fault wasn't principally mine. Due to an administrative error the renewal paperwork hadn't been processed and the maintenance contract had lapsed. Unfortunately, the god responsible for Contractual Obligations, who should have been attending to the matter, had taken extended sick leave, and the email of delegation, sent to me by Human Resources (a title that never fails to amuse), was arrested en route to my inbox and jailed by an over-zealous spam filter. Although the elders took the filter into consideration, still they found me negligent, citing my admission that for several months I'd failed to detect and overturn this blatant miscarriage of justice.

Escalifts was reassigned to a slightly more senior deity (in years and experience) who, I gather, resented having it added to her already heavy workload. I sympathise, though not to the extent that I'd petition for its return.

The most problematic task is Squeaky Hinges. I'm responsible for Squeaky Hinges not just on a small industrial estate or even, I wish, in the several schools and colleges near where I ply my trade. No. My territory is huge – every odd numbered house in Friern Barnet south of the North Circular, including sheds and garages. Hinges by the tens of thousands! At regular but irregular-seeming intervals, to avoid suspicion of tampering, I have to make one of those thousands of hinges squeak. Then weeks, perhaps months after that particular hinge on that particular door has been oiled, greased or given an aerosol blast of WD40, a nearby hinge must be made to squeak. Even if all the hinges on a door are oiled at the same time, nonetheless one of them must eventually be persuaded to raise its voice above that of its colleagues, if hinges can be said to have colleagues. Otherwise our fellow humans

For gods are also human
or more human than not.
They look like humans and behave like
humans and although they're vastly superior to humans
they try not to draw attention
to themselves.

would be in danger of lapsing into complacency. And we can't have that, now can we? Although, to be honest, I'm not sure why complacency is so deeply frowned upon. It's just something we're told to guard against. That's been the case ever since doors, windows and hinges were invented, and those hotheads, the thunderbolt throwers, eventually settled down to a life of domesticity and peaceful god-human interaction.

> Domesticity but not necessarily marital bliss.
> The divorce rate among gods
> is significantly
> higher than that
> of the general population
> in the western world
> and drug and alcohol
> abuse is rife.

Gods are notoriously fickle, mysterious and cruel, that's what children are taught. It's how you humans – sometimes disparagingly referred to as 'puny mortals' by gods in their cups, as all too often we are, having been driven to drink by the unremitting pressures of work – account for things that defy rational explanation. Life-changing, terrifyingly dangerous things such as earthquakes, wildfires, volcanic eruptions, nuclear meltdown, typhoons and tsunamis. All of which – let's be clear about this – are completely beyond our control. We don't cause them. Nor can we prevent them from happening. Or, for that matter, stop them once they've begun. I suspect we never could, though some of my fellow gods, those who've studied the history of our kind, say otherwise. The simple fact is, gods have a tendency to boast – always have done, always will – and humans attribute greater powers to us than we actually have or have ever had.

It's really only the small things in life over which we hold sway.

Untied Shoelaces, for example.

Occasionally, a lace that has come undone will cause the shoe wearer to stumble or trip, and trips can, as I'm sure you're well aware, probably from bitter experience, result in injury, sometimes severe injury, occasionally death. But not, *absolutely not*, as a result of the god who deals with Untied Shoelaces deliberately making it happen. On the contrary, he works hard, doing the best he can to keep laces tightly tied. He's conscientious to a fault and a staunch advocate of velcro. I know this for a fact because he's a longstanding companion of mine. Not a lover, we're just, as they say, good friends. He's gay and I'm not, but both of us lead celibate lives, it's simpler that way. Since the turn of the century we've shared a mansion flat just off Sloane Square. A good location, handy for the tube. Whenever we're able to set work aside for a few hours, we order a takeaway from a gloriously inauthentic but friendly Thai restaurant

A chippy in a previous incarnation
and a taverna and
a bistro
before that.
Same management and staff
in all phases
of its existence.

just off the Brompton Road, crack open a few beers and settle down to watch sports on TV, mainly footy, though for reasons unknown my friend supports Liverpool whereas I favour the infinitely superior – notwithstanding their lower ranking in the Premier League – Crystal Palace, which, when they play against each other, can lead to an occasional drunken argument. Friendly argument, of course. Hot air and bluster, dispersed by morning. Except for the inevitable hangover; the worst symptom of which is a mouth so parched the shrivelled tongue within feels like a corpse in a cocoon.

CUSTOMER: Very interesting, I'm sure. But what bearing does it have on the matter at hand?

~~~: I'll get to that in a moment. Let me first explain –

CUSTOMER: Wait. Before you go any further, I'd like to order an espresso doppio. And a panini – a croque monsieur, if possible. Where are the counter staff?

~~~: On a break. Back soon or soonabouts. But I suspect the paninis have all gone, they're a popular line with the desk-dinner crowd. While we're waiting, let me call my second witness.

CUSTOMER: [deep groan, obviously heartfelt]

> RADA-trained actors say that in the repertoire
> of groans this particular groan is one of
> the hardest to convey successfully
> whereas actors who've studied The Method
> by Strasberg out of Stanislavsky
> say it's as easy as rolling off a log.
> To prove the point
> in an instructional DVD that can be
> purchased from any good retailer
> several famous actors demonstrate the technique
> and Sean Penn
> always a stickler
> goes so far as to provide his own bespoke log
> from a tree he'd hewn and stripped
> in person
> grown from a sapling in his
> own back yard.

~~~: Enough of that! Let's get down to business.

Please state your name, age, present occupation and place of domicile.

SECOND WITNESS: Van de Plas. Austin P Van de Plas. I'd prefer not to say what the P stands for, if that's okay with you. Twenty-four next birthday. Used car salesman, luxury and vintage. What was that other thing you wanted?

~~~: Place of domicile.

VAN DE PLAS: You mean where I live, yeah?

~~~: Correct.

VAN DE PLAS: Frognal Parade, NW3.

~~~: Please tell us, Mr Van de Plas, in what capacity you know Jimmy Inkling.

VAN DE PLAS: According to the DNA results I got last year I'm ... I'm his son. 'Accurate to at least 99.999 per cent' it says in the brochure. Truth is, I still can't quite believe it, though I know it must be true. And that remaining 0.001 per cent niggles. It's a very small inaccuracy. Tiny, really. But when I asked the technician about it, he said it was just dodgy DNA, could have come from anyone, even, because of my build and hairiness, you know, a gorilla.

Actually, tell a lie, he said mountain gorilla.

That was embarrassing. Uncalled for. But I decided to laugh it off. I mean, what can you do? – maybe he meant it as a joke. I was born hairy. Long black silky hair, then as now. It's just the way I am. And let me tell you, some women really like it, they stroke me like a dog. One of them asked me to bark or howl when we ... you know. Just that once. But the technician was pissed off because I'd asked too many questions and was keeping him from his lunch – a quiche, straight from the oven, brie and bacon, I think, which I could smell even though it was on the far side of the room and wrapped in kitchen foil. But, come on, who wouldn't want to ask a few questions after being given devastating news like that?

~~~: The DNA sample was obtained how?

VAN DE PLAS: Mine or his?

~~~: Mr Inkling's.

VAN DE PLAS: From the handle and lip of a coffee cup and the shaft of a ballpoint pen.

~~~: Perhaps you'd better explain how this was done, so our expert witness, Mr Gatto, can –

GATTO: If I may briefly interrupt ... The explanation about accuracy that Mr Van de Plas has been given is arrant nonsense. Likewise the comment about dodgy DNA. I suspect the 'technician' to which he refers – a rather unpleasant fellow, it seems – is actually what we in the business would call a bench operator, a lowly worker ant, a creature of no significance in the overall scheme of things, except to the extent that this ant has woefully mis-led Mr Van de Plas, to whom, on behalf of the DNA industry worldwide, I offer a sincere apology.

The day that robots can do a bench operator's job will be a much better day for the human race, and the day that robots replace us entirely will be better still.

~~~: Thank you. I'm sure the apology is appreciated. Please continue, Mr Van de Plas.

VAN DE PLAS: Like I said: ballpoint pen and coffee cup. The pen was fresh from the packet, the cup had just come out of the dishwasher. When he left the office, having signed for a beautifully renovated vintage Bentley, a Sports Tourer Short Chassis six-and-a-half litre in racing green, I sealed them up in a ziploc bag.

GATTO: Did anyone else handle the materials?

VAN DE PLAS: Just me. I made sure of that.

GATTO: Which rules out the likelihood of contamination from other sources. Though one should bear in mind that the mountain gorilla hypothesis, as mentioned by the boorish bench op, though improbable, is not impossible. In the early 1970s an adult male exhumed in the Olsany ceme-tery, Prague, was found to have a small percentage of dung beetle in his DNA, enough to be worth writing about, as indeed I did. The article in question may be found in the pop-up and pop-out literary supplement to *Nature New Biology*, volume 242, number 119, if memory serves, though for the moment, annoyingly, the page numbers elude me. And in Japan a geisha who died in 1903 was discovered to have been part butterfly: Notocrypta Curvifascia, commonly known as the Restricted Demon. And as I'm sure you're well aware, medieval bestiaries are chock-a-block with monsters of various kinds, not all of which may be imaginary. The living world is full of surprises, so who's to say what's what and what's not.

~~~: Thank you. Most illuminating. Stand down, Mr Gatto. But please remain in the building until this witness has finished giving evidence, we may need to draw on your expertise again.

Now, Mr Van de Plas, what made you decide to collect a sample of Mr Inkling's DNA? I assume it isn't an unsavoury hobby of yours, something you do with all your clients.

VAN DE PLAS: Don't be daft, taking people's DNA without their knowledge or consent is a serious breach of protocol. The boss would have been appalled if he'd known what I was up to; he's a stickler for protocol. I'd never done anything like that before and never will again. No reason to. But during Mr Inkling's previous visit to the showroom we'd had our photo taken, him and me, all smiles, shaking hands. For promotional purposes. To be mounted on our Customer Wall of Fame alongside signed photos of Ralph Lauren, Elton John, Kate Moss, Hulk Hogan, Bob Geldof and the Sultan of Brunei. 'Like peas in a pod,' my boss said when he saw it. And it's true, though Mr Inkling is much less hairy than me and going a bit thin on top.

But it set me thinking. Something Ma said when she was alive, something that puzzled me at the time and kept on puzzling me. We were in the kitchen, having breakfast, and she was flicking through the Sunday scandal sheets, *The People* and *News of the World*, when she muttered something that sounded like 'That's the bastard maker', and drew a rough circle around the photo of a man who'd been caught doing something he shouldn't've. Everyone in those rags has been doing something they shouldn't've. Men mostly, needless to say.

She tore the photo out, folded it lengthways once or twice and stuffed it between the pages of one of the cookbooks on the table. Bread and cake recipes. She was especially big on cakes. And she often made comments under her breath about things she was reading and tore articles out of newspapers and magazines and used them as bookmarks. But what she said that day stuck in my mind, perhaps because it was such an odd thing to say. Not 'That's the bastard' or 'There's the bastard', which is what you'd expect and what I'd heard her say dozens of times before, but 'That's the bastard maker'. Unless I'd misheard. But I didn't think so.

When I got home that evening I dug the book out of the box the cookbooks got dumped in when she died, and there it was, in the section on yeasts and fermentation, a photo of CAPTION James Julius Inkling (aka Jimmy Jewels) on the steps of the Old Bailey, having been narrowly acquitted of a fraud so massive it could have sunk the fragile economy of Belize UNCAPTION, looking younger than he does now, though not much. He was the absolute spit of me, like an identical twin. I could hardly believe my eyes.

~~~: I take it that the paternal line was unknown, your progenitor a mystery.

VAN DE PLAS: If you mean I never knew the identity of my Dad, yes. Ma wouldn't talk about it. She took his name to the grave.

~~~: And you wanted to know who he was?

VAN DE PLAS: Yeah, I did.

~~~: Were you convinced that Mr Inkling was your biological father, even before you'd managed to obtain a sample of his DNA?

VAN DE PLAS: Pretty much. We were too alike for it to be a coincidence.

~~~: What did you do when you received the DNA results?

VAN DE PLAS: Got drunk. A mega-bender. Smashed out of my skull. Then a couple of days later, when I'd sobered up, I wrote him a letter. Friendly. Polite. Setting out what I knew, which was precious little apart from the DNA, and I didn't dare mention that because collecting it the way I did is what lawyers call a gross invasion of privacy, and I gather from what I've read that Mr Inkling's a very private person, some might even say secretive. Actually, that's what everybody says. But he never replied, which didn't surprise me. So about six weeks after I sent the letter – recorded delivery, to make sure he got it – I gave him a ring, all brazen like. I may have had a few drinks to set me up. Dutch courage. Quite a few drinks, probably. But he wouldn't speak to me. Refused point blank once he knew who was on the line. Though strangely enough he didn't hang up. I'm sure I could hear him breathing softly in the background

> Which could conceivably have been
> an echo
> or some other
> acoustic
> aberration.

while I spoke to a man who said he was his business partner, Derek Somebody-or-other, who said, once he'd heard my story, that his boss said that if I continued to harass him he'd sue the bollocks off me, or snip my bollocks off, one or the other – neither of which greatly appealed. So I left it at that.

~~~: Even though you had proof of paternity.

VAN DE PLAS: Yeah, well ...

~~~: Have you had any contact with him since that phone call?

VAN DE PLAS: Neither sight nor sound. Didn't expect to.

~~~: Thank you, Mr Van de Plas. Please stand down.

VAN DE PLAS: Hang on, there's one more thing ...

~~~: Yes?

VAN DE PLAS: Last month I got a cheque in the post, drawn on an obscure bank in the Cayman Islands. When I say obscure, I mean obscure even by Cayman standards. George Town is rife with banks like that. Quite a few of our customers use them, Mr Inkling included. Hole in the wall enterprises. Some, according to an article in *The Economist*, no bigger than a portakabin, and in one case housed in a garden shed. The account holder was anonymised and the cheque was for a substantial sum of money.

~~~: How substantial?

VAN DE PLAS: Enough to set up my own car dealership and cover the operating costs until the business starts to pay for itself. If that's what I decide to do. Which I should; I've got the experience, and demand always outstrips supply, especially with the Russians and Saudis. They buy up vintage cars sight unseen, or from catalogue, a dozen at a time. They seem to have nearly all the money in the world. By their standard, Mr Inkling was a small-scale collector. But he was very particular, knew exactly what he wanted, and he always paid bang on time, in total, without quibble. Which is why I've mentioned the cheque. The courtesy slip enclosed with it was marked 'In full and final payment'. Read into that what you will.

~~~: Thank you again for your testimony, Mr Van de Plas.

⊖

CUSTOMER: Frankly, this god business sticks in my craw.

~~~: Why so?

CUSTOMER: You claim that gods walk among us, unrecognised as such. Which may be true, though I've only got your word for it. Then you say the powers of these modern gods, though greater than those of mere mortals, are limited compared to the thunderclap merchants and earthquakers of yore. Well, fine, I'm willing to grit my teeth and suspend disbelief. To some degree. Or at least try to. But what do you and your god colleagues do with these suprahuman powers? According to you, nothing much. Trivial things. Make hinges squeak and try to keep shoelaces tied. Now that really doesn't sound like typical god behaviour to me, not at all. It sounds, if you'll forgive me for saying so, idiotic and demeaning.

~~~: Precisely! I'm glad you understand. One of our key roles as gods is to keep things running smoothly in this world: the simplest things, the fundamentals, all the way down to the molecular level, however idiotic that sounds. Which it does, I know it does. But that doesn't make it any less true. Another is to strive to succeed and have our strivings fail conspicuously for the betterment of humankind. We mirror your shortcomings and amplify them. We make you feel good about yourselves because our failings make your paltry achievements seem bigger and better than they really are. Although by nature we're far from humble, we're prepared to be demeaned, if that's what it takes. Needs must. The best way to illustrate this point is by calling my third witness. And before you start acting up: no amount of eyeball rolling will divert me from this course of action, so stifle those moans, groans and histrionic sighs, they'll be wasted on me.

CUSTOMER: [...]

~~~: Please state your name, age, present occupation and place of domicile.

THIRD WITNESS: God name: Δ≈ΔΔΔ°◇≥, which is unpronounce-
able in any of the seven thousand human languages currently spoken. A real tongue twister. If it's of any consola-
tion, speakers of languages now extinct fared no better,
though the ancients of Mesopotamia, Akkadian their lin-
gua franca, almost got it right. Even we gods find it hard
to pronounce, and let me tell you, spelling it is an
absolute nightmare, so the court stenographer will just
have to do the best she can. Human name: that's a doddle
– Charlie Taylor. In human years I pass for fifty-seven,
though, needless to say, I'm considerably older than that.
I was the mechanic who in 1903 helped Wilbur and
Orville Wright get their first powered aircraft off the
ground, having previously worked with the brothers in
their bicycle workshop. Happy days, those, all in all,
though the brothers, Wilbur especially, were stinting with
praise. Wages too, for that matter. But making them look
good was my brief, and if I say so myself I succeeded
admirably. I even received a scroll of commendation from
the Council of Elders, and when it comes to handing out
commendations they're a notoriously stingy bunch, as
well you know, so I can't rightly complain.

One of the key tasks I undertake nowadays is to slow
the Rate of Depletion in Inkjet Printer Cartridges. They
seem to last no time at all, to the annoyance and frustration of the consumer and the joy of cartridge manufacturers and their shareholders.

Also, Scansion as applied to Wills, Government Documents, Contractual Small Print for Electrical Appliances,
Academese and, hardest of all to deal with, the baroque
gibberish known as Artspeak (i.e. curatorial and critical
writings on the visual arts). To my considerable relief,
poetry and the poets themselves were hived off to another
god. Hers is a thankless task, poets being notoriously difficult to deal with, maddened by words, perpetually

drunk on them, and given to extravagant and unpredictable behaviour. Like toddlers, really, but with adult vices. Endangerment of self and others is often an issue. Byron set the template for such things. But that's not the worst of it. Their verse: ugh. Almost without exception: ugh. Such mangling and mauling of language. The words weep as poets bend them grotesquely out of shape and crack their tiny bones.

My hobby, when I find time to practise it, is Computational Fluid Dynamics, which in simple terms involves modelling the action of wet steam flow in large turbines using algorithms to automatically modify turbine blades during the simulation of the fluid flow. When you know what you're doing it's hardly more difficult than building a bicycle, or riding one, though the scientists I work with sometimes make such heavy weather of it I feel like giving them a slap. Which, of course, as you know, is allowed only in exceptional circumstances, if at all. Slapping hysterical women is now deeply frowned upon, and anyway there are fewer of them to slap, hysteria having largely been transferred from women to men, footballers in particular and their emotionally incontinent fans. And children can't be slapped, not now, not under any circumstances, more's the pity. Even the glove slap, as an aristocratic mode of insult, is no longer practised. Nor the duel, to which a glove slap nearly always led, unless the slap was administered by a woman. Soon the slap will be consigned to history, to be puzzled over and misunderstood by future generations of social scientists.

~~~: And your place of domicile?

TAYLOR: You know fine well where I live. As I recall, you attended our New Year bash and drank us under the table.

~~~: Just for the record.

TAYLOR: Yes, of course. Silly me. Vale Hall, a tiny hamlet on the

West Sussex coast, not far but thankfully just far enough from the boiling cauldron of sin that is Littlehampton. The great hall itself was demolished centuries ago, or fell down through neglect, and only the barns and estate workers' cottages remain, most of which are derelict. The sea will claim them eventually as the south of England gradually sinks and Scotland continues to rise. One of my neighbours, who manages the Wind-Blown Redistribution of Tilth, and as a hobby monitors Coastal Erosion (though in Norfolk rather than Sussex), gives Vale Hall one hundred and fifty years at most. But even he agrees that no-one will miss it when it's gone. It's already dropped off the map, a forgotten place. That's why he and I and other gods like living there, where the local authority, the police and the Post Office think no-one lives and we can go about our business unheeded and unhindered.
— Does that answer your question?

~~~: Fully, Mr $\Delta\approx\Delta\Delta\Delta°\diamond\geq$. As ever. Your attention to detail is celebrated far and wide.

TAYLOR: I aim to please and perhaps, on occasion, delight.

~~~: That you do. You do indeed. But the day is running away with us and soon night will fall, unleashing the murky horrors that swarmed through our childhood dreams and continue to plague our collective sleep. We need to wrap this up quickly. Succinctness would be greatly appreciated. Be pithy, if possible.

TAYLOR: I'll do my best.

~~~: I believe you had dealings with Jimmy Inkling some while ago, is that correct?

TAYLOR: Yes.

~~~: Unsatisfactory dealings?

TAYLOR: Very.

~~~: Perhaps you'd care to elaborate.

TAYLOR: Elaborate ... concisely?

~~~: If possible.

TAYLOR: I'll be as brief as I can. In a nutshell

Preferably walnut –
a peanut shell being too flimsy to
convey the gist of what he has to say
though during a thunderstorm
half a peanut shell can become a handy
canoe for an insect or two.

I first met Mr Inkling at the Battle of Windrush Valley. Not the one that took place in the early 1640s, its re-enactment. August 1994. Staged by members of the Sealed Knot Society. A blissful sunny day in what had been a hot, dry summer crackling with thunder. But the event ended abruptly when smouldering wadding ejected from a cannon burst into flames, setting fire to the stubble field in which the re-enactment was taking place. Fanned by a stiff breeze, the fire tore through the stubble and into an adjoining field that was being used as a car park, where it gutted fifty vehicles. Although more than a dozen people were injured, there were, thankfully, no fatalities.

According to one of the newspaper reports, Mr Inkling and I were QUOTE heroic in their efforts to save the lives of spectators caught up in the conflagration UNQUOTE. Typically, the journalist misspelled our names, even my human name, but most of what he wrote was correct. Amid thick smoke, tumult and confusion, with flames licking at our heels, we worked tirelessly, side by side, guiding people to safety, him in full Cavalier regalia – plumed hat, leather doublet, bucket-topped boots, shoulder-slung musket, etc. – me in my everyday spectator garb which, with enormous self-restraint, I'll itemise slowly and meticulously in my head while my verbal explanation moves on and gathers pace.

I was at Windrush Valley on assignment. An unrelated matter. God business, of course, but hardly worth mentioning, so I won't.

I saw Mr Inkling out of the corner of my eye just as the flames started to take hold. He was behaving ... how shall I put it? ... anomalously. Whereas his fellow Sealed Knotters were evidently following the society's code of conduct to the letter – i.e. during hand-to-hand combat, blows should be struck with the maximum *impression* of force rather than with *actual* force – Mr Inkling was laying into the Roundheads like a man possessed, using the butt of his replica musket to knock seven bells of Parliamentarian shit out of them. Much blood was spilt. Bones possibly broken. One Roundhead lost several teeth, or perhaps a dental plate, and was stretchered off, semi-conscious, by the St John Ambulance Brigade, ably assisted by a unit of Girl Guides who were attending the re-enactment on an historical-themed Adventure Day and got more in the way of adventure than they'd bargained for. Several of the Cavaliers had noticed Mr Inkling's violent behaviour and were trying to subdue him, the sight of which must have confused the spectators: Cavalier fighting Cavalier, a skirmish within the ranks at the very heart of the battle. But Mr Inkling broke free and slipped away.

> He's a slippery customer
> and that's a fact.

Next thing I knew he was helping me lift a very fat, very elderly gentleman suffering from smoke inhalation into the back of an ambulance.

It transpired that Mr Inkling wasn't actually a member of the Sealed Knot, or any of the other re-enactment societies,

> Who sometimes try to sabotage each other's performances
> as rival troupes of players did in Shakespeare's day
> [though that may be apocryphal].

he'd turned up hoping to let off steam after a major business deal had gone wrong, or, in his trenchant phrase, 'tits up'. He would, he said, have preferred to pummel the punchbag at his local gym for an hour or two, the heavy one, until even within protective gloves his fingers would be swollen and bloody, but it was booked solid by boxers doing their final preparations for a tournament that evening. And the Cavalier outfit? Just something he had in the wardrobe at his holiday cottage in nearby Chipping Norton. Apparently he bought all the costumes and stage props from Huntingdon's Cromwell Theatre when it fell into administration and sold most of them to the National Theatre at a handsome profit. He never did anything that was unlikely to turn a profit. And he never would have started to knock Roundheads about in the way he did if it wasn't for one of them getting uppity and aggressive with him,

Perhaps in jest
misjudged if so
but
quite frankly
who's to know.

saying his plumed hat was historically inaccurate, of a style that wouldn't become fashionable until at least three decades after the date of the battle, and calling him a rank amateur, an embarrassment both to the society and his mother, the latter of whom should have had him throttled at birth.

Being needled like that tripped, as they say, his switch.

Mr Inkling has a bit of a temper.

That's another thing to which he admitted, half shamefaced, half boastful, less than an hour after the last ambulance had quit the battlefield. The fire brigade was still hosing down the burnt-out cars (mine included) and preparing to clock up hours of valuable overtime. By then

Mr Inkling and I were in a local pub, the Swan at Ascott, drinking foul beer to wash the taste of smoke from our mouths. Because of the smoke, our taste buds were shot; everything tasted foul. Even the words we spoke were foul and tinged with smoke.

Here be dragons!

Mr Inkling was in his eighties at the time but looked not a day over fifty. Nor, from what I'd seen, had his strength and stamina declined with age. It was remarkable, and I said so. That's when he decided we'd be friends. Great friends. Bosom buddies. I had no say in the matter. It's how things got done, and probably still do, in Mr Inkling's circle.

I've since learned that a decade or two earlier he'd undergone treatment in Marseille with one of Dr Serge Voronoff's dwindling band of acolytes, a few of whom were country doctors, retired or disbarred, though most were vets working undercover to avoid the scrutiny of police, medical ethics committees and other ignoramus non-believers and authoritarian naysayers. Voronoff pioneered xenotransplantation, a technique that involved opening up the patient's scrotal sac in order to graft wafer-thin slices of baboon testicle onto the testes. Voronoff claimed it would offer the patient a greater span of years than three score and ten, improve memory, and maintain a peak level of virility into bleak old age. Unfortunately, several of his patients contracted syphilis as a result of the procedure, and critics have suggested that his interventions may also have led to the development of HIV, which spread rapidly during the 1980s. By which time Voronoff himself was long dead, having decided to forgo a baboon graft of his own.

Mr Inkling's extraordinary youthfulness set me thinking. It seemed unlikely, but … could he be one of us, you know, a god? Usually I can spot a fellow god a mile off. It's just something we gods can do. Whereas humans, who are much less perceptive and don't know what indicators to look for, identify us as one of their own. That's just as well; remaining incognito works to our advantage. Put simply, glamour is one of the major differences between gods and humans. Humans have less of it. They seem a bit grey and two-dimensional. Less vital. It's hard to explain so I won't even try. But Mr Inkling had a certain *je ne sais quoi* that lifted him out of the ordinary, by which I mean the human ordinary. He definitely had a touch of glamour. Sometimes, in humans, that's brought about by unshakeable self-belief. That may well be the case with Mr Inkling. I suspect he's never experienced a twinge of self-doubt in his entire life. But a god? Really? I decided to consult the registers of births, death and marriages at god HQ, to find out whether he and his parents were listed and, if so, in what capacity.

Quite frankly, my expectations were low. Even if I managed to find some trace of them in the archives, there was no certainty that what was recorded would be accurate. The potential for error is huge. I've heard of instances where the offspring of two gods has been given up for adoption at birth, and because of incomplete or inaccurate records (the files at HQ are in a terrible muddle and have been for several centuries) or bureaucratic incompetence (we're not infallible, despite claims to the contrary) the child has been offered to human parents rather than to parents of its own kind and even unto death remains ignorant of its status.

Then there's cradle swap, whereby newborns are mislabelled in the hospital nursery, sometimes by accident, more often maliciously, and given to the wrong parents to take home and raise as their own.

There are also occasions, thankfully rare, in which a god
has mated with a human and even secretly married one,

> The laws regulating god behaviour
> are very strict on
> this matter.
> Gods are permitted to marry and mate only
> with other gods
> to safeguard
> the purity of the bloodline.
> Though
> regrettably
> lapses occur.
> As mentioned earlier
> gods are all
> too human
> and let's face it
> love trumps law and probably
> always will.

but, because of slight chromosomal differences, god-
human couplings rarely have issue. When they do, the
child, nearly always male, will probably have no godlike
powers per se, though he's likely to lead a charmed life.
While his peers – humans who mistakenly think him
human – struggle to achieve anything of note and more
often than not fail miserably, the half-god will succeed
effortlessly, thereby countermanding much of our good
work. But if the half-god manages to produce an offspring
of his own, the child will be entirely human, lacklustre
and nondescript, as exemplified by your second witness –
I don't recall his name, the posh car salesman, or rather
the salesman of posh cars, who claims to bear Mr
Inkling's DNA and from his appearance may well do.

The registers, together with a small cache of letters I
chanced upon, plus a yellowed, barely legible newspaper
clipping, revealed what they could, which was precious

little. Mr Inkling was a foundling, abandoned when only a few hours old. His mother was never traced. He was left in the early hours of a bitterly cold winter morning on the doorstep of a house in William Mews, Belgravia, occupied by a Mr Rex Cribbage and his spry septuagenarian housekeeper Maeve. Snow was flurrying under the streetlamps and settling in drifts. Icicles hung thickly from gutters and eaves. The doorbell rang. Reluctantly, Maeve pulled on her dressing gown and answered the call. It was, in any case, almost time to stoke up the fires and prepare breakfast while Mr Cribbage slept on, as usual, dreaming of whatever men dream of.

On the doorstep she found a squalling red-faced infant swaddled like an Egyptian mummy. When unwrapped on the kitchen table, by a now roaring fire, with Mr Cribbage in attendance, the infant was revealed to be a well-made boy, blood-slicked from head to toe and with the umbilical cord still attached.

What was remarkable was that Mr Cribbage chose to adopt the foundling and raise him as his own, though he bestowed on him a different surname, having, as he said in one of the letters, 'no real inkling as to how difficult it would be to raise a son as difficult as James'.

By the way, the *Who's Who* entry for Mr Cribbage – a lowly civil servant at the time, working initially at the Foreign Office, later a cultural attaché assigned to a succession of insignificant countries below the equator

But as a god
responsible for Hurricane Lamps
Maize Yield and
Pinking in Two-Stroke Motorcycle Engines.

– lists him as a confirmed bachelor, which in the code of the Diplomatic Service usually means a discreet homosexual.

A fictionalised portrait of Rex Cribbage

Sir Rex
as he was dubbed
in June 2007
[dying of smugness
shortly
thereafter].

can, according to his biographer, be found in *Lefty Hangs a Right*, a decidedly odd, not altogether successful crime thriller, book #37 in the Jimmy Inkling series, about a gay getaway driver, Frederic 'Lefty' Freenham, trying to go, in both the criminal and sexual orientation senses of the word, straight.

The book's author, or rather its purported author, is Boss Dangerfield. Google him: you'll discover less than you thought you knew. There are no authoritative biographical details to be had online (or anywhere else, for that matter), just rumours that decades of repetition have hardened into fact. Nothing else is known. All you'll find are blurbs for his many and varied (in style, content and quality) novels, half-baked reviews of the books themselves and splurges of bizarre commentary. Most of the fanboy chat centres on the possible true identity and whereabouts of the author. Shakespeare is more mysterious than Dangerfield, but only just. Bigfoot is less elusive. His skill as a writer lies somewhere between the two. Dangerfield has never been photographed, never attended a book launch or embarked on a promotional tour, never, for that matter, visited any of his publisher's offices in London, New York, Dublin, Victoria (Aus), Toronto, New Delhi, Valparaiso, Rosedale (NZ), Johannesburg, Flying Fish Cove and Rome,

Where, in Vatican City, Pope Francis is known to be a hardcore fan
whose enthusiasm sometimes gets the better of him.
An early draft of his 2015 encyclical on man-made climate change
Laudato Si'
contained not one but
two quotations from Jimmy Inkling book #32
a tale of warring teenage street gangs
[a romantic tragedy, more Sharks and
Jets than Crips and Bloods]
in Judaea at the turn of the first century AD
entitled *The Dead Rise Not*
which his Council of Cardinal Advisers
advised him to replace with words
more apposite:
'What the Faithful, who dislike
innovation of any kind, especially in religious matters,
will expect, Holy Father –
perhaps by your namesake and
favourite saint, the first
recorded bearer of the stigmata
that noble sufferer dear to us all
Francis of Assisi'.

and in his long,

Undeniably so.

industrious,

Sixty-seven novels in less
than half a century
is by most people's
standards an exceptional
level of productivity.
But compared to truly prolific
authors such as
Barbara Cartland and Georges Simenon
Dangerfield is
let's face it
a slacker.

and illustrious

[hmm]

career he's given only one substantial interview: to *Paris Review* for their Writers at Work series. As David Foster Wallace notes in his brief prefatory comments, he and Dangerfield never actually met; the Q&A was conducted entirely via email and Dangerfield changed his email address answer by answer. Those email addresses, each used once only, are now dead letter drops, hacked and haunted by obsessive fans who send emails to themselves and each other in Dangerfieldese and post them online as though they're Boss' own words. But, as I say, perhaps that's how he wants it to be. He's determinedly reclusive. Like Emily Dickinson, JD Salinger, Harper Lee and Thomas Pynchon rolled into one, but with, in my opinion (Wallace seems to think otherwise), barely a grunt of their eloquence or a spark of their trail-blazing genius. And it's obvious that Boss Dangerfield is a nom-de-plume. In fact, because Lefty Freenham and Rex Cribbage are identical down to the smallest detail, including intimate details that would be known only by Sir Rex's nearest and dearest, which rules out everyone but his son and his biographer, and perhaps Maeve, long dead, I think we can safely conclude that the author of the Jimmy Inkling books is none other than James Julius Inkling, something he has always strenuously denied.

After the Windrush affair, I got to know Mr Inkling better. At his insistence. Usually he'd send a couple of burly minders to fetch me, and on one occasion, when I'd ignored his summons and been brusque with him on the phone, they carried me, still in my pyjamas, dead weight like a sack of spuds, down the narrow, rickety staircase of the cottage at Vale Hall and out through the shattered front door. An ignominious exit ... but what followed was worse. They heave-ho'd three times and threw me into the back of a dark limo. Having handcuffed me to a ring that was bolted to the limo floor, and folded themselves into the front seats, we sped off. Apart from the heave-hos, not a word was spoken, not even between the two of them. They put the radio on. World Service: a programme about the kidnapping of westerners by Kashmiri terrorists. I couldn't help but see points of comparison between my fate and theirs.

Mr Inkling's reasons for fetching me were nearly always trivial: to play Monopoly; to admire the recent additions to his stamp collection (using the illuminated globe by the side of his desk to show which obscure countries the stamps came from); to watch the sun rise over Canary Wharf; to help him feed his tropical fish. Very needy is Mr Inkling, very, very clingy. Perhaps even on his first day on Earth he was aware of being abandoned and alone.

Before we go any further, I'd like to counter the testimony of one of your earlier witnesses, the grumpy actor, and set the record straight. Mr Inkling is certainly tall, much taller than me and, for that matter, most people, but he doesn't bear a facial scar, terrible or otherwise, and in every photograph I've seen, and in all the time I've known him, he's been clean shaven. Moreover –

~~~: Must there be a moreover?

TAYLOR: I'm afraid so. We're fast approaching the nub of the matter and by the most direct route. Beans of great significance are about to be spilled. It would be foolish to stop now, before the beans, in their entirety, have been comprehensively spilled, the spilling of which –

⊖

CUSTOMER: If I may interrupt ...

~~~: You may not. Members of the jury are –

CUSTOMER: But there's only me!

~~~: – expected to remain silent throughout the proceedings, to concentrate fully on the evidence as presented in court, ignoring all external and extraneous factors, setting aside for the duration of the trial firmly held irrational beliefs and objectionable prejudices. There are other things jurors must not do: address the judge, the witnesses and the accused, eat smelly/crunchy/slurpy snacks, go walkabout, become intoxicated, break wind sarcastically, use mobile electronic devices, scratch as if flea- or lice-ridden, smoke, play footsy with fellow jurors, read books, newspapers or magazines, chew gum, sleep, and if sleep is unavoidable, snore. (A complete list, the so-called Verbotens Guide, has been placed on the table by the exit, the door to which is, as you've probably noticed, now locked. For reasons of security. To keep others out rather than keep you in: it's better that we remain undisturbed.) Notes may be taken as an aide-memoire but you must not pass notes to your fellow jurors, although jurors may ask the foreman of the jury to pass a note

Actually an
emoji:

to the judge should certain aspects of law require explanation.

CUSTOMER: But there is no jury, only me!

~~~: You are, therefore, elected as foreman of the jury. Congratulations! As foreman you must act as the chairperson and spokesperson for the jury and help your fellow jurors

to decide the facts of the case. The jurors' task is to decide whether the accused is guilty beyond reasonable doubt. Beyond reasonable doubt means – in case you don't know, and many don't, so don't feel embarrassed if you don't – that if there are two reasons given in the case, and both are possible explanations for what happened, taken together with the evidence presented the jury should give the accused the benefit of the doubt and return a verdict of not guilty. It isn't necessary for a jury to be unanimous in its verdict –

FOREMAN: But there's only me! Why won't you listen? There – is – only – me!

~~~: I appreciate that, Mr ... what did you say your name was?

FOREMAN: You never asked and I didn't say.

~~~: Tut tut. Remiss of me, I do apologise. You're hungry, hence grumpy and standoffish. Understandable. Something we need to remedy asap. The proprietor of this caff, Tiffany, together with her sandwich technician colleague,

Who she's secretly in love with.

will soon, despite the lateness of the hour, rustle up a ham and cheese toasty and a double espresso. In the meantime, please state your name, age, present occupation and place of domicile.

FOREMAN: No.

~~~: No?

FOREMAN: No.

~~~: Really, no?

FOREMAN: No!

~~~: May one ask why?

FOREMAN: It's none of your damn business.

~~~: But if you have nothing to hide ...

FOREMAN: That's not the point.

~~~: You're a doctor, am I correct?

FOREMAN: Yes, but ...

~~~: Of medicine?

FOREMAN: Yes. Well, no. Not a general practitioner. Dental and Oral Health Care Sciences, Paediatrics. But how did −?

~~~: Spirit mediumship with a dash of the psychics, as I explained just a moment ago. Useful skills, especially when seeking evidence from those who've ridden the Necropolis line to the terminus.

FOREMAN: Does that mean what I think it means?

~~~: Communing with the dead? If so, yes. Each spirit has a tale to tell of its own unique death. It's the last and therefore the most important thing any of them can recall, and once they start prattling on about it it's hard to shut them up. Luckily, those who've been dead for a couple of decades or so get tired of reviewing their mode of despatch, and having nothing better to talk about

Why?
Because according to *Lonely Planet* and *Fodor*
The Afterlife is situated in the densely
populated one-horse town of
Dullsville-upon-Bore
in the dead centre of a
vast plain bereft
of memorable
features.

they lapse into silence and stay resolutely mum. Anyone who claims to be able to contact Cleopatra, Boudicca, Rasputin and Hitler, giving them voice in laughably bad, heavily accented English, a language none of them spoke, and colloquial English at that, as heard on the proverbial Clapham omnibus or the Blackpool tram, is an out-and-out fraud. Or fool. Or non compos mentis. But who better to give testimony in a murder trial than the victim.

FOREMAN: Let me get this straight. This is a murder trial?

~~~: If you insist. Manslaughter may also be considered.

FOREMAN: Someone has been killed?

~~~: A not unreasonable assumption.

FOREMAN: By Mr Inkling? Is he the accused? You and the witnesses have said an awful lot about him, some of which would be considered defamatory if uttered anywhere but in a court of law, if indeed this is a courtroom –

~~~: Hastily convened, but yes.

FOREMAN: – which I very much doubt, despite what you say. At the outset you declared he was king of the criminal underworld, but I'm sorry, that doesn't ring true, not to my way of thinking, despite the no-smoke-without-fire slur of him having been put on trial in 2007 for a fraud involving timeshares and money laundering in the UK and Belize. A trumped-up charge, of which, let me remind you, he was acquitted. In fact, I remember reading that the judge in his summation admonished the DPP for bringing the case to trial based on nothing but the flimsiest of evidence, evidence that Mr Inkling's barrister said was QUOTE the most outrageous tissue of lies I've heard in all my years at the bar UNQUOTE. I mean, hasn't Mr Inkling done vast amounts of high profile work for charities in the UK and elsewhere, Afghan Orphans, Médecins Sans Frontières, the Prince's Trust and suchlike? Isn't he also a UNICEF Goodwill Ambassador, following in the dainty footsteps of notables such as Cat Deeley and Jemima Khan?

~~~: He *was* involved with UNICEF, but no longer.

FOREMAN: Look, I hate to harp on about it, but are you absolutely sure we're talking about the same Jimmy Inkling, the Jimmy Inkling who donated one of his kidneys to the adult twin daughter of a friend of his, the father of the twins having already donated a kidney to the other twin, a son?

~~~: I believe so.

FOREMAN: A selfless act, one that had tragic consequences, as many selfless acts do. Endowed with a new kidney and restored to good health, physical if not mental, didn't the daughter become infatuated or, more accurately, obsessed with Mr Inkling? Wasn't she hell-bent on getting him to marry her, despite their disparity in age and his indifference to her wiles and charms, an indifference that gradually curdled into loathing? Having rebuffed her time and again, firmly but gently, wasn't Mr Inkling forced to go abroad for a month or two, whereabouts unknown, to escape her erratic and increasingly violent behaviour? Didn't she then embark on a killing spree of middle-aged lotharios she met through online dating sites

All of whom
the victims
coincidentally or not
bore at least a passing resemblance to Mr Inkling
[according to the press reports].

prior to shooting herself

In the heart
no less.

on a small industrial estate near Macclesfield as the police closed in, leaving a note that said, as I recall, 'His kidney made me do it'?

~~~: Yes, that's the Mr Inkling in question. Though the exact phrase was: 'His evil kidney goaded the devil in me'. Same difference: five men dead, none of whom deserved to die the way they did, i.e. horribly.

For someone who hasn't actually met Mr Inkling, you know rather a lot about him. Much more than I thought. But I suspect my next witness will still be able to offer a surprise or two.

Mr $\Delta{\approx}\Delta\Delta\Delta^{\circ}\diamond{\geq}$, would you step outside for a moment?

And while you're there, I'd be greatly obliged if you'd call Mr Honeyman to the stand.

⊖

~~~: Please state your name, age, present occupation and place of domicile.

FOURTH WITNESS: Paul Honeyman, biographer, sixty-two next birthday. St Peter Port, Guernsey, is where I make my home, but between now and next Thursday you can reach me at the Athenaeum. Extremely comfy beds at the Athenaeum, which is why I always stay there, though I prefer to eat at Snowy White's. Don't tell anyone, but the head chef at Snowies, a Ukrainian overstayer, is worth his weight in gold, and he's a man of considerable girth who has trouble squeezing through doorways, so that's an awful lot of gold. No-one who has sampled his *cuisine exquis* would be inclined to tip off the UK Border Agency – jealous lesser chefs excepted.

~~~: Indeed. But I wanted to ask you about Sir Rex Cribbage. You are, I believe, his biographer.

HONEYMAN: Unofficial biographer. Or, in his own words, before he slammed the door in my face: 'rogue biographer, a rogue who writes biographies'. He refused to cooperate. Denied me access to his papers. Told his friends to give me short shrift, which most of them did. That meant I had to seek information almost exclusively from his enemies. I was surprised by how many there were, his son foremost among them.

~~~: I assume you mean his adopted son, James Julius Inkling, unless there's a son we know nothing about.

HONEYMAN: No, that's the fellow. Jimmy Jewels. Quite a character. A trouble and a caution, as they say. Or worse. Actually, very much worse. I spent some time in his company and got to know him pretty well. As well as anyone can, under the circumstances.

~~~: The circumstances being ...?

HONEYMAN: He's a veritable iceberg. The big, important stuff hidden below the waterline. His business empire is vast, and the illegal parts of it were, as I discovered to my astonishment, vaster still. Fingers thrust knuckle-deep in every iffy pie in nearly every country worldwide, especially those in Africa and Latin America. Corrupt politicians and heads of state in pocket. The police his private army, the army his secret police. On the surface he's a one-man charm offensive, quick with a handshake, a smile, a good-fellow-well-met slap on the back. He's a decorated war hero, a hugely successful legitimate businessman and philanthropist, a man who, when the camera is on him, is unfailingly kind to dumb animals and dumber employees, that sort of thing. But I wouldn't like to cross him. There's a dark side. He casts a long shadow, and anyone so much as grazed by it is likely to sicken and die.

I decided early on in our relationship that for the sake of my health my investigation into Mr Inkling's affairs would have to be conducted under an impenetrable cloak of secrecy, and whatever I discovered would have to remain unpublished during his lifetime. Or if I felt exceptionally brave or reckless, published during his lifetime but anonymously, with all links to the source scrupulously erased and a plethora of false links inserted, to try to confuse and confound Mr Inkling's ex-GCHQ snoops. I have a dossier on him that's as fat as Arkady Bredyuk's neck – he's the chef I mentioned a moment ago – locked up in a bank vault, the location of which is known to me and only one other person.

Let me be clear: that other person has no obvious connection to me. It's not my wife Tamsin nor either of our sons: I would never do anything to put their lives at risk. It's not my bank manager, solicitor or accountant. Nor even is it Arkady Bredyuk, who, were I sentenced to be shot at dawn by a squad of Mr Inkling's 'special ops', would be asked to prepare my last meal on Earth. I dare say no more for fear of reprisal, which Mr Inkling would undoubtedly relish.

~~~: Then perhaps you'd be so kind as to tell the court why, as Sir Rex Cribbage was your subject, you were investigating Mr Inkling.

HONEYMAN: It's standard practice. Meticulous biographers need to know whether their informants are trustworthy and, if so, to what extent. Would the information Mr Inkling supplied about Sir Rex be accurate, despite his negative bias? I suspected not, though I hoped it would be. But the simple fact is that truth is elusive and often, despite our best efforts, nowhere to be found. That's why most biographies – even those written by a number of my esteemed colleagues, some of whom are also dear friends – are fact-lite semi-fictions that try, with bulldozer rhetoric and masses of superfluous detail (i.e. padding) to convince the reader that they portray their subject accurately in the context of our shared reality. As for autobiographies, they are, almost without exception, fiction masquerading as fact. Fun reads, nothing more. Everyone in the publishing industry knows this. Most readers do, too.

What I think I've consistently achieved as a biographer – something that all biographers hope to achieve, apart from the slipshods and ne'er-do-wells who've swelled our ranks of late – is accuracy with regard to the facts. My accomplishments speak for themselves. Of course, facts are notoriously slippery, meaning, as they do, different things in different contexts. The sea of information is in constant flux; one can all too easily drown in the churning waves and vicious undertow. No wonder there's so much confusion in the world, which in turn breeds anxiety and despair. Of all the emotions, despair ranks supreme. And writers, melancholic and solitary by nature, often hitting the bottle before or instead of breakfast, are the most prone to despair.

Not
[as suggested by Srinivasa Ramanujan
or someone claiming to speak for him]
cutting-edge
mathematicians who
requiring clarity of mind at all times
even while asleep
tend to be abstemious with
regard to alcohol and
other stimulants
and intoxicants
but are
on the whole
surprisingly jolly
the life and soul of the party
though they couldn't crack
a joke if their life depended on it
and they only laugh at things
no-one else finds funny.

According to stats compiled by PEN International, during the last quarter century biographers have steadily ranked five per cent higher in the suicide stakes than the writerly norm, and the writerly norm is a whopping seven per cent higher than the nearest contender in the suicide stakes – doctors. No wonder the I-SOB (International Society of Biographers) annual conference is such a glum affair and local AA meetings are standing-room only. No wonder the phones at the I-SOB members' hotel have the number for the Samaritans on speed dial.

Once I'd completed Sir Rex's biography I vowed I'd never again tackle a living subject. I'd ghost books only or write about the definitely deceased.

Corpse dug up and
silver stake
hammered
through heart
is the traditional method
used by biographers
to check whether
their subjects are dead.

Ghosting frees you of constraint and responsibility. If you've made it a contractual stipulation that your name won't appear anywhere in the book, your reputation can't be sullied and, quite frankly, it seems any old rubbish will do. It's what the public expects. It might even be what they want, I honestly don't know. But I do know that publishers couldn't care less as long as the book sells by the containerload. It will be read, forgotten – each new page erasing from memory the one that came before – and pulped by the containerload, all within a year or two of publication. Such is the brainwashing power of the vacuous subject and the ill-written word. Don't think for a moment that MI6, the CIA, MOSSAD and other intelligence agencies aren't aware of it.

Since Sir Rex's biog, I've ghosted the autobiographies of three medal-winning sportspersons (two men, one woman – a rugby player, a javelin thrower and a sprinter); a gobby, thoroughly obnoxious one-hit wonder from the '80s with a louche, some might say depraved, lifestyle in the Balearics; and a career politician in a safe seat who, for donkey's years, has toed the party line without question or qualm, has sleepwalked through life, and is so tedious and lacking in intelligence I occasionally nodded off while transcribing our conversations.

The politician's trophy wife, neglected, bored and sultry, freely admits, off the record, to having had dozens of affairs, mainly with tennis coaches and pilates teachers, male and female. Her husband knows all about them but has, she says, chosen not to know. She stays in the country and rides horses. He prefers taxis and town – and if the malign whisperers in the Commons' Pugin Room and Strangers' Bar are to be believed, as indeed they are, rent boys.

Husband and wife meet occasionally for lunch on neutral ground (Le Gavroche in Mayfair or The Glasshouse, Kew) and, says wife, the conversation is desultory. They have no interests in common other than Earl Grey tea and the weather. Not that they seem unhappy with their lot. Theirs isn't a dysfunctional marriage, just a coldly functional one, a marriage of convenience. Many's the time, while listening to his witless drone, I've wished I were being paid to write about her rather than him. But commissions are commissions, few in number and much sought after. We humble hacks are obliged to feast on whatever scraps are tossed our way.

~~~: So I gather. But we seem to have strayed from the business at hand, the reason why we're here today: Mr Inkling.

HONEYMAN: I do apologise.

~~~: Mr Honeyman, don't beat about the bush. If, as you're suggesting, Mr Inkling is a criminal, some evidence of criminality is required. And from your own experience; first hand only. Hints and hearsay simply won't do. After all, as you said a little earlier, you pride yourself on your 'accuracy with regard to the facts'.

HONEYMAN: True. Even, I suppose, the pride bit, though that's not quite what I said.

~~~: Then tell all. Give us the facts, Mr Honeyman. Let the cat out of the bag, or as many cats as the bag contains. Let them out, Mr Honeyman!

HONEYMAN: I can't.

~~~: Can't or won't?

HONEYMAN: Both.

~~~: You do realise you're duty bound to answer my questions truthfully, holding nothing back. If you fail to divulge vital evidence while under oath –

HONEYMAN: I'm not under oath.

~~~: – which was administered by the polygraph operator earlier in the day –

HONEYMAN: Look, I was naked at the time, shut up in a room in which boxes of crockery and various other catering items were being stored. A room that felt as cold as a refrigeration unit. And I was distracted by the presence of the camera crew. We were all crammed into that horribly small space, constantly bumping into each other. The director was bullying his poor cameraman. Tempers were short and egos were being shredded. It was disorientating. Upsetting. I hardly heard a word of what was being said and would have agreed to almost anything to get the ordeal over and done with.

~~~: – under, I admit, less than ideal circumstances –

HONEYMAN: I can't tell you anything.

~~~: – I'll have no alternative but to hold you in contempt of court, the penalty for which –

HONEYMAN: I don't care. Do your worst. I daren't tell you anything.

~~~: – is incarceration for a period of no less than two months and no more than three years.

The cost of detaining you at HM's pleasure will be calculated to the nearest pound sterling and items equal to that sum will be seized from your Guernsey abode by court-appointed bailiffs. And I believe you also own a pied-à-terre in Richmond, tenanted by a young Chinese woman, a logistics and inventory control manager at Muji.

The second-hand retail value of said items will be averaged from prices achieved for similar items in similar condition on eBay and when sold at a car boot sale in a middle-class suburb of a quintessential English town on a surprisingly mild Sunday afternoon at Summer's end. Excess funds from items sold will be held in trust during your period of incarceration and surrendered to you on release. Any shortfall in funds will result in a second round of seizures and sales.

If the sentence imposed is on the harsh side – as it will be! – your house and apartment may be forfeit. Also your car, a rather elegant Bentley Flying Spur, currently parked on double yellow lines outside Claridge's, ticketed by a traffic warden and due to be towed within the hour.

You will, because of the contemptible nature of the offence, be denied time off for good behaviour. Visits from family and friends will be limited, cancelled at ridiculously short notice or disallowed entirely. There's every likelihood you'll be sent to Ashfield Prison in Pucklechurch and banged up unsupervised with adult sex offenders, gerontophiles to a man. Standard perks and privileges, such as quilted toilet paper, petroleum jelly and in-cell TV, will be withdrawn for the duration of your sentence. The work assigned to you, the undertaking of which is compulsory, will consist of hard labour and nothing but. While your fellow inmates sit in a cosy workroom, listening to Radio 2 and hand-printing vaguely Oriental pearls of wisdom on rice paper for placement in fortune cookies, you'll be at the quarry in all weathers for up to nine hours a day breaking rocks. Is that really what you want?

HONEYMAN: Don't be absurd. Everyone knows that prisoners no longer break rocks. That was outlawed decades ago.
~~~: They do when they've been locked up for spoliation of evidence. It's a major contempt. Special rules apply.
HONEYMAN: [...]
~~~: I'm waiting.

HONEYMAN: You don't scare me, not like Jimmy Inkling does. I'm saying nothing.

~~~: Tut tut. Such stubbornness. But let that not be your final word. I'll give you one hour in which to reflect on your situation. — Usher, please escort Mr Honeyman to the cells and ask Mr Δ≈ΔΔΔ°◇≥ to return to the dock.

USHER: When you say Mr Δ≈ΔΔΔ°◇≥, do you mean Mr Taylor?

~~~: I do.

USHER: Okay, Chief.

⊖

FOREMAN: There are cells in this building?

~~~: In the basement. It's a former police station. Scenes from *The Shawshank Redemption* were filmed here. Also *The Silence of the Lambs*. And Stanley Kubrick was so taken with the claustrophobic look and feel of the cell block, he constructed a scale replica of it (two-thirds actual size) in the basement of his Hertfordshire home, Childwickbury Manor. It's currently used as a wine cellar, but at the time of his death he was working on a screenplay about a prison planet populated entirely by dwarfs.

⊖

~~~: Now, Mr Δ≈ΔΔΔ°◇≥, let's pick up where we left off. You were, as I recall, on the verge of telling us about the unsatisfactory dealings you had with Mr Inkling. Yet hadn't you and he become, as you put it, 'bosom buddies'?

TAYLOR: Not bloody likely! I couldn't stand him. It was a one-sided relationship, if you can call it that. More akin to stalker:victim. Him getting into every aspect of my life and controlling it by stealth or force, mostly force; me trying to put significant distance between us. While I was tied to a chair in one of his apartments, he –

~~~: Say again. He tied you up?

TAYLOR: One of his henchmen did. On Mr Inkling's orders.

~~~: Why was that?

TAYLOR: So I wouldn't escape.

~~~: [...]

TAYLOR: It was the sensible thing to do. I'd tried to escape on several previous occasions. Once I even succeeded; managed to shimmy down a drainpipe from a third-floor office in a Rotherhithe warehouse that backed onto the Thames; dropped straight into the water from the broken end of the pipe; swam to the Wapping shore and ran to my sister's house in Pennington Street, less than a mile away. As luck would have it, Mr Inkling had made me strip to my boxer shorts before locking me in, taking all my other clothes with him. Said he had to visit the floor below to answer a call of nature. As I eased down the pipe, past the lavatory window, making as little noise as possible, I saw him relieving himself into a cracked urinal. He had his back to me, but something, some queer intuition, made him turn his head. For a second or two our eyes met. His bewilderment turning to outrage was a joy to behold. I felt like sticking my tongue out at him, childish though that sounds. He ran to the window but couldn't get it open. Yanked at the handle and it came off in his hand. As I slid further down the pipe I could hear him hammering with it on the meshed glass and bellowing furiously. Flakes of glass showered down as I dropped the last twenty feet or so into the water. Fully clothed, swimming would have been impossible, I might well have drowned. But, as I say, I was lucky: the tide was high and the streets were deserted at that late hour. Only a handful of people saw me and they didn't seem surprised. According to my sister, soaking wet near-naked men running as though their lives depend on it is a regular occurrence in Wapping, especially after the pubs close. She's lived there for thirty years and knows what she's on about.

~~~: Very interesting. Illuminating, even. But please tell the court about the occasion when Mr Inkling's henchman tied you up.

TAYLOR: Occasions. More than one. Lots of times, in fact, using lots of different things: washing line, a regimental tie, various leather belts, a shirt sleeve, a dressing gown cord, duct tape, sellotape, VHS tape and masking tape, a bull whip, an extension cable (plug at one end, socket the other), clingfilm, boot laces, speaker cable, pantyhose – you name it. Almost the only thing he didn't use was barbed wire. Not on me, anyway.

~~~: I see. Forgive me for insisting, but there seemed to be one particular occasion you had in mind. Shall I have the court stenographer read your words back to you, to jog your memory?

TAYLOR: That's kind of you but quite unnecessary. I'm not known on the amateur magician after dinner circuit as Mr Mnemonic for nothing. If shown a sequence of one hundred objects for three seconds each I can, for example, up to six months later, reel them off at breakneck speed, in strict alphabetical order, averaging ninety-eight per cent accuracy,

> According to Srinivasa Ramanujan
> [or someone claiming to speak for him]
> that two per cent can easily be accounted for:
> an occasional table can be
> mistaken for a night stand
> a clementine for a tangerine
> a sock for a glove
> a pip for a squeak.

and I've never once lost my car keys or forgotten to take my books back to the library on time. In fact –

~~~: I know thoroughness is your watchword, Mr $\Delta\approx\Delta\Delta\Delta^\circ\diamond\geq$,

but please try to be concise and keep to the point.

TAYLOR: My apologies. I'll do what I can.

> An empty sardine can
> afloat in a flood
> a lifeboat
> for a half-
> drowned bug.

But there's so much to tell, I hardly know where to begin.

~~~: Just do your best.

TAYLOR: Actually, tell you what, let's skip the tyings-up and jump straight to the kidnappings, which always involved physical restraint of some kind. Such as, for example, the situation I mentioned just a moment ago, when two thugs broke down my door at Vale Hall, blindfolded me and threw me into the back of a limo. Before speeding off, they handcuffed me to the aforementioned ring on the floor of the vehicle. Despite the limo's excellent suspension it was a bumpy ride (temporary road surface on the M23, junction 11, near Pease Pottage), and the blindfold, a length of black crepe, folded twice, wound several times around my head and knotted behind my left ear, gradually rode up. By tilting my head back I could just about see where we'd got to. And as we began to approach London's inner suburbs, it was possible to guess where we were going. Maida Vale. Elgin Avenue. To one of Mr Inkling's favourite haunts: The Marbles – once a Trustee Savings Bank, now a gastropub. According to reliable sources he stores valuables and 'items of interest' (my sources wouldn't say, or didn't know and didn't care to know, what those items might be) in the pub's walk-in safe.

I'd been taken to The Marbles twice before, for a lock-in. Mr Inkling and I hardly spoke during those sessions, but it didn't seem to matter. What he wanted was company, not conversation; someone to sit with him and match him drink for drink, hour upon hour. We drank until we were, as some of my working class friends say, completely bladdered, and the dawn chorus (cars, people, a few asthmatic sparrows) started up.

What I couldn't understand was why, on this occasion, they'd bothered to blindfold me when we were obviously going somewhere I'd been before. The Marbles hardly qualifies as a secret location, now does it? You've been there too, at Mr Inkling's behest – don't deny it, I saw your name in the visitors' book. Nothing to be ashamed of. Many people have supped with Mr Inkling at The Marbles. But why this was happening at sunrise, rather than at midnight, the more appropriate time for a lock-in, I had no idea. It made no sense.

~~~: And their names?

TAYLOR: Whose?

~~~: The thugs you mentioned.

TAYLOR: They neglected to offer a calling card and weren't terribly sociable. I didn't get to know their names until later. Their clothes reeked of stale tobacco smoke, so think of them as Lambert and Butler, Benson and Hedges, Lucky and Strike, as I did. Now please stop interrupting!

~~~: [...]

TAYLOR: Good.

~~~: [...]

TAYLOR: Anyway, while we motored along I was able to peer through the gap between the two front seats. A limited vantage, blocked on three sides, what with the headrests, blindfold and all, but adequate. Then something swam across my field of vision, an arm sleeved in sharkskin, and he – Lambert or Hedges, whichever one of them was occupying the front passenger seat – pinched me hard on my inner right thigh, up near the groin.

Did he think, because my head was tilted far back, that I was napping? Was he under strict orders to keep me awake and fully alert at all times? If so, why? Surely, transporting an abductee while he's drowsy or asleep and therefore passive

Apart from the parasomniacs
some of whom rape
kill
set buildings alight
derail trains and sink ships
while fast asleep
upon waking have no knowledge
of the terrible things they've done
and while reading the
morning news
tut and
sigh
appalled
by the boundless depths of
human folly and
the rampant
imp of the perverse.

is preferable to having him wide awake, agitated (as I most certainly was) and therefore potentially trouble-some (as I was determined to be, given half a chance).

But I'd got it all wrong.

As Strike's or Benson's or Lucky's or Butler's or who-ever's arm withdrew, I noticed something clamped in his fist. It was the briefest of glimpses but I'm sure of what I saw: a hypodermic syringe, his thumb on the plunger, the plunger fully depressed.

That's when things began to get a little hazy. The car hit a bump and seemed to lurch into the air. Having taken flight and achieved optimum cruising speed, it continued to motor along, an inch or two above the road, the engine note becoming as small and distant as a wasp trapped in a bottle. Then the bodywork began to fade. Soon it was as transparent as the windscreen. As, for that matter, were the blindfold, the seats in front of me and their bulky occupants. For a few seconds after that, all I could see, ghostly white, like contrails etched against grey cloud, was the car's chassis, its spinning wheels and throbbing engine. Then even they were gone, and I was travelling through the air by the seat of my pants, the tarmac speeding under me in a dizzying blur.

What happened next is something I can't explain, not even to my own satisfaction.

I was standing in a room I'd never been in before. The blindfold had slipped down over my nose. Someone behind me crooked my arm and pushed my elbow, hissing into my ear: 'Give it to them if they don't do what they're told.' As if powered by leaky hydraulics, my hand rose slowly and none too steadily to chest height, and to my astonishment there was a gun clasped in it, a gun pointed at two small, dark-skinned individuals standing close together, a man and a woman.

A glass-topped wooden counter stood between us laden with confectionery, chewing gum, scratch cards, newspapers and a collection box for an obscure charity, something to do with glands – renal, I think. Behind them were shelves stacked to the ceiling with tobacco and spirits.

The couple had their hands raised and looked scared. Angry, puzzled and scared, to be precise. Mainly angry. I couldn't blame them, but in truth I experienced none of the emotions they were feeling. Numb was how I felt. Untouched by circumstance. Even though what I seemed to be doing was unlawful. Perhaps because the situation was controlling me, rather than vice versa. There I was holding a gun – some kind of revolver (I'm no expert, but that's what I think it was), with a fat cylinder in the middle like a beer keg and a snub nose with a rounded bump at the end

A pug-ugly-
looking thing.
The Ernest Borgnine
of weaponry.

on two people who were so alike they were probably siblings rather than husband and wife.

'Fuck's sake, try to look mean!' growled the voice in my ear, which belonged, I assumed, to the elbow pusher. (But where was his accomplice? There can be no Hedges without Benson, no Strike without Lucky.)

'Grimace. You look like a rabbit caught in the crosshairs. Bare your teeth. We've knocked one out and chipped the one next to it, to make you look more dangerous.'

And so they had. When I probed with my tongue I found jagged edges and a canine-shaped gap. The funny taste in my mouth was blood.

'Say "Gimme the money and don't fuck about."'

'Give me the money.'

'And ...? And ...? Come on, where's the rest of it?'

'Don't mess about.'

'Again. Louder, you pussy. More menacing. And get the words right, this isn't a fucking dress rehearsal.'

'Give me the money and don't fuck about.'

'Again. In a Glaswegian or Cockney accent, preferably Cockney – you're too posh to be convincing. Try to sound like metal scraping on metal. Squeeze the words out rapidly, loud and proud, like machine gun bullets: ratt-att-att-att-att.'

'GIMME-THE-MONEY-AND-DON'T-FUCK-ABAHT!'

'Terrible. An absolute fucking shambles. But it'll have to do. You really aren't cut out for this line of work, are you!'

Because I didn't know what to say, I said nothing. Did nothing. I froze in motion like one of the ash-smothered citizens of Herculaneum. We might well have remained there to this day, in tableau vivant, but the woman broke the spell with an angry outburst. 'Go on then, take all our hard-earned cash. Take it and get out, you despicable little turd!' 'Little' was pejorative and just plain wrong – she was four foot eleven if an inch, and although I'm only of average height I towered over her without meaning to. But I was glad to receive instruction.

She jabbed at something under the counter and a till drawer clattered open, bouncing off its rubber retards. As I reached out with my gunless hand – slowly, none too steadily – to take a fistful of notes from the twenties pile, she lunged at me, tore the blindfold from my face and pointed at something high on the wall. Foolishly, I looked at what that something was and found myself staring into the lens of a CCTV camera. I couldn't take my eyes off it. Nor did it take its beady eye off me. (I feel as though it's kept an eye on me ever since, following me everywhere I go, even deep into Epping Forest where I shared a yurt with Mr Inkling. Were I to land on the far side of the moon, as the founder and sole inhabitant of a New Earth colony, it would already be there, waiting for me. I suspect it will follow me to my grave, into the coffin itself, and together we'll be buried six feet under, to rot and rust, each to his own. — If there's a crumb of comfort to be gleaned from that thought, please tell me what it is.) The pitiless glass eye held my gaze. I blinked first and felt crushed. My heart stopped beating. It's the last thing I can recall before the room started to spin and I slipped gratefully into unconsciousness.

I found myself back at Vale Hall, in bed, nursing a monumental hangover – if that's what it was. To my knowledge, the strongest thing I'd drunk the previous evening was decaf coffee. Or might it have been the evening before? Time and memory were no longer in sync.

There was a polite tap at the bedroom door, scattering my thoughts. Probably Livvy – Olivia Strang, my next-door neighbour, god of Midlife Crises, Arguments About Arguments, Angry Walkouts, Irretrievable Marriage Breakdowns and Parental Child Abductions and/or Abandonments – who held spare keys to my cottage, 'just,' she said, 'in case' (but of what?). She was always forgetting to buy milk, always popping round to borrow some, and after a while I got accustomed to doubling the quantity I bought. But neither my kindness nor the milk were taken for granted; she invariably gave or did something in return.

For example, after Lambert and Hedges broke down my door, she offered to fix it and did an excellent job, as one would expect of someone who'd previously been the 'portcullis' (so-called – not an official title) god of Door Bars, Latches, Locks and Bolts. (Her favourite lock being the five-lever mortise deadlock, conforming, so she told me – which for some reason I've remembered and probably always will – to BS 3621. That was the type of lock she fitted to my door. Two of them, for added security.) The fortified hinges I myself supplied and to the best of my ability fitted.

Livvy was a good friend, if occasionally intrusive and somewhat eccentric. Helpful in her own peculiar way. While I was far from home, on god business, she watered the plants and spent quality time rearranging my socks and underwear, colour coding them in accordance with the days of the week.

'Hello?' Not Livvy. A man, someone I didn't know. 'Hello. May I come in?' The door opened an inch or two.

'You're already in, whether I like it or not. What do you want?'

'Are you decent? Oh, I see you are, if a little rumpled. I'm here to inform you that Mr Inkling requests the pleasure of your company at a private screening.'

The depths of my sigh must have shifted tectonic plates and set boats bobbing wildly on the Tasman Sea.

'Tell him thank you but no. I've got a diary shoehorned with appointments today. And tomorrow, for that matter. And I'll be away at the weekend.'

'That's unfortunate,' he said, 'but irrelevant. I'm afraid attendance is compulsory. And Mr Inkling stressed that you need to be presentable. He noted that your standards of hygiene, dress and even deportment have become slipshod of late, something he absolutely cannot abide or allow to continue. Your manner, too, leaves a lot to be desired. He told me that, then told me to tell you what he'd said, which is what I'm doing. I'm also recording our exchanges' – indicates a voice recorder poking out of the breast pocket of his jacket and a thin wire leading to a microphone, disguised as a poppy, clipped to the lapel – 'in accordance with Mr Inkling's instructions, so that on playback he may be satisfied that his orders have been carried out to the letter, as indeed, for the sake of my health, I hope they have. He also said that as a courtesy I should explain about the voice recorder. Which I've now done. That's the niceties taken care of.

'Please shave, shower, brush your teeth, comb your hair – a left parting, the side Mr Inkling favours

According to Paul Honeyman
Rex Cribbage's biographer
any man with
a well-trimmed moustache and slicked down
dark hair
much longer on top than sides and back
who parts it on the right
reminds
Mr Inkling of
Hitler.

– and put on your Sunday best. I'll wait in the car.'

When I inspected my teeth in the shaving mirror, I saw the gap recently occupied by my canine friend: a tooth once proud and strong, who lorded it over his fellow teeth – master of the molars, boss of the bicuspids, etc. I mourned him then, the one I suddenly realised I loved best, better than all my human friends (than all of them combined, truth be told) and family too. I swore that his death would not go unavenged!

~~~: Condolences on your loss, Mr $\Delta \approx \Delta \Delta \Delta° \diamond \geq$. In a minute or two we'll hold a one-minute silence, which will allow us to reflect on the sacrifice made by your enamel-coated friend. Then we'll sound *Reveille* – one of our witnesses is a trumpeter who, luckily for us, was expecting to attend a rehearsal this evening and has his instrument with him – followed by a solemn recitation of the *Ode of Remembrance*. We'll then sing several rousing choruses of *O Valiant Hearts*, a perennial favourite in the Harris version (though Holst's and Vaughan Williams's settings are a tad more adventurous), and conclude with *The Last Post*. As to how you may gain legal redress for your missing tooth –

TAYLOR: Not missing, murdered! Murdered! There's no other word for it. But thank you. I'm grieving to this day, hence the black armband. Occasionally, still, stricken by grief, I'll come to an abrupt halt on a crowded street, a rock in a fast-flowing stream, people surging around me, giving me the wary eye and as wide a berth as possible, even to the point of stepping into traffic, while I stand there forlorn, weeping unashamedly. Youngsters jeer, getting right in my face, the callous little bastards, and take pictures with their mobile phones. They also take selfies – of themselves and me. Some drape an arm across my shoulders while doing so, but in mockery not sympathy. Just last week one of them pretended to lick and bite my neck while winking lasciviously at the camera, while I stood stock still, like a wooden Indian. Caked white makeup, panda eyes, black lipstick: vampire chic. A Goth girl. She showed the pic to her giggling corpse-faced girlfriends, then posted it on Facebook and Instagram and who knows where else. Said it would go viral, whatever that means.

~~~: I confess, because you've always been known, at least in god circles, as something of a style guru, I assumed the armband was a fashion statement. Mr Inkling's charge of slovenliness must have rankled. But can we, just for one moment, concentrate on the screening? That would seem to be the nub of the matter. To start with, where was it held?

TAYLOR: In a small editing suite – I believe that's what they're called – in a building on Sutton Row, just off Soho Square. A windowless room. Not a speck of dust anywhere, the way Mr Inkling likes it. He's extremely fastidious, as well you know. Seating for five: two mismatched chairs up front, by a canted, wraparound mixing console, all knobs and sliders and winking LEDs; three behind, flip seats, standard cinema issue. Directly above the console were two wall-mounted flatscreen TVs, or computer monitors, butted edge to edge. I was pushed into the newest-looking (price tag still attached) of the two chairs at the front and told, gruffly, not to touch anything or

QUOTE Mr Itchyfingers' fingers will be severed joint by joint UNQUOTE. The threat of violence was typical. It was also unnecessary: I've never been an inveterate tinkerer.

After my minder left the room, locking the door behind him, I sat there brooding. You would too, given the circumstances. I still felt emotionally numb from the shenanigans of the day before. Drained of all energy. Desperately hungover. But I noticed immediately that the chair had excellent lumbar support. It mirrored the knobbly contours of my spine as if bespoke, which, as I discovered later that morning, it was. Despite the many factors that weigh heavily in his disfavour, Mr Inkling is often kind and considerate: the chair was a present for my fifty-seventh (human years) birthday. And it was, I have to admit, extremely comfortable. Too comfortable. I dozed off almost immediately and almost immediately (or so it seemed) Mr Inkling shook me awake, saying, with hearty enthusiasm, 'Come on, Charlie-boy, rise and shine, there's a good lad. I've something really special to show you.' Indeed he had. Special but by no means welcome. I was –

~~~: I hate to stop you there, Mr $\Delta\approx\Delta\Delta\Delta°\diamond\geq$, in characteristically full flow ('when it comes to words he's a veritable force of nature: an avalanche, a tsunami, a raging forest fire, all occurring simultaneously in the same crowded space', to quote from your recent peer-to-peer performance review, which I just happen to have open in front of me, written, I see, by our old pal Temerity Tench, god of Superlatives and Soft-Soap [you really did luck out when you got him as your line manager]) – but hush, now's the time to pause and reflect.

ONE MINUTE SILENCE

TAYLOR: Thank you for that. I can't tell you how much it means to me. But as I was saying –

TRUMPETER STANDS IN THE DOORWAY AND PLAYS *REVEILLE*

TAYLOR: I was –

USHER RECITES FROM MEMORY THE *ODE OF REMEMBRANCE*
SONOROUSLY AND WITH GREAT CONVICTION

TAYLOR: What I wanted –

O VALIANT HEARTS, VERSES 1-3, SUNG BY THE FOLLOWING:
JUDGE, TRUMPETER, USHER, STENOGRAPHER, DR ANON [Dental and Oral
Health Care Sciences, Paediatrics], AND BELATEDLY, THROUGH
A MOUTHFUL OF GRAVEL BECAUSE HE
KNOWS HARDLY ANY
OF THE WORDS,
MR Δ≈ΔΔΔ°◊≥

TAYLOR: You're really too kind. But what I was about to say was –

TRUMPETER SOUNDS *THE LAST POST*, HIS CRACKED NOTES
SUGGESTING STRONG EMOTION
RATHER THAN POOR MUSICIANSHIP

TAYLOR: From the bottom of my heart, thank you. Never in the
history of humankind – and godkind, for that matter –
has a tooth been so honoured. Very touching. My late
lamented tooth's fellow teeth would have wept, if weep
they could.

> Although the emotional range of teeth is large
> much larger than dentists are willing to acknowledge
> their means of expression are severely limited.

Instead they ached in sympathy, from root to crown. Now
where were we?

~~~: The screening room? Sutton Row?

TAYLOR: Ah yes. Where the depth of my disgrace was made plain. An edited recording of the failed hold-up was played again and again – slightly speeded up, if I'm not mistaken – in a demented loop. We must have watched it fifty times, Mr Inkling and I. He cackling throughout, saying, 'The look on your face – absolutely priceless!' And: '"Don't fuck abaht" – what kind of accent is that? Cockernee? You're a regular potty-mouthed Dick Van Dyke, Charlie-boy. Look, here it comes again, cracks me up every time. If you had an Equity card they'd be demanding it back pronto, with menaces. "Don't fuck abaht" – I'll make that the ringtone on my mobile.' Slapping his knee. Doubling up with laughter. Fat tears rolling down his cheeks, wiped away with the back of his hand.

Let misery be unconfined, at least on my part: Mr Inkling was having a whale of a time.

After he'd drunk deep of my humiliation and slaked his thirst we sat in silence, each absorbed in his own thoughts. The temperature in the room had plummeted, to match my icy mood.

'This,' he said eventually, in sombre tones, 'is a grave situation, Charlie. Very worrying. I had no idea you were criminally inclined. You've led my boys astray and they've gone on the run. Fled the UK for the Costas, never to be seen again. Good riddance. No-one will miss them apart from their mothers, and even then probably not. In fact, because of Deke's lurching gait, general misshapenness and many, many scars (which he claimed were the result of falling off a mountain – a likely story, he wasn't the outdoors type, he didn't even like visiting garden centres), I thought he was an experiment gone wrong, pieced together by a mad scientist from butchers' offcuts and graveyard finds, sparked into life with a lightning bolt, and never had a mum at all. So good riddance to him, he wasn't a prime business asset.

'Nor, really, was Attila – the perfect name for someone with iron fists and a short fuse. Always getting into scraps, that one. Killed his older brother, the kiddie fiddler, beat him to death for some other reason and served eight years of the tariff. I suppose I'd better give his parole officer the bad news, not that she'll be surprised. I'm a sucker for the idea of rehabilitation and always employ her top no-hopers.

'But, fighting apart, Attila was a good chauffeur. He never put so much as a scratch on any of my vehicles. From time to time, when I'd had a few bevvies over the limit, I let him, as a treat, drive me home in one of the vintage models. His double-declutching was textbook, like Fred Astaire dancing lightly on the pedals. He'd learned it from an old pro – an old Etonian, in fact – who stole vintage trucks and delivery vans to order, mainly for Russian oligarchs. Anyway, that's sewage under the bridge, as they say. Those two are gone and we're here and you're in, to say the least, a wee bit of trouble. So what are we going to do about it?'

He genuinely seemed to expect an answer to his question, but I had none to give. The situation was beyond my control. I'd been stitched up as tight as Oliver Hardy in Stan Laurel's shroud, to comic effect, though I didn't find it even remotely amusing.

'Now,' he said, 'apart from "Don't fuck abaht", which tickles me no end, I'm happy to delete the CCTV footage. A touch of the button and it's gone. That's what friends are for. But' – heavy sigh – 'the couple who run the shop aren't anywhere near as amenable. They've tucked a copy away in a safe place and have said they'll take it to the police unless we supply them with wampum, plenty wampum. I coughed up the initial sum of money they demanded (a hefty sum at that, Charlie; repay me at your leisure) but I should've strung them along, I know I should. It was a considerable error of judgment on my part, for which I apologise. I should've stalled and quibbled, dragging the whole process out to an inordinate degree, grinding the buggers down until, exhausted but triumphant, they settled for iron pyrite thinking they'd hit the mother lode. More fool me. I was deeply concerned for your welfare, Charlie. Keeping you out of jail was all that mattered. But because I panicked and folded immediately, they thought infinitely richer pickings were to be had. Greed is their god. They worship filthy lucre in all its forms: the pound, the dollar, the euro, the yen and, I wouldn't be surprised to discover, the cowry shell and the Palau holy water coin. Demands for wampum are still being made, hour upon hour; the text messages are coming in thick and fast, the threats increasing in magnitude, and' – heavier sigh – 'I'm bound to conclude that no amount of wampum will suffice. Not even the untapped reserves of the bank of England could satisfy their money lust.

'Something radical needs to be done, something – how can I put it? – terminal.

'They live over the shop in five shabby rooms. There's no fire escape and the building is in terrible condition, a death trap. I should know: I own it. Antiquated electrical wiring smoulders in the walls. The heat it generates easily outtherms the so-called heating system, which is of similar vintage. Better still, there's a leaky gas valve in the basement, right next to an open fusebox. One day soon, according to the most recent inspection report, which I had to have suppressed, the whole shebang will go up in flames. It's inevitable. But why wait? Why not make it happen now, tonight, while the moon is a sliver and, by special arrangement, the two nearest steetlamps are broken? Strike while the wiring is hot, eh, Charlie. What do you say?'

I said no.

When I got home, I contacted our local field representative, Bernie Rawlings, god of Shovel Hardened Hands and Elbow Grease (the traditional concerns of all trade union shop stewards), who forwarded my request for an intervention to the Council of Elders, marked urgent. But to save you asking, which will derail my train of thought, something you seem determined to do, let me tell you what transpired. Nothing.

~~~: What ... nothing at all?

TAYLOR: Nothing means just that: nothing. Not a sausage.

~~~: That's highly irregular.

TAYLOR: Quite. I've lodged an official complaint with the ombudsman. Or, to be precise, ombudswoman.

~~~: Antonia Huff?

TAYLOR: How did you guess?

~~~: I heard her speak, the year before last, in Bognor Regis, at the three hundred and forty-first plenum of the central committee of the UK Council of Elders, which I attended as a humble usher.

An extremely formidable woman, Tonya. Very bracing. She'd been invited to give a keynote speech on a topic of pressing concern, though for the life of me I can't remember what it was. But I do recall the powerful impression she made. I'd never experienced anything like it. When she got to her feet to address the delegates you could hear spines stiffen throughout the auditorium. The cracking of synovial joints as they popped back into place, in strict alignment, sounded like an orchestra of castanets. And when everyone stood up to leave, I swear they were two to three inches taller than when they came in, me included, an effect that has lasted to this day.

So it's hardly surprising that a dozen or so of the delegates who'd been working as chiropractors claimed to have witnessed a miracle cure, having seen their fellow gods permanently relieved by Tonya of all manner of chronic back ailments, including, allegedly, a case of advanced myeloma

Although
a week or two later
the delegate in question
Jack Bissonnette
god of Unfashionable Wall Coverings [anaglypta and
flock, in particular]
died
having been riddled like a colander
or Swiss cheese
[or Swiss cheese plant]
with the following cancers:
bowel
liver
prostate
brain
kidney
lung
breast
throat
colon
pancreas
and
eye.

and shortly thereafter founded a religious order to worship her spine-stiffening image.

Gods worshipping gods?
What's
the world coming to?
It'll be gods
worshipping humans
next.

They burned or shredded their M.Chiro certificates and became Celebrants of the Healing Cult of Tonya – Huffists as they're known to the outside world – and took up the lease on a small steading near East Grinstead. It's now a house of spiritual retreat. Prayer and contemplation, that kind of thing. The celebrants don't go into town and keep themselves very much to themselves, which engenders curiosity and suspicion. When non-god chiropractors turn up, wishing to join the cult, they're politely but firmly turned away. Door-stepping journalists, the scum of the earth, are rebuffed violently. That's why newspapers love to publish anti-Huffist stories, the more lurid and apocalyptic the better. But because no-one has defected or been ejected from the cult, and Tonya has steadfastly declined to be interviewed, the hacks have nothing to go on other than idle gossip and wild speculation.

Periodically the journos root through the Huffists' refuse and recycling bins, searching for 'incriminating evidence', something on which to lavish a thousand gilded words, something perhaps worthy of a byline. It's wasted effort. All they find is the humdrum debris of a larger-than-average household, the members of which prefer pasta to pizza and Indian takeaways to Chinese.

Increasingly desperate, they prowl the steading at night, shining torches through windows in the hope of catching the celebrants doing weird and worrying things – stripping down, oiling and reassembling a large cache of illegal firearms, for example, while wearing condoms on their heads like beanie hats, or packing excrement into hollowed out copies of the Bible, the Koran and other holy books.

Luckless hacks; one could almost feel sorry for them. Having nothing worth writing about, with deadlines looming, they invoke their patron saint, Francis de Sales, who never fails to sanction the use of creative licence when facts are few or, as with the Huffists, non-existent.

TAYLOR: Anyway, as I was saying, my response to Mr Inkling's murderous proposal was no! No no no! Absolutely not! But I could tell he wasn't listening. When he doesn't want to hear something, it simply doesn't register.

'Y'know what, Charlie,' he said, 'I completely forgot to show you my eels. What a scatterbrain I am. New stock. Delivered yesterday while you were busy at the newsagent's. Right little beauties they are, too – you'll see.' So saying, he took me by the arm and led me out into the noise and bustle of Soho.

I assumed that a limousine would be waiting for us at the kerb, the one that brought me from Vale Hall, its engine purring contentedly; that we'd be chauffeured to Canary Wharf, to his penthouse, where, as you know, he keeps tanks of tropical fish in the reception area and boardroom. Instead, we crossed Soho Square and walked a little way down Carlisle Street, then turned into a blind alley I'd never noticed before. He stopped, produced a key almost as large as a bishop's crosier, and inserted it into the lock of a door sunk deep into the wall. 'Tradesman's entrance,' he said, by way of explanation. The door opened onto a short corridor, which led to a windowless room suffused with a faint, unearthly glow. The corners of the room were distant and in darkness. The ceiling was as high as the sky and painted with white, fluffy clouds. From the glitterball hanging overhead, at the end of a long length of chain, I realised this must once have been a ballroom, or perhaps a nightclub.

There was nothing in that vast space other than an aquarium, the size of which astounded me. Tall, deep and wrapped around three of the four walls, it filled almost the entire room. 'Most zoos can't handle tanks this big,' he explained. 'Almost two million gallons of sea water. I had to have the floor reinforced. Foundations, too. As well as the buildings to either side. Not to mention the hassle of having to bring liquid refreshment up the Thames every few days from out in the North Sea: a spot midway between here and Denmark where conditions are just right. The tank is divided into three compartments so one can be serviced while the other two are occupied. This is where the boys are housed.' He pointed to a section of tank that was dimly lit. 'In case you're wondering, it has to be kept like this. They won't come out to gambol about if the light's too bright. Sensitive creatures is what they are, though judging by their table manners you wouldn't think so. Here, let me show you.'

He clapped his hands twice and immediately, out of the gloom, stepped a man in a white lab coat, pushing a catering trolley with a squeaky wheel. The front of his coat was smeared with fresh blood and fish scale. As were his hands. On the top shelf of the trolley was a lidded ceramic pot the size of a small dustbin. 'Say hello to Ingo Peck, marine conservator. I poached him from Deep Sea World, up in bonnie Scotland, where it rains incessantly and his eel-wrangling skills were under-appreciated. His wife-beating skills, too. Ingo, this is my pal Charlie Taylor. He's here to see the boys tuck into their lunch, or' – consulting his watch – 'elevenses. Actually, you can call it whatever you like, eels couldn't care less and they're always hungry.'

Peck and I touched palms, each wary of the other, and some of the slime on his hand transferred to mine. Surreptitiously I wiped it off on the seat of my pants.

'Y'see, Charlie,' said Mr Inkling, 'congers are shy. Sensitive and shy, just like you. Proper little wallflowers. Isn't that right, Ingo?' The conservator grunted; obviously a man of few words. Whereas, when the topic was hot, as now, Mr Inkling was not.

'This,' he said, indicating the tank, 'is a faithful replica of the bed of the North Sea at the sweet spot I mentioned earlier. Take my word for it: I've been down there recently to check. Can't be too careful. Things change when you least expect it, and when they do it's rarely for the better.' Rocks, sand, weed, silt and a few lethargic fish, survivors of the EU fishing quota, wondering where all their finny friends had gone. The surface of the water was choppy, agitated by a machine I could faintly hear but not see.

'The boys are in their element, as happy as ... well, clams, I suppose. Can you see them yet?' I screwed up my eyes, as though concentrating (I'd left my spectacles on the bedside table at Vale Hall), and shook my head. 'Take a closer look. Over there. Those small, shadowy crevices in among the rocks.' He pointed. Obediently I followed where his finger led. There was nothing to see but murk and, as he said, rocks, fuzzy rocks piled upon fuzzy rocks, barren as a moonscape.

I was beginning to think he was teasing me, something he enjoyed doing, the more cruel the tease the better. But apparently not. He gave a small grunt of irritation. 'Fuck's sake, Ingo, help him out or we'll be here all fucking day.'

In one fluid motion, the conservator removed a folding aluminium stepladder from the lower shelf of the trolley and erected it with a well-practised flick of the wrist. Taking a large scoop of food from the pot, he scrambled up the ladder, lifted a gunmetal hatch in the top of the tank, and cast wet gobbets of it into the choppy waters. As the meat sank towards the rocks, most of the blood stayed behind, in suspension, blossoming into clouds that gradually dispersed, turning from ruby red to watery pink before disappearing completely. Still nothing happened. The meat fell through the water in slow motion, shivering in the machine-generated current.

'Any minute now,' said Mr Inkling. That was when I saw something that perhaps I wasn't supposed to see and wish to this day I hadn't. Something that froze the marrow in my bones.

Among the half dozen or so lumps of meat that were slowly sinking to the bottom of the tank, one was slightly larger than the others. But that wasn't why it grabbed my attention. Em-oh-tee-aitch-ee was why. MOTHE: a word inked in gothic script, jet black, missing its final capital. It was identical to a tattoo I'd seen only yesterday, on the nape of the gorilla who drove me to the newsagent's from Vale Hall. The bottom two-thirds of MOTHER had been hidden by his shirt collar and bisected by a greasy ponytail, but I'd had ample time to view it while peeking out from under the blindfold.

And now, because the flesh on which it was inscribed was sinking incredibly slowly, as if in a medium much denser than water, I had ample time to view it again. I tried to persuade myself that I was mistaken, in shock, that what I was seeing in the tank was a hallucination, a toxic residue of the drug I'd been injected with. No such luck. It was precisely what I thought it was.

That's when something long and greeny grey surged out from among the rocks, grabbed MOTHE in its powerful jaws and wriggled back, tail first, into its lair. It happened so quickly I didn't see where the creature came from. The gaps in the rock looked too narrow to accommodate something as big as that. Other eels were now emerging and feeding voraciously, but they were small compared to the monster I'd seen, two-and-half metres long, its muscular body as thick as a man's thigh.

'Impressive specimen, isn't he?' said Mr Inkling, as the conservator ladled out a second helping of food, then a third. The eels disposed of it in a matter of seconds, seething the water and churning up great clouds of silt, obscuring everything in that part of the tank, for which, though I'm not usually squeamish, I was grateful.

So much for the theory that Deke and Attila had fled to the Costas ... though Mr Inkling's prediction that they'd never be seen again was, at least for one of them, correct. And two was more likely than one. They'd been chopped up for fish food, probably by Ingo Peck, on Mr Inkling's orders. What they'd done to deserve such a fate I had no idea, but I wasn't about to ask.

The following morning, when I switched on the radio, there was further shocking news. Fire had gutted a three-storey building in a row of shops on Holland Park Avenue, claiming two lives, a man and a woman, both found in bed, burnt to a cinder. Their names were being withheld until next of kin had been informed.

A fire scene investigator said faulty wiring was probably to blame, though arson couldn't be ruled out. There was, however, something odd: the batteries were missing from the smoke alarms. Not just one or two – all of them. The discarded batteries were found in a bin at the rear of the premises, in a locked yard only the shopkeepers had access to, and when tested they were found to be almost fully charged. Moreover, the shop was well stocked with batteries of that kind, so they could easily have been replaced.

Why, he was asked, did he think the batteries had been discarded? And why would anyone choose to disable not one but all of the smoke alarms?

He said he didn't wish to speculate, those were matters for the police and the coroner to decide.

~~~: Quite right!

TAYLOR: I'm sorry ...?

~~~: The arrogance of these so-called journalists, always asking ill-formulated, idiotic or irrelevant questions.

[81]

Always?
Don't the two
just mentioned
pass muster?

Invariably failing to provide a pertinent follow-up question.

[ahem]

Barely listening to whatever answer is being given before interrupting and breathlessly asking another question, then another, in stunningly swift succession, piling them up as a bulwark against knowledge and truth.

Only death can stay their tongue and sometimes not even then. It's no secret that when mediums in the Spiritualists' National Union hold a séance, they live in dread of summoning up the spirit of a journalist, especially one recently deceased and understandably perplexed, knowing that their questions will be met by a torrent of counter-questions arriving faster than a greased planchette, and nothing even remotely useful will be learned.

A recently published wide-ranging occupational study found that the only adults likely to ask more questions in an average working day than the police and psychotherapists – the latter passive-aggressive inquisitors par excellence – were journalists. Most revealing of all was the study's tick-box section. From a long list of descriptors, pro and con, the box-tickers, a focus group drawn from all walks of life, were asked to select the defining characteristics of various trades and professions. Journalists came out badly. Worst of all, in fact. Even worse than politicians. Insensitive, slippery and charmless were the descriptors most often attributed to them. In the Additional Comments box, one anonymised box-ticker wrote that given the choice of having a terrorist or a journalist as a next-door neighbour, he/she would plump for the terrorist.

An unlikely scenario, but that's as may be.

The greatest inquisitors of all, as everyone knows, aren't journalists, they're four-year-olds, girls in particular, who on average ask three hundred questions per day, many if not most of which are profound and unanswerable.

Clinical psychologists are puzzled as to why journalists seem
never to have outgrown this childish trait.
Perhaps because of autism.
Though factors such as inadequate weaning and an
obsessive compulsive disorder
or two
may be contributory.

Shakespeare, Ghandi, Hypatia of Alexandria, Confucius and Mary Wollstonecraft, working as a brains trust under the chairmanship of King Solomon, would struggle to satisfy the average four-year-old's craving for knowledge. But at least, when an answer is given, the child is usually able to make sense of it and put aspects of this new-found knowledge to good use. Not so journalists, who seem unable to fully comprehend anything they're told, as one can immediately tell from the repetitive, woefully garbled copy they submit, written in clunky prose that only estate agents and the authors of tax forms and lift maintenance manuals would find aesthetically pleasing.

TAYLOR: Three hundred questions? Really? That's an awful lot. Didn't I read, and quite recently too, in *Scientific American* or *Reader's Digest*, that just thirty pertinent questions asked of the right individuals, living and dead, would elicit answers sufficient to explain the intricate workings of the universe and the nature of human existence? But the scale of enquiry in this court is very much smaller. Tiny, really. Jimmy Inkling: he alone. And you've asked, according to my rough estimate, thirty-three questions (two of them rhetorical, so perhaps they don't count), yet we seem to have got almost nowhere.

~~~: You're right. I hang my head in shame. But my intentions were pure. All I wanted to do was enlighten Dr Anon, he of Dental and Oral Health Care Sciences, Paediatrics, if possible.

TAYLOR: He's asleep.

~~~: Fast asleep?

TAYLOR: So it would seem. I can hear him snoring – the light, fluttery snore of a shrew, or a small rodent of some kind. He's indulging in a spot of REM, unless I'm mistaken.

~~~: Since when?

TAYLOR: Sleep – hmm – about forty minutes ago, shortly after *The Last Post* was sounded. REM – just now. A swifter descent through the sleep stages than one would expect. He's obviously exhausted.

~~~: Then all this has been in vain. That's a depressing thought. Many's the time I've been overwhelmed by such thoughts. In my bleakest moments, were I to find myself alone in a room with a hangman's noose dangling from a sturdy beam

And just how likely is that?

I'd be sorely tempted to thrust my head through it, tighten the knot and launch myself into space, by which I mean, of course, oblivion.

TAYLOR: Oblivion?

~~~: Blessed oblivion. Nothingness, if you prefer. The dreamless sleep of sleeps.

TAYLOR: I can't believe I'm hearing this. You're saying you don't believe in an afterlife? You, a spirit – or is it psychic? – medium!

~~~: Despite my bluff exterior, Mr $\Delta \approx \Delta \Delta \Delta° \diamond \geq$, I'm constantly assailed by doubts. I consider myself the rankest of rank amateurs, a hobbyist who, because of pressures of work,

devotes hardly any time to his hobby and has therefore, unsurprisingly, limited success. Very limited success. Almost none, in fact. We gods are overworked and undervalued even by our fellow gods, especially by the Council of Elders, as well you know. I don't own a crystal ball or a ouija board or any of the other props that professional clairvoyants and mediums, especially the flaky ones (i.e. most of them – perhaps, to be brutally honest, nearly all of them, myself included), consider essential. Cross my palm with silver and you'll probably be throwing your money away.

But caveat emptor and all that. Let's hear no more about it.

Under the circumstances, the best course of action is to keep busy, to drive away those suicidal thoughts. They quickly sully the air in a locked room such as this and have a deleterious effect on everyone in it. That's why prisons are so dangerous for guards and inmates alike. Which reminds me ... Usher, please bring Mr Honeyman up from the cells. I'd hate to think of him giving way to despair. We probably should have confiscated his belt and shoelaces, just in case.

TAYLOR: Don't worry. He was wearing double buckle slip-ons. Italian. Terrifically stylish for a biographer; they're usually the down-at-heels type. He may, of course, try to beat himself to death with one of them, but I doubt it. And no belt.

~~~: If you say so. Your powers of observation are extraordinary, Mr $\Delta \approx \Delta\Delta\Delta°\diamond\geq$. As prodigious as your memory, which I suppose it would have to be.

TAYLOR: What about Dr Anon, shall we wake him?

~~~: Best not. He'll only start complaining about the lack of refreshments. — But what's this I see? No sooner mentioned than here they are, bang on time. Thank you, Tiffany. Yes, mine's the double-shot latte. Mr Usher, Miss

Stenographer, you're both teas, aren't you – one with, one without.

USHER: I'm the without.

~~~: Help yourselves to sugar if you're not sweet enough already.

USHER: Shall I fetch Mr Honeyman, like you said?

~~~: On second thoughts, no. Let him stew a bit longer, it'll teach him a valuable lesson.

USHER: And the witnesses out in the corridor that have yet to be called?

~~~: Well, there's plenty of tasty things to go round, a veritable feast of sandwiches, pastries, and cake. Whatever we don't eat, they can have. But didn't we order two croque monsieurs? I see only one. You'd better have it, Mr $\Delta\approx\Delta\Delta\Delta°◇\geq$. Get it inside you while it's still piping hot. A cold croque, in my opinion, is fit for nothing but the dustbin.

TAYLOR: Wasn't it ordered for Dr Anon?

~~~: It was, but let him sleep, he obviously needs it more than he needs to be fed. In fact, it looks like he could do with shedding a pound or two. Or more. I hate to say it, but he's verging on obese. And it really isn't necessary for him to be awake; we're recording the proceedings so he can listen to them later, before delivering his verdict. Or perhaps after. So perhaps not in vain after all. But there's lots of good eating to be had before then. Help yourselves. Come on, tuck in!

Second Session

~~~: Welcome back, Mr Honeyman. Am I to assume from your look of disgruntlement that the bunk in your cell was uncomfortable? Substantially less comfortable than the beds at the Athenaeum? I do hope so. Claustrophobic in its narrowness and way too short, the bunk

> Brought to you by the same
> people who configure
> airline seating
> economy class.

is designed to punish you while you sleep, assisted in this noble endeavour by a thin, lumpy mattress and sandpaper sheets, the top sheet overlaid with scratchy wool blankets and a leaden grey coverlet of indeterminate cloth that, miraculously, feels even worse than it looks, i.e. as hard as lead and every bit as heavy. Standard issue, along with the bedbugs.

> For prison service use only.
> Specially bred from
> mutated eggs
> at Porton Down.

Unsusceptible to insecticides
impervious to radiation
and with no
known predator.

Old lags say you get used to them in time, that their bites are just love bites, softer than a baby's kiss. It's a lie, all swagger and swank. But time in abundance is definitely what you'll get unless you quit stalling and answer my questions.

HONEYMAN: Don't count your chickens. I told you before, I'm keeping schtum.

~~~: Ah ... but that was, as you say, before. Things have moved on and circumstances have changed. During the recess a cycle courier arrived bearing gifts – important documents, legally binding. Once they've been signed, you, your wife, your children and grandchildren –

HONEYMAN: Grandchildren?

~~~: – will enter the Witness Protection Scheme. You'll be relocated en bloc to the outskirts of a large town or small city, to a street on a new-build housing estate where new faces won't arouse suspicion because everyone's face is new. There you'll be kept safe from retribution at the hands of Mr Inkling and his gang. Cosmetic surgery, to substantially alter your appearance, will be provided free of charge, and following psychiatric evaluation some protectees opt for gender reassignment. Think of that: you could become a woman; your wife, Tamsin, a man. As you're roughly the same height and of similar build you wouldn't even have to buy new clothes, you could just swap wardrobes. Essentially, you'd be given what most people crave but can't have: the opportunity to start over with strong financial and psychological support, a clean slate, and the benefit of hindsight. You could ditch writing, it's an awful faff, and become a crane driver or a bingo caller, the kind of fun job you'd always dreamt of

having but never had the courage to try. How could you? You knew your parents would disapprove. They'd given you food rich in vitamins, minerals and dietary fibre; moral guidance by example rather than diktat; a happy home and a sound education: so, naturally, they expected nothing but the best of you. Of course they did. And you didn't have the heart to disappoint them, did you? But now they're gone, dead and buried –

HONEYMAN: Cremated, actually.

~~~: – whereas you're alive and well, footloose and fancy free. You can choose to become whatever you want. Those, Mr Honeyman, are the not inconsiderable benefits of Witness Protection. — And the downsides? For you, only one. Due to cuts in funding and sky-high overheads, pets have had to be excluded from the scheme. That has implications for your cairn terrier who, I gather, is faithful to a fault, as terriers often are. Name of Bonnie, correct? Or Bernie. I can't read my own handwriting.

HONEYMAN: Boswell. He answers to Bozzie.

~~~: Ah yes. Bozzie. But rest assured, rehoming isn't out of the question. Finding him a loving family near his favourite beaches, parks and pissing posts – that can be arranged. But only if you cooperate fully. Otherwise he'll be taken to one of the less scrupulous vets in St Peter Port and, let's not mince words, destroyed. That would be a terrible thing, wouldn't it? Happy, healthy animal that he is, and a much loved family pet. It would weigh heavily on your conscience.

HONEYMAN: How did you know I had a dog?

~~~: Brindle hairs on your trousers, Mr Honeyman, all below knee height, which, credit where credit's due, Mr Δ≈ΔΔΔ°◇≥ brought to my attention. (Though I think he only noticed them because he was gazing admiringly, perhaps enviously, at your shoes.) Also, the snapshot of a dog in your wallet.

HONEYMAN: You've been rummaging through my wallet? When did that happen?

~~~: Yesterday afternoon, while you were naked and wired up to the polygraph machine. But that's not important. What I find interesting – some might say downright peculiar – is that you don't carry photographs of Tamsin, your children and their children –

HONEYMAN: That's because I have no grandchildren.

~~~: – just a pic of whatsisname, Buzzy.

HONEYMAN: Bozzie.

~~~: And I think I can guess why. Did he, by any chance, save your life?

HONEYMAN: Twice, actually.

TAYLOR: Sorry to interrupt, but there's another photo you should know about. A mugshot: full face and profile. Slipped, perhaps hidden – not terribly well, if so – between the twenties and fifties.

~~~: Of Mr Honeyman? A selfie?

TAYLOR: No.

~~~: Surely not of Mr Inkling!

TAYLOR: Of an extremely large man in a chef's hat. Slavic features. The wickedly curved lips of a depraved voluptuary. Arkady Bredyuk, I presume.

~~~: What do you say, Mr Honeyman? If conjugal visits are allowed, will the lovely Arkady visit you in jail as all dutiful wives should? Of course he won't. Because by the time you begin your lengthy sentence he'll already have been dragged, squealing like a stuck pig, out of the kitchen at Snowy White's, taken to Heathrow in handcuffs and bundled onto the next available Aeroflot to Kiev, there to stay forever and a day.

Such are the dire consequences of keeping schtum.

I don't doubt that on being released from Ashfield Prison you'll immediately apply for a Ukrainian visa, but your application will be turned down flat, without explanation, as will all subsequent applications.

To sum up: you'll never see Arkady again, never hear his whispered endearments in the exotic accent and charmingly broken English you've come to know and love, never smell his peculiarly gamey smell, an intoxicating blend of full-strength pheromones, sweated lard and pound shop deodorant, never sample another mouthful of him or his *cuisine exquis*, never –

HONEYMAN: Stop it! Stop browbeating me! You've got it all wrong!

~~~: Then perhaps you'd better explain.

HONEYMAN: On the first occasion, Bozzie –

~~~: Wait-wait-wait! Please don't tell me this is going to be a shaggy dog story.

HONEYMAN: You said you wanted an explanation. That's what I'm trying to give you. And I'd succeed, too, if only you'd stop interrupting.

~~~: A *relevant* explanation, Mr Honeyman. *Relevant*. Not about a terrier, no matter how brave and loyal he is, or of such formidable intelligence he's been invited to join Mensa. Even though he saved your life not once but twice, which must be some kind of record. Pitch it to Disney, they'll lap it up. But let's hear no more about it – not here, not now. Preferably not ever. Mr Inkling is our subject. Tell us what you know about him.

HONEYMAN: You must be joking. No means no. And why do you keep banging on about grandchildren? As I said just a moment ago, I don't have any.

~~~: Ah, but you will, you will, just as soon as you sign the relevant documents. In that green folder. There, by your right hand. The youngest-looking undercover officers – baby-faced, with girlish skin and bumfluff rather than stubble – often find themselves embedded in a Witness Protected family for a year or two, until things settle down. The role they enact is that of young teen grandchildren to middle-

aged clients such as Tamsin and yourself. Their dedication to duty is so absolute it's scary. They're the professionals' professionals. Sometimes they get so deep into the character they're portraying it's hard to winkle them out again. It means you'll have weapons-trained minders with you at all times. What a comfort that must be.

Their mere presence will help to throw Mr Inkling's hit squad off the scent. If, for example, on Christmas day (an ideal time to catch a family together, slightly tipsy and off guard) they suddenly arrive at your door, expecting to ambush six of you – i.e. you and Tamsin plus two grown-up children, both with spouses – but find instead a family of eight, including two mystery grandchildren, they'll pause. That's all it takes: a sliver of doubt. And the cosmetic surgery you'll have had will fatten that sliver. They'll compare the face in the identity photo they've been given with the new, improved you standing before them. Then they'll do the same with Tamsin. Seeing no resemblance whatsoever, they'll brush the snow from their shoulders, offer sincere if gruff apologies for the misunderstanding, give the women a kiss and a sneaky feel under the mistletoe, shake hands crushingly with the menfolk, pat the undercover officers on the head, and go their merry way.

Bear in mind what everyone says about Deke, Attila and the like: they're of low mental wattage. They can just about count to ten using fingers and thumbs, and they skip over the long words in comic books. Outmanoeuvring them should be easy.

HONEYMAN: And if I don't sign?

~~~: We'll have someone sign for you. Probably Grace Zappettini, one of the world's leading forensic handwriting analysts and the founder of Decoded Scrivenings, an organisation of which I'm sure you'll have heard, working, as DS does, on high-profile cases with international crime-fighting agencies such as Interpol and Europol.

Professoressa Zappettini is a remarkable woman with, so I'm told, an hourglass figure and the charisma and sensuality of Sophia Loren – the Loren of forty years ago, around the time she made *Sex Pot*. She's here today as an expert witness. Having told the historian Hugh Trevor Roper that the so-called 'Hitler Diaries', on which he'd been asked to pass judgment, were forgeries, citing inconsistent nib flexion, the absence of microscopic, period-specific ink riffles, and, most tellingly, the blotting of line rather than sentence, her reputation was made. If only, for the sake of his reputation, Roper had taken her advice. So let's hear what she has to say about your diary entries, Mr Honeyman – tone, content, flexion, riffles, whatever.

Usher, please call Professoressa Zappettini to the stand.

HONEYMAN: You have my diaries?

~~~: Facsimiles. But only for the years 1980 to 2011. According to the entry for 17th July 1980 – I have it before me – you'd just finished feeding all your earlier diaries, page by page, into a bonfire in your parents' back garden while you were house-sitting and they were in Tenerife. A destructive act that suggests you had something to hide.

HONEYMAN: Why?

~~~: Why what?

HONEYMAN: Why do you have my diaries?

~~~: Let me spell it out, to avoid further misunderstanding. What we have are facsimiles. Not the diaries themselves, which are right where you left them, in the bottom drawer of your Biedermeier bedside cabinet. Facsimiles only. The diaries are off-limits unless obtained with a search warrant, and we didn't have time to apply for one. Nor sufficient grounds, probably. But those are the strictures under which we operate. The law is the law and must be applied to all in equal measure, by brute force if necessary.

HONEYMAN: You still haven't answered my question.

~~~: Mr Honeyman, your ignorance is deplorable and, quite frankly, irritating. You seem to have no understanding of legal procedure, especially with regard to the functioning of the court. This is how it works: I ask questions and you answer them truthfully, in full, without hesitation. If you don't do that, I'll hold you in contempt. Under no circumstances am I obliged to answer your questions. Nor shall I, unless, for reasons of my own, requiring no explanation, I deign to do so. Is that clear?

HONEYMAN: [...]

~~~: I'll take that sullen nod as a yes. Mark it as such in the written record, Miss Stenographer, and let's move on.

HONEYMAN: The court stenographer's name is Miss Stenographer?

~~~: [...]

HONEYMAN: Ah, I see: no answer unless you feel like giving one. And on this occasion, apparently, you don't.

⊖

~~~: Please state your name, age, present occupation and place of domicile.

FIFTH WITNESS: Grace Zappettini, fifty-three years old, forensic handwriting analyst, Via Pasquale Calvi, Palermo.

~~~: We were lucky to find you visiting London, Professoressa. Thank you for agreeing to help us out at such short notice.

ZAPPETTINI: My pleasure. And please call me Grace.

~~~: Thank you. Now, Grace, you've spent several hours in your hotel suite perusing Mr Honeyman's diaries and raiding the minibar's limited range of salty snacks, the cost of which, of course, we'll gladly cover. Based solely on his handwriting – the soul-shrivelling contents of the diaries we'll tackle later, if there's time – could you give

us a brief summary of your findings? What manner of man is he?

ZAPPETTINI: Duplicitous and potentially dangerous. Charming. Manipulative. Devious.

~~~: I see.

HONEYMAN: No you don't!

~~~: Let her speak, Mr Honeyman. You'll get your turn.

ZAPPETTINI: In assessing my suitability as an expert witness, I assume you will have read some of my published articles, conference papers and best-selling true crime books, in addition to pieces written for newspapers worldwide, including your *Telegraph* and *Daily Mail*. You will also certainly have browsed the contents of my website, Spiedo Centrale,

Skewer Central
named
presumably
after the unusual mode of despatch
in J Lee Thompson's
1981
slasher movie
Happy Birthday to Me.

which rarely receives fewer than six thousand visitors per day, give or take a handful, many of them blocked writers of crime fiction searching for inspiration –

~~~: Indeed.

ZAPPETTINI: – then you'll know that in the field of graphology my area of expertise is the penmanship of serial killers, paedophiles and rapists, the megalomaniac leaders of various death and religious cults, war-mongering political narcissists, killer-cannibals and all extraverted personas harbouring an antisocial psychotic core as defined in the psychodynamic diagnostic manual, an ebook version of which I carry round in my purse although, having read it so many times I can quote it chapter and verse, there's no real need.

As Mr Honeyman has not, to my knowledge – please correct me if I'm wrong – murdered anyone or committed an act of extreme physical violence, with or without sexual or sadistic overtones, he falls into the latent category, as do most individuals of the types just mentioned. They and he are psychopaths nonetheless.

HONEYMAN: Now wait a minute!

~~~: Not yet, Mr Honeyman.

ZAPPETTINI: Only one in a hundred of the sixty-four-point-six million people currently living in the UK can be categorised as dangerously psychopathic, though most psychopaths are, needless to say, men. While going about his everyday business, the psychopathic male may seem perfectly normal: a good husband, father and friend, a blood donor, an avid recycler of glass, cardboard and plastics, a man who pats dogs and strokes cats, who neatly mows and edges his lawn then does his disabled neighbour's lawn too, unbidden, apparently out of nothing but the goodness of his heart. He's civic minded, a seemingly selfless do-gooder whose neighbours, even the habitual grudgers, hold in high esteem. But how he seems is not what he is, and his handwriting often gives the game away.

HONEYMAN: I protest! This is nothing but a crude attempt at character assassination! I've a good mind to sue!

~~~: You can't. Please sit down, Mr Honeyman, or I'll have the usher handcuff and gag you. As you ought to know, but obviously don't, though it's common knowledge, any statement made in open court that is relevant and pertinent to the matter under enquiry is protected by absolute judicial privilege unless spoken with malicious intent. Have you, at any time, either socially or professionally, made the acquaintance of Professoressa Zappettini?

HONEYMAN: Not that I'm aware of, but I –

~~~: Communicated with her?

HONEYMAN: Never.

~~~: Visited her website or read anything she's written?

HONEYMAN: Well ... no.

~~~: Categorically?

HONEYMAN: Yes.

~~~: Professoressa, Grace, have you read any of Mr Honeyman's scribblings?

HONEYMAN: Hey!

~~~: Be quiet, Mr Honeyman.

ZAPPETTINI: Until late this afternoon, when the photostats of the diaries were delivered to my hotel, I was unaware of his existence.

~~~: You see, Mr Honeyman, there's absolutely no reason to assume the comments we've just heard were made out of malice – neither the Professoressa's nor mine – so I advise you to calm down and, better still, pipe down. Grace, please continue with your evidence.

ZAPPETTINI: Thank you. I was particularly struck by the extravagant flourishes in the Hell Zone (lowest level) of Mr Honeyman's script, in particular the jays (j), jeez (g), wise (y) and zeds (z) rather than the peas (p) and queues (q), letters that begin unostentatiously, one might even say normally, in the Earth Zone (middle level), and which are reminiscent of the hand of the 'Co-Ed Killer' Ted Bundy. Several distorted letters, repeated with small variations, are similar to those one finds in Bundy's script, and although the spacing between words is even and of average width and to the untrained or inobservant eye would suggest nothing unusual, they have a clenched quality typical of the hand of Josef Fritzl, who imprisoned his daughter Elisabeth in the basement of his house for twenty-four years and fathered seven children on her. Even in photostat, a poor substitute for the original pages, one can detect the near-microscopic ink spatters and the Fritzlian build-up of intense, emotional, nib-bending pressure that Mr Honeyman applies to certain key words, many of the same words on which Joseph Stalin's depraved henchman Vyacheslav Molotov lay stress in his death warrants, a characteristic shared by Osama bin Laden.

The invented, somewhat schizoid lettering of Swiss outsider artist and paedophile Adolf Wölfli, who spent most of his adult life locked up, first in prison then in an insane asylum, can occasionally be found in Mr Honeyman's script, particularly when he's under duress. But the strongest similarity is between Mr Honeyman's hand and that of Donato 'Angel Voice' Bilancia, the opportunistic killer of seventeen individuals on the Italian Riviera. In fact, astonishingly, Mr Honeyman's hand matches Bilancia's in almost every detail, achieving 'dittos' (graphologist-speak for points of correspondence) of eighty-six-point-two per cent on the Crepieux-Jamin Scale and throwing up only a handful of discordances, minor ones at that – something I'd heard was possible but never thought I'd live to see.

Most telling of all is the absence of lettering in Mr Honeyman's Heaven Zone (uppermost level). His finials are so malnourished they evoke pity, as one would feel for a starveling child – unless, that is, one is a psychopath. There are no flourishes of note at the crest of the els (l) and effs (f), not even flourishes that are half-hearted or strive to succeed but fail.

Based on the evidence, I can only conclude that Mr Honeyman is a Catholic with a fear of losing control, especially in the confessional booth, and not just emotionally but physically: bowel, bladder and, what's the word – blubbing?

~~~: Sobbing, weeping, bawling, snivelling, wailing – tearful,

in general. Blubbing, though of less common usage, will do nicely. Your English is superb, Professoressa. Please continue.

ZAPPETTINI: I wouldn't be at all surprised to learn that he was a chronic bedwetter –

HONEYMAN: How dare you!

~~~: Mr Honeyman!

ZAPPETTINI: – well into his teenage years, having been systematically abused by a member of the clergy, a man he'd confided in, trusted, revered, possibly even loved. Deprived of the confessional and unable to gain absolution, alienated from his fellow religionists, including, while they were still alive, his parents, he knows he has fallen from grace and will never enter Heaven, not even by the back door. Nor is it possible for him to achieve Heaven on Earth. His life is but a living Hell, and he knows the afterlife will be more of the same and for all eternity. He's a man without hope, with nothing to lose. That's what makes him potentially dangerous, especially if you back him into a corner.

~~~: Such as now?

ZAPPETTINI: From what I understand of the situation, yes.

~~~: Ease off the gas, as our American cousins say.

ZAPPETTINI: That would be advisable.

~~~: Thank you, Professoressa.

ZAPPETTINI: Grace.

~~~: Grace. And thank you for your insightful analysis of Mr Honeyman's character.

ZAPPETTINI: You're welcome. But please bear in mind that my findings are preliminary, based on only a few hours' evaluation in less than ideal conditions – the lighting in hotel rooms is often feeble, designed to enhance mood rather than work by, and the day, so typical of London, midweek and midwinter, has been uniformly dull.

~~~: Enlivened somewhat, I hope, by our little show trial.

HONEYMAN: Did you just say show trial? You did, didn't you!

~~~: I did not.

HONEYMAN: Yes you did!

~~~: I assure you, Mr Honeyman, I did not.

HONEYMAN: You did, I know you did. I'm not imagining things. I heard it, plain as day. Have the stenographer read your words back to you, see if I'm right.

~~~: Miss Stenographer, if you would be so kind ...

STENOGRAPHER: 'Enlivened, I hope, by our little trial.'

~~~: There, Mr Honeyman. Satisfied? Now can we get on, I have one or two leading questions to ask of the professoressa.

HONEYMAN: Did you say leading?

~~~: Once again you have misheard, Mr Honeyman. I do wish you'd pay attention. Miss Stenographer, please –

HONEYMAN: Don't bother.

~~~: Then let's waste no more time. Professoressa –

ZAPPETTINI: Grace.

~~~: Yes, of course. Forgive me. Grace ... a lovely name ... my mother's name, as it happens, though she failed to live up to it. Anyway — Yes, Mr Honeyman?

HONEYMAN: If I'm not allowed to question you, may I at least ask one or two questions of the so-called professoressa?

~~~: Your sarcasm does you no credit, Mr Honeyman, and the dismissive term 'so-called' is unwarranted. Professoressa Zappettini's credentials are perfectly in order.

HONEYMAN: So ... may I?

~~~: If you feel you must, though it's highly irregular.

HONEYMAN: Professoressa, if that's what you are –

~~~: Mr Honeyman, I warn you! Any more of that and permission to cross examine will be withdrawn. My patience is wearing thin. Do you understand?

HONEYMAN: You'll be aware – as a professional graphologist you could hardly fail to be – that the Crepieux-Jamin Scale was discredited decades ago.

~~~: Venting spleen, Mr Honeyman, or stating a fact? If it's fact, back it up. If not, shut up.

HONEYMAN: It is and I can. During a low ebb in my career, circa 1985, I ghosted the autobiography of Elvira Petulengru of Margate. A very short autobiography as her life was exceedingly dull. Cash in hand. Not quite enough cash to make it worthwhile. The book to this day remains unpublished. It was declined by a dozen reputable houses and by a fat handful of the less reputable ones, as I knew it would be, though I decided not to tell her so in case she stiffed me on the fee.

Elvira Petulengru wasn't one of the Cromer Petulengros, proper Romanies, Egyptian in origin, so they say, though people will say just about anything. In fact, she wasn't a Petulengro at all, she'd just adopted the name and swapped an oh (o) for a you (u), which, notwithstanding the one-letter difference, incurred the wrath of the Cromer clan who felt Elvira was bringing the family name and business into disrepute. They trundled down to Margate in their lane blockers, large, well-equipped touring caravans, known in the trade as rolling bungalows, and on reaching Dane Park, Elvira's usual pitch during the summer season, they encircled her tiny gypsy-style van and made threatening noises, stampeding her usually placid horse and scaring off all but her most determined and loyal customers.

But Elvira's elder brother, George, who ran Bounce Around, a doorman supply agency staffed mainly by hardened ex-cons, was having none of it. He mustered his entire workforce, some forty strong, and rousted the Cromerians, sending them back up the M2 under escort to Norfolk, where they belong and where he advised them to remain.

Anyway, unlike the true Petulengros – if the Cromer lot are true, something the Blackpool branch of the family disputes – Elvira wasn't a palmist. Nor did she claim to be clairvoyant, which is just as well because she wasn't. With her it was all about love letters. That was her shtick: analysing a letter-writer's handwriting and its 'emotional residue' to determine whether the sentiments expressed in the letter were sincere. Mostly they weren't, but often she claimed otherwise. 'It's better to send a client away reassured,' she told me, 'though not entirely. Always plant a tiny seed of doubt in her mind. That way she'll come back for more.'

A shrewd, unlikeable woman.

Nonetheless she had a devoted clientele among the lovelorn, one or two famous faces among them, mostly female, mostly showbiz types, all emotionally fragile and some verging on certifiable, especially the thesps – none of whom wished it to be known that they were consulting Elvira. She named names in her autobiography, but only of those who'd passed away, and – to get to the point, because I can see you're itching to interrupt – she analysed the letters they'd brought along using the Crepieux-Jamin Scale, which she referred to scathingly as the Crap-Jam method. Over the years she'd, as it were, 'jammed' a number of wealthy, neurotic clients out of a sizeable portion of their disposable income. Several deluded fools were so grateful they made her a beneficiary in their will.

Being, as I am, then and now, a keen researcher, when Elvira mentioned the Crepieux-Jamin Scale, which I admit I'd never heard of, I popped round the corner to the British Library to look it up. This was, as I say, 1985, prior to the widespread use of PCs, when authors in general viewed them as vampiric machines, designed to suck the life and soul out of a well-turned sentence and turn brilliant ideas into zombie mush. Typewriters and libraries were king. Still are, as far as I'm concerned.

Anyway, in the British Library I found two meticulous studies dating from the late 1960s, one overlapping the other in its field of enquiry, in which the Crepieux-Jamin Scale had been investigated thoroughly and tested to destruction. Highly elaborate though it was, Crap-Jam was well-named: it failed miserably on all counts. Several of the major handwriting journals, including *The Graphologist*, published edited highlights of the studies, and within a decade the Crepieux-Jamin Scale had fallen into a crack of history. It was graphology's very own Piltdown Man, a hoax, a source of embarrassment to those who'd once sworn blind that its accuracy was peerless, its insights magisterial.

Only a few elderly diehards continued to use it after that, Elvira among them. By the time I came to ghost her book, most graphologists had switched to the Hilliger System or one of the reliable alternatives. She was probably the last Crepieux-Jamin practitioner in the UK, which of course gave her a certain cachet among the gullible, the needy and those of scattered wits who believed that 'ancient knowledge of inestimable value' was being suppressed by 'the powers that be', whoever they are, for reasons of vested interest and/or to facilitate mind control. I know, I know: it takes all sorts.

So, Professoressa, perhaps you'd care to explain why you're still using the Crepieux-Jamin Scale, despite its inefficacy?

ZAPPETTINI: [...]

HONEYMAN: I thought so.

~~~: Professoressa ...?

ZAPPETTINI: Grace.

HONEYMAN: *Dis*grace, more like.

~~~: That will do, Mr Honeyman! Professoressa, please stand down. I believe there's a taxi waiting outside, ready to take you back to your hotel. See the professoressa out, Mr Usher.

STENOGRAPHER: Should I ...?

~~~: Just a moment, Miss Stenographer. — Right, she's gone. Strike her testimony from the record and let's take a breather. We'll resume in thirty minutes.

HONEYMAN: More an autumnal Gina Lollobrigida than a summery Sophia Loren, in my opinion.

~~~: On that, at least, we can agree, Mr Honeyman. Now off you go back to the cells, there's a good chap. Mr Usher, if you please ...

Third Session

~~~: Feeling suitably refreshed are we? Ready to capitulate and cooperate fully?

HONEYMAN: Don't be ridiculous. And wipe that silly grin off your face. Despite its horrors the rugged bunk treatment hasn't broken me; never can, never will. And until I know all there is to know about the Witness Protection Scheme I won't sign a damn thing. What you said about weapons-trained, baby-faced undercover officers was disconcerting. Trigger-happy youngsters prowling round the house, inside and out, using the utility room (assuming there is one) or the kitchen (which there will be – at least I sincerely hope so) as their command HQ? Can't say I like the sound of that. And Tamsin, a staunch pacifist and longstanding member of Guernsey CND, would, I know, greatly disapprove.

~~~: For Heaven's sake man, there'd only be one or two of them and for a couple of years at most! And the officers the WPS have assigned to you are mature in both outlook and years – to save you asking: thirty-two and thirty-five – although, because of their god genes, they can easily pass for teenagers, young teens at that.

HONEYMAN: Whoa. Scroll back a bit. *God genes?* What in blazes is that all about?

~~~: Ah. Of course. You don't know, do you?

HONEYMAN: If I did I wouldn't be asking. God genes?

~~~: Okay. Look. I think, to save us having to go over old ground, which will slow down the proceedings to such a degree it will feel like we're wading thigh-deep through treacle, you'd better skim-read the explanation I gave Dr Anon. Has our preliminary session been translated from stenographese into standard English, Miss Stenographer?

STENOGRAPHER: Assuming that the auto-transcriber is working properly and the function setting has been switched to sten-eng-auto/save-print, yes. The printer is in Tiffany's office. It's ancient but still seems to be limping along. Shall I fetch the relevant pages?

~~~: Leave out the bits about Escalifts and the Thai takeaway on the Brompton Road.

STENOGRAPHER: Didn't you say it was 'off' the Brompton Road?

~~~: On/off/in/near, who cares.

$$\ominus$$

~~~: Any questions, Mr Honeyman?

HONEYMAN: None.

~~~: Really? Not even a teensy-weensy question, a questionette?

HONEYMAN: As your explanation made absolutely no sense, there's no point wasting time on it.

~~~: Good. Back to the WPS undercover officers then. They've both been trained to SAS standard and one of them, code name Shortman, had a brief career as a race horse jockey before his true vocation was revealed in the kick of a horse's hoof. He was thrown by a filly at Leopardstown, got trampled by the rest of the field, and spent several weeks in a coma, as a result of which he's become a highly sensitised equinophobe, said by his colleagues to be able to detect the tiniest morsel of horsemeat in a purportedly

beef lasagne even when it's frozen – a claim I take, like my lasagne, with a pinch of salt. But unless Mr Inkling's men gallop into the close like the Wild Bunch storming the Ford County Bank in Spearville, Kansas, his phobia won't be an issue. For full biographical details consult the hefty information pack the WPS has provided.

HONEYMAN: Where?

~~~: There. Red folder. Next to the green one.

HONEYMAN: Oh.

~~~: As to firearms, they'll be kept somewhere on the premises under lock and key (not, as once was the case, in laxer times, on a high shelf in the greenhouse or hidden beneath an upturned flowerpot by the back door), except, of course, when they're required for the weekly siege and evacuation drill, in which you're all expected to partici-pate, and during target practice, which takes place monthly though on a different day to siege drill and at the nearest Police Specialist Training Centre.

The inconvenience of having WPS officers in the house will be minor, I promise. Because of their chameleonlike nature – the reason they were drawn to undercover work in the first place – they'll blend in seam-lessly with you and the family, and to make life easier they'll stay in character throughout, even during siege drill and at the shooting range. After a month or two you'll start to think they really are your grandchildren. Or rather you'll gradually cease to think of them as under-cover officers masquerading as children. From what I gather this period of transition can be disorientating. But as they'll do what young teens do – i.e. look sullen and be surly, make a discordant racket on guitar or drums, refuse to bathe regularly and keep their rooms tidy, be argumentative about nearly everything but especially matters of no importance, get drunk on rough cider and vomit in the cucumber frame, skip family meals and snack straight from the fridge in the middle of the night leaving the fridge door open when they shuffle off to bed – despite all that, you'll soon get accustomed to having them around.

Most of the time you'll be hard pushed to know they're there. For four or five hours a day they'll be in their bedrooms playing what look like Xbox or Playstation games but are in fact bespoke SAS siege simulations based on the precise configuration of your new house and the topography of the surrounding streets, all rendered in such exquisite detail you can count the leaves on the trees and the veins in the leaves – assuming that the contractors have, as stipulated by the local authority when building regs approval was backhandered, actually planted some trees. If not, the WPS will plant some for you, for screening purposes.

So don't worry about the officers. You'll soon find, despite the annoying habits they'll gleefully cultivate, that you're really rather fond of them, will perhaps in time come to love them, and when they're at school or visiting friends the house will feel unnaturally quiet, cold and empty, a lonely place.

HONEYMAN: They have to go to school?

~~~: Of course. Nothing in their lives must be out of the ordinary lest it draw attention. Their grades have to be kept strictly average. In fact, to be average in all things is the principal aim, even though they're smarter and savvier than all their teachers put together. Probably more handsome too (though not, of course, too handsome). The slightly taller officer assigned to you, Brett, Grady, Leon or Drake (his cover name has yet to be established by the WPS in-house focus group), code name Skinnyman, has a PhD in astrophysics, though to look at him, all gangling limbs and floppy fringe, knock-off Gucci trainers and strategically torn, ill-fitting jeans from Primark, you'd

think he was best suited to a career in burger-flipping.

HONEYMAN: Hang on, something's being skipped over here, something really important ... Teenage boys, as I know all too well, though presumably you don't, are randy little buggers who'd screw knotholes in trees if nothing better was available. What about girlfriends, are they allowed?

~~~: Civilian girlfriends? Definitely not. That would neither be ethical nor, if they're underage, as they probably would be, legal. One of the Scheme's female officers assumes the girlfriend role. She'll be housed with a Scheme-supplied family on another part of the estate and enrolled at a neighbouring school rather than the one your WPS officers will attend. Because young love is mercurial and young men so fickle, several officer-girlfriends may have to be deployed in the course of a year. Creating a semblance of authenticity is a highly labour intensive and expensive undertaking. In some cases, though rarely, a boy-boy relationship is allowed to develop, again with a fellow WPS officer, but only in a non-homophobic environment where such things are neither frowned upon nor punished and where peer-group bullying is unlikely to occur. There are very few places where the criteria have been met in full, though the situation is, I gather, improving. The scripts –

HONEYMAN: You mean, as in playscripts?

~~~: Indeed so. According to the information I've been given by Deputy Assistant Commissioner Starkey, the WPS employs several brainstorming teams, each consisting of six writers in early middle age, all male, all functioning alcoholics, whose banal and clichéd ideas are neither better than average nor worse. The team that will be allocated to you, known as the Alpha Betas, meets fortnightly at The French House in Dean Street, an arty pub for self-consciously arty types, which is what these writers are. They think they've been hired by a new-kid-on-the-block

media production company to generate start-up plots and scripts for a youthcentric soap opera that will air on Sky or Netflix or perhaps, if the big money baulks, Channel 4.

The pay is so good they're disinclined to ask why, after months of preparation, having worked on hundreds of character outlines, family trees and elaborate storyboards, every element of which has been greeted with cries of exultation by the senior script editor, there's still no news as to when the show will go into production. But they're always paid on time; they receive occasional, unexplained bonuses; the liquor is plentiful (and marked down, quibble-free, to expenses); and in between bouts of brainstorming they relax, crack feeble jokes, and revel in each other's self-inflicted ailments and comically exaggerated domestic woes.

They're having as much fun as they possibly can and so, in consequence, might you.

But if the standard of a team's work nosedives, or, as can happen, though rarely, it improves, and to the extent that it's markedly better than average, the team has to be disbanded and new writers sought. That's not a problem: there's always plenty more where they came from.

HONEYMAN: Let's see whether I've got this straight. Adult deep-cover firearms officers –

~~~: Yes.

HONEYMAN: – in the guise of randy schoolboys, both gay and hetero –

~~~: Yes.

HONEYMAN: – are given scripts to learn and enact in real time.

~~~: And not just them. You and Tamsin too, though not to the same degree. Just until you get so fully into character you begin to generate scripts of your own. Impromptu scripts. Actually, scenarios might be a better term. I apologise if I've misled you, Mr Honeyman, that wasn't my intention.

The scenarios are loosely plotted and officers are

expected to improvise on and around the written material as events unfold. Improvisation workshops with stand-up comedians are a fundamental part of their training, and one or two former officers have gone into showbiz on the bear-baiting wing of the comedy circuit, either as a wittily scathing rent-a-heckler or a comic whose act consists mainly of squelching such hecklers in the cruellest way possible.

Sometimes, in circumstances such as those, it's hard to say who is stooging whom.

But that last gobbet of information has, I'm afraid, completely exhausted my knowledge of the Witness Protection Scheme, so I think we'd better call Deputy Assistant Commissioner Starkey to the stand.

$$\ominus$$

~~~: Please state your name, age, present occupation and place of domicile.

SIXTH WITNESS: Starkey, William Galen, fifty-nine last April, Deputy Assistant Commissioner in the City of London Police, seconded since July 2015 to the UK Protected Person's Service (UKPPS), part of the National Crime Agency. For security's sake I won't reveal my home address.

~~~: Understood.

STARKEY: Look, I hate to rush you, but we've been hanging around for several hours and I'm scheduled to attend a meeting of Cobra at midnight. The Home Secretary, who's chairing it, is fanatical about punctuality, a vicious scold if one is late, and my taxi is waiting, engine idling, the meter clocking up hundreds of phantom miles. Time is of the essence. What do you want to know that isn't in the information pack?

~~~: Over to you, Mr Honeyman.

HONEYMAN: Me? But I haven't had time to look at the pack. How could I possibly know what is or isn't in it?

~~~: You said just a moment ago that you weren't happy about having armed undercover officers in the house.

HONEYMAN: Well, yes, now that you mention it, I did.

STARKEY: So should we just provide them with high-pressure water pistols? Faithful replicas of assault rifles and handguns that shoot jets of bleach or some other toxic liquid? Is that what you're suggesting?

HONEYMAN: No. Definitely not. I don't know where you got that idea from. It's not something I've –

STARKEY: Because, let me tell you, we tried that. We being they, the MoD, because they have all the research funding and facilities and we, the police, have next to none. The MoD has tried and tested almost everything you can think of and lots more besides. They developed a chemical agent that was essentially a nerve gas in liquid form, a new, slightly less deadly variant on sarin, that could be delivered by high-pressure water pistol. Guaranteed to turn enemy agents, terrorists, rioters, demonstrators, rubberneckers and innocent bystanders into gibbering wrecks, some permanently. Years of R&D went into it. The investment was huge. But no matter how much the formula was tweaked it continued to breach the EU directive on dangerous substances and fell foul of the Chemical Weapons Convention (CWC) and the Organization for the Prohibition of Chemical Weapons (OPCW). To appease those agencies the formula was tweaked and diluted again and again, to such an extent that by the time its use was approved it was no more effective than plain old H_2O.

Homeopaths have, however, been using it with great success
as an adjunct treatment of
sadness
apathy
and constipation

[with few adverse reactions other than night sweats
raised blood pressure
mild Tourettish outbursts
arrhythmia
blackouts
and a skull-splitting headache]
especially when patients have
responded poorly or
inappropriately
[a sudden loss of inhibition resulting in
aggressive touchy-feeliness
that could easily be
and often has been
mistaken for sexual assault]
to applications of
Viscum Album
a semi-parasitic plant whose
host trees are
Malus [apple] and
Quercus [oak].

And ice, bullets of ice – they tried those too. The prototype gun designed to fire them was highly innovative and an engineering marvel. Take a gander at the blueprints at the patents office, you'll see what I mean. But as you can't, because you're stuck here in court, I'll explain how it worked.

A precisely calibrated measure of water was forced out of the reservoir of the gun by a burst of compressed air and snap-frozen in a mould by a jet of liquid nitrogen. It was delivered to the breach as an extremely hard, well-formed pellet, identical in shape and size to a 5.56x45mm NATO-approved round, though of lighter grain. A powerful gas ram charge then sent the projectile on its way. The weapon was serviceable, but because of the vacuum flask in which the liquid nitrogen was stored, the multi-litre water reservoir, and a compressed air cylinder, it was unwieldy. Two strong men were needed to position it on a swivel mount in the back of an open-topped utility vehicle. Once locked in position it was capable of firing an ice bullet every two-point-oh-six seconds. Not fast, you might think, compared to an L85A2 gas-operated assault rifle, and you'd be correct.

But lack of speed wasn't the major issue. Because of bubbles of air trapped chaotically in the ice, which the MoD lab rats were unable to eliminate completely, the bullets tended to be unstable in flight.

Which led
though the Deputy Assistant Commissioner
won't say so
[actually can't say
because it's classified
part of a military programme of
which he has no knowledge]
to the development of the
so-called boomerang bullet
which returns
almost immediately
to sender.   ·
An aerodynamic miracle.
British ingenuity at its best.
When 'accidentally' dropped as AK47 ammo
behind enemy lines
the enemy eagerly uses it
and self-annihilates.

During a 2015 NATO exercise at Ustka, Poland, there were numerous incidents of friendly fire, many more than the statisticians had predicted. Nearly all were attributable to the ice gun. Adjusting the rifling in the barrel and the length of the barrel did little to improve the accuracy of the projectile or its effective range – calculated to be less than three hundred metres average in tropical climes where, particularly at midday and during seasonal high temperatures and periods of near-maximum humidity, surface melt and evaporation would be a major issue. The ice gun was found to work best in the temperate zone, from late autumn to early spring, which simply wasn't good enough to satisfy the MOD.

Eventually it was donated to the Imperial War Museum for their Failed Prototypes section, though it has yet to be put on display. Ask Lara Bream – I think that's her name, a curator in the Department of Collections – for a private view. And send flowers with your request; they soften many a bureaucrat's heart, male and female alike, mine included.

I hope that addresses your concerns and sets your mind at rest.

~~~: Mr Honeyman ...?

HONEYMAN: I really don't know what to say.

STARKEY: Then best say nothing. Loose lips sink ships and all that. As good a slogan now as once was. Or, if you prefer, put a zip in it, and if a zip isn't available then button up. Now, may I stand down? I have urgent business to attend to in Downing Street, the security of the nation is at stake.

~~~: Of course. And thank you, Deputy Assistant Commissioner. But before you go ...

STARKEY: Yes?

~~~: I don't think Mr Honeyman was concerned about the type of weapon per se. He was merely wondering why officers assigned to his household would need to be armed at all.

STARKEY: Isn't it obvious? Mr Inkling is an extremely dangerous man, as are the people who work for him. If you've done your research well, Mr Honeyman, as we suspect you have, which is why we need the valuable information you've acquired and why we're offering you the WPS's deluxe family package, you could hardly fail to be aware of that. We've got files on Mr Inkling as fat as a goat-fed anaconda going all the way back to the 1970s, plus some remarkably good intelligence on his current activities. But we need to know what you know in case it's something that, for some reason, we don't know, because, needless to say, we don't always know what we don't know.

Not that we've been idle or negligent. We've built a case so strong that even the habitual waverers at the DPP have been won over. But additional information is always needed to shore up the few remaining gaps in our knowledge.

Although nowadays most of Inkling's business concerns are legitimate, in the sixties he and his agoraphobic partner Derek Noone were kings of the underworld. That's the period we need to know more about. Nothing criminal in that distant epoch happened without their say-so, and if it did, woe betide the criminal who'd stepped out of line. Inkling and Noone had the Kray twins well under thumb, though you wouldn't know it from what was said at the twins' trial. Hotheads, the Krays. Thugs, not thinkers. Pure id in the case of Ronnie, driven by his ungovernable lusts. They were arrogant and reckless and bound to come a cropper eventually. Likewise the Richardson brothers, who, it has to be said, were smarter than the Krays though no less unpleasant. But Inkling and Noone outsmarted and outlasted them all.

They ran all the major rackets: prostitution, drugs, pornography, gambling and extortion. Slum landlording too, which Inkling is involved in to this day. But nothing was too small-scale for them if it was capable of turning a profit. For example, London's street teams of pickpockets, card sharps, shell game operatives and attendant shills were, until the mid-'70s, trained personally by Noone, who, before illness kept him indoors, had been a stage magician – a good one, by all accounts. He even managed to win over the patrons at the Glasgow Empire, and they were a notoriously tough crowd, belligerent, often drunk and incomprehensibly (except to fellow

Glaswegians) abusive – ask anyone who's ever had the misfortune to work there, they'll tell you.

Noone and Inkling practised sleight of hand every which way, and it helped them no end that so many police officers were willing to take backhanders and wear blinkers (a copper's pay being wholly inadequate then and not much better now, though that's no excuse). In fact, though it pains me to say so, during the '60s and '70s most Met officers were as, if not more, villainous than the villains, tampering with and destroying evidence (especially material relating to Inkling and Noone's activities – one of the reasons they've never been brought to book), stealing and fencing property from the evidence room, blackmailing upper-crust homos long after homosexuality was legalised, renting out untraceable firearms by the day, demanding protection money from businesses the length and breadth of the high street, committing acts of arson and fraud, perjuring themselves in court, setting up raids on banks, bookies, off-licences, etc. Inkling and Noone gave them free rein providing they received a cut of the proceeds.

The few incorruptibles in the Met who wouldn't turn a blind eye to those activities soon found themselves in compromising situations and forced to resign. Or they got transferred to regional backwaters, Norfolk and the Dales – sheep-shagger country, as it was known.

Inkling even managed to become a Mason and regularly attended the prestigious Westminster lodge – hobnobbing, would you believe, with the likes of Prince Philip – having been recommended for membership by two corrupt members of Parliament, one a Liberal, the other Conservative, both since publicly disgraced and both now deceased, one apparently by his own hand (or perhaps a victim of foul play – the coroner's findings were inconclusive).

~~~: Well, Mr Honeyman, does that tally with what you know of Mr Inkling?

HONEYMAN: [...]

~~~: I see. You don't wish to commit yourself. Still pussyfooting around and wasting the court's precious time. You do realise, don't you, that yesterday Tamsin signed up to the Witness Protection Scheme on the assumption that you'd have the good sense to do so too.

HONEYMAN: That can't be!

~~~: Can and is.

HONEYMAN: She wouldn't. Just wouldn't. I know Tamsin better than I know myself. She wouldn't.

~~~: Already has, Mr Honeyman. What you think you know is wrong and no amount of denial will undo what's been done. Open the WPS information pack – yes, the red folder – and turn to pages forty-six and fifty-seven. Tamsin's signature can be found at the foot of those pages, countersigned by unimpeachable witnesses, a bishop and a retired judge.

HONEYMAN: No!

~~~: Ah, but yes. Yes yes yes. Moreover, your sons Jasper and Kiddling (the latter of whom prefers, understandably, to be known as Ian) have signed. As have their wives. Jasper was desperately keen, describing it as QUOTE a once-in-a-lifetime opportunity to become a new, better, happier me UNQUOTE, before bursting into tears. He does that an awful lot, doesn't he? Years of tears have etched arroyo marks in his cheeks. His bookshelves are crammed with self-help books, all well-thumbed, page corners turned down, numerous passages heavy with yellow highlighter or underscored in red, sometimes both. Many a therapist has given up on him; even, after a decade or more of twice-weekly sessions, the Freudian, and Freudians are shakedown artists par excellence, they never give up until the client dies or the money runs out.

But the books and the therapy have proved worthless. That's what Jasper thinks, and Katharina, his wife, who you're inordinately fond of, agrees. They're at crisis point. Theirs is a marriage heading for the rocks unless the WPS can turn the ship around. Surely that's what you'd want for Jasper and Cat, isn't it? – to be given a fresh start, to be as happy as they were when they were newlyweds.

HONEYMAN: You're browbeating me again, and what you've just said amounts to blackmail. I simply won't have it!

STARKEY: Ahem.

~~~: Yes, Deputy Assistant Commissioner?

STARKEY: If I may ...

~~~: Please do.

STARKEY: There's something you should bear in mind, Mr Honeyman, something that is little known and may influence your decision. The WPS has, in recent years, expanded in scope to cover areas that the founders of the service never dreamt of. Once upon a time, several decades ago, it was assumed that all one had to do was remove an individual whose life was in danger from near proximity to that danger. Putting distance between the warring parties was sufficient, along, perhaps, with a change of name. Of course, villains were much more territorial in those days; they guarded their manor zealously and rarely strayed beyond it except to go on holiday or wage a brief, bloody turf war with a neighbour whose manor they coveted or whose incursions, accidental or deliberate, had become intolerable. So if a WPS client was relocated from London to, say, Leeds, and told not to register to vote, not to allow his name, original or new, to appear in the phone book, and obviously not to consort with any of the local villains, family included, because villainy tends to run in families, one could usually guarantee his safety. The Scheme provided the client with lodgings and pin money until he was able to find regular work and became self-sufficient. His movements were loosely monitored by a designated WPS officer at police HQ, though the officer, dressed in civvies, would usually meet the client elsewhere, on a bench in Roundhay Park, near the duck pond, for example, unless the weather was foul, as often it is in Leeds, in which case they'd rendezvous at a neutral indoor location, such as House of Fraser's kitchenware department, by the egg slicers. If the client kept his nose clean and his head down, all would probably be well.

But in the intervening years things have got much more complicated. The major villains are internationalists now and far from stupid. They know how the Scheme works. Distance and a change of name are no longer adequate safeguards. Hence the offer of cosmetic surgery, of which the biggest take-up is for tattoo removal. Nothing identifies someone more readily than a distinctive tattoo, though happily you yourself have none, and Tamsin has, I'm led to believe, only a small bluebird in an intimate place. Is that correct?

HONEYMAN: And a likeness of Yosemite Sam. On her right ankle.

STARKEY: Yosemite who?

HONEYMAN: Sam. A diminutive cartoon cowboy with a fierce disposition. Known for his extravagant moustaches, twenty-gallon hat, short, bandy legs and bulbous nose. When riled, as he nearly always is, he has a tendency to blaze away with six-guns at the floor to either side of him, the recoil lifting him off his feet like a levitating mystic.

STARKEY: The significance escapes me.

HONEYMAN: We had a stillborn child before Jasper and Kiddling came along. A boy. We were going to call him Sam – Samuel Carson Honeyman, in full. Among his baby clothes was something we'd chosen specially: a cowboy outfit, bought in Carson City while we were on holiday, travelling through the Sierra Nevada mountains. In fact,

Carson City was where he was conceived. Tamsin knew immediately that she was pregnant – she said she just *knew*. She carried him to term and he died in the breach. The tattoo was her way of commemorating him, to have him with her always.

STARKEY: She'll have to have it removed.

HONEYMAN: I think not.

STARKEY: Tattoo removal isn't particularly painful.

HONEYMAN: That's really not the point.

STARKEY: Unless, of course, we instruct the tattoo artist – they call themselves artists, God knows why – to adjust the laser to the least efficient wavelength and gradually reduce the effectiveness of the cooling system, at which point, when the patient starts to squirm, the tattooist (actually a WPS officer, though the client won't know that) casually shifts from vacuous chitchat about holidays, sport, soaps and celebrities to asking questions about things we, the WPS, are curious about, and things that may help the police with their enquiries.

HONEYMAN: But surely that's torture.

STARKEY: Absolutely not. I resent that accusation. We operate within strict legal guidelines as ratified in the 1984 UN Convention against Torture and Cruel, Inhuman or Degrading Treatment or Punishment, to which our government, no matter which party is in office, subscribes wholeheartedly. And we err on the side of caution. But as Tamsin knows nothing about Mr Inkling, none of this is relevant.

HONEYMAN: By the same token, surely Mr Inkling knows nothing about Tamsin.

STARKEY: I wouldn't bet on it. He knows something, a twisted or warped something, a grubby, shameful, under-the-carpet something, about everyone –

HONEYMAN: That's impossible!

~~~: Hold your horses, Mr Honeyman.

STARKEY: – everyone *of interest* to him. I don't wish to cast aspersions, Mr Honeyman, but that may even apply to Tamsin. He has a great many interests, as you know.

HONEYMAN: My Tamsin has nothing to hide and therefore nothing to fear!

STARKEY: Glad to hear it. Your loyalty, warranted or not, does you proud.

HONEYMAN: So what about jailhouse bunks?

STARKEY: What about them?

HONEYMAN: I was told in this room less than an hour ago that their uncomfortableness was a form of punishment. Surely that's a serious breach of the UN convention.

STARKEY: Only if the uncomfortableness is intended to degrade. Which it isn't. You've been misinformed.

HONEYMAN: But surely you can't deny that the bunks are uncomfortable.

STARKEY: For whom, Mr Honeyman? The princess who can detect something as small as a pea under her mattress? The Indian fakir accustomed to sleeping on a bed of nails? Not all sleepers are equal and their needs vary considerably.

~~~: I think, gentlemen, we're drifting off course.

STARKEY: Then I'm afraid I must jump ship and swim to shore. But before I do, let me finish what I was saying about the increasingly complex nature of Witness Protection, from its humble beginnings in a portakabin at the back of New Scotland Yard, etc.

Tattoo removal isn't the only thing new to the Scheme. We offer a wide range of services. Consider, for example, clients suffering from male pattern baldness who may, if their heads aren't as barren as the surface of the moon, qualify for and benefit from a hair weave. If the degree of hair loss is more significant, however, implants rather than a weave may be necessary. The cost of such treatments is borne by the grumbling taxpayer who will always grumble no matter how little he's obliged to pay. But what the taxpayer doesn't appreciate is that the benefits to society far outweigh the cost. Of course, as a means of disguise neither hair weaves nor implants are particularly successful. No-one but a blind man would dispute that. But what the taxpayer doesn't know – because for obvious reasons our work must remain secret and subject therefore to myth and rumour – is that the case files are chock-a-block with hair-related success stories.

To give you just one example. There is, or was, an extremely dangerous villain, a former associate of Mr Inkling, name of Ball-Pein John,

Not his baptismal name
needless to say.
One conferred by the WPS in accordance
with its prime coding directive for
moles
squealers
noses
supergrasses
blatters
snouts
grievers
biffs and
stool pigeons:
nothing
must be revealed
by the code name
other than
the client's gender and
weapon of choice.

whose life was turned around because of receiving a course of WPS-sponsored hair implants. Ball-Pein John was a man of no education, and he came from a brutal home. He was inarticulate, charmless and bereft of common sense, quick to anger, with a tendency to solve life's problems, large or small, with a disproportionate degree of violence, leaving a trail of mangled victims in his wake stretching all the way back to kindergarten and beyond. His twin sister swore on a polygraph machine, then again under hypnosis, and finally under oath (we interviewed her three times because we couldn't believe what we were hearing) that her brother gave her a savage beating in the womb. Given that she was born with multiple bone fractures and a cauliflower ear, there may be some truth to it, though foetal alcohol syndrome and a botched abortion can't be discounted.

In the Scheme's initial psychological assessment of Ball-Pein John, he was written off as a lost cause. He'd never been adequately socialised as a child and it was now too late to begin that process. He lacked empathy (didn't even seem to understand the concept) and had no qualms about drowning sacks of kittens or throttling howling infants until they lapsed into unconsciousness. Women – prostitutes, in the main – submitted unwillingly to his bestial embrace, fearing for their lives if they didn't give him what he wanted. Rape, to him, was just spicy sex, which is exactly how he liked it. He'd committed more crimes than you've had hot dinners and had spent more time in jail than out.

Public opinion has it that he and others of his kind are beyond redemption; they should be kept shackled in solitary confinement, on a starvation diet of mouldy bread and ditch water, until they can be dropped into an unmarked grave and given a farewell golden shower, courtesy of the gravediggers and, if so inclined, the priest. Until very recently, I too was of that opinion. But once I'd made his acquaintance I realised that rehabilitation was possible, even for someone as monstrous as Ball-Pein John.

He was loathed by all and sundry, Mr Inkling

included, as well he knew. But his self-loathing was greater still, so extreme and so explosive it was almost impossible to be in a room with him for more than a few minutes without wanting to crawl under a low table, wrap your head in your arms, and wish for the world to end.

That's how things stood for him prior to receiving hair implants. But once in possession of a full head of wavy chestnut hair, capable of being sculpted into any number of fashionable styles, he underwent a radical transformation. This was, to say the least, unexpected. The senior psychologist who'd assessed him was so unnerved by this turn of events she took early retirement and devoted her remaining years to long, aimless walks and thumb-twiddling. As for Ball-Pein John, his self-esteem, once rock bottom, was restored to what it might have been if only he'd had the benefit of a 'normal' upbringing. His confidence received a monumental boost, and the distorting mirror in which one sees oneself as one thinks others see one – i.e. with contempt, disgust and barely suppressed rage – was, in his case, shattered into a thousand pieces.

~~~: Precisely one thousand pieces? No more, no less?

STARKEY: So I'm led to believe.

~~~: That's useful information. Please continue.

STARKEY: Cameras had been installed behind the mirrors of the safe house he'd been allocated, enabling us to observe his behaviour first hand. Once the implants had bedded in he began to spend several hours a day on personal grooming, teasing his hair first this way then that, experimenting with a huge range of gels, oils, waxes, dyes, tints and mousses. He spent more on hair products per week than he did on food, despite having expensive tastes and a gargantuan appetite. To everyone's surprise, once he had a full head of hair styled just the way he liked it, he became a model WPS client and even took to religion, declaring himself QUOTE a Lamb of God, the meekest of the meek,

no longer a threat to society UNQUOTE – unless you cate-
gorise doorstep evangelising as a threat rather than just
an irritant, as I and many of my colleagues do.

Not that his new-found piety gave pause to his
grassed-up and banged-up former associates (Mr Inkling
not among their number, more's the pity), some two
dozen of them, who from their cells in maximum security
jails across the land placed a bounty on his head, a substantial sum of money that in decades past would have
caused many a Met officer to stray from the righteous but
unremunerative path of law enforcement.

HONEYMAN: May one ask what this Ball-Pein John character
did for Mr Inkling?

STARKEY: You may. He broke skulls to order.

HONEYMAN: Anything else?

STARKEY: No.

HONEYMAN: And now?

STARKEY: That's something I'm not at liberty to reveal. But I can
confirm that he's definitely put skull-breaking behind
him. Nowadays his principal weapon is prayer.

HONEYMAN: I've a feeling I met him when I was looking into Mr
Inkling's affairs. He's a tall man with a ruddy complexion
and broad shoulders, thick through the chest, am I right?
Wears at least size twelve shoes? Has a nose bent to the
left, with a slightly tilted tip? Smokes torpedo-like roll-
ups filled with Charles Fairmorn Dark Fired Shag which,
as I know from the Athenaeum prior to the implementa-
tion of the smoking ban, has a good room aroma and
works well in combination with a robust port or strong
black coffee? Wears a full set of dentures that are whiter
than white? Knows the words by heart to only one song
other than the National Anthem, *Nellie Dean*, made
famous by his aunt, who he never met and who probably
wasn't actually his aunt, just someone his mother knew in
childhood, or knew of, Gertie Gitana? Has never fully

mastered the art of cutlery? Is so unlettered he's effectively illiterate? Doesn't drink except to excess? Climbed into the big cat enclosure at London Zoo just before feeding time, for a bet, and emerged unscathed, having left the lions cowering in a corner? Collects toenail clippings from stars of stage and screen and presses them into wax effigies? Dreams of almost nothing but white, fluffy clouds and talks about them incessantly? Surely that's our man – the white, fluffy clouds are the clincher.

STARKEY: I think you're getting him mixed him up with another of Mr Inkling's mob: Arturo 'Artie' Banditti, a man of advanced years, much troubled by arthritis, who walks with the aid of a stick but to this day is still one of the world's most accomplished shoplifters. He's banned from every business on the Holloway Road, including the undertakers. His convictions, such as they are, are for trivial offences of other kinds, such as urinating in public fountains at home and abroad, the Trevi Fountain in Rome being a particular favourite, as indeed it is for most of us.

HONEYMAN: No, not him. The fellow I'm thinking of is younger.

STARKEY: How young?

HONEYMAN: Late thirties or so. Fifty tops.

STARKEY: With a droopy moustache, like a 1970s porn star?

HONEYMAN: As I recall, yes.

STARKEY: As you yourself once had.

HONEYMAN: What are you insinuating?

STARKEY: Nothing, nothing at all.

HONEYMAN: Good. Because many of us had droopy moustaches at the time, especially Italian waiters – or, should I say, waiters in Italian restaurants pretending to be Italian. I'm talking about *British* Italian restaurants. The waiters in Italian restaurants in Italy, particularly in Rome, and, come to think of it, Florence, often seemed to be trying to pass themselves off as French, even in backstreet trattorias. Why, I've no idea. A veneer of sophistication, perhaps. Or perhaps they were of French/Italian parentage and mostly spoke French at home. Such things aren't uncommon, though things, even common things, are rarely what they seem.

STARKEY: I'm glad you realise that, Mr Honeyman. It's Witness Protection's guiding principle. We hold that things should be hidden in plain sight, where they're least likely to be found. And it isn't just waiters who, for various reasons, try to pass as French. Do you remember the Murgerson-Dart trial of 2005? The Old Bailey was as packed as the black hole of Calcutta. The accused's fellow chartered accountants, tax specialists to a man, were waiting to see whether the loopholes they'd long been exploiting for the benefit of their wealthy clients would be deemed morally indefensible, and even if not actually illegal (it's a grey area) subject from then on to uncomfortably close scrutiny by HMRC. But because there was evidence of money laundering on a grand scale, nearly all of it attributable to Dart, Murgerson turned Queen's evidence, and Dart, whose principal clients were Jimmy Inkling and his iffy lot, got banged up for eight years. Dart, deeply embittered and a thug whose best friends were even more thuggish than he was, all of whom used the services of ultra-thugs such as Attila Urban and Ball-Pein John, swore revenge. We have him on tape – inadmissible as evidence, unfortunately, because the recording quality is so poor – trying, in the weeks leading up to the trial, to organise a hit on his former partner. It came to nothing, we saw to that. But Murgerson was deeply shocked when he heard the recording. And there was no reason to assume that Dart would drop the matter once he was released from jail.

Dart served six years of the tariff, was a model prisoner by all accounts, and by the time of his release Murgerson, renamed Joubert, had been in the Scheme for several years. Where did we hide him? In plain sight: the third floor Chelsea apartment right next to Dart's. Culford Gardens, near the back of Peter Jones.

Only a thin party wall separated them. They shared a stairwell and a front door and they bumped into each other on a fairly regular basis. In that typically British way of dealing with awkward social situations, they strenuously avoided eye contact and offered only a brief nod or a mumbled greeting as they collected their mail or squeezed past each other on the stairs.

Murgerson was understandably fearful of what might happen if Dart recognised him, but prozac and sessions with a WPS hypnotherapist calmed his jitters, and we took the precaution of having an invisibility screen installed in a corner of the lounge. We also, during their first few encounters, had armed response officers stationed nearby, ready to intervene should things get ugly. But nothing untoward happened: Dart failed to recognise Murgerson, which is remarkable considering that he looked little different from how he'd looked when Dart last saw him, as chief witness for the prosecution.

The changes made to Murgerson's appearance were subtle but significant. A former contact lens wearer, he now wore spectacles, lightly tinted, with heavy black frames; his skin tone was darker (Type 4 on the Fitzpatrick scale, with the slightly olive cast of a Type 3) and kept that way with regular sunbed top-ups; and his hair was longer and greyer than it had been when he and Dart were partners. He'd lost quite a bit of weight (due to stress, despite the prozac), and his attire was now smart-casual rather than formal, as befits a man who seems not to have to work for a living.

We provided him with a live-in girlfriend, a willowy, elegant WPC name of Vasseur, Jacqueline Vasseur (not her real name, needless to say), who spoke several European languages fluently. In the evenings, when at home, they were instructed to converse in French interspersed with broken English, but mainly French. That was the key factor. Hearing French being spoken in the apartment next door threw Dart off the scent. He and Monsieur Joubert have now lived side by side for several years and Dart seems none the wiser. Either that or he's craftier than we think and playing the long game.

Murgerson is currently a special adviser on tax evasion to both HMRC and the WPS – poacher turned gamekeeper, as they say – and he's been keeping an especially close eye on Dart, who, despite having been struck off by the Institute of Chartered Accountants, has continued to work illegally for many of the dodgy clients he'd had prior to his conviction. Evidence of criminality is accumulating and Dart's days as a free man are numbered. Perhaps those of his clients, too. One can only hope.

HONEYMAN: You mentioned a little while back something I'd never heard of, an ... now what was it? An invisibility something-or-other.

STARKEY: A slip of the tongue, nothing more. Perhaps you misheard me. Anyway, it's of no consequence, and as time is of the essence, let's move on ...

HONEYMAN: No, wait. I'm sure of what I heard. Can we have the stenographer confirm what the Deputy Assistant Commissioner said?

STARKEY: There's really no need.

~~~: Miss Stenographer ...

STENOGRAPHER: Erm, 'we took the precaution of having an invisibility screen installed in a corner of the lounge'.

HONEYMAN: Thank you, that's what I thought I heard. But what does it mean?

STARKEY: I'm not at liberty to tell you. Not unless you agree to sign up to the Scheme. As have, may I remind you, the rest of your family.

HONEYMAN: I won't even consider signing until I have all the relevant information, this included.

STARKEY: It's really not important.

HONEYMAN: It is to me.

STARKEY: [...]

HONEYMAN: [...]

~~~: Perhaps we should have a short recess to –

STARKEY: *No-no-no-no-no*, let's not do that! There's no time. Haven't you understood what I've been saying? – I have to get to Downing Street. I should already *be* in Downing Street. We've got to resolve this now, as a matter of urgency. My chariot awaits, unless my charioteer, thinking I've abandoned him, has returned to the cab rank or gone home in a sulk – in which case I'll have to hoof it. The Home Secretary will be mounting the stairs, preparing to enter the Cabinet Room, briefing papers in order, lipstick meticulously applied, hair stiff with spray that smells curiously of almond-scented furniture polish

> Which has led to a wicked rumour
> that as some kind of glandular
> defense mechanism
> her skin
> secretes cyanide
> as toads
> do
> bufotoxins.

and wearing, perhaps, those snakeskin or croc hide shoes that are her sole concession to femininity, though they look incongruous, as everyone but her husband agrees, and even he may just be being diplomatic – after all, he is a diplomat. She'll want to know whether you've signed the WPS papers, Mr Honeyman. The Inkling case is uppermost in her mind; it's not on Cobra's agenda this evening but we'll be discussing it afterwards. What am I to tell her?

HONEYMAN: That I refused to sign because you wouldn't give me all the relevant facts. That you stonewalled throughout our negotiations. That the responsibility for failing to secure my cooperation is yours and yours alone, and as an honourable man (I'm giving you the benefit of the doubt) your resignation will be on her desk first thing tomorrow, though I suspect it already is tomorrow.

~~~: It is.

HONEYMAN: So. This invisibility thing, what is it?

STARKEY: You're a stubborn man, Mr Honeyman.

HONEYMAN: [...]

STARKEY: Can we not agree to set it aside for one moment? If only you'd pick up the pen and sign on the dotted line, just above where Tamsin has signed. Two signatures, that's all that's required. Surely it's not too much to ask.

HONEYMAN: [...]

~~~: Mr Honeyman ...

HONEYMAN: Not until I know what I want to know, and perhaps not even then.

STARKEY: Now you're just being petulant.

HONEYMAN: [...]

STARKEY: All right, I give in. But I want your assurance, Mr ~~~, that nothing of what I'm about to say will be entered into the trial's official transcript.

~~~: Take a comfort break, Miss Stenographer. Ten minutes or so. I'll pause the audio equipment for the duration.

STARKEY: And I want you, Mr Honeyman, to sign an affidavit saying that I revealed the information reluctantly, and *only after* you'd signed the WPS papers. Is that agreed?

HONEYMAN: Perhaps.

STARKEY: Perhaps isn't good enough. I need your assurance.

HONEYMAN: What if, in a year or two, Tamsin and I decide we want to leave the Witness Protection Scheme?

STARKEY: You may do so, but at your peril. I would strongly advise against it. And anyway, why would you? The WPS isn't just there to keep you safe from harm; it's a warm and supportive organisation, more akin to a happy family than a soulless bureaucratic machine staffed, as in most government departments, by jobsworths, makeweights, drones and zombies. Our profiling system, employing the most sophisticated dating agency computer algorithms the world has ever known, and finessed by a technical team capable, one-on-one, of out-intelligencing Einstein, is foolproof. We carefully match officers and clients to ensure they get along famously; which they do. So famously it's sometimes hard to get an officer to relinquish his assumed identity and disembed himself. Playing a role is much more satisfying than eking out the years under leaden skies as one's plain old less-than-satisfactory self, as any actor will tell you. On occasion we've had to snatch officers off the street who'd 'gone native' or 'rogue' and repeatedly ignored the command to return to HQ for debriefing. It's as though they'd been brainwashed – self-brainwashed, if that makes sense. Some of them never wholly relinquish their adopted persona; they keep slipping in and out of character at inconvenient moments and have to be put on restricted duties or even, if all else fails, pensioned off.

But clients such as yourself and Tamsin can stay in role for as long as you like. Really now, what could be better than that! And if, in previous comments, I may have given the impression that the Scheme is only for bad people fearful of having bad things done to them, consider this: In April next year, Murgerson and his WPC girlfriend are going to be married. They plan to honeymoon in, I think, Hawaii. Or Iceland. Somewhere romantic, rocky and volcanic.

Why not
Venus?
It ticks
all the boxes.

Don't get me wrong: the WPS is not a dating agency. It's one of the few services we don't provide. In fact, we discourage trysts and/or sexual relations between fellow officers, also between clients and officers, as invariably it leads to trouble. But love, true love, cannot be denied. I may even be persuaded to act as Murgerson's best man, given that he's had to sever ties with his family and void all friendships made prior to his conviction. He's also had to delete his Facebook and Twitter accounts. Such are the demands the Scheme makes of us. But the rewards are so abundant they make the demands seem piffling.

HONEYMAN: Glad to hear it. Now, without further ado, as you're supposed to be elsewhere, I'd like to know more about the invisibility curtain. More than I currently know, which is, precisely, nothing.

STARKEY: Not curtain. Screen. Three-panelled, folding. A product of the emerging technology that led to the development of the stealth bomber. Same principle, though I can't claim to fully understand the science underlying it: a combination of passive low observable features and active emitters to fool the observer into thinking the screen and whatever's behind it isn't actually there. It's mostly used in safe houses that, for one reason or other, can't accommodate a so-called panic room or even a panic alcove.

The panic wardrobe
a free-standing unit
bullet- and bomb-proof
oxygenated and fire resistant for up to one hour
employing an internal lock
accessible only by
the WPS client
was hauled away
and dropped into a nearby lake
where it sank immediately.
The client escaped
swam to shore

and was shot
as he raced towards the
shelter of the tree line.
The panic wardrobe has since
been mothballed.

Technicians place the screen in a relatively dark, out-of-the-way corner, connect it to a power socket and adjust the 'chameleon clade' emitters until the screen blends into its surroundings. You really wouldn't know it was there unless you happened to bump into it. If you're hidden behind the screen when Mr Inkling's men burst through the door, they'll think the room is empty. The screen is also fitted with an elaborate array of small noise-cancellation loudspeakers that work on the principle of destructive interference to mask any sound you might make. They're fine-tuned to block body sounds in particular: breathing, sniffing, coughing, sneezing, burping, etc. Remain perfectly still behind the screen and your chances of being detected are almost nil.

But its effectiveness will be void if the villains of this world get to know of its existence. Hence the high level of secrecy. One of the newspapers got whiff of it a couple of years ago but we managed, through a so-called 'dispassionate intermediary' (i.e. someone of major influence not known to be on our payroll), to persuade the journalist and her editor that the supposed whistleblower was living in cloud cuckoo land. Luckily for us, the whistleblower had a well-documented history of delusional behaviour. He'd already spent the best part of a decade in Rampton Secure Hospital having stabbed two individuals with unusually pale skin to establish, out of curiosity and without malice aforethought, whether they were already dead. One of them died on the spot, the other survived, which left the delusionist none the wiser. He's back in Rampton now, following an unrelated incident, and may never be released.

HONEYMAN: So how did he, of all people, get to know of the existence of the invisibility screen?

STARKEY: He didn't. It was all in his imagination, the product of a cruelly warped mind.

HONEYMAN: Yet it exists.

STARKEY: Of course it exists, haven't I just said so?

HONEYMAN: And the screen would be fitted as standard in a corner of the lounge.

STARKEY: More likely the utility room, if it's relatively free of clutter. Or the attached garage which, given its puny dimensions, an average-sized family car will no longer fit. Or, at a push, the small room upstairs that estate agents call an occasional bedroom, though the only way even a cot could be squeezed in there is by standing it on end or dismantling it and leaving it dismantled. But –

HONEYMAN: Yes?

STARKEY: – there's no guarantee you would receive the screen. Not unless you met the criteria. Due to swingeing cuts and other deep austerity measures, we have at present only one invisibility screen, and for nearly a month it's been in the workshop for routine maintenance. We're awaiting a replacement part that's in transit from Hangzhou, the electronics capital of China's Zhejiang Province. It was sent by the slowest modes of transportation possible: a combination of bicycle rickshaw, sampan and small feeder container ship, and on a zigzag route that would dizzy a bee, even though we specifically requested and paid for couriered air mail and were promised delivery within three working days.

The company has flatly refused to despatch a replacement part by our preferred mode of transportation until the first part can be confirmed as lost rather than just delayed in transit. They haven't even offered to refund postage and packing.

I'll be taking the matter up with the Home Secretary

and – as the Chinese seem to have done this deliberately, though they claim it's just a communication error – the Foreign Secretary, both of whom will be attending the Cobra meeting. If the matter isn't resolved quickly it could escalate, resulting in a major diplomatic row, tit-for-tat expulsions of embassy staff, the collapse of hugely important trade deals, etc.

But I won't lie to you: even when the screen is fixed it may have to be deployed elsewhere. It's allocated to whichever client has the greatest need according to the perceived level of threat (which we calculate using the sliding scale you'll find among the appendixes in the WPS pack), and, unlikely though it sounds given Mr Inkling's track record, someone's need may be greater than yours.

HONEYMAN: No screen, no deal.

STARKEY: Mr Honeyman, you're being unreasonable. You can't wring further concessions from us, there's nothing more to give.

HONEYMAN: In which case ...

STARKEY: Look, Mr Honeyman, I'd hoped that by appealing to your sense of decency and fair play – very British conceits, of which Johnny Foreigner has little understanding – I'd win you over. But perhaps, like the Chinese, you're deficient in those qualities. Or, though unlikely, my argument wasn't strong enough. Either or both, it matters not a jot. Something needs to be done, and the only tool left in my toolbox is threat. So ... does Tamsin know about the truly disgusting activities you engaged in during the droopy moustache era, and the mutated strain of papillomavirus you contracted and passed on to her (fewer than thirty confirmed cases worldwide since the early 1980s), which, although it's hidden in the nooks and crannies of your body and is nothing but an occasional irritant when your immune system is low, may – in fact, probably will – be the death of her?

As you're well aware, having researched the issue thoroughly, in women the virus triggers a highly aggressive form of cancer that's unsusceptible to treatment by the time it's detected. You also know that analgesics offer the patient little relief. No relief at all, to be precise. A dose strong enough to quell the pain would kill the patient five times over. Tamsin, the love of your life, will die in agony. Have you told her that?

HONEYMAN: [...]

STARKEY: Well, have you?

HONEYMAN: [...]

STARKEY: Your silence could hardly be more eloquent, Mr Honeyman. You've lived with this guilty secret for much of your adult life and tried desperately to cover your tracks. Using the advance you received on your first book, a thriller (and a complete stinker: unheralded, unreviewed, unpurchased, the entire edition long since pulped), you bought up the extant copies of *Cinderella's Balls, Arse over Tit, Wicked Wang Wooing* (in which you played a coprophile Fu Manchu-type pirate captain) and other depraved epics in which you were the star attraction, and destroyed them all. You doused them with lighter fluid and set fire to them in your parents' back garden while they were on holiday, feeding the flames with incendiary diary entries.

Unfortunately for you, copies of *Cinderella* and *Wang* slipped through your fingers and fell into our hands. By 'our' I mean the Met's. We've been using them for decades as Vice Squad induction material and a source of drunken ribaldry at office parties. I love the moment in *Wang* when, on being startled by mutineers creeping up on you, pantomime fashion, you exclaim, 'Shiver me timbers and fuck me with a fig tree!' – and as there just happens to be a fig tree on the poop deck, growing in a tub ...

Although not as incongruous as the wristwatch in *Ben Hur*
[which may just be a shadow – its existence is hotly disputed]
this is still a cine-goof
as any arborologist will tell you.
A fig tree couldn't survive
more than a few days on deck
while a vessel is at sea
as
according to the script
the Bachelors' Delight is supposed to have been
for six whole months
long enough for the crew to become
malnourished
dehydrated
scurvous and stir crazy.
Prunus Serrulata
would cope slightly better
in those conditions
and
'fuck me with a flowering cherry'
wouldn't significantly diminish the power
of the captain's oath
though even the best of actors might stumble
over the crammed-in syllables
at the end of the line.

I believe you also wrote the screenplay, such as it is, despite your name being absent from the credits. Not much in the way of dialogue and most of it laughably bad. Prentice work. Still, we all have to start somewhere.

HONEYMAN: For your information, Deputy Assistant Commissioner, *Wicked Wang Wooing* is an acknowledged lost classic of world cinema. The film critic Maurice Roche said so, and in *Cahiers du Cinéma*, no less.

STARKEY: That was you writing under an assumed name. We know all your tricks, Mr Honeyman, don't think we don't.

HONEYMAN: That's a cheap shot.

STARKEY: Which doesn't make it any less true.

HONEYMAN: [...]

STARKEY: Cat got your tongue?

HONEYMAN: [...]

STARKEY: Well ...?

HONEYMAN: Tamsin knows everything.

STARKEY: Does she now.

HONEYMAN: Of course she does. We keep nothing from each other.

STARKEY: I don't think so.

HONEYMAN: Well, you're wrong.

STARKEY: What about your built-for-comfort-not-speed Ukrainian lover, Arkady Bredyuk?

HONEYMAN: That's a wilful misunderstanding of our entirely platonic relationship. Sheer mischief-making on your part. You ought to be ashamed of yourself. Once Arkady's indefinite leave to remain in the UK has been granted, he, Tamsin and I will be entering into partnership to open a swanky restaurant in St Peter Port. We've already leased premises on the High Street. The builders have reconfigured the interior in accordance with the architect's plans, and the shopfitters are itching to get to work. It's an exciting project. But if Arkady's right to stay is denied, we'll opt for premises within la citadelle, St Malo, and perhaps that would be for the best. The French won't turn him away, I know they won't; they have a keen appreciation of *cuisine exquis* and, trust me, no *cuisine* is more *exquis* than Arkady Bredyuk's.

STARKEY: I'll take your word for it. But it's irrelevant, because his leave to remain won't be granted – not unless you sign the WPS papers. And we'll have a discreet word with our French counterparts. Bredyuk will be flagged up as an undesirable alien, a known security risk, a suspected cell member of a hitherto-little-known terrorist organisation that has links to al-Qaeda. Mere suspicion will get him locked up for several weeks pending enquiries, followed by expulsion. Destination Kiev, where the authorities, entertaining similar concerns, will treat him in a similar fashion, though more harshly, as is their way. After a year or two in solitary confinement, perhaps he'll land a cushy job in the prison kitchen, peeling spuds. After all, he looks like one.

HONEYMAN: But Arkady's no terrorist!

STARKEY: That's as may be. But one really can't be too careful when national security is at stake. Which reminds me ...

~~~: Yes, of course. Downing Street. Cobra. Black cab, meter ticking. We haven't forgotten.

HONEYMAN: If I sign the papers, will we be able to proceed with our restaurant?

STARKEY: That's entirely up to you. Though for security's sake you'd have to choose a new location, somewhere on the UK mainland where you're not well known, not that you're well known even in St Peter Port. How about Edinburgh? It's the only city in Scotland where a restaurant of the quality you aspire to is likely to succeed and an English accent is the norm rather than, as they say, 'a thistle in the ear'. They're tribal and chippy, the Scots, resentful of all things English. To them, the Act of Union was a shotgun wedding, no love lost nor subsequently gained, and centuries of familiarity have bred nothing but contempt.

HONEYMAN: And Arkady will get leave to remain?

STARKEY: He will.

HONEYMAN: Definitely?

STARKEY: You have my word.

HONEYMAN: Tamsin, Jasper and Kiddling have signed?

STARKEY: They have.

HONEYMAN: Cat, too?

STARKEY: Yes.

HONEYMAN: And what about Kiddling's sweet but wittery wife, the sometimes exasperatingly indecisive Belle?

STARKEY: Even Belle, though she dithered a bit, as you'd expect.

HONEYMAN: […]

STARKEY: Everyone has signed up to the Scheme but you, Mr Honeyman. For the first time ever you're out of step with your family. You're holding them back rather than, like Moses, boldly leading them through the bureaucratic wilderness to the Promised Land, aka Caledonia. And Jasper will never forgive you if you spurn this golden opportunity; his life depends on it. Sign the papers, Mr Honeyman. You know it's the right thing to do.

HONEYMAN: Can't we keep Bozzie with us? It would break my heart to leave him behind.

STARKEY: I really ought to run it past the Home Secretary. To include Bozzie would exceed the cap on a single case spend and stretch the WPS budget to breaking point. — But she's said to be a dog lover, or at least someone who doesn't actually hate dogs, and these are exceptional circumstances, so … yes. I'll skimp on someone else's spend. Or reduce the number of specials on the menu in the staff canteen, especially the two most expensive dishes, fugu nabe (no deaths so far this year) and quasi of veal with alba white truffle. Or cut by half the gargantuan stationery budget. You wouldn't believe how many printer cartridges we get through every month. Presumably some get stolen for domestic use or end up for sale on market stalls and at car boot sales. Or perhaps, when no-one's looking, they sprout little legs and scurry back to the manufacturer's warehouse. Homing cartridges: it's as good an explanation as any.

But if we include Bozzie he'll have to have a change of name. Barkin? Bony? Baxter? Biscuit? Boo-Boo? Bradley? Bucky? Binky? Something beginning with Bee that he'll quickly get used to.

HONEYMAN: Biscuit would probably work. He's biscuit-coloured, more digestive than bourbon.

STARKEY: Then Biscuit it is!

HONEYMAN: And the invisibility screen?

STARKEY: Yours if I can swing it, once it's been repaired.

HONEYMAN: And Arkady's leave to remain will definitely be approved?

STARKEY: Yes. Though, like you and Bozzie, it would be best if he changed his name. And nationality. He'd look good in a kilt, though there's unlikely to be a tartan for Clan MacBredyuk in the *Vestiarium Scoticum*. I'll have one of my officers trot over to Snowies this afternoon to discuss the matter with him. Okay with you?

HONEYMAN: Err, yes ... Thank you.

STARKEY: Anything else? I hate to rush you into making such an important decision, but ...

HONEYMAN: Well ...

STARKEY: Spit it out, Mr Honeyman.

HONEYMAN: Will I still be able to publish?

STARKEY: Under your new name, whatever that will be, yes. Luckily your writing style is so style free – that's merely an observation, by the way, not a criticism – it could belong to almost anyone, and only one of Mr Inkling's close associates is much of a reader, though he rarely reads anything apart from racing tips in *The Sun* and, while eating breakfast, the list of ingredients on cereal packets, both of which he declaims, between mouthfuls, to his largely indifferent cat in a velvety, sinister voice not dissimilar in timbre to that of Vincent Price. We bugged his flat for a month and that was the only intelligence we gained.

So you're unlikely to be detected. But if I were you I'd steer clear of biography and, needless to say, autobiography, and turn my hand to literary fiction. If you do we can probably ease you onto the Man Booker longlist and, who knows, if it's a poor year, as often it is, you might make the shortlist. We can't allow you to win the prize, of course. Nor attend the awards dinner. Even after having had cosmetic surgery, you'll still be obliged to keep a low profile. We'll excuse your absence by saying you're incommunicado, on a spiritual retreat in Lhasa, or digging wells in the Horn of Africa – something along those lines.

HONEYMAN: You can do that, get a book placed on the longlist?

STARKEY: No problem at all. There aren't that many good books published in a single year, perhaps only one or two, and if past years are anything to go by those will be overlooked.

Actually, you'd be amazed to learn how many former Booker nominees are WPS clients – and that doesn't include that annoying Rushdie fellow. He dithered almost as much as Belle and never actually joined the Scheme, though everyone assumes he did. Somehow he managed to wangle an armed police guard, 24/7, consisting of officers drawn from the Priceway-sponsored wing of Special Branch.

HONEYMAN: What's that ... Priceway? The supermarket chain?

STARKEY: *Defunct* supermarket chain. Swallowed up by one of its now defunct competitors. Don't sound so surprised, Mr Honeyman, most major UK retailers sponsor policing. Anonymously, of course, and with no expectation of favour. It's an open secret. At one time our canteen cutlery came from Woolworth's – not best quality, to be honest, made in Taiwan rather than Sheffield, but gratefully received. Pens courtesy of BIC. Truncheon oil from Ronseal in those far-off days when truncheons were made of rosewood. You get the picture.

But the WPS currently lacks sponsorship. Our negotiations with Posycar (motto: luxury fragrances for the automobile in your life) failed because of a disagreement over terms and conditions which, after weeks of fruitless haggling, our legal team and theirs tried to resolve with a friendly game of five-a-side football. But even after a full hour of stoppage time the game ended in a goalless draw

– neither side being fit enough to stage a penalty shoot-out.

The referee later said that never, since the heyday of gladiatorial combat in the second century AD, had so many egregious fouls been committed in the name of sport, any sport. At the end of the match, team members on both sides had to be hospitalised, one of the Posycars with a stab wound. Lord knows how that happened; everyone, including the referee and the linesmen, had been patted down immediately before kick-off and relieved of their weaponry. A frustrating outcome. Hence the austerity measures.

But to get back to the main point ... Rushdie's decision wasn't based on who sponsors what, though he could probably tell which way the chill wind of austerity was blowing. My personal opinion is that, with all the perks we offer, only a handful of which I've outlined for you, he would still have been better off in the WPS. But what's done is done.

The WPS is of particular benefit to authors because, quite simply, it removes them from their immediate social circle, which limits the scope of their vices, thus providing them with more time to write. Once they've had breakfast and a slug of Jim Beam and run through their extensive repertoire of delay and displacement activities, what else can they do to stave off boredom? People with regular jobs don't have that luxury. Nor might you if the restaurant takes off in a big way.

HONEYMAN: I can't believe what I'm hearing. You're telling me the Man Booker Prize is a stitch-up?

STARKEY: *Certainly not!* That's *not* what I'm saying! Just because some clients of ours are writers of so-called literary fiction, and their books get longlisted every few years, doesn't mean the fix is in. Frankly, it would be better for us if they wrote fewer books. Or less well-written ones.

Two made it to the shortlist in one year alone, both critically lauded and given short odds by the bookies. Faced with the distinct possibility that one of them might win, despite our best efforts, we had to draw up contingency plans. Obituaries were prepared for each of them. The unlucky winner would be said to have died suddenly, tragically, while en route from Lhasa to the awards ceremony, of a heart attack or a stroke. There'd be a private funeral and an empty casket cremation. Our client would then have to undergo yet another tiresome change of name and location, and perhaps a further round of cosmetic surgery.

Thankfully it didn't come to that because the judges harboured a viper in their midst. Not a WPS ringer, just an arrogant refusenik who loathed consensus. She – that year it was a she – was incensed that her favoured book, written by one of her best friends, didn't make the salmon leap from longlist to shortlist; so incensed that she did everything in her power to disrupt the proceedings. There were shouting matches so loud they could be heard out in the street, vile insults flung, rumours of scuffles in the corridor outside the judging room. At the awards dinner the chairman bore a scratch on his cheek so livid that even pancake makeup couldn't hide it.

The prize that year went to a hefty novel no-one really cared for, written by a non-WPS author on a topic so dull, or rendered in such a dreary manner, it has since been called the Booker's Blooper of Bloopers. That's its sole claim to fame, the reason people still remember it.

A survey undertaken among readers of Kindle books found that of the hundreds who'd been encouraged by favourable but frankly lunatic reviews to buy the book, only nine per cent read beyond page fifty and only two per cent actually finished it.

I suspect the Booker judges were also nine-per-centers, though none of them, not even the refusenik, has admitted as such.

HONEYMAN: Well, I never.

STARKEY: Never say never, Mr Honeyman. No-one knows what the future may bring, not even Mr ~~~ who regularly communes with discarnate entities or spirit beings and travels extensively on the astral plane. Or thinks he does. The top-notch psychics we employ say otherwise.

Now, gentlemen, if you'll excuse me ...

Fourth Session

~~~: Ready are we, Miss Stenographer?

STENOGRAPHER: Hang on a sec. The stenotype roll has run out.

~~~: So those who say that all things must come to pass, even stenotype rolls, are right after all. Ah well, take your time, we're in no great hurry.

STENOGRAPHER: [...]

~~~: From the look you've just given me – eyes flashing daggers, as the lady romance novelists say – I suspect my comment has been misunderstood. If it seemed sarcastic or ironic, I apologise; it was neither.

HONEYMAN: Point of order, Mr ~‡◊.

~~~: Yes?

HONEYMAN: I apologise for constantly mangling your name. Bit of a tongue-twister, to say the least. Almost as bad as Mr Taylor's. It might help if I could see it written down. — Ah. Oh dear. What a pity. No help at all. I suppose I'll just have to call you Mr Squiggle.

~~~: I'd prefer it if you used my real name. In fact, I insist.

HONEYMAN: Not going to happen. But look, there's something important you need to know. During the recess Mr Taylor and I somehow ... I'm not entirely sure how it happened, but ... well ... there we were standing at the urinals, bumping elbows because it's a really tight squeeze in the little boys' room, and to mask the sound of urine splashing on porcelain and gurgling down the drain we began to chat, comparing notes about Jimmy Inkling, sharing memories, painful memories. Let's face it, with Jimmy Jewels that's the only kind there are. We wept manfully, as men do, and, having zipped up and thoroughly washed and dried our hands, we fell to consoling one another with Iron John hugs.

Catharsis has never felt more cathartic.

Our red-rimmed eyes tell you everything you need to know.

We also experienced pangs of guilt, knowing that one of the principal verbotens in the Verbotens Guide states that witnesses should, except when giving evidence, aspire to the remorseless silence of lichen, and must not, under any circumstances, by any means or mode of communication whatsoever, discuss the case with any other person, *especially not with fellow witnesses*, either prior to or during the course of the trial. Words to that effect.

The confessional booth
psychiatrist's couch
and
one-sided
graveside
chats
are excepted.
Likewise
talking in one's sleep
or to someone
suffering from
locked-in syndrome.

We did what we were explicitly told not to do, for which we beg the court's forgiveness.

But while we were giving and receiving emotional support – of, as mentioned, the bluff, manly kind – and blotting each other's tears with paper towels, something potentially useful occurred to us, something that we hope will redeem us in your eyes.

Many of the terrible things that Mr Taylor and I experienced at Mr Inkling's hands, or at his behest, are remarkably similar (though Mr Taylor suffered considerably more abuse than I did), and they overlap to a significant degree, so much so that we thought it might benefit the proceedings if we gave evidence together rather than one after the other. It would, we think, enable us to provide a more detailed account of Mr Inkling's criminality. Also –

~~~: *Alleged* criminality, Mr Honeyman.

HONEYMAN: Yes. Alleged. Innocent until proven guilty, which I'm sure he will be. Found guilty, I mean.

~~~: That's for the jury to decide, not you.

HONEYMAN: The jury is asleep.

~~~: Asleep or awake, it makes no difference. Whatever verdict the jury reaches will be binding. Now kindly finish telling me why hearing evidence from you and Mr Δ≈ΔΔΔ°◇≥ in tandem –

HONEYMAN: Not in tandem. That implies that one of us would be steering and pedalling the evidence while the other merely pedalled. Whereas, in reality, both of us would be steering and pedalling. Hmm. I'm not sure whether comparing the delivery of evidence to riding a bicycle is terribly helpful, though what Mr Taylor and I propose may well be. We're hoping to avoid tedium, the tedium of repetition that might plunge the jury into an even more profound sleep than it's in right now. It would also speed up the proceedings, something we thought you'd approve of.

~~~: Mr Honeyman, not only do I not approve, quite frankly I'm appalled. By rights, I should dismiss you and Mr Δ≈ΔΔΔ°◇≥ as witnesses, invaluable though you are, for

having had a discussion about Mr Inkling while the trial is ongoing ... and in the lavatory of all places. What were you thinking? The proper course of action would be to jail you for contempt of court and declare a mistrial. And had you not just signed the WPS documents, that's precisely what I would have done. But starting the trial again from scratch and trying to persuade former witnesses to cooperate might be difficult. In some cases impossible. I'm thinking, in particular, of Rodney Blenkinsopp, the 'actor' from Kew, and Professoressa Zappettini.

HONEYMAN: But their evidence was worthless! One was a know-nothing, the other a flake and a fraud.

~~~: Perhaps so. But for due process to succeed we have to follow established procedure. Who's to say that, at the trial's denouement, when the evidential threads are drawn ever tighter and fashioned into an elegant noose, their testimony won't become increasingly relevant, perhaps even of vital importance, in ways that would have seemed unlikely when it was given and, with some justification, laughed out of court.

HONEYMAN: Oh, *come on*! You've got to be kidding me.

~~~: Most certainly not, Mr Honeyman. If we don't follow established procedure, chaos will ensue.

STENOGRAPHER: Okay. Fixed.

~~~: Thank you, Miss Stenographer. Let me apologise again for my earlier gaffe –

STENOGRAPHER: No worries, shit happens.

~~~: Indeed it does. Eloquently put. But stay your hand, if you will, just for one moment. There's something I need to explain to these gentlemen before we proceed ...

You say, Mr Honeyman, that by giving evidence simultaneously with Mr $\Delta{\approx}\Delta\Delta^\circ\diamond{\geq}$ you can speed up the proceedings. You and he assume that doing so would be desirable. I hate to have to tell you: your assumption is false. During the last recess I became aware that courtroom time was passing more swiftly than it should; faster than standard time. That's highly unusual. And worrying.

A somewhat eccentric but utterly brilliant theoretical physicist, McCreedy Byrne, gave the problem of perceived temporal relativity (PTR), which is what this is, considerable thought. In fact, he dedicated much of his life to it and in the end it was the death of him. More than a million pages of work in progress filled the rooms of his house from floor to ceiling. In 2002, when a minor earthquake near the town of Dudley sent ripples from its epicentre to his home in Gospel End, shaking the building violently for several seconds, the paper columns, almost as heavy as the trunks of giant redwoods, toppled and fell on him, stifling his mortal spark.

None of Byrne's work was published
during his lifetime.
Nor much of it afterwards.
His speed of thought was such that
he was incapable
of finishing one sentence
before starting another.
The few things that have seen print
posthumously
are
largely unpunctuated
gnomic utterances
such as:
'whereas a ball rolling downhill can || dearth of gut flora will'
and
'consider the fated jurors || thunderbolts in a box'
and
'sparks of the desire magneto || to able-bodied seamen'
and
'imagination stumbles || memory quips'
which none but writers
of an experimental bent
seem to comprehend
and appreciate fully.

Before scholars were able to get their hands on Byrne's written legacy, his ignorant, unappreciative next of kin consigned it to landfill. She said she needed to clear the house quickly so it could be sold. The few fragments of his work to survive were found in the potting shed. Rejected drafts, apparently, some of which were wrapped around plants that had been lifted from the garden to protect them from frost. Lifted, wrapped and forgotten: the plants weren't just winter dormant, they'd been dead for years. Those drafts are being pored and puzzled over to this day.

Being neither a physicist nor a philosopher, I can't hope to do justice to the rich complexity of Byrne's thought, but as you require some kind of explanation, however feeble, here's my best shot.

Byrne's contention was that trial time should, on average, run six per cent slower than standard time, allowing sufficient time for a jury to weigh up the evidence without feeling rushed; whereas cine time, by which he meant the time spent engrossed in a movie, especially during a matinee screening, will always be faster than standard time, perhaps by as much as twenty-four per cent.

I'm sure you can recall trying to be the first person to leave the cinema as the end titles began to roll, launching yourself from your seat and into the aisle, walking briskly from the dimly-lit auditorium into dazzling sunshine, the rest of the audience hot on your heels, and feeling that hardly any time had passed since you'd entered the building. That's when perceived temporal relativity is most obvious.

Byrne attributed this example of PTR to the way movies are edited, cramming more time into a single minute of standard time than a minute usually holds. Less than three hours of screen time may contain a span of thousands, if not millions of years, as in, to use Byrne's example, *2001: A Space Odyssey*.

But what's appropriate for cinema is wholly inappropriate for a courtroom. If courtroom time speeds up and somehow gets ahead of standard time, it can and probably will lead to disorientation among members of the jury and produce eccentric or perverse verdicts. Such, one could argue, was the case with OJ Simpson. His trial ran for nine months and one week but the deliberations on his fate took less than four hours.

Four measly hours! Four days would have been more appropriate; a week better still.

The Simpson jury, having been sequestered for almost a year, was probably experiencing the stressful psychological condition known as cabin fever, and their desperation to be discharged was reflected in the speed of deliberation and the verdict they reached.

That's why the jury room is often called the decompression chamber. It's the place where trial time reverts to standard time, gradually, without haste, to avoid giving jurors the bends. That's why judges in their summing up always stress that deliberation *must not be rushed.* They know that most juries are capable of reaching a verdict in less than ten minutes, and unless inhibitors are put in place that's precisely what will happen. Jurors want to get home to their loved ones, if they have any, or their animals, or a TV dinner-for-one, a bottle of wine and a soap opera. Which is why, in the UK, one of the jurors on any trial expected to run for thirty working days or more is a stooge, a courtroom official working incognito, whose job it is to slow down deliberations in the jury room by, if necessary, grandstanding, naysaying, point-of-ordering, filibustering, and being argumentative to an annoying but necessary degree.

HONEYMAN: So ... look ... I'm not sure whether I understand. Cinemas are fast and courtrooms slow, is that what you're saying?

~~~: I am. Or rather Byrne is. Was.

HONEYMAN: Which is how things ought to be.

~~~: Ideally.

HONEYMAN: And the proceedings in this courtroom are accelerating and in danger of speeding out of control.

~~~: Like a coach with failing brakes on an Alpine pass with numerous hairpin bends and a drunk at the wheel.

HONEYMAN: Leading to dire consequences?

~~~: Obviously.

HONEYMAN: Such as?

~~~: The death of every passenger on board. Mainly sick children and their parents en route to Lourdes. The driver and his co-driver too. Fragments of their bodies mingled with their luggage and scattered widely over rocky terrain accessible only by helicopter, weather permitting. Those who aren't mingled and scattered will be incinerated in the twisted shell of the vehicle, assuming that it goes up in flames, which it almost certainly will because that's what happens, and not just in the movies, when a fuel tank gets ruptured and a fine mist of diesel is ignited by sputtering electrics. Death will be nigh instantaneous for all concerned.

HONEYMAN: I meant dire consequences in the jury room.

~~~: And beyond.

HONEYMAN: Meaning what?

~~~: Regina vs Brinkmann, 1997, if memory serves, in which Roger Brinkmann, accused of murdering his terminally ill mother, Erin, was found not guilty after barely half-an-hour's deliberation. One of the jurors, a Sikh, name of Panesar, a man apparently of sound mind prior to the trial, went home and slaughtered his entire family before impaling himself on the ceremonial sword with which he'd killed them. He was a closet claustrophobe who'd suffered a violent attack of the bends. An internal enquiry concluded that what happened happened because the jury stooge was thought to be having a heart attack

and had to be excused. Consequently, jury time sped past standard time.

STENOGRAPHER: Should I be recording any of this?

~~~: Not until I give the nod. This is a sidebar conference, a private exchange of views. Frank and forthright; no quarter asked, none given.

HONEYMAN: And yet, just a short time ago, you were reprimanding both of us – Mr Taylor in particular – for slowness, badgering us, setting a furious pace and whipping us along, demanding that we deliver our evidence faster, faster, faster. And not just because Deputy Assistant Commissioner Starkey had a prior and pressing engagement. Isn't that so, Mr Taylor?

TAYLOR: It is.

~~~~: Hindsight can be a terrible thing. What I know now I knew not then.

HONEYMAN: That's just a fancy way of saying 'I'm an idiot'.

~~~: Don't push your luck, Mr Honeyman. Any more of that and I'll land on you like the veritable ton of bricks.

HONEYMAN: Would that be an avoirdupois ton or a metric tonne? Not that it matters. Consider me well and truly crushed.

~~~: *Mr Honeyman!* Desist!

⊖

HONEYMAN: Okay, then. Let's open the mystery box and see what guilty secrets lie within. Earlier on, Mr Taylor quoted from a letter written by Rex Cribbage, Jimmy Inkling's adoptive father, indicating that – and I'm paraphrasing – he didn't have an inkling as to how difficult it would be to raise Jimmy as his son.

~~~: How could you possibly know what Mr $\Delta\approx\Delta\Delta\Delta°◊\ge$ said?

You weren't in the courtroom during his testimony.

HONEYMAN: He told me. While we were weeping and hugging by the urinals – which, by the way, reek to high heaven. To think that food is being served on these premises and I actually ate some. Tsk! It's an absolute disgrace. Someone should notify the Food Standards Agency. — But let's move on ... As Deputy Assistant Commissioner Starkey acknowledged, I'd done my research and done it well, so I knew about the letter anyway.

~~~: I see. Please continue.

HONEYMAN: Well, there's more to the choice of surname than the letter indicates. While studying at Oxford, Cribbage was one of the lesser members of an exclusively male club known as The Inklings, the participants in which were keen on God, beer and the reading and discussion of literary work in progress – interests that Cribbage hoped to inculcate in Jimmy. The club's leading lights were CS Lewis and JRR Tolkien, whose books are so well known there's probably no need to read into evidence a list of key titles. Unless, that is, you think it necessary.

~~~: I don't. Please continue.

HONEYMAN: Cribbage was a poet; not, apparently, a good one. Edward Tangye Lean, the club's founder, called him a Hopkins manqué, as unsprung as a Skid Row mattress. We'll just have to take his word for it; none of Cribbage's poems were published during his lifetime and none were found among his papers after his death. Perhaps Jimmy, who, surprisingly, inherited all, destroyed them out of spite. It's entirely possible. Even when Sir (as by then he was) Rex was on his deathbed, there was no reconciliation, nor even the faintest possibility of one. Jimmy ignored the death-rattle summons, though he lived close by and would probably have heard it had he flung a window open and cocked an ear. But he didn't. Nor did he attend the funeral or send a floral tribute. What he does, however, by special arrangement with Capita, the cemetery management company at Hendon Park, is vandalise Sir Rex's gravestone every now and then, using a sledgehammer, to show how much he cares, then he pays for the stone to be replaced, presumably so he can have the pleasure of vandalising it again.

~~~: Very interesting, I'm sure. But what bearing does it have on Mr Inkling's alleged criminal activities?

HONEYMAN: I'll get to that in a moment. Let's not rush things; we don't want time to tie itself in knots, or whatever you say it does.

~~~: Not knots. And the claim was McCreedy Byrne's, not mine. Though poorly understood, PTR is a matter of grave concern. Jury room measures wouldn't've had to be taken to counter its influence were that not so. It poses a major threat to the integrity of the British criminal justice system which, let me remind you, is renowned worldwide and for very good reason.

HONEYMAN: Yadda yadda yadda.

~~~: Your facetiousness is tiresome in the extreme, Mr Honeyman.

HONEYMAN: Deary me. That won't do at all, now will it?

~~~: [...]

HONEYMAN: [...]

~~~: That was a rhetorical question, surely.

HONEYMAN: Well spotted! Glad to see you're paying attention, despite the lateness of the hour and your zombie demeanour – though perhaps that's how you always are. Anyway, as I was saying, Rex Cribbage was a member of The Inklings, though how often he attended the group's twice weekly meetings isn't known. Unlike most clubs or literary societies The Inklings operated without rules, officers, agendas or elections. An informal register was kept by Lewis, sporadically, on beer mats.

Little known fact:
CS Lewis was a tegestologist
one of the
foremost beer mat
collectors of his day.
Between 1929-1945
he amassed nearly two thousand mats
some American but most of them British.
On his death in 1963
his executors offered the collection to
Oxford University
for their Bodleian archives.
Shockingly
the university declined the offer
despite the fact that Lewis
wrote draft fragments of
Out of the Silent Planet
in a squirrely scrawl
on thirty of the mats
those with a greater area
of blank space
such as Tetley Mild
rather than those of his regular tipple
Morrells Varsity Ale.
The mats are now in the hands of a private collector
a Russian
whose anonymity has been guaranteed.
Lewis researchers wishing to consult the mats can
according to Srinivasa Ramanujan
[or someone claiming to speak for him]
go whistle.

Cribbage's name appeared only once, spelled Cribbidge, so I think we can safely assume that Lewis didn't know him well. What we do know, because Cribbage mentioned it in a letter to his mother, was that it was at an Inklings meeting, in the snug of the Eagle and Child public house (aka the Bird and Baby), that he made the acquaintance of Piers Anthony Urquhart.

Urquhart was a literary dilettante living off a trust fund set up by his parents, both of whom had succumbed, he said, to lassa fever during an epidemic in Kenya when he was barely four years old. Or they'd been mauled to death by lions. Or leopards. Or their canoe had been flipped by an angry hippo and they'd drowned and been eaten by crocodiles. Truth was a concept alien to him. What was verifiable was that his trust fund was lavish. He'd never have to work for a living unless he wanted to, which he didn't.

Cribbage, demonstrating a gift for discretion befitting a future diplomat, allowed Urquhart to tell his tales again and again without once interrupting, though they were riddled with inconsistencies and subject to outrageous embellishments. Perhaps he judged them harmless and, all things considered, really rather amusing – Urquhart being, according to those who knew him, a great raconteur. Anyway, however it came about, he and Urquhart struck up an immediate friendship and were frequently seen dining together in town.

Several months later they moved to London and took a flat in Pimlico. Cribbage had, upon graduating, been offered a job in Whitehall, and almost immediately thereafter, or so it seemed, he was headhunted by the Secret Intelligence Service and put in charge of Section N, which manages the exploitation of foreign diplomatic bags.

What Cribbage didn't know and never, it seems, for one moment suspected, was that Urquhart was a Soviet sympathiser. Nor that he was also a talent spotter for the SIS. In fact, Cribbage owed both his Whitehall job and the invitation to join the SIS to his friend. As for Urquhart, he soon moved on to Cambridge where he had an aunt, he said, very elderly – he had no such thing – who'd been a source of great comfort when his parents were trampled by a rogue elephant while on safari near Lake Manyara in the company of Ernest Hemingway. The aunt had broken a hip, developed pneumonia, and wanted Piers to tend to her affairs while she recuperated.

Within a couple of months of arriving in Cambridge, Urquhart had tipped off the Soviet agent Anthony Blunt about two excellent prospects for recruitment, both of whom were members of the Cambridge Apostles discussion group: John Cairncross and Guy Liddell. So successful were Cairncross and Liddell that, even when their fellow spies Burgess, Maclean and Philby were exposed, they managed to remain undetected. As did Urquhart, at least during his lifetime. Cribbage, who shuffled off this mortal coil only a month or two before Urquhart's coil was shuffled, never got to know of his friend's treasonable activities.

There is, by the way, no suggestion that Cribbage was a Soviet agent, or even a Communist sympathiser. He was given a thorough vetting by MI5 prior to being offered a knighthood. The only stain on his record was that of association with his adopted son Jimmy, from whom he'd long been estranged. This was shortly before Inkling legitimised much of his business empire and threw himself into the charitable and philanthropic work that made him a media darling and, after his stint on reality TV, a household name.

~~~: The estrangement between father and son that has now been mentioned twice, I think, during these proceedings … what was the cause of it?

HONEYMAN: God only knows.

~~~: I was addressing Mr Δ≈ΔΔΔ°◇≥, Mr Honeyman.

HONEYMAN: Good, because no-one –

TAYLOR: Well, actually …

HONEYMAN: – was willing to talk about it, especially not Jimmy himself.

TAYLOR: That's not what he told me.

HONEYMAN: Inkling spoke of the rift?

TAYLOR: Yes.

HONEYMAN: Didn't just say 'there was a rift' before changing the subject, as he does?

TAYLOR: No.

HONEYMAN: A properly detailed account, eh? You must have charmed him something rotten.

TAYLOR: Well I sincerely wish I hadn't. Our chance meeting at Windrush Valley turned out to be one of the worst days of my life.

~~~: Please tell all, Mr $\Delta\approx\Delta\Delta\Delta°\diamond\geq$.

TAYLOR: Of the rift?

~~~~: For now.

TAYLOR: Okay, I'll do my best.

> Leafcutter ant
> on a leafy raft
> heading
> for the
> rapids
> fast.

According to Mr Inkling, if one can believe a word he says, it wasn't just one terrible event that caused the rift, it was a build-up of niggling things that began in early childhood and ended in adolescence when he ran away from home, never to return.

HONEYMAN: Not that Cribbage would have wanted him back. Not from what I heard.

TAYLOR: Agreed. But given the circumstances, that's hardly surprising. At age three, Jimmy clambered over a spike-topped wall into the garden next door, climbed an apple tree, plucked the largest and juiciest-looking fruit and bit into it with his now fully developed primary teeth. During the previous weeks, as the teeth had come through, he'd been testing them out – playfully, in the main, to see how strong they were, what use they could be put to, and what damage they might inflict – on Mr Cribbage, his house-keeper Maeve, and the household's fierce unneutered ginger tom, Mouser.

Actually
according to the tag
on his collar
his name was
Mauser
a ship's cat
who'd jumped ship
in Tilbury
from the
[again
according to
the tag]
German cargo vessel
SS Claus Rickmers.

But this was the biggest challenge his teeth had faced: an apple so big he was obliged to hold it in both hands. Opening his mouth as wide as he could, he sank his teeth into the flesh, flattening his nose in the process. But something was wrong. A fat maggot writhed near the heart of the apple, bitten in two. Enraged, he spat out the maggoty gobbet and smashed the apple again and again against the trunk of the tree, then hurled the pulped fruit to the ground. The following year the tree sickened and died, swiftly followed by the elderly householder. In both cases poison was suspected, but the crude forensics of the day were no match for the infant poisoner's wiles.

On his fourth birthday, dissatisfied with the expensive present he'd been given (a tin pedal car from Harrods, with electric headlights), he stole a five pound note from his father's wallet – a considerable sum of money in those days, more than a week's housekeeping, the absence of which was bound to be noticed, as well he knew. A job-bing painter and decorator doing work in the house was accused of the theft, then exonerated when Jimmy not only confessed but asked for eleven similar offences to be taken into consideration. He wouldn't say what he'd spent the money on

Top-quality Cuban cigars
Padron Serie 1926
from Sautter
of Mount Street.

and he stubbornly refused to explain his actions or, for that matter, apologise.

While his fellow five-year-olds ran around with wooden swords, cap guns and water pistols, Jimmy collected bayonets and First World War revolvers with ammo to match. Webley Mk IVs, the latter. No-one knows how he got hold of them. Maeve chanced upon his arsenal while putting towels away in the linen chest. The guns were hidden under several layers of blankets, coverlets and sheets. All were loaded, their safety catches off. His bayonet collection, the blades honed to scalpel sharpness, lay undiscovered on top of the wardrobe until Maeve began her quarterly top-down clean.

At six, using a beefed-up junior chemistry set, he destroyed the Alpine-style summer house at the bottom of the garden. The size of the explosion was a mistake, but what Jimmy learned from it was of inestimable value. In the following weeks the reinforced back door of a sub-post office in Hounslow was blown off its hinges. Although explosives were also used on the post office safe, it held fast. Post offices in Wembley, Enfield and Sutton weren't so lucky.

A witness to the Enfield burglary, wending his way home from the pub, told police they should be looking for a dwarf or midget and two larger-than-life accomplices, all of them male and perhaps showmen or roustabouts. (The Bertram Mills Circus was camped in Broomfield Park at the time.) He said the little chap was definitely the one in charge, smoking a fat cigar and angrily bossing the other two around.

The witness, habitually drunk and on occasion disorderly, was placed in a cell overnight to sleep it off. His statement was binned, the thieves never caught.

But when Mr Cribbage came across bundles of high-denomination banknotes in the attic, wedged behind the cold water tank, and had the serial numbers checked against those recently stolen, his suspicions were confirmed. While Maeve was out shopping he burned the money in the hearth, one fat bundle at a time, breaking up the hot ashes with a poker to ensure that not even the tiniest scrap could be identified. Jimmy watched, incandescent with rage.

Not much happened the following year, apart from Jimmy getting expelled from the first of three boarding schools, all of which he loathed. Although no official reason for his expulsion was given, perhaps it was because of thefts from the chemistry lab, bursar's office, tuck shop, staffroom and student lockers. Or because the cricket pavilion, in which fireworks were being kept under lock and key until Bonfire Night, burst into flames and exploded, shattering the windows of nearby buildings and blowing tiles off their roofs. Or because of shoplifting sprees in nearby towns targeting easily resalable gentlemen's accessories (wristwatches, cufflinks, hip flasks, fountain pens, calfskin wallets, tie-pins, cigarette cases and lighters), said by the investigating officer, admiration discernible in his voice though he tried his best to suppress it, to have been carried out with almost military precision by a schoolboy mastermind and his criminal gang. Or because the brakes on the headmaster's car were tampered with, though he wasn't seriously injured in the ensuing crash, and because, once the car had been repaired, sugar was poured into the petrol tank, all four tires were slashed, and a potato was rammed so far up the exhaust pipe it could neither be seen nor retrieved. (Jimmy said that if he'd done it, which he might have, though he couldn't remember whether he had or not, he would have inserted the potato using a broom handle.) Or because a shy, thoroughly homesick Greek whose cot lay adjacent to Jimmy's in the dormitory, hung himself in one of the lavatories using the school tie taken from Jimmy's bedside cabinet. Or because, on more than one occasion, ground glass was put in the breakfast porridge and caustic soda in the milk. Or because the school mascot, a magnificent cockerel, failed to greet the dawn with gloriously raucous fanfares, his head having been torn from his body, and the hens, perhaps in mourning, flatly refused to lay for several days afterwards. Or perhaps, who knows, because it rained incessantly for almost forty days and forty nights, flooding the school basement, causing considerable damage to the boiler room and knocking out the heating system, the blame for which had to be laid at someone's door, a particular someone who'd adopted the occult practices of the so-called 'Great Beast 666' and rather than read aloud from Genesis 6:9-8:22, as instructed by the rector, had instead, during a highly memorable morning assembly, spat out a foul-mouthed delugial curse on the school and its inhabitants.

~~~: Did similar things happen at the other schools?

TAYLOR: Similar, yes. But in certain respects worse.

~~~: How so?

TAYLOR: There were a greater number of suicides and accidental or unexplained deaths. Even more than one might expect of an English boarding school in that dark era.

Suicides, in particular, were always worryingly high, much higher than in the prison population, even among lifers – and those were the days when *life actually meant life*.

~~~: Were any of the deaths attributable to Jimmy Inkling?

TAYLOR: Not directly, insofar as one can tell, and Jimmy wouldn't say. But they were hushed up. Suicides are bad for business. Few are the parents who would willingly enrol their child at Slaughterself Manor.

~~~: Few?

TAYLOR: Cruelty comes in many guises and often from the least expected quarter. Not all children are lovable or loved.

~~~: I see. Please continue.

TAYLOR: Well ... Piers Anthony Urquhart, who Mr Honeyman mentioned just a moment ago, took Jimmy under his wing at the behest of his friend Rex Cribbage, who confessed he was at his wit's end because of his son's ungovernable behaviour.

One could argue, with some justification, that from then on Urquhart's role in Jimmy's life was greater than that of his adoptive father, that Urquhart moulded Jimmy in his own warped image and made him the man he is today, the man the public know and love despite, or perhaps because of (in fact, almost certainly because of) his chequered past. He's a man of the people: flawed, as are we all, but somehow inexplicably better than us. Admirable, even. So what, his supporters say, if he was once involved in a little harmless illegality – tobacco and alcohol smuggling; clocking cars; selling high quality knock-offs (cosmetics and perfumes, mainly) on market stalls throughout the land; eventually scaling up his operation and encouraging middle-managers with more surplus income than sense to buy off-plan timeshares in unapproved developments (many of which were never built or have since been demolished) on the Costa del

Somewhere-or-other, the contracts for which just happened to lack, because of an oversight, more down to carelessness than calculation, a get-out clause. Minor stuff, really. And no charges brought except for that money-laundering one relating to, where was it, Spain, Portugal? Somewhere warmer and sunnier than Margate, that's for sure.

HONEYMAN: Belize.

TAYLOR: A charge of which, as his supporters are always quick to remind you, *he was acquitted!* And anyway, they say, the smuggling fulfilled a social need and righted an obvious wrong. Taxation in the UK is cripplingly high. Always has been. Especially on alcohol. France: much lower. So why should Jimmy not do as he did: buy goods over the channel that people want over here and sell them at less than the artificially inflated high street price. Just like duty free, eh? Where's the harm in that? If, in consequence, the exchequer loses a bit of revenue, so what; they'll claw it out of our wallets and purses some other way, they always do. Rip-off Britain, that's the consensus; the less you earn the more they take. Were it not, say his supporters, for entrepreneurs like Jimmy, oiling the wheels of capitalism and pulling a few corrective levers, the beleaguered, downtrodden masses, hugely resentful of the soft-buttocked bunch who lord over us, would rise up, howling and spitting with rage, and put Parliament to the torch. They'd massacre all the politicians they could lay their hands on, mount their heads on poles, carry them in triumphal procession across Westminster Bridge, and dump them in an ugly heap on the mortuary floor of St Thomas'.

That's what Inkling's highly vocal and often surprisingly high-profile supporters say, not all of whom are deep in his pocket (though some would like to be, of course). I've even heard it said, po-faced, entirely irony-free, that if Robin Hood fathered a son on Mother Teresa their offspring would turn out to be just like Jimmy Inkling.

> To which
> the mind
> fair
> boggles.

Since his winning appearances (who'd have thought he could be so devastatingly funny!) on the TV hit show *Guess Who's Coming to Dinner* and ... that other one, what on Earth was it called?

HONEYMAN: [...]

~~~: [...]

TAYLOR: You know, the one about digging up the past ...

HONEYMAN: *The Golden Grave*? I don't own a television set, spawn of the Devil that they are, but a pal of mine wrote a long article about it. A peculiar hybrid: gameshow-cum-documentary. Half a dozen contestants parachuted into Cambodia, armed with machetes, bug spray, anti-venom and trowels, each of whom has a GPS fix on where hidden treasure is likely to be found. Tomb raiding, in common parlance. From what I gather, points were to be awarded not just for the quality of the haul – mostly 12th century brown-glazed stoneware ewers, bottles and jars – but for the ingenuity with which contestants contrived to smuggle it out of the jungle and back to Blighty, the competition winner being allowed to keep one special item from the spoils as a memento, the rest going to the V&A for their Ceramics Study Galleries Collection.

> In a giddy fit of enthusiasm
> Display Case J
> Room 137
> in the Asia and Europe section

was cleared in
readiness for the new arrivals.
The case's former contents
were dusted off
wrapped carefully
and placed in storage
apart
from one item
lost in transit
presumed stolen.
[A former museum employee
recently extradited from Spain
is said to be helping
police
with their enquiries.]

TAYLOR: Uh-uh, not that. Jimmy wasn't in that one.

HONEYMAN: Are you sure?

TAYLOR: Definitely. He was asked to participate but snubbed the offer. Took to the high moral ground on his hobbyhorse, if you know what I mean. Said on Radio 4's PM programme that *The Golden Grave* was both irresponsible and deeply disrespectful, a slap in the face for Cambodia; that the country's ancient artefacts should stay where they are, where they belong, hidden from grubby-fingered nighthawks with their self-justificationary rhetoric and baseless air of moral superiority. What the show planned to do, he said, was hardly more edifying than a smash and grab raid (something it was generally assumed he knew quite a bit about).

Then he rounded on the British Museum and successive UK governments for holding on to the Elgin Marbles when they weren't ours by right. Poor old Greece, Jimmy said, fobbed off with weasel words time and again. Lord Elgin was nothing but a criminal toff addicted to plunder whose name should go down in the annals of infamy. — Strong stuff and plenty of it. That's what prompted Athens to award Jimmy an honorary citizenship.

It was a particularly slow news week that week. No gruesome murders, plane crashes, major financial scandals, female Royals photographed topless, soap stars entering/exiting rehab, floods or fires, high-profile divorces, motorway pile-ups, tarantulas lurking in bunches of bananas, pointless awards ceremonies, epidemics or pandemics, weapons of mass destruction in the hands of foreign despots, paedophile rings in high places, cats stuck in trees, and likenesses of Jesus found in the textured surface of naan bread and the creases of a drying sock. In the absence of anything more headline-grabbing, Jimmy's comments ended up splashed across every newspaper front page from Land's End to John o'Groats.

So ferocious was the critical storm whipped up by the press that government ministers got involved, albeit reluctantly. Pressure was applied behind the scenes. *The Golden Grave* was cancelled just as the first contestants were about to exit the plane over the least explored and therefore most unexcavated region of the hundred temples of Koh Ker.

Of course, as was soon revealed, the whole thing had been cooked up by Channel 4 and the Cambodia Tourism Board with the complicity of a senior departmental administrator at the V&A (who admitted he'd been a willing dupe, resigned his post and fled the country). The grave goods that the contestants would have uncovered, had they actually managed to land on Cambodian soil, were fakes. A companion documentary series was nearing completion which showed the fakes being made and by whom: highly skilled former employees of Wedgwood who, since being made redundant in 2009, had been engaged in relatively unskilled work – sweeping the streets of Stoke-on-Trent or till jockeying at Asda. Yet another programme (awarded the Grand Jury Prize at Sundance in the category World Cinema Documentary) examined the issues around their plight and the failure to make *The Golden Grave.*

No, the show I'm talking about is the one in which he attempted to find out who his mother was and who his and her famous ancestors were, all the way back to Boudicca and her hubby King Prasutagus. The show boasting a telegenic female historian wearing a divide and conquer bra under a blouse so diaphanous it was rumoured not to exist,

From the
Empresses' New Clothes
range at
Aquascutum.

a foppish astrologer with a syndicated daily column in English language newspapers worldwide, and a creepy past-lives hypnotherapist who was later accused of adjusting the clothing of several of his female clients ('to make them more comfortable,' he insisted) while they were under his sway and helpless to resist and he, according to their sworn statements, was heavily under the influence of Johnnie Walker or one of his friends.

HONEYMAN: *Who Were You?*

TAYLOR: Not quite.

HONEYMAN: *Who Do You Think You Were?*

TAYLOR: That's it! A hammer blow bang on the head of the gutter spike! Well done! I knew we'd make a formidable team.

~~~: And did he find out who his mother was?

TAYLOR: Of course not. Though they did reveal that he wasn't his adoptive father's biological son, which some cynics had suggested he might be. But anyone who knew Rex Cribbage knew the cynics were wrong. Put simply: women were of no carnal interest to him. Nor – let's scotch that evil rumour – were little girls. When the

show's presenter suggested that Cribbage might have dallied awhile

Dallied?
A word
from the lexicon
of a Victorian prig.

with a chambermaid or shopgirl and got her pregnant,
Jimmy laughed; it was a ludicrous notion.

No-one but Jimmy's mother knows who and what she
is and why she chose that particular doorway in William
Mews. But I wonder ... was the Cribbage household carefully selected or chosen at random? Things might have
worked out differently had the infant Jimmy been left at
the house next door, or next door but one. Perhaps he'd
have become an airline pilot, a window dresser, a commis
chef, a priest, a cardiologist, a snooker referee, an actor, a
lion tamer. Perhaps even a motor mechanic who ended
up working for his own illegitimate son, the vintage car
salesman you spoke to earlier, neither of whom, despite
their startling physical resemblance, had realised who the
other was. He might have become Prime Minister; someone has to be luckless enough to do that job. Each and
every doorstep offered myriad possibilities.

I'm sure there are hundreds of Jimmy's victims who
wish he'd been abandoned elsewhere that bitterly cold
winter night: on the upper deck of an empty tram return-
ing to the depot, or cast adrift on the Thames in a leaky
wooden apple box. Or that the doorbell failed to summon
Maeve (she was hard of hearing even in her younger days,
stone deaf in her dotage) and the snow kept falling on the
infant until he was covered to a depth of several inches
and shivered his last. Had the poor wee mite been buried
in the paupers' section of Kensal Green Cemetery under a
simple wooden cross inscribed 'Precious little Angel,

Known to God', perhaps the world would be a better place.

~~~: So what did the show discover, if anything?

TAYLOR: In terms of hard facts: not a sausage. Though it generated lots of wild and woolly speculation. Only in the narcissistic cocaine-fuelled fantasyland of low-budget no-talent daytime television would genealogical methods so slapdash be taken so seriously. Jimmy was, they said, an almost direct descendent of Henry VIII.

~~~: He of the six wives.

TAYLOR: That's the fellow. Perhaps not the best role model for young men wishing to marry and procreate, but famous for having written *Greensleeves*, if indeed he did.

~~~: What evidence did Dr Voluptuous and her colleagues draw on?

TAYLOR: Evidence? You must be joking. The Henry claim was, as you'd expect of such a tacky show, without merit,

What they found
using a suspect DNA profile
and a complex genealogical chart
crammed to the margins with bastardy
was that Inkling was
related not to Henry
himself
but to Henry's
most faithful courtier and foremost
jousting and hunting companion
Charles Brandon
who
in May 1515
married Henry's sister
Mary Tudor
Queen Dowager of France.
But it was thought
that a direct link
to Henry
would wow the audience more

['Chuck Brandon? Never
heard of him!']
and cater to their
short attention span
wilful ignorance
and tendency to channel hop as a way
of killing time
relatively painlessly
while awaiting death
they skewed the evidence
in that direction.

and the astrological enquiry was more preposterous and rigour-free than the genealogical one. To pass over it in silence is a kindness undeserved, but I'm feeling charitable, so, as they say, mum's the word.

Anyway, the real issue was what happened next. The studio lights dimmed and the creepy presenter, clad entirely in black, stepped out from behind a black velvet curtain swinging a gold fob watch in a short arc at the end of a gold chain. Increasing the rate of oscillation, he loop-de-looped the watch twice, then reversed the loop in a figure of eight and flipped it neatly into a snug little waistcoat pocket that seemed smaller than the watch itself.

Cue canned applause, whoops and whistles.

Then, to show it wasn't a fluke, he did it again, this time using his left hand, flipping the watch into a pocket on the right hand side of his vest. Scores if not hundreds of hours of practice must have gone into perfecting the manoeuvre. It was – I'm sure even he wouldn't deny it – his crowning achievement.

When, mid-whoop, the sound man killed the applause, Mr Creepy explained that just a few moments earlier, using a combination of the power pendulum method, some aeons-old mystical passes of proven worth, and his own radical variation on the psychic energy field technique known as magnetic hands, he'd sent Jimmy down to the basement level of hypnotic trance, then into the sub-basement, then lower and lower still, cautiously, by slow degrees, to strata unknown, where the richest seam of past-life memories gets laid down for all eternity, including, he hoped, memories of the time when Jimmy was Henry. For safety's sake he'd been obliged to do the hypnosis off-camera. Some viewers, he said, were highly susceptible to the powerful mesmeric resonance he was capable of generating, even at one remove. There was a risk they'd slip into a trance, be declared dead, and end up buried alive – something he and the show's legal team strenuously wished to avoid.

That said, he drew back the curtain and there was Jimmy, seated in a high-backed wing chair of Cordovan leather, looking relaxed in a semi-foetal Stephen Hawking kind of way, eyes closed, the suggestion of a smile playing on his lips. So far so good. But that's when Mr Creepy's luck ran out. No matter what he said or did, he couldn't coax Jimmy to reveal any past-life memories. In fact he barely got him to say anything at all. The seconds in passing seemed shackled to lead weights. Time dragged by. I believe it's called car crash television, in which everything appears to be happening in excruciatingly slow motion. Still nothing or next to nothing from Jimmy: monosyllabic answers, grunts, yawning silence. In desperation – you could see the fear in his eyes, sweat starting to bead on his brow – Mr Creepy blurted out a question that obviously hadn't been scripted, about something Jimmy had always steadfastly refused to discuss: his tempestuous six-day marriage to the late Tuscaloosan peanut oil heiress Wanda-Mae Weissman.

Actually a five-dayer.
Mr Creepy said six
in an attempt to establish
some kind of

correspondence with
Henry's six wives
thereby missing a trick.
Jimmy had
according to Boss Dangerfield in
Sinai Assault Weapon
[book #59
in the Jimmy Inkling
once bestselling
crime and thriller series]
acted as a go-between
an 'honest' broker
between warring factions
courting danger
and
dodging bullets
while conducting steamy love affairs
with women on both sides
of the 1967 Arab-Israeli conflict
also known as the
Six-Day War.

His and Wanda-Mae's drunken dash from the marriage ceremony (at the Doo Wop Diner Wedding Chapel, Las Vegas, the officiant a hip-swivelling embodiment of Elvis Presley) to the sober confines of a semi-derelict, earthquake-stricken divorce court in Port au Prince, was followed, barely a week later, by news of her death, tragically young, in circumstances that are still far from clear.

~~~: Suicide, as recorded.

TAYLOR: Indeed. Though as the coroner noted, her mode of despatch was such that she couldn't have achieved it singlehandedly. It had to have been an assisted suicide. That's pretty much all that is known.

~~~: No charges were brought?

TAYLOR: There wasn't enough evidence to charge anyone. Jimmy, the prime suspect, had the ultimate watertight alibi: at the time of Wanda-Mae's death he was webcam-ming a live feed to YouTube at the controls of a Triton 6600/2 submersible, some seven hundred metres down on the bed of the North Sea, in the company of the eel-wrangling wife-beater, Ingo Peck.

Attention then focused on Wanda-Mae's previous ex-husband, a bare knuckle MMA cage fighter and domestic tyrant

Various 911 call-outs.
Officers told to stand down after the 'victim'
apologising profusely
through bloodied lips
said it was all a terrible mistake
an accident
she'd slipped in the bath
then tripped and fallen downstairs
then banged her head on an open cupboard door and
understandably
got a bit confused.

who was known to suffer from steroid-induced psychosis and frequent, sometimes day-long blackouts. After several massive bust-ups she left him for good and he wasn't, to say the least, best pleased. He made death threats. Most unwise. Jimmy said he'd had to have him 'spoken to'.

But the alibi he provided was almost as sound as Jimmy's. Apart from being nearly four thousand miles away from where she died, he was hospitalised with septicaemia from an appendix-rupturing kick. He'd been badly beaten in an unprovoked attack while taking a midnight smoko-stroll near his hotel. By whom and for what reason the beating was administered, either he wouldn't say or didn't know.

~~~: Did Jimmy, while under hypnosis, reveal anything that would implicate him in his ex-wife's death?

TAYLOR: Of course not. He was as inscrutable as ever. Not even a bout of exquisitely drawn-out torture at the hands of Josef Mengele would have loosened his tongue. But even if it did he'd only have said what he wanted to say.

~~~: And did he inherit any part of Wanda-Mae's fortune?

TAYLOR: After a lengthy legal tussle with one of her distant relatives, yes. And by distant I mean a second cousin twice removed. Perhaps thrice. It was a complicated family relationship that no-one really understood, which was probably the claim's undoing.

~~~: So ... let me get this straight. He inherited all even though he and Wanda-Mae were no longer husband and wife?

TAYLOR: Correct. Wanda-Mae's will was highly unusual. Without precedent, even in Haitian law. It was drawn up the day after their divorce became absolute. Jimmy was named as her sole beneficiary, and in his will, drawn up on the same day, she was his. That's love, I suppose.

~~~: Was the legitimacy of the wills challenged?

TAYLOR: Only by her previous ex-husband. His suit got nowhere. Since then he's been in hiding, supposedly from his creditors.

~~~: And the fortune that Jimmy inherited, was it small, medium or large?

TAYLOR: To be honest, I'm not sure. Large probably, though the exact sum has never been disclosed. Mr Honeyman, do you know?

HONEYMAN: It was, by anyone's standard, extremely large. Large enough to make Croesus look like an indigent and guarantee a thousand lifetimes of luxury for a typical Russian oligarch, assuming there is such a thing. The fortune Jimmy inherited from Sir Rex and the one he'd made from a life of crime were piddling compared to the wherewithal that was now at his disposal. He could easily afford to buy whole cities (downtown Detroit at the bottom of the recession, for example), Croatian or Indonesian islands, a famous mountain or two.

He was rumoured to be looking for a sufficiently large tract of land (a minimum of 60km2, roughly the size of San Marino) in which to found his own nation. He'd drafted a constitution. Jasper Johns had designed a wibbly-wobbly flag. A composer of world renown (said to be Ennio Morricone) was commissioned to write a National Anthem – martial but jaunty was the spec, with perhaps some celebratory gunfire near the end. But nothing came of it. All the best plots – those enjoying an equable year-round climate, sandy beaches, a deep harbour, at least one mountain, a forest, arable plains and a navigable river – had already been taken by people of wealth even greater than his, who didn't particularly want to sell, even under pressure.

But of course, because of his fabulous fortune, Jimmy no longer needed to engage in criminal activity, other than for the pleasure of teasing and thwarting HMRC by constantly moving his money around, whack-a-mole style, and as a hobby, a distraction.

~~~: You're being facetious again, Mr Honeyman. A hobby?

HONEYMAN: Not at all. He gets bored, and when bored he drinks, and when sufficiently drunk he becomes impulsive and reckless, by which I mean increasingly reckless, drink by drink by drink.

TAYLOR: I can vouch for that.

HONEYMAN: Recently he's started taking risks he hasn't taken, nor had to, for decades. The riskier the better. He can't seem to get enough of it. The fact that he's got so much to lose, if caught, heightens the thrill. There's an adrenalin surge while the crime is being committed, a blissful release of endorphins when it's done. Better than any drug, so I'm told. Also, he's nostalgic for the halcyon days of bent coppers and good honest crooks, when everyone respected authority and knew where they stood in the pecking order. The last time Jimmy mugged anyone was in the 1950s, perhaps even earlier, but I've heard he's taken it up again.

TAYLOR: It's true. And, if you're interested, I know the precise date when he originally stopped committing street crime ...

~~~: If it's relevant, Mr Δ≈ΔΔΔ°◇≥, please enlighten us.

TAYLOR: It is. At least I think so. Just before we set out (him in a state of unbridled enthusiasm, me heel-draggingly reluctant, both of us drunk as skunks) on a similar excursion, he showed me an entry from his 1952 diary which, with my superbly-honed retentive skills, as discussed earlier, I memorised in its entirety, punctuation and all:

December 7th

Waylaid three sinners on their way home from Evening Mass. 'Stand and deliver!' None of them laughed, miserable buggers. Relieved them of their valuables at knifepoint and gave the woman, elderly, smelling of lavender water, a peck on the cheek. She didn't flinch, much to my surprise. And not too bad a haul: Four pounds eight and six in cash and a fine mink stole. Derek will be pleased, he likes quality mink. While all this was going on the Old Bill were just a few yards away. I could hear them stumbling around, blowing whistles, trying to direct traffic and keep people, drunks mostly, from falling into the Thames or tumbling down the steps to the underground. Good luck to them, they can't see much of anything right now. Most importantly, they can't see me and my fellow highwaymen going about our unlawful business. And business is, I'm glad to say, good.

That was written during one of the last of the great London fogs, pea-soupers as they were affectionately known, the colour of mustard into which a quantity of excrement had been stirred. It tasted mainly of sulphur but with a long finish, metallic and bitter, like a cold foretaste of Hell. No-one could escape it. Indoors and out the fug was much the same. Film screenings and football matches had to be abandoned. To anyone with weak lungs it was a torment. Those with TB or lung cancer dropped like flies, as did a significant number of asthmatics and pneumoniacs. Even delicate toddlers suffering from croup. It was said that if your pet canary died, you'd almost certainly be next; and many were. But not all was doom and gloom. As one might expect, London's undertakers did a roaring trade.

Perhaps that's why Jimmy gladly took ownership (in lieu of a gambling debt, so I'm told) of a popular chain of funeral directors in Shoreditch, Hainault, Buckhurst Hill and Theydon Bois, the last three branches situated conveniently on the fringes of Epping Forest. He sacked the staff he'd inherited en masse and replaced them with his own people, none of whom had BIFD or NIFD approved qualifications in funeral operations and services. It raised a few eyebrows and one or two hackles but no-one said a dicky-bird – not to Jimmy, anyway. Regulation of the funerary trade was extremely lax in those days. Bribery the norm. An undertaker could, if he so wished, easily store and/or dispose of 'inconvenient' material, including, so I've been told, corpses. Whether Jimmy's undertakers did so, I really can't say.

Herewith
a selection of useful terms from
Thanat
a dead language
once used exclusively by Funeral Directors
of a criminal persuasion
in London and parts of the South-East
[not to be confused with

Tanatos
the slang language
also dead
of limestone and flint workers on the Isle of Thanet]:

Fire Exit
Crematorium.

Blocked Fire Exit
[aka *Cardinal Singe*]
A crematorium whose management won't allow
undertakers to slyly recycle coffins.

Double-Deckering
Placing two skinny corpses in a sealed coffin
where a fat one ought to be.

Late Harvest
Stripping a corpse of valuables
including gold teeth
immediately prior to the coffin being sealed.

Slumgumming
Disguising bullet holes with a plug of flesh-tinted beeswax that
if and as required
has hair from the victim's
buttocks
[short, wiry]
or shoulder
[slightly longer, somewhat softer]
pressed into the surface layer.

The Batcave
[aka *Santa's Grotto* and *Aladdin's Cave*]
The rectal cavity.

Hard Stool
Something of value [jewels, guns, etc.]
inserted into the rectum of the deceased
for retrieval at a later date.

Ex-Lax
The process of *Hard Stool* retrieval.

Flux
[aka *Soft Stool*]
A rectally stored drugs cache.

Sloshwork
Unpleasant *Hard Stool* and/or *Soft Stool* retrieval
when a corpse is
badly decomposed.

Beggar's Banquet
Cannibalism.
Once said to be rife among undertakers
supplementing their meagre wartime rations
and supplying nearby butchers
with a range of choice cuts.
[N.B. may be apocryphal]

Mulchman
A corpse
or part thereof
nourishing the roots of a tree in Epping Forest.

Meatball
Ground-up human testicle
sold worldwide
as an aphrodisiac
to hopeful impotents.

Oh yes, Jimmy loved smog. As did many a London villain. The Clean Air Act spoiled all the fun. But as we set out that evening, reeking of alcohol, in the guise of pub-crawl contestants in a three-legged race (that, he said, if questioned by the police, was our cover story), we −

~~~: Hang on, Mr Δ≈ΔΔΔ°◇≥. Sorry to have to put you on hold just as you were about to regale us with details of your and Mr Inkling's little excursion. — Mr Usher, please tell

whoever is banging at the door to sit down and shut up. It's extremely annoying. We can't hear ourselves think. And don't, whatever you do, open the door more than a crack. Use your foot as a wedge.

USHER: Will do, Chief.

~~~: And make it quick. If Mr Δ≈ΔΔΔ°◇≥ loses the thread we'll never find our way out of his labyrinth of words.

USHER: [mumble mumble mumble]

~~~: So, who is it and what does he want?

USHER: Not him, a her. Approximately five-three, 120lbs, early thirties, Caucasian, a faint South Yorkshire accent, blue-grey eyes, blonde hair held in a shoulder-length ponytail, what used to be called American teeth when British teeth were always yellow and snaggly, unblemished skin, pierced ears but no earrings or other visible jewellery, cheek bones to die for, well turned out in a grey herring-bone business suit (trousers not skirt, neither too sexy nor too frumpy), and sent, apparently, by the WPS. What Arnold the Viking would have called a comely wench. Says she has to have immediate access to you, you lucky dog.

~~~: A finely detailed description. I can picture her so clearly I feel I probably don't need to see her in person, so I won't.

USHER: Thanks, Chief. I'm what's known as a super-observer, capable after little more than a sideways glance at grainy CCTV footage of picking out hooligans in football crowds and putting names to faces. It's more fun than ushering, to be honest. Pays better too.

~~~: I appreciate your plain speaking, Mr Usher, but don't address me as Chief. It demonstrates a clear lack of respect and the court will not stand for it.

USHER: Oh. Okay. For some reason I thought you were less of a stuffed shirt than the other judges on the circuit.

~~~: Well I'm not, so cut it out.

USHER: Rightio.

~~~: So, how do we know she is who she says she is?

USHER: [mumble mumble] ... [mumble mumble] ... Yeah? Okay.

~~~: Well?

USHER: From the security pass she's shown me, it looks like she's legit: a fully accredited Witness Protection officer, clerical division.

~~~: Clerical, eh? Tell her she'll have to wait, Mr $\Delta \approx \Delta\Delta\Delta°\diamond\geq$ is currently giving evidence.

USHER: [mumble mumble] ... I see. Uh-huh ... [mumble mumble] ... [mumble mumble mumble mumble mumble]

~~~: Oh, for God's sake, man, stop all that mumbling and slam the door in her face. We don't have time for such nonsense.

HONEYMAN: It might be a better class of nonsense than the nonsense we've heard so far.

~~~: Give it a rest, Mr Honeyman. Your behaviour is tiresome in the extreme. By the powers vested in me by the Council of Elders I'm the senior authority figure in this room – the godhead, so to speak – so I'll be the judge of what's timely and what's not.

USHER: She says it can't wait –

HONEYMAN: Are gods always this tinpot?

USHER: – and she has a letter –

~~~: Your poisoned barbs cannot puncture, dent or even scratch the righteous armour of my divine authority, Mr Honeyman. Give it up, you're making a fool of yourself. Or should I say, *even more of a fool than you've already proved yourself to be*. Now what's that about a letter?

USHER: From the pen of Deputy Assistant Commissioner Starkey. For your eyes only. Sealed with a wax seal and marked URGENT.

~~~: Give it here. [...] Hmm. [...] Hmm. [...] Oh. Hmm. [...] Hmmmm. Ah. [...] Right, while I decide what's to be done, let's take a break. Court will reconvene in twenty minutes. — Lock the door, Mr Usher. Let no-one in, no matter what.

Fifth Session

~~~: Now, where were we?

TAYLOR: I was trying to explain what happened when Mr Inkling and I, bound or rather shackled, yes, shackled, that's the word I was looking for ... shackled together by handcuffs at wrist and ankle like conjoined twins, were –

~~~: Unless I'm mistaken that's the first we've heard of handcuffs in these proceedings.

TAYLOR: I think you'll find ... if you cast your mind back to our opening session ...

STENOGRAPHER: 'Having handcuffed me to a chain that was ...'

~~~: Yes yes. Thank you, Miss Stenographer, but please don't prompt me unless I ask you to do so. Though not quite the remarkable instrument that Mr $\Delta{\approx}\Delta\Delta\Delta°\diamond\geq$ plays so consummately, my memory is, I promise you, equal to the task. — Yes, it's all coming back to me. You, Mr $\Delta{\approx}\Delta\Delta\Delta°\diamond\geq$, were abducted from Vale Hall by two uncommunicative thugs and handcuffed to a chain that was bolted or welded (you didn't say ... no, my apologies, you did: bolted) to the floor of a limo as it drove you, innocent as a newborn, drugged and incapacitated, to a corner shop en route, so you thought, to a rendezvous with Mr Inkling at a gastropub in Maida Vale.

But you were mistaken on all counts.

The point of the exercise was to force you to commit a serious criminal offence: armed robbery – a robbery that not only failed but failed miserably and, worse still, was recorded for posterity, or at least for use by blackmailers, both of whom, a him and a her, lost their lives soon afterwards in an inferno that bore the hallmarks of a professional torch job. — Am I right or am I right?

TAYLOR: Almost. It was a newsagent's, situated mid-row in a parade of shops.

~~~: Same difference. Please continue.

TAYLOR: Mr Inkling is very fond of handcuffs, new, old and antique.

Especially the model
patented in 1862
by WV Adams.
Cuffs of adjustable
ratchet design
the first of their kind.
He owns three pairs.
Also a pair of Orson C Phelps cuffs
[very rare
purchased from a member
of the devolved Phelps family]
which improved on
Adams' design
and
after a tweak or two by John Tower
[the double lock mechanism in particular]
became industry standard
for three quarters
of a century.
He also has a set of manacles
dating
from the time of
Elizabeth I
fastened
by Elizabethan-era bolts

to the 21st century wall of
his inner sanctum at Canary Wharf.
Mr Inkling says
those were the manacles used
on John Donne's friend
Robert Southwell
by Elizabeth's
chief
investigator/torturer
Richard Topcliffe
a man who dearly loved pain
[though not
of course
his own].

He's got boxes and boxes of new cuffs, a cupboardful of them, gold-plated rather than standard issue molten chrome steel, each pair bearing the Brandon coat of arms. I was going to mention them just before the recess, but I'd barely got started on my explanation when you told me to hang on. And that's what I've been doing, hanging on, and it's been a long and frustrating wait, let me tell you. So ... handcuffs. And, of course, legcuffs. That's how we were conjoined. I'm right-handed and he's a lefty so, sensibly, he locked my left to his right, all the better to coordinate our movements and keep the dominant –

~~~: I'm sorry. Hang on again, Mr Δ≈ΔΔΔ°◊≥ ...

TAYLOR: – hand free.

~~~: What on earth is the WPS woman doing? That's a fearsome racket she's making out there. Samson toppling the pillars of the Temple of Dagon must have gone about it more quietly and with greater consideration for those living nearby. And before you jump in, Mr Honeyman: yes, I'm fully aware that Samson destroyed the temple during office hours, and noise, both here and in Gaza, is more tolerable then than after sundown.

HONEYMAN: I wasn't going to say a word.

~~~: How refreshing. Let's hope it sets a precedent. Not that I'd be able to hear you properly given the noise. — Find out what she's doing, Mr Usher. Use the peephole. Don't open the door again, whatever you do, we don't want her in here, not yet.

USHER: It looks like ... hmm.

~~~: Speak up, man. What does it look like?

USHER: Hmm. Hard to say. Everything's distorted and badly out of focus. Peephole manufacturers use such poor quality lenses –

~~~: I don't care a damn about the inadequacies of peephole lenses! Just tell me to the best of your ability what she's doing.

USHER: Okay, keep your shirt on. It looks ... hmm.

~~~: How did she get into the building anyway?

USHER: Beats me. The street door is still, as far as I can tell, firmly locked. I've got the keys right here; they've never left my hand.

~~~: Yet there she is.

USHER: Indisputably.

~~~: So how did she get in without keys or the ability to walk through walls?

As subatomic particles can
in a process called
quantum tunnelling
although
according to Srinivasa Ramanujan
[or someone
claiming to speak for him]
anyone
from the WPS
attempting to quantum tunnel
through a wall or door into
say
a coffee shop
or impromptu courtroom

                    would
            at the molecular level
    be bound to experience considerable
          perhaps insurmountable
                  difficulties.

USHER: Based on what I can see, which is precious little, I'd say
    she probably broke in through the transom. Chipped out
    all the glass back to the frame so she wouldn't cut herself.
    She certainly looks slim enough and fit enough to squeeze
    through the transom without too much difficulty. 'Of cat
    burglar physique is she/with skills aplenty,' the poet says.
    Which poet, I don't recall. Just something we learned at
    school. Yes, now I come to think of it, I'm almost certain
    the noise we heard a little earlier, just before she handed
    me the letter to give to you, was glass being broken. Let-
    ter in one hand, hammer the other – that's what I saw.
    Which at the time struck me as odd, by which I mean
    incongruous.

~~~: And now ...?

USHER: She and three of the six witnesses who've been waiting
    to give evidence, the strongest and fittest of the bunch,
    are hurling all the chairs towards this end of the corridor.
    One of the witnesses is stacking the metal ones and
    breaking up the others. Looks like he's enjoying himself,
    venting spleen and letting off steam. Now, using chair
    legs as levers, they're trying to prise a wooden bench
    away from the wall. Yep. Done. Brackets broken. Easy
    peasy fart and sneezy. Now they're carrying the bench
    over to the street door. Actually it's a pew, not a bench;
    probably salvaged from St Nicholas the Wondermaker,
    the church just round the corner. When I was a nipper we
    called it Nicky the Wonderhorse because of the saint's
    long face. The adults did, too, except in the presence of Fr
    Anton, whose harmless fixation with choirboys was com-
    mon knowledge. It seemed funnier then; but in those

days we hadn't a care in the world and we'd laugh at anything, even cancer.

~~~: The origin of the pew is of no consequence, Mr Usher, and therefore of no interest whatsoever. And spare me your dewy-eyed reminiscences. What I want to know is what she's doing with it?

USHER: Not she, they. Swinging it back and forth, end to end. Getting the feel of it. Judging how much kinetic energy it might generate and unleash. [BANG!] Now they're using it as a battering ram on the street door. [BANG!] That's the pounding you can hear. Like someone thrashing an empty wooden-ribbed travelling trunk with [BANG!] a cricket bat or, if sport isn't your thing, the back of a yard broom. [BANG!] Yes, the door's buckling. Have at it! [BANG!] Once more, with feeling! [BANG!] And again, my lovelies! [BANG!] Go on, you can do it, you [BANG!] know you can! And again! [BANG!] Again-again-again-again! [BANG!] Yay! Great teamwork! Job done! They've knocked the door off its hinges and thrown it into the street. The witnesses are, as I speak, fleeing as though pursued by demons. Not so the amazon from the WPS. She's waving them off and wishing them good night, safe journey home, etc. Looks like ... yes, she's leaning over a crumpled biddy in a wheelchair and giving her a twenty or a fifty. Cab fare, I presume. Now she's heading our way, and ... Aha! Is that what I think it was?

~~~: Yes?

USHER: I may be wrong, but ... it very much looked like she was tipping me the wink.

~~~: Winks are not material to these proceedings, Mr Usher, as well you know. Save them for your memoirs, which rattle-brains throughout the land and the few members of your family who can read will, I'm sure, find enthralling. So, tell me, what's happening now?

USHER: Did you hear that?

~~~: What?

USHER: That's her knocking to be let in. A gentle, one-knuckle tap, softer than the footfall of a shrew in felt slippers. Demonstrating remarkable restraint given what she was doing just a moment ago. Wait ... That was her knocking again. Did you hear it?

~~~: I did. Just. I think so – my hearing isn't what it used to be.

USHER: What's even more remarkable is that despite her exertions she's barely broken a sweat. No sign of fluster, not that I can see. Nor a hair out of place. I think I'm in love, and just a little bit afraid. That's the true basis of all intimate relationships – those destined to last, anyway.

HONEYMAN: I'll second that.

~~~: Keep to the point, Mr Usher. This is a court of law and you're no longer a marriage guidance counsellor.

USHER: What? How did you know that?

~~~: Clairvoyance, Mr Usher. Clairvoyance. Plus I skim-read your CV: a work of fantasy fiction, surprisingly well written for a man of meagre education, though not entirely convincing.

USHER: And ... you know why I'm no longer a counsellor?

~~~: I do. That bit wasn't in your CV. But if you fulfil your duties promptly and to the best of your ability it will remain our little secret. Let's have no more of your asides and reminiscences; no-one here is remotely interested in anything you have to say. You're a functionary, hired to do a few basic things at near-minimum wage, such as opening and closing doors. Things that, with a modicum of training, an ape could do just as well. Or better. But as the ape would cost considerably more to employ, feed and house-train ...

> They're notorious shit-flingers and masturbators
> apes
> even more so than Salvador Dali.
> Avida Dollars

as André Breton
anagrammed him
because of his
money-grubbing ways.
And
of course
as every ape knows
especially those
who know their Freud
shit = money.

USHER: Whoa! Harsh words. And a none-too-subtle threat. Ask yourself: 'Is this the best way to inspire loyalty among my employees and have them gladly give their all? Does my leadership engender goodwill and command unconditional respect?' — Let me answer on your behalf: No way, Jose! Epic fail! Your people skills would make Dale Carnegie shudder. Not to mention Henry V. (You could learn a lot about inspirational leadership from his speech in act 3, scene 1, lines 1-34: 'Once more unto the breach', etc.) But if you believe that insults and intimidation will always produce the best results, despite a mountain of evidence to the contrary, continue to do what you've been doing, especially if you want to die a bitter, twisted man, alone, unloved and unlamented. In the meantime I'll tug the forelock respectfully but resentfully and keep my thoughts to myself. That's it. End of tirade. Let's crack on.

~~~: [...]

USHER: So-o-o-o-o ... now that you've had time to mull things over, shall I let the WPS woman in?

~~~: Certainly not! We'll brook no further interruption, not from her, you or anyone else. We're in lockdown mode until I say otherwise. — Continue with your evidence, Mr $\Delta \approx \Delta\Delta\Delta°\diamond\geq$. You were drunk, you say, and shackled to an equally drunk Mr Inkling, and ... there was something about a three-legged race ...

TAYLOR: Pub crawl contestants in a three-legged race. He asked me to memorise the prize list, which I did, to keep on his good side. Herewith: 'First prize: a dirty weekend in Walton-on-the-Naze. Second prize: a wet weekend in Clacton-on-Sea. Booby prize: permanent exile, living on benefits, in an unheated shack with an outside toilet in the least salubrious quarter of Jaywick Sands.'

~~~: But that was just a cover story?

TAYLOR: And meant as a joke. O how Mr Inkling likes his little jokes. He laughed himself silly when I fed that one back to him. Said it really tickled his funnybone.

~~~: Did you laugh along with him?

TAYLOR: Not uproariously, and not without feeling thoroughly ashamed of myself. But remember, we were drunk. Not that I'm trying to excuse either of us. We got drunk at Mr Inkling's insistence, a joyless glugging of vodka straight from the bottle, half a bottle each in one fell swoop. He said it would make our cover story seem just that little bit more plausible. 'Verisimilitude,' he said, 'gets us reasonably far, but vodka will get us further still.'

Has an eye for detail does Mr Inkling.

Then he had one of his people flick stale beer at us, so we'd smell right, for even greater verisimilitude. 'Send me the dry-cleaning bill, Charlie,' he said, 'and I'll set it off against what you owe me.

'By the way, I hate to have to mention it, but your monthly instalment is late, and I've had neither a word of explanation from you nor hint of an apology. Second month in a row, Charlie; twice on the trot. It simply won't do. If you borrow money you have to pay it back. You needed a new car after your old one got gutted at Windrush Valley, and I made sure you got one, a good one, and at knockdown price. Look, I'll waive the vig this time, but don't let it happen again. Another delay or, Heaven forefend, a skipped payment would negatively impact our friendship and lead to considerable unpleasantness.'

What he meant by considerable unpleasantness I didn't wish to discover. His attempts at pleasantness are unpleasant enough.

So ... a three-legged pub crawl race. The story, fleshed out, was that we'd got separated from our fellow contestants, presumably because they drank beer at a much faster rate than we did. Or they'd cheated – bribed some of the race stewards and skipped a pub or two on the designated route. In addition to which we'd say, if asked, that we'd had to stop for an urgent comfort break; and one of us – to spare his feelings I won't say whom – had to sit down to experience that feeling of comfort; and because the disabled toilet in The Moon on the Water was temporarily unavailable we'd had to squeeze into one of the regular stalls, and not even in the Gents, which was being given an emergency clean, no, the Ladies, for which there was already a long queue of women shuffling tipsily from foot to foot. That was embarrassing. And time-consuming. No, we'd say, we don't have the keys to the cuffs (because they're bound to ask; asking awkward questions is what police officers do, it's their raison-d'être), they're in the safekeeping of the race organisers, at our final destination, if we ever get there. Where's that? The Dolphin's Arms, Bash Street Mews, Colliers Wood. And your fellow contestants, where are they? Good question, officer. If only we knew. Probably supping ale in a pub in Balham. Or, if they've managed to get even further away from us, somewhere in the vicinity of Tooting Broadway Station.

That's what Mr Inkling said to say if we were stopped by the police, which luckily we weren't. But he also said that as he was the brains of the outfit he'd do all the talking. Fine by me.

~~~: Were you armed?

TAYLOR: Muggers always are, it's obligatory. If you're asking for money, with or without menaces, and don't have an offensive weapon on or about your person, it's officially classed as aggressive begging, a lesser offence.

Muggers and beggars don't get along. Muggers despise beggars, especially the authorised ones who clutter up supermarket doorways, rattling their charity tins in a passive-aggressive manner.

But the clipboard-wielding gangs who blockade whole streets and ambush shoppers, picking off the stragglers, the weak and the vulnerable, are worse than that. More like jackals and hyenas. Muggers mug them on principle. But they also do it because they can't stand their gung-ho manner, by which I mean their relentlessly cheery patter, their ludicrous and wholly inappropriate attempts at mateyness (guaranteed to bring out the misanthrope in everyone, even someone as benign as the Dalai Lama), their inability to understand a crisply enunciated No! unless it's screamed in their face five times in swift succession, and their tightly scripted attempts at emotional blackmail. (I have it on good account that they're all failed actors, i.e. bad actors who've previously failed at being waiters.)

At best their methods grate on the nerves; at worse they trigger paroxysms of rage. Bystanders often burst into spontaneous applause when clipboarders are relieved of their ill-gotten gains – those valuable sequences of account numbers and sort codes – and see them turned into confetti. If violence is involved it can even raise a schadenfreude cheer.

Anyway, Mr Inkling had a boning knife in a sheath strapped to his ribs, and he gave me some brass knuckles. He has a drawerful of the latter, various sizes. Says he likes to keep a set on the boardroom table as a paperweight during tense negotiations. I tried three or four until I found one that was a snug fit and unlikely to chafe. As I walked up and down the room, swinging them at the

end of my arm, accustoming myself to their weight, I seriously considered knocking him to the ground and making
a run for it. Actually, I thought of killing him, or trying to.
But I knew, deep down, my courage would fail. I've never
knowingly taken a life. As I'm sure you'll have heard in
one of the many gossip rooms at god HQ – my, how gods
love to gossip! frankly, it's a miracle that any godwork
gets done – I don't even kill spiders that have fallen into
the bathtub by flushing them down the plughole.

~~~: Your advanced escapology kit for spiders large and small
is, as you've guessed, common knowledge in god circles,
sniggered at by some but lauded by the Jains among our
number, a surprisingly large number (of Jains, I mean),
one of whom is the god of Poisonous Things (Animal, not
Vegetable or Mineral), Connie Ripple – for the sake of
one's health a woman best avoided.

TAYLOR: Let those who wish to snigger snigger. Let them laugh
up their sleeves. Let them bray like drunken donkeys for
all I care. If they think I'm holier than thou, it's because
I'm holier than they, and by a margin as wide as Cheddar
Gorge.

~~~: An admirable sentiment, if expressed a tad pompously.

TAYLOR: That's rich, coming from you.

~~~: Mr Δ≈ΔΔΔ°◊≥, we're all friends here, let's not bicker.
There are important issues still to be dealt with and a spat
between colleagues can do nothing but hinder our
progress. Continue giving evidence, if you please ...

TAYLOR: Oh, I please, I most certainly please. And this time I
don't expect to be interrupted, no matter what – *capisce?*

~~~: You have my word.

USHER: She's tapping again. A two-knuckle job. Slightly louder
than before.

~~~: Ignore her. Please continue, Mr Δ≈ΔΔΔ°◊≥ ...

TAYLOR: So there we were –

USHER: She's straightening a hairpin and ... no, it looks like there's another hairpin. Two hairpins. Hmm, I can't quite see what she's up to. Whatever it is, it's taking place below peephole level. No, wait, I can hear a scritchy-scratchy sound, more muffled than faint. I think ... hmm ... well, unless I'm very much mistaken, she's trying to pick the lock.

~~~: Quick! Put your key in the barrel and give it half a turn clockwise so it can't be pushed out. That should give her pause.

USHER: Okay, Chief. Consider it done.

~~~: Well? Is it done?

USHER: Of course it's done – you just watched me doing it. I put the key in the lock and gave it precisely half a turn clockwise, as per your instructions. I withdrew my hand and the key stayed where it was, in the lock, half turned.

~~~: Are you sure?

USHER: You really are exasperating. Shall I do it again, with a running commentary, to demonstrate that I've done it properly? Perhaps, to be certain, you should bloody well do it yourself. But I suspect even that wouldn't satisfy you.

~~~: Don't you dare take that tone with me! I'll dock your pay, don't think I won't!

USHER: In the immortal words of Mr Honeyman: 'Yadda yadda yadda.'

TAYLOR: Have you two quite finished?

~~~: […]

USHER: […]

TAYLOR: Good. As I was saying, there we were, clumping three-leggedly down Balham High Road, looking for some poor sap to mug. Absolutely anyone would do. In my troubled state of mind I would have, as Mr Inkling put it, 'nobbled an infant or brass knuckled a nun'. I just wanted to get the whole thing over and done with so I could go home, fall into bed and stuff my head under the pillow.

I wondered, not for the first time since meeting Mr Inkling, whether it might be possible to smother myself with it; the pillow, I mean. Perhaps with the help of Livvy Strang, an advocate of assisted suicide who donates a quarter of her salary to Dignitas. I know for a fact she'd be happy to put me out of my misery, she's said so on several occasions, out of the blue, when we've been discussing a completely unrelated matter, sock management or houseplant hydration.

Death-obsessed is Livvy.

My death in particular.

She covets my cottage, I'm sure of it; hers being even more cramped and dark than mine, and so damp the books on the shelves swell to twice their size and become wedged in place. Some can only be removed with the use of a crowbar.

As for Mr Inkling, he wasn't in the least bit miserable. He was enjoying every bit of our little adventure. That's what he called it, 'our little adventure', as though we were kids indulging in harmless mischief, the sort of thing for which one would receive a tongue-lashing or a clip round the ear from a responsible adult (although, according to Mr Inkling, there's no such thing as a responsible adult, not south of the river). But that's not at all what he had in mind. He was intent on serious criminality.

I'd had a really bad day and was thoroughly pissed off by the time we reached Clapham South. That's when the cuffs were ratcheted into place. As we trotted up and down the common, keeping well away from lit paths and cruising spots, trying to get our strides in sync (Mr Inkling is taller than me, with longer legs, and of course, as I said just a moment ago, we were drunk), I could feel the cuffs starting to bite into the flesh above my ankle, even through thick layers of moleskin trouser and thermal sock. I tried to get him to loosen the cuff by at least a notch, but he wasn't having it. I pleaded with him, but it made no difference. 'Fuck's sake, Charlie, stop whingeing, you're getting on my tits.' A former UNICEF Goodwill Ambassador ...

Tenure brief
departure unexplained.
But there were rumours
of a major conflict
of interest
[sourcing sweatshops
to make replica handguns
while on official UNICEF business
in Bangladesh and China]
and gross irregularities
with regard
to expenses
[the Lear jet hire
for weekend jaunts
from London City Airport
to Ponta Delgada in
the Azores where
he has a holiday home
being the least of it].

his words verbatim. Diplomacy not his strong suit.

Having completed our dry run on the common, we ventured onto Balham High Road. Mr Inkling's car began to shadow us at a discreet distance, driven by one of his less prepossessing minions. The man in question was one hundred per cent thug, as I could tell at a glance. A slack-jawed mouth breather with a boxer's snout squashed like a tomato across his face. Part of his left earlobe had been removed, not surgically. His name wasn't revealed to me (although, to be fair, I didn't bother to ask) and I never saw him again.

Presumably, given his age, he was out on licence, a beneficiary of the Offender Rehabilitation Act (which Mr

Inkling supports wholeheartedly) rather than a callow YTS inductee, soft and pallid as so many of them are, bone idle and slothlike, drawn grudgingly from darkened bedrooms into the workplace by the threat of benefit sanctions. 'Good for making tea and opening mail, the YTSers, especially the suspect packages that might explode or contain poison,' quoth Mr Inkling. 'I get a lot of those. Most celebrities do, especially since the newspapers explained how to make ricin out of nothing but sodium hydroxide and castor beans – simple enough that even a five-year-old could do it. But as for the quality of the tea the YTSers make: yuk. Often so foul it might just as well be poison.'

~~~: Or the deviant doings of the venomous Connie Ripple, she of reptilian gaze and scaly skin, the latter of which she claims is a mild form of psoriasis. 'Tell it to the marines, sister,' I said, 'though they won't believe you any more than I do!' Meant as a joke but she took it badly. I laughed. She didn't. Nor did anyone else in the room. No sense of humour, that's their trouble.

HONEYMAN: Forgive me for butting in ... I suspect, with regard to the YTSers and their foul-tasting tea, it's probably not the work of a god gone bad –

~~~: Not bad, mad! Paranoid. Dangerous. Batshit crazy. Call it what you will. She's voided her sacred oath. The spread of the deadly Asian giant hornet is one of her pet projects, and a recent WHO report stated that cross-species venom levels have increased worldwide by two-point-three per cent during the last decade. *Two-point-three per cent!* Every percentage point of which is attributable to her selective breeding programme based on applied Nazi logic and arms-race-style proliferation.

Death by dunny spider has become almost commonplace throughout Queensland and the Northern Territory, and Britain's only poisonous snake, the adder, has grown larger in population and become much more aggressive, almost hooliganish, attacking sheep and dogs with gay abandon.

Despite prayers of intercession to St Patrick, adders have, according to the *Irish Times*, been encountered in moorland, rough grassland, open woodland and coastal areas as far apart as Limerick and Cork. Ripple releases them in the dead of night, a hundred at a time. She's out of control, a danger to herself and others.

When I aired my concerns with the Council of Elders, they were unusually quick to respond. They'd obviously been keeping a wary eye on her. Even as we speak she's confined to quarters and under investigation.

HONEYMAN: – just bad tea-making technique: water long off the boil in a rusty old kettle, twice-used teabags of the floor sweepings variety, milk that tastes like UHT though it's straight from the teat of a cow parked outside, mooing happily and cropping clover.

~~~: That's how Italians used to make it between the wars. Although they loved coffee and were masters of the blended bean, they disapproved of tea, so took little care over its preparation. In cafés, I mean.

But to the English such things matter greatly. Freshly drawn boiling water poured over best-quality leaves in a pre-warmed pot: those are the basics. Stir once, wait between four to seven minutes depending on the size of the leaf (bigger necessitates longer, generally speaking), stir again, pour. Milk, if required, should be added to the cup after the tea has been poured, not before.

Only the Japanese are more tea fussy, despite the fact that theirs tastes horrible.

TAYLOR: Yes, Connie Ripple went off the rails years ago. She's a liability. And prayers of intercession to Patrick are a complete waste of time; they're never answered. He's a flake. Always has been, despite his astonishingly good rep. *He was made a saint, wasn't he, so he must have been a saintly man.* That's what most people think, and it's about as deep as their thinking goes. In private, St Columba called him the laziest Irishman that ever was (though he wasn't actually born in Ireland). Ragged of hair and beard, often scruffily dressed, and invariably the worse for wear from the home-distilled poteen he drank like water, he was considered an absolute disgrace by his parishioners and fellow clerics.

Criticisms not repeated in
Adomnán's
Vita Colum Cille
[Life of Columba]
though Adomnán was well aware of Columba's opinion
and may even
have secretly shared it.

But that's by the by. Let's go back to the driver. Whether on licence or not, I could tell he was incredibly nervous. Distracted. Constantly checking his rear view mirror as though the police were hot on his tail. His driving from Mudchute to Clapham had been erratic, jerky through the gears. He'd twice wandered out of lane and got honked and sworn at by enraged drivers of oncoming vehicles. His driving was, in other words, nowhere near the exemplary standard set by his predecessor, Attila, he of the smooth runnings and dancing double-declutch technique. No, the old boy wasn't a patch on Attila and probably never would be. Que sera, sera, etc. His employment with Mr Inkling was bound to end in tears, though the end came sooner than I expected.

While bringing the Bentley to a halt outside the tube station, he cut in sharply between parked cars and scuffed the nearside front wheel against the kerb. The vehicle hopped onto the pavement and off again with a loud and painful rasp as the alloy rim ground against stone. Mr Inkling stiffened in his seat; the driver slumped low in his, so low his head, with its tonsure of lifeless grey hair and what looked like an early stage basal cell carcinoma on the upper crown, disappeared below the headrest. Nothing was said, but from the look on Mr Inkling's face I suspected the eels would soon be getting an unexpected treat.

What struck me as peculiar was how empty the streets were. The common, too. I mean completely empty. No-one out and about as far as the eye could see. Not that I could see very far. As usual I'd left my spectacles at home on the glass shelf in the bathroom, one of the three places I regularly leave them.

~~~: Are you sure you need to wear spectacles? If you do, I've never seen you with them on; not once in all the years I've known you.

TAYLOR: That's because I always forget them.

~~~: Always?

TAYLOR: Unfortunately, yes.

~~~: Short-sighted or long?

TAYLOR: Unusually short.

~~~: So you can't see objects clearly at a distance.

TAYLOR: That's what I just said. Hardly any distance at all. Even you, not ten feet from where I'm standing, are a blur. A familiar blur but a blur nonetheless. If you were any further away you'd be indistinguishable from some-one or something of roughly similar shape and size. I once mistook a bull for a horse and had to leg it out of the field when it took umbrage at my presence and charged. Bad-tempered animals, bulls, especially when sexually frustrated, as often they are, and as that one obviously was.

~~~: You don't take your spectacles when you go out?

TAYLOR: Never.

~~~: Why's that?

TAYLOR: They pinch my nose something rotten.

~~~: So why not get the bridge or the nose pads adjusted? Any one of the opticians on the high street would do it for you gladly, without charge.

TAYLOR: I keep forgetting to pick them up when I leave the house. In fact, they've never left the house in all the time I've had them.

~~~: Do you wear them at home?

TAYLOR: No need. The rooms are very small. Not doll's house small, that would be a ludicrous claim to make. But not much bigger than that: playhouse small, treehouse small. Everything is conveniently near at hand and I always know where everything is except when Livvy, in one of her arranging moods, re-arranges everything. But mostly she sticks to socks and underwear, ties and shoes. Those are ... I suppose you'd call them her specialities. Or obsessions. Why do you ask?

~~~: I was wondering whether Balham High Road was as empty of people as you thought it was.

TAYLOR: Oh, I see what you mean. Actually, that's a good point.

HONEYMAN: Is it? We're getting bogged down in trivialities. Neverworn spectacles – what on earth has that got to do with the matter under discussion?

~~~: Let me explain, Mr Honeyman, since you seem even slower off the mark than usual. If people stand stock still, at or beyond a certain distance from someone who is short-sighted, they effectively blend into the background, assuming there's a background to blend into. It's what ophthalmologists call the fresco effect.

HONEYMAN: Are you suggesting that Balham High Road was just as heavily populated as usual but everyone was standing stock still?

~~~: It's just a theory. One that merits consideration.

HONEYMAN: Why? What's all this about?

~~~: Gregory Crewdson, Mr Honeyman: the post-Hopper Edward Hopper, the uberHopper, the Hopperphile's post-Hopper Hopper. A photographer who creates stylised tableaux of seemingly ordinary but, on second glance, extraordinary aspects of small town American life. Eerie images. Disquieting. His work often shot at twilight, suffused with the blue of melancholy.

HONEYMAN: Never heard of him.

~~~: I suspect he's never heard of you either, Mr Honeyman. But Mr Inkling owns perhaps a dozen of Crewdson's best-known images and has expressed considerable interest in his working methods, especially the use of actors. For location shoots, Crewdson marshals a technical team some forty strong, and his set-ups are little different from those of the motion picture industry. The mise-en-scènes are elaborately staged and exquisitely lit. But it's lights: camera: inaction. The actors have to remain perfectly still, in whatever pose Crewdson specifies.

HONEYMAN: You're suggesting ... let's see whether I've got this right ... you're suggesting that Mr Inkling, or rather his henchmen, cordoned off a main South London thoroughfare –

~~~: Permits can be sought for such things. Sought and easily obtained if one knows who to ask and which palm or palms to grease. Needless to say, Mr Inkling does.

HONEYMAN: – and populated it with actors.

~~~: It's not impossible. Not even that difficult. Actors are ten a penny, as are scriptwriters, biographers and other arty types, most of whom live hand to mouth, seeking work of any kind that doesn't compromise their much-vaunted artistic integrity.

HONEYMAN: Not impossible, I grant you that, but hardly likely.

~~~: Nonetheless ... just think if he had, which indeed he may have. It would chime nicely with his theatrical interests and the plays he wrote under his, as we've established,

regular nom-de-plume, Boss Dangerfield.

HONEYMAN: Ah. Now. That's something I do know something about. During the 1970s two of Dangerfield's plays were staged – one at the Royal Court, the other somewhere in Leeds – to neither critical acclaim nor box office success. Both playscripts have since been withdrawn from circulation and, I suspect, destroyed by the author. Or perhaps they're tucked away in the safe at The Marbles. But for the sake of his reputation, such as it is, destruction would probably be the better bet.

According to an anonymous reviewer of *The Teasmaid* in the *Yorkshire Evening Post*, even though Dangerfield QUOTE whips up a soufflé of sub-Pinter menace out of nothing but verbal tics, the action is almost non-existent and the dramatic arc is flatter than Norfolk UNQUOTE.

The other play, a one-act special, the title of which is on the tip of my tongue ... two words, the first beginning with ess ... *Split Infinitive* or *Spinning Jenny*, something like that –

TAYLOR: *Spitting Blood?*

HONEYMAN: Got it in one! Well done, Mr Taylor. *Spitting Blood.* I can't think why it didn't immediately spring to mind. Such a good title, and by far the best thing about the play, so I've been told. I was, as luck would have it, sunning myself in Nice during its brief run at the Royal Court, when it was dismissed by an acerbic critic in *Time Out* as QUOTE a tedious, charmless, utterly witless gabfest UNQUOTE.

Those damning reviews sealed Boss' fate as a dramatist. When the impresarios and producers stopped taking his calls, which they did immediately after *Time Out* hit the newsstands, he went back to writing the trashy novels for which he's best known, featuring his most popular character, Jimmy Inkling.

~~~: Trashy? That's unduly harsh. The Second World War trilogy has, may I remind you, been republished by Oxford

World's Classics.

HONEYMAN: Well, his recent books have all been stinkers. So say the bookchat columnists and even some of his fans. His ranking on Amazon has slipped from the top one hundred to the hundred thousands and continues to drop month by month as the one-star reviews trickle in.

As for cordoning off a street for the purpose of creating a quasi-theatrical experience in which Mr Taylor and Mr Inkling were to have starring roles ... I just don't see it. Really, I don't.

~~~: Yet it happened.

HONEYMAN: Something happened, I'll grant you that.

TAYLOR: Perhaps I could explain what that something was, or at least try to.

~~~: Please do, Mr $\Delta \approx \Delta\Delta\Delta°◊≥$.

USHER: She's gone, by the way. The WPS woman. I thought you should know.

~~~: Don't interrupt the proceedings, Mr Usher. Speak only when you're spoken to.

USHER: Taking her straightened-out hairpins with her.

~~~: That's enough! I won't warn you again!

USHER: You spoke, so I spoke. That's what you just told me to do, so that's what I'm doing.

~~~: You've deliberately misunderstood what I said. The meaning was clear. Step away from the door. Perhaps, Mr Honeyman, you could take his place at the peephole.

HONEYMAN: If you wish.

~~~: See if you can rustle us up a cup of coffee, Mr Usher.

USHER: Can't Mr Honeyman do it?

~~~: No. I want him here, he's still capable of giving valuable evidence despite his uncooperative nature. Go make some coffee.

USHER: I'm not very good at coffee.

~~~: I don't care. Just do it.

USHER: I'd rather not, if you don't mind. I'm allergic to coffee.

And milk. Even the smell of them, especially when they're mingled. Sometimes just the sight of them mingling gives me the collywobbles – a nasty griping pain like a bayonet in the gut. Not that I've ever had a bayonet in the gut; those that have don't usually survive. But it doubles me up it does. Some people faint when they see blood, even the fake blood they use on stage and screen – well, that's what happens to me when I see milk, even skimmed and condensed milk, though not, for some reason, UHT. But there's not a drop of UHT on the premises; I looked everywhere for it during the last recess because Miss Stenographer wanted some.

By the way, I'm almost certain that when the camera crew left they swiped at least a dozen sacks of coffee beans that were tucked behind the storeroom door. Perhaps they also took the UHT, I wouldn't put it past them.

And steam ... the steam from boiling water sets me off badly. I suffer from post-traumatic stress disorder because of being burnt on the arm when I was five. Take a look, there's the scar. It has, I grant you, the appearance of a badly faded tattoo of a scar, but it's an actual scar.

And because I have Type-1 diabetes, sugars of all kinds are a no-no. Seeing them doesn't worry me greatly, but the smell, especially of muscovado, rapadura, demerara, sucanet, turbinado, panela, chancaca, jaggery and piloncillo, not to mention kokuto, which is extremely rare, I've come across it only once, in a market in Okinawa – the smell alone sends my blood sugar rocketing. If I obey your order to make coffee there's a strong possibility I'll slip into a coma and die. Not something you'd want on your conscience, I should imagine, but perhaps I'm wrong about that.

It would also contravene the General Duties of Employers to their Employees section of the Health and Safety at Work Act 1974, in particular sub-section 2b, QUOTE ensuring, so far as is reasonably practicable, the safety and absence of risks to health in connection with the use, handling, storage and transport of articles and substances UNQUOTE. Use, handling and substances are the key words here.

So all in all I think it would be best if someone else made the coffee.

~~~: Mr Usher, I've asked you to make coffee – a perfectly reasonable request, one would have thought, and despite your qualms, caveats and dire prognostications an incredibly low risk undertaking – and why? because it's the middle of the night, our spirits are flagging, bodies fatigued, minds frazzled. We're desperately in need of something to perk us up, and, most important of all, you're the only one here with nothing to do now the witnesses have bolted.

USHER: Still, I'd rather not.

~~~: Motion denied! Make the coffee and make it strong. Mine's black, one level teaspoon of demerara, well stirred, no gritty residue in the dregs, please. Shoo! Get going! Go-go-go!

And finally
reluctantly
but
yes
there he goes
hangdog
sullen
dragging his heels
but he's going
going
going
[...]
gone.

Au revoir, Mr Usher! Five coffees, at your earliest convenience.

HONEYMAN: I can't see a damn thing.

~~~: What?

HONEYMAN: Through this peephole.

~~~: Why? What's wrong?

HONEYMAN: I'll tell you what's wrong: there's nothing to see. Not because the field of vision is too narrow or shallow or distorted ... there's nothing, *absolutely nothing*. It's all black, like ... what did Stephen Hawking call it? ... 'the timeless nothingness before the big bang'. Perhaps not word for word but something like that. Or was it Stephen Jay Gould? Stephen Somebody-or-other. Definitely a Stephen and probably, given the topic, an astrophysicist or suchlike.

To me it looks like the inky blackness at the bottom of a well, insofar as I can imagine such a thing, never having looked into a well. I hope that analogy helps. Or, better still, black as the floor of the Mariana Trench, the section known as the Challenger Deep. Or perhaps what I had in mind was an oil well, an even blacker black.

~~~: I think I get the picture, such as it is.

HONEYMAN: Look, I'm loath to cast aspersions, but I really don't think, peepholewise, Mr Usher was telling the truth, the whole truth and nothing but the truth as per the courtroom oath – do you?

~~~: Not that he was under oath. But that's what happens when you contract an employment agency drone to do an unsocial hours job at extremely short notice. You get what you get and you always get less than you hoped for, though things usually aren't quite as bad as this. The recruitment consultant obviously took Mr Usher's CV at face value, despite significant dissonances and one or two glaring anomalies with regard to his employment record and academic qualifications. In particular the claim that he works part-time for the Met as a super-observer.

Ridiculous. He must think we're as gullible as loons. Mr Honeyman, ask him to come out here and explain himself, if he can, though I suspect he can't. The coffee will just have to wait.

STENOGRAPHER: [...]

FOREMAN: [...]

TAYLOR: [...]

~~~: Come on, come on, what's taking so long? ... Ah, there you are, Mr Honeyman. So where is he?

HONEYMAN: Mr Usher?

~~~: Who else.

HONEYMAN: Scarpered. Flown the coop. Lit out for the territory.

AKA
Tower Hamlets
where London's
highest concentration
of muggers live
in row upon row
of squalid
crack dens
the majority of which
are serviced by
Rashomon Solutions
listed
in Companies House
as a wholly owned subsidiary of
Inkling Inc.

Crashed the metal bar on the emergency exit and sped off into the night, leaving the door gusting back and forth on squeaky hinges.

TAYLOR: Squeaky hinges, eh? Your handiwork, I presume, Mr ~~~. Or that of a colleague.

~~~: The latter.

HONEYMAN: And it's raining quite heavily.

~~~: 'As the garden breathes, so do we. Let that be our solace.'

Rain in Autumn. Longfellow, I think. Mr Usher isn't the only one who can spout a few lines of poetry at inappropriate moments.

HONEYMAN: So it would seem.

~~~: Okay, let's take a break. In the absence of an obliging minion I'll make the coffee, despite the considerable risk to life and limb.

Sixth Session

~~~: May I remind you that you're still under oath, Mr Δ≈ΔΔ°◊≥.

TAYLOR: Understood.

~~~: Okay then. Let's set aside for one moment the evidence about spectacles, photography, the theatre and Mr Inkling's nom-de-plume, Boss Dangerfield. Just before the recess you were telling us about Mr Inkling's unsatisfactory new wheelman and conjecturing how he might end his days. Prompt, please, Miss Stenographer.

STENOGRAPHER: Just a sec. Mmm-mmm. — Got it: 'From the look on Mr Inkling's face I suspected the eels would soon be getting an unexpected treat.'

TAYLOR: Yes indeed. So ...

HONEYMAN: Wait-wait-wait-wait-wait! Sorry to butt in, but I have a confession to make. While you were busying yourselves in the kitchen, I turned the key in the lock, sallied forth along the corridor and out into the street, brazen as you like.

~~~: *You did what!*

HONEYMAN: To see what was on the other side of the peephole. Couldn't resist the temptation. But guess what I found ... Go on, guess ...

~~~: I couldn't care a hoot. Not even half a hoot. I gave Mr Usher strict instructions to lock the door. On no account was he to open it again unless I specifically asked him to do so, and I assure you, Mr Honeyman, I did nothing of the sort.

HONEYMAN: But as I'm not Mr Usher ...

~~~: The injunction applied to all of us. Everyone in the courtroom at the time. All, Mr Honeyman. Without exception. Even the mice in the wainscot understood that, so you could hardly fail to.

HONEYMAN: Yes, but –

~~~: No ifs or buts, Mr Honeyman.

HONEYMAN: Do you really not want to know what I discovered? You're the grand inquisitor here; aren't you feeling just a teeny-weeny bit inquisitive?

~~~: What I want is for you to cooperate fully with these proceedings in pursuit of the truth about Jimmy Inkling. That's something you've failed to do, despite your WPS pledge.

TAYLOR: Actually, I wouldn't mind knowing what you found, Mr Honeyman, if it's relevant, and if Mr ~~~ doesn't mind.

~~~: But Mr ~~~ *does* mind. He minds very much.

HONEYMAN: It has a direct bearing, I promise.

~~~: Oh, for Heaven's sake! All right then, go ahead if you must. But keep it simple and make it snappy.

HONEYMAN: Thank you. The situation in the corridor was, I found, pretty much as Mr Usher described it, despite the fact that he couldn't see a damn thing and must have had to guess what was going on from the confusing mishmash of bangs, scrapes, grunts and exclamations he could hear. No easy task that, listening through a solid wood door. But his hearing was obviously pin-drop acute and his echo location skills almost to bat standard.

Front door smashed out of its frame: check.

A wooden pew half in the corridor, half out on the pavement: check.

The fact that he failed to mention the rain hammering down is immaterial. He probably couldn't hear it because of the fearsome racket being made by Ms WPS and her fellow escapologists.

And escape they did: the corridor was empty, the street as people-free as a city street can be – unless, of course, there was actually a large crowd of actors out there, standing perfectly still, soaked to the skin, who'd somehow contrived to blend into the scenery.

~~~: Less of the sarcasm, Mr Honeyman.

HONEYMAN: The transom was, however, intact. So, regardless of how Ms WPS got in, she'd still had to batter her way out. Or perhaps that's how she likes to make an exit, in grand style.

But a shattered door and an undamaged transom weren't the only things of note. Stuck fast on the corridor side of the peephole was a wad of chewing gum that covered the lens completely. Despite my squeamishness I prodded the gum with a fingernail. If I'd had a pen on me I would have used that instead, then wrapped the pen in my handkerchief and, at the earliest opportunity, discarded them both in a receptacle for contaminated waste. One can't be too careful in times like these when antibiotics are hardly more effective than sugar pills and prayer – yes, prayer – has, according to a recent study, twice their efficacy.

The gum itself was stalagmite or stalactite hard, I don't know which. Ms WPS hadn't put it there today. She could, of course, have stuck it on the lens six months ago, on the assumption that it might somehow be of use to her six months hence. But, all in all, that seems unlikely.

TAYLOR: Six months?

HONEYMAN: A guesstimate. I don't know whether carbon dating

would enable us to pinpoint accurately when the gum was applied, though I suppose it might. It's an area of science I know little about.

~~~: Nothing at all, I would say, from the comment you've just made.

TAYLOR: Ah, but it might be possible to determine the flavour of the gum, even after all this time, hence perhaps the manufacturer. Residual DNA could also provide a valuable clue if the details of the person who applied the gum to the peephole have been logged on the DNA register of the police national computer. We could always ask Deputy Assistant Commissioner Starkey to have one of his people run a search, I'm sure he'd oblige.

~~~: And that would avail us how, exactly? Let's stick to what we know, gentlemen. Or think we know. Continue with your evidence, Mr $\Delta \approx \Delta \Delta \Delta^\circ \diamond \geq$.

TAYLOR: Would it help if I told you that Mr Inkling is an inveterate gum chewer? Nicotine gum since he gave up smoking a year or two ago. Although, to be precise, he still enjoys the occasional post-prandial cigar – top quality Cubans only. If the gum stuck on the peephole proved to be a nicotine brand it might suggest Mr Inkling's involvement.

~~~: Pure speculation, Mr $\Delta \approx \Delta \Delta \Delta^\circ \diamond \geq$. And if the WPS woman couldn't possibly know six months ahead of time that this coffee shop of all the coffee shops in London would become an impromptu courtroom, how could Mr Inkling? And anyway, what purpose could obscuring the peephole serve, then or now? It's a red herring. Put it in the same box as the spectacles, photography, playscripts, etc. and tamp the lid down tight. We need to focus exclusively on the three-legged pub crawl race down Balham High Road – that, surely, is the nub of the matter.

You told us, Mr $\Delta \approx \Delta \Delta \Delta^\circ \diamond \geq$, that you were drunk on neat vodka and had been splashed with stale beer, to give your cover story added authenticity, or, what did you call it? – verisimilitude. But did you visit any of the pubs en route to Colliers Wood, as per the race schedule?

TAYLOR: Of course not. We didn't get anywhere near Colliers Wood. Not even as far as Balham underground station. We passed, at a stumbling trot, the Parson's Nose, followed by the Organ of Corti, then, almost next door, a spit and sawdust, hole-in-the-wall boozer known to locals since time immemorial as The Leper's Spots (i.e. The Leopard's Spots), and finally we reached that wittily named Scandi-themed gastropub, the one that scored a perfect ten in the 2012 *Good Food Guide* but dropped off the page after the head chef topped himself – Smorgasbord.

~~~: Wittily named?

TAYLOR: The building had once been a cooker showroom for what was, in the 1970s, the British Gas Corporation: the gas board as it was colloquially known.

~~~: How did you know it was a former gas board showroom?

TAYLOR: A large plaque above the entrance. I'd seen it before and knew what it said.

~~~: Good. Please continue.

TAYLOR: You do realise, don't you, that we weren't going to cross the threshold of any of the umpteen watering holes along the route. It was a pub crawl in name only, a pretence, a ruse. There were no competitors, no stewards, no prizes. In short, no race. Just me and Mr Inkling, handcuffed together, armed and dangerous. We'd ventured onto the High Road for one reason only: to find someone who was, as Mr Inkling put it, 'gagging for a mugging' – a phrase he was particularly fond of.

~~~: I'm cognizant of those facts, Mr Δ≈ΔΔΔ°◇≥. Frankly, I'm surprised you'd think I thought otherwise. Despite the lateness of the hour my mind is like a well-oiled steel trap, its teeth not dissimilar to those I have in my jaw.

Little wonder my dentist looks nervous when she has to put a finger in my mouth. I haven't bitten her yet, not even a playful nip or an 'accidental' nibble, but her exorbitant fees make me wish I had, and one day perhaps I shall.

TAYLOR: Yes, well, those were Mr Inkling's actual words: 'gagging for a mugging'. He told me that some people, whether they realise it or not, are always on the lookout for someone to mug them, just as muggers, even when off-duty, are always looking for someone to mug. It's habitual. Ditto murderers and their victims. According to Mr Inkling it's a yin-yang kind of thing (he explains it so much better than I can, so I won't even try), unfathomable to all but those such as he, few in number even among the world's top criminologists, who have dedicated their lives to the understanding of such societal checks and balances ... and in his case their exploitation for personal gain. 'Crime,' he said, 'fulfils a need for both the lawless and the law-abiding. Everyone gets what's coming to them when they finally get what they want.'

~~~: He's fond of spouting guff like that. Fortune cookie social philosophy, influenced by Debord, I suppose, or someone of his ilk, and of little or no relevance to the topic under discussion, which is, or was until just a moment ago, Balham High Road. Let's get back to it. Did you eventually find someone to mug?

TAYLOR: No. Something unexpected happened. It even took Mr Inkling by surprise, which would prove he hadn't set the whole thing up. Or if he had, the set-up had gone horribly wrong. And, if so, I knew there'd be hell to pay and I'd be the one to pick up the tab.

As I'm sure you're well aware, Mr Inkling never takes responsibility for anything that goes wrong, not when someone else is available to shoulder the blame; and if not a person, an animal; and if not an animal, something inanimate – a gun, a knife, a spade, a rock.

~~~: One of the classic character traits of the psychopathic male, alas.

TAYLOR: Alas indeed. Anyway, we'd just reached Smorgasbord, in which there were hardly any customers, and I think I know why. Because of some extremely unsympathetic 'feature' lighting, the diners in the showroom window eating their Scandi-food looked not quite human, more like waxwork dummies. Unless, of course, they were waxwork dummies. Or, because they seemed to be moving (albeit more slowly than people usually do unless they've been hypnotised or debilitated by a stroke), automata. Or perhaps they were participants in a time-and-motion study to find out how long it takes the average adult diner to complete each course of a three-course meal without feeling harried or neglected by the waiter. Or perhaps they weren't particularly hungry, or the food wasn't sufficiently appetising.

HONEYMAN: Or, conversely, the food was so delicious they were savouring each and every mouthful, drawing the meal out inordinately in the hope that it would never end.

TAYLOR: I suppose that's possible, despite some of the unenthusiastic recent reviews on TripAdvisor. But I'm still not convinced that the window people weren't automata, part of a striking display designed to lure customers onto the premises. If so, it wasn't working terribly well. Although, to be fair, apart from me and Mr Inkling there weren't any passing punters to lure. None that I could see.

But as for automata … the giveaway would be if they repeated the same simple gestures, in sequence, at fixed intervals, over a period of, say, ten minutes.

HONEYMAN: They could, of course, be production line workers eating at the speed of their work. Don't discount that possibility.

TAYLOR: Another giveaway would be if they were still sitting in the window after all the lights had been switched off, the security grilles pulled down, the burglar alarm set, and the restaurateur, his head chef, kitchen and waiting staff had gone home for the night, or to a nightclub, or a brothel. Chefs in particular are partial to brothels and brawls, as a quick scan of any local rag will confirm.

HONEYMAN: That, I grant you, would be conclusive.

TAYLOR: Unfortunately, although it was nearly closing time, I wasn't able to hang around to find out. Mr Inkling was speeding up and, having no choice in the matter, I sped up too. It was a downhill stretch, so that may account for it, but suddenly we were running full tilt, out of control, both of us puffing and panting, neither of us quite as young and fit as we once were, me especially.

~~~: You recently celebrated your one hundred and thirty-fifth birthday, if the records at god HQ are to be believed.

TAYLOR: Hundred and thirty-seventh.

~~~: Ah. Not to be believed. Apologies.

TAYLOR: No need. The years fly by once you top the ton. It's hard to keep a tally and there's very little reason to do so. Have you ever tried to blow out more than a hundred candles in one go? Of course not, you're almost four decades younger than me. I quickly ran out of puff and had to use a fireside bellows. And the cake itself was enormous, more than a metre in diameter and thirty centimetres tall. It needed to be that big to accommodate all the candles. Livvy couldn't get it in the oven in one piece, so it was baked in sections, then assembled and exquisitely decorated. She's a veritable Picasso with the icing bag.

But then she realised she wouldn't be able to get the cake through the doorway of her cottage to bring it next door to mine, not without tilting it to the vertical, in which case it was bound to fall apart. So we cut a couple of hefty slices and ate them in her kitchen; just the two of us, sitting on padded stools (for which I was grateful) at a dining table that was hardly bigger than a stool head, our knees interleaved because in a space that small there was nowhere else for them to go. Much too intimate for my liking, though despite her interest in the contents of my underwear drawer Livvy didn't try to flirt. Never has, come to think of it. Perhaps I'm not her type. I'm not sure I'm even my own type.

HONEYMAN: Unlike Mr Inkling. A perpetually preening mega-Narcissus. Vanity writ monstrously large. Another of the classic character traits of the psychopathic male, as I'm sure Mr Squiggle will agree.

~~~: That's not my name, Mr Honeyman. It's ~~~. Your lack of good manners reflects badly on you.

TAYLOR: It's true, though, about Mr Inkling. I've never known a man surround himself with so many mirrors. Hundreds of them. Though the ex-villain that Deputy Assistant Commissioner Starkey told us about, Ball-Pein John, may run him a close second. But what's unusual about Mr Inkling's use of mirrors is that eventually he wears them out. In all my years I've heard of no-one else capable of doing that, have you?

Even the obsidian mirror he owns
one of the largest and
most perfect
ever found
Anatolian
dating from circa 6,000 BC
and the envy of
curators at
the British Museum
began to pit and flake
as though his facial features
were gradually being
etched into its surface.
This he attributed
to a curse

placed upon it
by King Anitta of Kussar
and
more prosaically
the ravages
of time.

~~~: No.

HONEYMAN: Nor me.

TAYLOR: Has he shown either of you his funfair labyrinth at
Canary Wharf?

HONEYMAN: [...]

~~~: [...]

TAYLOR: No?

~~~: [...]

HONEYMAN: [...]

TAYLOR: Never heard of it?

~~~: Frankly, no.

TAYLOR: Well, you must have remained in his good books,
that's all I can say.

~~~: Are you sure about this ... this labyrinth?

TAYLOR: Absolutely. It occupies an entire floor of his suite of
offices. Or perhaps two floors, it's hard to tell. Accessible
only by a private lift from his inner sanctum, it's a thing
of snakelike undulations, forking paths, dead ends and
sudden drops. The lights go out briefly every few minutes
and in pitch darkness the walls glide into new, unpredictable configurations. There are no doors other than at
the beginning and end, though the end may also be the
beginning and vice versa. The walls are lined throughout
with distorting mirrors salvaged from funfairs and theme
parks the length and breadth of Europe. And not just the
walls; there are mirrors on the ceiling and the backs of
the doors. Even the floor is mirrored. Once the door has
closed behind you there's no way of telling what's where
or even which way is up. Take two steps and you'll be lost

forever, though your chances of living to see another day are small. Even to peer into the labyrinth from the doorway is a dangerously disorientating experience.

Mr Inkling uses it to punish members of staff who have, in his menacingly bland phrase, 'failed to give satisfaction'; and anyone else who incurs his wrath, deliberately or otherwise. With hidden cameras he monitors their descent into madness, a process that rarely takes longer than thirty minutes. When he judges that the punishment is equal or equivalent to the offence (that yin-yang thing again, so hard to describe), which is often just a tad short of total mindmelt, the victims are either led or stretchered to safety by the Retrieval Squad – blind employees, hired in compliance with the Equality Act 2010 – and placed in the recovery room, a womblike space of replicated orbicular muscle, loose, soft and blood warm, with filtered light and comforting womblike sounds, from which some of the labyrinth's victims flatly refuse to leave and have to be dragged out by a burly obstetrician using adult-size forceps. Should a forceps delivery be unachievable, there's a caesarean zip.

If the degree of punishment is gauged incorrectly, no amount of time in the recovery room will undo the harm that's been done. In which case Mr Inkling arranges for the victim to be installed in a privately run mental health facility, the Nightingale Hospital, City of London, no expense spared, until there are signs of improvement and the patient can safely be discharged into the care of his loved ones. But if, after several months, there's no discernible improvement, as has happened on a couple of occasions, and long-term 24/7 care is needed, the patient is handed over to the NHS.

Not an enviable position to be in. Because of budgetary constraints the NHS relies heavily on fetters and pills. The Nightingale is akin to a five-star hotel, the NHS a prison. But as Mr Inkling explained:

'None of this would have happened if I'd known those ex-employees were cracked vessels. It wasn't divulged on their application form, as it should have been, under the heading: *Are you able to perform the essential job functions of the position you are applying for with or without reasonable accommodation(s)?* Can't get much clearer than that, now, can you?

'Both of them denied needing reasonable accommodation(s) at the job interview, and they got away with it despite being wired to a polygraph machine.' (He often uses the polygraph in interviews, despite its unreliability; it's one of his favourite toys.) 'They lied through their teeth, the duplicitous little shits, and for what? – to get a job from which they knew their incompetence would soon get them sacked. But they did it anyway. They weren't even competent enough to cover up their mistakes or blame them on others. I mean, c'mon, how stupid can you be? They've got no-one to blame but themselves for the pickle they find themselves in.'

HONEYMAN: Pickle, eh? A master of understatement is Mr Inkling.

~~~: Mr Honeyman, I've warned you before and I won't warn you again. If I hear one more sneery comment from you I'll have you removed from the courtroom and taken down to the cells.

HONEYMAN: Who by? Or rather, by whom? Mr Usher came to his senses and legged it.

~~~: By Miss Stenographer, if necessary.

STENOGRAPHER: That's not in my job description.

~~~: By me, then. Needs must when the Devil drives, etc. Pray continue, Mr $\Delta \approx \Delta\Delta\Delta°\diamond\geq$.

TAYLOR: Mr Inkling spends hours in the labyrinth once or twice a week. It has, he says, therapeutic value, akin to one of the fundamental aspects of meditation: a realisation of the identity of the self. Samadhi, I believe it's called. He claims he's the only man alive who can't be driven insane by the labyrinth's frequent shape-shifting and warped selfie onslaught … though one has to wonder whether that's true given his increasingly erratic behaviour of late.

When he led me to the door and, without a word of explanation or warning, flung it open, I recoiled instinctively, lost my footing and crashed down onto the floor – polished concrete, the hardest substance known to man.

Not so.
The hardest substance is
wurzite boron nitride
which has a similar structure
to diamond
though made up of different atoms.
It's used as an electrical insulator
and in crucibles
reaction vessels
moulds
and evaporating boats
but never
in flooring
not even in high tread areas.

I'd sat down so hard I'd fractured my coccyx. You may have noticed the doughnut cushion I carry around with me, to ease the pain of sitting. But sometimes I prefer to squat, as I'm doing now. Most people view it as nothing but a harmless eccentricity, especially at the theatre when I squat in the centre aisle or in the area (I've no idea what it's called) between the stalls and the orchestra pit where, during the interval, the ice cream sellers roam as they have done, mother and daughter, for generations.

But those who know my history think it's a legacy of the time I spent at Sri Harmandir Sahib, Amritsar, several decades ago, mistranslating (I'm not much of a linguist; precisely the reason I may have been chosen for the task) the thousands of verses of the Guru Granth Sahib into Polari. (Every half millennium or so the Council of Elders has us poke around in the various world religions, to stir them up a bit. I've no idea why.) But people can believe whatever they like.

Despite the fact that I was writhing in agony, Mr Inkling found my pratfall funny. I'm glad someone did. He laughed a nasty laugh and quickly closed the door.

Showing me the labyrinth was his way of suggesting that if I didn't buck my ideas up there'd be consequences, dire consequences. A threat, what else? It's what he specialises in. But given that his lexicon of love is so malnourished, his threats are often better understood as perverse terms of endearment, as I would argue they were on this occasion. I don't think for one moment that he intended to pitch me into the labyrinth – scruff of neck, seat of pants, like a pub landlord ejecting an obnoxious drunk – he just wanted to savour its destructive potential and my horrified reaction to it.

'It is,' he said, when we were back upstairs, sipping a restorative single malt, him sitting comfortably, the swine, me standing and still in agony despite having received a powerful shot of morphine from Inkling Inc.'s Syrian in-house medic, Dr Syringe (not his real name – at least, I don't think so), 'an instrument of torture beyond the limited scope of the medieval mind, as typified by the Inquisition, an organisation fixated on exquisite pain, a form of suffering exemplified by our saviour on the cross.

'And the torture strategies of intelligence agencies worldwide – MOSSAD, the CIA, et al. – are based almost exclusively on breaking the victim's will to obtain intelligence, secure a confession, or both. A pointless exercise: the intelligence will be nonsense, the confession insincere.

'Happily, the labyrinth serves neither of those purposes. Its sole function is to derange the senses. Which it does. Magnificently. The design concept alone is worthy of a Nobel Prize, though in what category I can't rightly say. Peace, perhaps. Its victims are entirely at one with themselves and made blissfully unaware of anything else.'

HONEYMAN: Rimbaud would have loved it.

~~~: This Rambow, Rameau or whatever – I didn't quite catch the name (I do wish you wouldn't mumble) – who is he? Or she?

HONEYMAN: Doesn't matter.

~~~: Things that don't matter have no place in this courtroom, Mr Honeyman. Keep such thoughts to yourself. You're holding up the proceedings with these fatuous remarks.

HONEYMAN: Tut tut. I don't know what came over me. Right hand smacks left wrist. Ouch! Lesson learned. Continue, please, Mr Taylor.

TAYLOR: Shall I, Mr ~~~?

~~~: How kind of you to ask, Mr $\Delta\approx\Delta\Delta\Delta°\diamond\geq$, and how appropriate given that I'm the one in charge of these proceedings and Mr Honeyman, though he'd like to persuade you otherwise, is not. — So yes, please do.

TAYLOR: Okay. Well, umm … Six or seven years ago a newly hired cleaner strayed into the labyrinth, almost certainly by accident, probably thinking it was where mops and buckets were stored, and just as she crossed the threshold a gust of wind – it probably was a gust of wind, not human agency, though one can't entirely be sure – slammed the door shut behind her. No handle on the inside, of course. The door opens electronically on verbal command: a meow and two woofs.

The cameras, triggered by someone entering the labyrinth, recorded what happened next … which doesn't bear thinking about.

That was a Friday. The cleaner wasn't found until the following Monday. By then it was too late, much too late.

Blood everywhere. She'd clawed her eyes out and there were more than a hundred additional self-inflicted injuries.

Mr Inkling offered to show me the footage and the death scene photos, but I declined and he didn't insist. That too was a loving threat – an affectionate tease, if you prefer.

I've no idea how the cleaner's body was disposed of. Mr Inkling didn't say and that suited me just fine. I've always tried to be as uninquisitive as possible in his company: three wise monkeys rolled into one. But sometimes, especially in his cups, he's hell-bent on revealing all. I suppose he expects me to keep his secrets locked in my head like a safe deposit box, as a father confessor would, or a psychoanalyst, or a sin eater. Yet here I am spilling the beans. What kind of man that makes me, I really don't know.

~~~: A man answering difficult questions as truthfully as he can, heedless of the consequences, which, knowing Mr Inkling, there will be. You should be as proud of yourself as we are of you. A fitting epitaph, yes? Let's hope it won't be needed. Not soon, anyway.

HONEYMAN: Hear hear!

TAYLOR: It is and it isn't. I'll explain what I mean once I've finished telling you about the labyrinth. He was determined to talk about what had happened to that poor woman, and short of thrusting a napkin in his mouth or bread in my ears I had no way of stopping him. (We were in a restaurant at the time, occupying a quiet corner between the emergency exit and the toilets, Mr Inkling facing the main door so no-one could ambush him – an arrangement he always insisted on when booking a table.)

The cleaner was, he said, just one of the hundreds of thousands of people who go missing every year in the UK, a small percentage of whom are never heard from again.

He said he'd sent an anonymous donation to her husband – bloodwit, he called it – and, the following year, a smaller but still substantial sum, five figures, to Whereabouts, the charitable trust the family set up to investigate cases of missing persons the police had dropped for lack of resources and, one presumes, enthusiasm.

Later still, as if by accident, he bumped into Whereabouts' CEO at a rural fundraising event in the Cotswolds, somewhere between Splat the Rat and the Wheel of Fortune

Which aren't
by the way
nicknames
given to quaint
little
honeystone villages
by their
inhabitants.

and declared himself a staunch supporter of the trust's work. After they'd chatted for a while in the back of Mr Inkling's limo and consumed several large brandies from its well-stocked cocktail cabinet, he offered his services as a trustee. An apparently spontaneous gesture that the CEO assumed was just the drink talking.

'No-no,' Mr Inkling insisted, 'absolutely not. I'm serious. To be able to help in any way would be an honour. Even stuffing envelopes or cold-calling dotty pensioners, if necessary.'

Family and trust alike, wowed by his celebrity status, his extraordinary business acumen and the sheer magnitude of his financial interests at home and abroad, welcomed him with open arms.

At the next board meeting but two (playing the long game, cunning fox) he suggested that perhaps, as the post was vacant, he might, just might, if the board found the idea acceptable, take on the role of Finance Director, just, you know, for a little while, a couple of months, six at most, to keep things ticking over until a more suitable candidate could be found.

Not only was the vote in favour unanimous, the search for a new Finance Director was immediately scaled down and eventually, quietly, dropped.

Having got his hands on the accounts, Mr Inkling began the serious work he'd intended to do all along: siphoning off a sum of money equivalent to the amount he'd originally donated and plumping it up with a super-inflationary but not quite loan shark rate of interest. 'Mustn't be greedy,' he said. 'It's a charity, after all.'

~~~: He's not entirely heartless, Mr Inkling, though his heart isn't necessarily in the right place, if you know what I mean.

HONEYMAN: I do.

TAYLOR: Certainly not worn on his sleeve, that's for sure.

HONEYMAN: Nor in his chest.

TAYLOR: Probably kept for safekeeping at a nearby cryopreser-vation unit, ready to be thawed out quickly if required.

HONEYMAN: 'Quoth the Raven, "Nevermore".'

~~~: That'll do, gentlemen! We're straying off piste again. Let's return to the pub crawl on Balham High Road. Continue where you left off, please, Mr $\Delta \approx \Delta\Delta\Delta^\circ\diamond\geq$.

TAYLOR: Yes. The High Road. Well … when we ran past Smor-gasbord I noticed that Mr Inkling was trying to check his reflection in the window. He wasn't seeing what I was seeing, not at all. Not that it mattered. What happened would have happened anyway.

~~~: Which was?

TAYLOR: Hard to explain, but I'll try. Much of what I know has been gleaned from the police accident report and various newspaper articles. But I clearly remember us running downhill, full tilt, outer arms flapping like windmill sails in a hurricane. It was all we could do to stay upright. We were losing coordination, becoming ragged, our three legs trying to become four again. The cuffs were managing to keep us in sync, but only just. It seemed inevitable that unless we reduced speed we'd trip over our own three feet and come crashing down, one of us dragging the other after him.

But as I said earlier, what happened wasn't at all what I expected, and I assume that's also true for Mr Inkling given the life-threatening injuries he sustained. Perhaps he should have worn his favourite stab-proof vest, the one with the purple and yellow paisley lining that, he said, always reminded him of the 1960s and especially Carnaby Street. Throughout that decade and beyond, he and his partner Derek Noone looked down on Carnaby Street from the windows of their top-floor import/export business (actually a money laundering operation) on Great Marlborough Street.

Happy gangland days.

Mr Inkling really does yearn for them.

And for Derek Noone, too: declared dead in absentia on the seventh anniversary of his disappearance. If still alive, whereabouts unknown. But Mr Inkling is so convinced that Noone is dead, he bought him the plot next door to Sir Rex's at Hendon Park, and a nice headstone too. Mr Inkling is the only cemetery visitor who regularly arrives with flowers in one hand and a sledgehammer in the other.

~~~: And the incident on Balham High Road, Mr Δ≈ΔΔΔ°◇≥?

TAYLOR: Of course. Forgive me ... We were blindsided. No better way to describe it than that. Out of the corner of my eye I saw something large and white moving towards us at high speed. We were struck amidships by whatever that thing was and flung over a low wall, through a hedge and into a small suburban garden. At the time I was too shocked to realise what had happened. Or perhaps I was unconscious. Frankly, I don't know.

According to the accident report, the vehicle that struck us was a catering van, stolen that morning from outside a delicatessen in Winchmore Hill. It mounted the kerb and, from the lack of tire marks on the pavement, it seems to have been airborne when it knocked us through the hedge. The occupants of the van were never traced. After they'd done what they came to do, they roared off into the night. That was the last sound I heard before ambulance and police car sirens converged on us from opposite directions. But before the emergency services reached us, the men –

~~~: Men? How many?

TAYLOR: Two, of course. One with a Birmingham accent, the other Caribbean, probably Jamaican. At a guess. It could only be a guess; I was lying face down, unable to move, so I never caught sight of either of them.

'That fucka's dead,' said the Brummie – meaning, so I thought, Mr Inkling. 'Stick the other one and let's get the fuck away from here.'

Fuck he pronounced fook.

There was an effortful grunt and a muffled thud

How appropriate.
Muffled Thud
is the title of
Boss Dangerfield's
most recent novel
[#67 in the Jimmy Inkling series]
published a couple of years ago
a revenge thriller
about hapless hitmen
their very
unhappy endings
and

                    the even unhappier
                    endings of those who'd
                    commissioned
                    the botched hit
                    on our suave
                    and gallant hero.
                    'Life imitates art far more
                    than art imitates life'
                    according to Oscar Wilde.

as the knife went into Mr Inkling's chest, glancing off one of his ribs and narrowly missing his heart.

HONEYMAN: Which, luckily, wasn't in his chest, but stored, as we established earlier, at a cryopreservation unit.

~~~: Nothing of the kind was established, Mr Honeyman. It was mere surmise on Mr Δ≈ΔΔΔ°◇≥'s part, a comment more facetious than factual.

HONEYMAN: If you say so.

TAYLOR: Next think I knew, he and I were lying side by side in Accident and Emergency. They'd pushed two of the metal-framed cots together because they were unable to separate us.

I was viewing events as they transpired from a far corner of the ward, up near the ceiling, to one side or perhaps actually inside a small security camera. It didn't occur to me to think this was unusual.

Someone said that the keys to the cuffs hadn't been found and Neville had gone to fetch bolt-cutters. No surprise there: the keys had been left in the safekeeping of Mr Inkling's driver, the kerb scraper, Mr Clumsy.

~~~: So what was the driver doing while you were being attacked? Wasn't he supposed to be shadowing you?

TAYLOR: Apparently, when he saw the van crash into us, he panicked and abandoned the Bentley in the middle of the road, engine running, driver's door flung wide. All that remained of him was a whiff of cheap aftershave that did little to disguise his body odour, rank with fear.

Less than a minute after he exited the vehicle, someone hopped in and drove off. The following morning the
thief and the Bentley turned up at a second-hand car
dealership in St Albans that was under surveillance by
Hertfordshire constabulary's car-smuggling unit. Some
people have no luck, not even the dumb sort.

~~~: But the men in the catering van had left you both for
dead.

TAYLOR: That was certainly their intention.

~~~: And they thought they'd succeeded.

TAYLOR: Yes. Though they were wrong on one count: Mr
Inkling survived.

HONEYMAN: Wait a minute! You're telling us, right here, right
now, that you're dead – *actually dead?*

TAYLOR: Technically, yes.

HONEYMAN: Meaning?

~~~: Pipe down, Mr Honeyman. As you recently pointed out,
I'm the grand inquisitor here, so let me do my job. —
Meaning, Mr $\Delta\approx\Delta\Delta\Delta°\diamond\geq$?

TAYLOR: I was declared dead on arrival at the hospital. Once
they'd managed to snip through the cuffs I was covered
with a sheet and trundled down to the morgue. Although
I seemed completely and utterly dead, irrefutably dead,
halfway across the Styx on a one-way ticket to Hades,
obviously I wasn't, otherwise I wouldn't be here to tell
you this.

I came to on a gurney by the side of the mortuary
table, ready for the pathologist to turn up and begin the
autopsy – *my autopsy*. That didn't seem like such a good
idea. I could hear voices in an adjoining room, so, holding
on to anything that might help me stay upright, my head
spinning and every shuffling step wracked with pain, I

gradually made my way to where they were. In my confusion I didn't think to cry for help.

Not that it would have made any difference: the voices were emanating from a small transistor radio that was chattering away to itself. From what I could see, the office had only recently been vacated. A brown suede jacket was draped casually over the arm of a typing chair, and a mug of tea – freshly made, still steaming – stood on the desk. I sat down gingerly, though my coccyx was probably the least sore part of me, took a sip of tea and found it was just the way I liked it: strong, three sugars and heavily milked, full-fat at that. I drank it while awaiting the return of whoever's office it was, but no-one came.

The only other item on the desk was a box of paracetamol. I popped two caplets from the blister pack and managed to gulp them down with sips of tea. Then, a few minutes later, once my mind had cleared a bit, it occurred to me that the recommended safe dose was unlikely to be effective, so I took another six. That's all there were in the box. Had there been twenty caplets, or even a hundred, I'm pretty sure I would have taken them all and died yet again, this time permanently.

After what seemed like hours but was probably no time at all, I stood up and set off in search of help, stumbling down a series of long corridors and opening every unlocked door I could find. Nobody about. Just rooms full of trapped air and that strain of melancholy unique to the NHS.

Eventually I found myself in a staff-only car park at the rear of the building, standing amidst cigarette ends, late autumn leaves and snotted tissues.

I was exhausted, unable to take a single step further. To one side of the exit, at the head of a short alleyway, stood a recycling bin for cardboard and paper. I lifted the lid and looked inside. It was full almost to the brim with thin ribbons of paper that had been put through a shredder, thousands of pages worth, a major clearout, and it looked so soft and inviting I used my remaining strength to drag my half-dead body over the lip and topple in. The shreddings sank by fifty per cent and moulded themselves to the shape of my body. I'd barely snuggled down when the lid was lifted and further shreddings were tipped in, covering me from head to toe.

Cocooned, I slept, unaware of the security alert that had been triggered by my absence from the morgue. The police were searching everywhere for me, working on the not unreasonable assumption that my corpse had been stolen, perhaps by rogue taxidermists (frustrated owl stuffers wishing to tackle a larger, more challenging subject) or as an end-of-term prank by drunken medical students.

By the time the police arrived, hospital security staff had turned the place upside down. They must surely have given the recycling bin the once over during their search, but I was hidden from view and didn't notice them looking, so deep was the sleep I'd fallen into. A dreamless, recuperative sleep. A coma in all but name.

The following afternoon I made my way on foot to my sister's house. Already I was feeling a bit better. Most of yesterday's sharp pains had dwindled to dull aches, though I must have looked awful – bloodied, battered and bruised, desperately in need of a shave, and dressed like a stumblebum in torn, grubby clothes. But no bones had been broken, no organs ruptured, and there was no obvious sign of concussion. I'd been lucky.

Not that Nessa agreed. She tutted and raised an eyebrow when she saw the terrible state I was in. 'You need to ditch that nasty, good-for-nothing friend of yours,' she said, guessing instantly what had happened. An easy guess, considering what she knew of my previous experiences with Mr Inkling, including the perilous leap from the Rotherhithe warehouse and my midnight swim across the Thames. 'Mark my words, Charles, one day that man will be the death of you!'

Happily, that day has yet to come. Gods are hard to kill, as you know. We're much more robust than our fellow humans.

HONEYMAN: Actually, I didn't know. This is all new territory to me, hard to take in.

TAYLOR: Not only more robust, quicker to heal too, coccyx, for some reason, notwithstanding. Within a couple of days I was back at Vale Hall, packing a few things, essential items only. With heavy heart I kissed the doorknocker and waved my cottage goodbye. I knew that if I remained there Mr Inkling's henchmen would eventually come looking for me. He has a very suspicious mind does Mr Inkling. The lack of a corpse would trouble him. He'd worry it up into a major obsession, an itch he'd be unable to resist scratching, and once he started scratching he'd scratch right down to the bone. I knew he wouldn't be satisfied until he'd seen me lowered into a grave at Hendon Park as near to Sir Rex as possible; preferably right next to him, on the opposite side to Derek Noone's vacant plot, so he could keep an eye on me. I'd have to lie low until he accepted the fact of my demise. That could take a good long while and might, worse case scenario, never happen. It's said that hope springs eternal in the human breast, but with regard to Mr Inkling I sincerely hope it won't.

A disused granary on the far side of Vale Hall has become my new home, but mostly my days are spent elsewhere, trying to catch up on god business. Recently I wrote to the Council of Elders, asking to be relieved of one of my principal tasks – slowing the Rate of Depletion in Inkjet Printer Cartridges. I explained that Mr Inkling had 'borrowed' my work diary and memorised my itinerary. He knows where I'm scheduled to be on every inkjet cartridge workday between now and 2035 (though inkjet printers will be obsolete by then, dead and buried, and I for one won't mourn their passing). I requested a substitute task of similar onerousness, one that would keep me as far away from Mr Inkling as possible. Not too much to ask, surely. But I've yet to receive a reply, even though I marked my request URGENT and sent it special delivery.

~~~: Did you phrase it in the stilted semi-legalese they use in upper-echelon Council communications?

TAYLOR: I did.

~~~: I've even heard of requests being binned because of a single inappropriate use of the semi-colon. They're sticklers for such things at god HQ.

TAYLOR: My semi-colons were meticulously placed throughout, I can assure you, and used only when necessary.

~~~: Flattery and special pleading also seem to help.

TAYLOR: I provided a measure of both, together with a full and frank account of my relationship with Mr Inkling. I'm conscientious to a fault, as you know, Mr ~~~, but because of him my work had suffered badly, something the Council of Elders couldn't have failed to notice.

HONEYMAN: Did Mr Inkling really memorise your itinerary for the next couple of decades?

TAYLOR: Probably not, though he said he had. He spieled off a couple of pages, just enough to convince me that he might have. It's the kind of thing he likes to do, a form of coercive persuasion.

For example, once, while I was drunk (not of my choosing), he wheedled out of me, drink by drink, the names of my early childhood toys – Ned, Stumper, Cunty, Wally Oink, Vlad, Growl, Chatterbox, et al. – and since then he's regularly discussed them with me, asking me what I think they might be doing nowadays – as though they'd have shucked off their toyness and metamorphosed into adult humans.

According to Mr Inkling they'd be just like everyone else: QUOTE saps, drones and marks UNQUOTE. He said they'd probably have suffocating, unfulfilling careers from which they feel they can't escape; an unhappy home life; a large mortgage and a plethora of debts that will either be carried over to the afterlife or burden their next of kin, assuming their kin inherit; a tendency towards substance abuse (alcohol mainly, being so readily available); and a hundred thousand scattergun woes, the kind that puncture one's self-esteem and lead to ulcers, insomnia, chronic fatigue and depression.

One or two of the more reckless toys may have met with an untimely death, even a violent one. 'Tragic, of course,' said Mr Inkling, 'but,' shrugging his shoulders, 'that's life.'

His outlook is unremittingly grim, and because I choose not to contradict him I assume he assumes I feel the same way too. He always thinks the worst of everyone and frequently reminds me of the disparaging things that, so he says, I've said about the toys, Wally Oink in particular (my least favourite toy, I admit), but have, despite my superb retention of facts, figures, etc. which he acknowledges, simply forgotten.

If indeed I actually said those things.

He could well be making them up in a bid to destabilise me and make me feel anxious, unsure of what's real and what's not. I wouldn't put it past him.

HONEYMAN: It's called gaslighting.

TAYLOR: Well it's scary, whatever it's called. Did I really have a toy called Cunty? Surely not. Mother would have been appalled by that name and told me in no uncertain terms not to use it. And Nessa, three years older than me and with a memory almost as capacious and retentive as mine, says she has no recollection of my owning such a toy – a doll, no less, an impossibly slim, long-legged doll wearing high heels and clad in nothing but white lacy knickers and a wispy black negligee, who, in Mr Inkling's latest scenario, has become a high-class call girl with a neurotic Siamese cat by the name of Princess Yowl, undiagnosed HIV and an 'Imeldific'

Pertaining to
Imelda Marcos
purported owner of
2,000+ pairs of shoes
and other footwear
ranging widely in style from
flippers
to
brothel creepers
to
kitten heels
to
wellington boots
and grand patron of the
Marikina City Footwear Museum.
What she wears around the house are
million dollar
slippers
by Stuart Weitzman
made to look like
scuffed
canary yellow
heavy duty boots
the kind worn on building sites
and by road menders
and refuse collectors
thus demonstrating solidarity
with her fellow countrymen
the poor
rough-shod
hard-working Filipinos
of whom she once said

disingenuously or deludedly
'I am my little people's
star and slave'.

collection of Manolo Blahniks, Louis Vuittons and Jimmy Choos, none of which she finds comfortable to wear because of her bunions.

Surely I could never have had a toy called Cunty, it's impossible. Yet there she is, as solid a memory as Growl and the others. Perhaps more so, as I can't recall whether Growl was a tiger or a lion – a vagueness that irritated Mr Inkling no end.

Which, in turn, pleased me no end.

Revenge, however meagre, is sweet.

One day he asked me which of the toys had been my favourite. 'Stumper,' I replied, without hesitation. We were drunk again, of course; if not I would have held my tongue. 'I knew you'd say that,' he said, and reached into a bag that was tucked under his chair.

What he drew from it was something wholly unexpected. I couldn't believe my eyes. Stumper, in person. Not a new toy that looked a bit like Stumper, based on the series of detailed descriptions and numerous drawings to scale he'd made me do, but the original Stumper, the true Stumper, the Stumper of my distant childhood, who'd slept on my pillow by night and went everywhere with me by day, who was as much me as I was him.

As you can imagine I was stunned. Stumper was exactly as I remembered him, down to the tiniest detail. I'd been born with one leg slightly shorter than the other and had an operation to fix it while barely out of infancy. Afterwards I had to wear an adjustable leg brace for several months. Father fashioned a mini-version of it in leather and steel for Stumper to wear. He still had it on, although, like me, he no longer needed it. And the most astonishing thing was: I'm sure I hadn't said a word to Mr

Inkling about the brace. Nor had I included it in any of the drawings.

It was uncanny. How could he have known?

But all I could think of was Stumper ... *Stumper Stumper Stumper!* I never thought I'd see him again, though I dreamt of him often. Yet there he was, a bit smaller than the Stumper of yore; but I'm much bigger now than I was then, which would account for my skewed perception. I could feel fat tears starting to well in my eyes, though I managed to hold them back. I knew that if I broke down and wept, Mr Inkling's scorn would be monumental; he'd rip into me with gusto and tear me to shreds.

As I reached out for Stumper, to draw him to my breast, Mr Inkling snatched him away. 'Uh-uh,' he said. 'Not so fast, Charlie-boy. There's something we've got to do first. A little game. A role play. You'll enjoy it.'

That I doubted, but for the love of Stumper I knew I'd have to go along with whatever he said.

'Role reversal, to be precise. You'll be me and I'll be you. You okay with that?'

It wasn't really a question.

I nodded, wondering what this was all about. Whatever it was, it was bound to involve a degree of humiliation. He thrives on humiliating others, especially those of whom he's particularly fond.

HONEYMAN: He has a funny way of showing it. Fondness, I mean.

TAYLOR: It's one of his many quirks of character, most of which are unendearing.

~~~: So what happened during the role play?

TAYLOR: Mr Inkling stood Stumper on his knee, holding him firmly under the arms with both hands. 'Show me where he touched you,' he said.

'What?'

'Show me where he touched you. You're me, remember. Show me where he touched you. Show me now. On Stumper.'

I wasn't sure what was expected of me, so I gently touched Stumper's chest. 'No no no,' said Mr Inkling, irritably, 'that's where he *licked* you. All around the nipples. Smeared with honey and licked clean. Said it was a special bedtime treat. Try again.'

His eyes were hooded and his colour had risen. He looked feverish. When I didn't respond he said more forcefully, his voice steady, 'Try again, and get it right this time.'

I pointed a shaky finger at Stumper's groin. That's when I noticed he was rather more well-endowed than I seemed to recall. Was that really how he'd always been and I hadn't though anything of it? Apparently so. Stumper is as Stumper was, penis, testicles and all – anatomically correct, though his penis is disproportionately large for his body and permanently semi-tumescent. That's what, years later, in the toilet stalls at school, where penis comparisons weren't just unavoidable they were all but obligatory, we used to call a 'soft lob'.

Once upon a time I'd walked around holding Stumper by the penis and never thought to question why his widdler was so big or even why he was naked. Obviously he wore no clothes because he didn't need to; he was made of wool and the wool kept him warm. If sheep didn't need to wear clothes, why would Stumper? A child's mind is wonderfully accommodating and child logic can square the circle – something it needs to be able to do to make sense of those most irrational of beings, adults.

Mr Inkling let out a low moan and said, in a raspy voice, 'Tell me what he did.'

'But,' I said, 'I don't know what he did.'

'Yes, you do.'

'Really, I don't.'

'You do. No-one else knows what he did, *but you do!* Tell me about it. Now. In detail. Tell me *everything.*'

He was so insistent I knew I had no choice but to comply. What came out of my mouth surprised and appalled me. It was as though the words were being whispered in my ear by a malevolent spirit and all I was doing was repeating them. What I recounted was an explicit tale of child sexual abuse, pure filth, utterly degrading, the kind of thing that has stirred the loins of paedophiles since Adam and Eve began to beget and brought children into the world.

As I repeated what I was hearing, word for word, trying not to think about what those words meant, I noticed Mr Inkling's right hand glide surreptitiously into his fly and begin to squeeze and caress his genitals. Eyes closed to thin slits, brow knotted in concentration. He slumped a little lower in his chair. A sheen of sweat appeared on his forehead and top lip. Stumper was now sitting lopsidedly in his lap, loosely held. With the forefinger of his visible hand, Mr Inkling was gently stroking all around the glans of the woolly penis and sliding up and down the shaft. And unless my eyes deceived me, Stumper now had an erection, a full, throbbing erection.

This was so disturbing I tried to look away, but found I couldn't. Nor could I stem the flow of words, though they curdled on my tongue.

After what seemed like an eternity but was probably no more than ten hellish minutes, just as my story seemed to be reaching a truly appalling climax, Mr Inkling let out another low moan. His body stiffened and his eyes opened briefly, seeing nothing, then rolled back in his head.

He seemed, in the throes of orgasm, to have completely forgotten about Stumper. Sensing that this was a once in a lifetime opportunity, I snatched him up and ran for the door, which for once wasn't locked. Mr Inkling had become complacent. Perhaps he thought I had no fight left in me, that I was now his creature, slavish as a whipped dog.

Hearing the sound of footsteps running towards him, one of Mr Inkling's henchmen – a soft-spoken, well-mannered bruiser with the ramrod spine of an ex-guardsman and the unlikely name of Humphrey Rattlebone – stuck his head out into the corridor to see what was happening.

As I ran past, I stiff-armed his nose with the heel of my hand and felt the septum crunch and flatten. I sat down heavily, as though I'd run into a brick wall, and he staggered back into the room, tripped over a leather sofa and reverse-somersaulted to the floor. I'm ashamed to say I didn't stop to find out whether he was badly hurt. In fact, I didn't stop until I'd managed to lose myself among the throngs of rush hour commuters at Liverpool Street station, one homeward bound worker ant among many, distinguishable only because I was clutching a sexually aroused toy to my chest.

~~~: Are we to assume from this account that Mr Inkling was abused as a child?

HONEYMAN: It might explain the strong antipathy he felt towards Sir Rex. If there's another reason, I don't know of it.

TAYLOR: Nor me.

HONEYMAN: It might, of course, have nothing to do with Sir Rex. There's not a shred of evidence to suggest he was a paedophile.

TAYLOR: Nor that Mr Inkling is one – apart from the seamy episode I've just related.

HONEYMAN: Quite the conundrum, isn't it?

~~~: Perhaps we should seek advice from our foreman of the jury, Dr Anon, he of Dental and Oral Health Care Sciences, Paediatrics. He's sure to know a thing or two about

children and can perhaps shed some light on the subject.

HONEYMAN: One would imagine so, even if, throughout his long working life, he's done nothing more than peer into children's mouths and ignore everything else about them.

TAYLOR: Ah, but what he won't know about milk teeth and canker sores probably isn't worth knowing.

~~~: Let's ask him anyway.

STENOGRAPHER: Too late. He's dead.

~~~: *He's what?*

STENOGRAPHER: Dead. Died about fifteen minutes ago. He took a much deeper breath than usual, held it for a few moments, then let it out in a really long sigh. He slipped away between that breath and the next. I'd like to go like that, when I have to.

~~~: Why on earth didn't you say something?

STENOGRAPHER: I would have, at the first opportunity, which would probably have been during the coming recess. Interrupting the proceedings is strictly forbidden, as well you know. If one of you had said, 'Dearie me, Dr Anon seems to have stopped breathing,' the conscientious court stenographer's correct response – *my response*, in other words – would have been to record that statement, not act upon it. Acting upon it is someone else's job. Each to their own. *The Good Stenographer's Guide* is clear about such things, though thankfully courtroom deaths are rare. In fact, this is my first and I hope my last, even though it was a good death, not at all unpleasant. But that's by the by. Accurate record-taking is what I've been hired to do, and it's what I was doing when Dr Anon expired. Mr Taylor was getting a bit agitated at the time and yammering away twenty to the dozen. Keeping up with him was difficult. My fingers were tired and sore and I'd broken a nail.

Let me remind you: we haven't had a proper break for quite some time. Not that you care. As your behaviour throughout this trial has shown, you're oblivious to everyone's needs but your own. And even when you do notice you turn a blind eye unless it suits your purpose. But to get back to the main point: health and safety isn't my responsibility. It's not included in my job description and I've never been trained in even the most basic first aid procedures, have you?

~~~: Well, look ... Okay, now you mention it, no, I haven't. But it wasn't necessary. Suitable arrangements had been made. Mr Usher was hired to be our designated first-aider and fire officer for the duration of the trial. He was contracted to do a single twelve-hour shift, paid in advance at the unsocial hourly rate, double time, no quibble, rather than standard rate, even though I had every confidence that we'd be able to reach a verdict in less than ten hours. Same goes for you: double time, no quibble, paid in advance and in full. Most generous, don't you think?

STENOGRAPHER: [...]

~~~: I chose Mr Usher from among a handful of applicants specifically because he claimed to have had appropriate training in both fields. Expertise that none of the others could provide. As for the job of court usher ... well, as I said earlier, any fool can do it.

STENOGRAPHER: Your exact words were: 'You're a functionary, hired to do a few basic things at near-minimum wage, such as opening and closing doors. Things that, with a modicum of training, an ape could do just as well. Or better.'

~~~: Your point being ...?

STENOGRAPHER: The insulting tone. Comparing Mr Usher unfavourably with an ape. Even were he not black, that would still be unacceptable.

~~~: I can't say I'd noticed the colour of his skin.

STENOGRAPHER: Really? He could hardly be blacker if he tried.

~~~: That's as may be, but it's irrelevant. Some of my best friends are black.

STENOGRAPHER: Of course they are.

~~~: The Nubians, especially.

STENOGRAPHER: Nubians, eh? Martians would be just as likely.

~~~: Their skin is perhaps the blackest of all the dark-skinned races. Much blacker than Mr Usher's.

STENOGRAPHER: So you did notice his skin colour after all. Keep digging, Australia is barely a shovelful away.

~~~: I'm afraid you're the one digging a hole. Although the official language of South Sudan is English, I'm fluent in three of the country's indigenous languages: Dinka, Bari and Nuer.

STENOGRAPHER: What's that got to do with anything?

~~~: If you can bring yourself to stop interrupting, I'll tell you. Languages are a hobby of mine, an interest that, along with football, my flatmate and I share. While I wash and he dries and we stack the dishes away, we converse in Dinka. Actually, to be precise, we crack jokes in Dinka, about football. It's a household ritual. I also have a smattering of Zande, just enough to hold a basic conversation.

STENOGRAPHER: Good for you. But so what?

~~~: I'm a volunteer liaison officer at the Highgate branch of a Juban NGO that supplies bovine medicine to hard-pressed Sudanese cattle herders. In my spare time. Such as I have.

STENOGRAPHER: You really don't expect me to believe that, do you?

~~~: You should. I'm being serious. Liver fluke, worms, foot-rot, trypanosomiasis, east coast fever, brucellosis and foot and mouth disease are significant problems for the South Sudanese cattle herder. If his herd sickens and dies, the herder starves. Not just him, his family too. These are poor people with few resources and no reserves to speak

of, and years of inter-tribal conflict have made an already bad situation worse. One does what one can to help.

Perhaps that's a concept you don't quite understand.

Now ... if you've finished making a fool of yourself, let's press on. We were, as I recall, discussing Mr Usher's credentials. He presented what he said was a current Emergency First Aid at Work certificate from St John Ambulance at which, I admit, I barely glanced. But for good reason: I wouldn't have known whether it was authentic or not. It's the only certificate of its kind I'd seen, so I had nothing to compare it with. But I acknowledge that perhaps, just perhaps, I should have given his CV closer scrutiny, to winnow fact from fantasy and determine whether he was likely to be reliable and a good team player – which he wasn't.

STENOGRAPHER: So you didn't bother to take up the references he provided?

~~~: Why do you assume that? You've been hostile from the outset, seething away behind your stenograph machine. But to answer your question, though it doesn't really deserve an answer: I did, but his referees haven't replied. Nor have yours, for that matter. And because the trial was convened at such short notice there wasn't time to chase them up. Even though we gods can live for two hundred years, there are always one or two niggling things that remain undone when we find ourselves suddenly at death's door. Life's a messy business and an infinite source of regret.

STENOGRAPHER: Is that an admission of guilt?

~~~: Certainly not, I merely –

STENOGRAPHER: Oh no. No-no-no. Stop right there. I don't like the wheedling sound of that 'merely'. Before you start flicking through your rolodex of excuses to see which of them might best apply, let me outline the situation as I see it.

~~~: If you must, though it's a waste of the court's time.

STENOGRAPHER: I'll be the judge of that.

~~~: How droll. I wouldn't have thought you had it in you. Okay, go ahead ...

STENOGRAPHER: Don't try to stop me.

~~~: The brakes are off, you're freewheeling downhill.

STENOGRAPHER: So ... Dr Anon died because Mr Usher fled, having had what was almost certainly a panic attack, a health problem that, if you'd bothered to read his CV carefully, was listed under the heading: *Are you able to perform the essential job functions of the position you are applying for with or without reasonable accommodation(s).*

As there was no longer a first-aider on the premises once Mr Usher made his exit, the trial should have been halted and a suitable replacement sought. The rules about this are clear. And I quote: 'If a replacement first-aider cannot be found, the trial must' – note: must – 'be aborted and rescheduled, and the retrial should begin as soon as possible, at the same location, preferably during the next term of the legal year.'

As the senior court official, that's what you should have done but inexplicably failed to do. The responsibility for Dr Anon's death is therefore yours and yours alone. Wrongful death: an extremely serious breach of workplace law.

Once my union rep has lightly spiced up her report and submitted it to the Metropolitan Police, and the police have forwarded it to the CPS, and the CPS prosecutors have decided whether the case satisfies both parts of the Full Code Test and there's a realistic prospect of conviction – which, in my opinion, there is –

~~~: What a formidable legal mind you have. You're wasted as a stenographer. I'll ask Deputy Assistant Commissioner Starkey to put in a good word for you at the CPS.

STENOGRAPHER: – along with supplementary material such as

the transcript of this trial and the depositions of various
witnesses, including Messrs Honeyman and Taylor, and
probably Mr Blenkinsopp, all of whom you spent time
bullying and insulting, I wouldn't be at all surprised if the
charge got bumped up to gross negligence manslaughter.
And once it comes to court and the jury has heard how
you've behaved throughout these proceedings, by which I
mean appallingly –

~~~: What a truly horrible man I must be. It's a wonder I can
sleep at night.

STENOGRAPHER: – I really wouldn't like to be in your shoes.
You'll get three to five years if the judge – a proper judge,
not a pompous windbag wannabe like you – is in a good
mood, though judges rarely are. Nor would any of us be if
we had to hear what they hear on a daily basis. I'm lucky:
the evidence is in my head for almost no time at all, just
until I've put it on record, then it's gone, forgotten –

~~~: In one ear, out the other, and nothing but emptiness in
between, as they say.

STENOGRAPHER: But judges have to keep the whole thing
securely in mind until a verdict is reached, which can take
weeks. It has huge implications for their wellbeing, particularly their mental health. Same goes for the jury. The
difference being that judges have to undergo this gruelling process umpteen times a year, year upon year,
whereas most jurors do it just once in a lifetime. No wonder judges are so warped and crabby; theirs is one of the
most dangerous jobs in the world, on a par with contain-
ment and cleanup workers at Fukushima. I wouldn't wish
either job on anyone but my worst enemy, who, to save
you asking –

~~~: I wasn't going to.

HONEYMAN: Ahem. Forgive me for interrupting, but ... should-
n't we call the police and, I suppose, an ambulance, even
though Dr Anon is beyond medical help?

TAYLOR: It's probably the right thing to do.

STENOGRAPHER: And it's not as though the trial can proceed without a jury.

~~~: Why ever not?

STENOGRAPHER: Because … well, because no verdict can be reached without a jury to reach it. Surely that's obvious.

~~~: I take back what I said about your formidable legal mind. You're obviously the complete dunderhead I first took you to be. In case you hadn't noticed, Mr Inkling is unable to be here to defend himself. His unfitness to plead is incontrovertible. Since the incident on Balham High Road he'd been recuperating, or trying to, at a secret location, attended round the clock by a team of medics, care assistants and discreetly armed bodyguards (on the assumption that another attempt would be made on his life). But yesterday he took a turn for the worse and was readmitted to hospital.

HONEYMAN: How could you possibly know that? More of the voodoo that you do so well?

~~~: The letter delivered by the WPS woman, from Deputy Assistant Commissioner Starkey.

HONEYMAN: Ah. Of course.

~~~: He was writing to inform me that Mr Inkling is in a coma, wired up to a life-support machine and being treated for pneumonia and sepsis. The doctors say he probably won't last the night. But even if he does, his mental capacity will have shrunk to that of a four-year-old, mainly due to the cerebral hypoxia that occurred when the catering van assassins left him, bleeding copiously, for dead, but compounded by something that we have been made aware of by Mr $\Delta \approx \Delta\Delta\Delta°\diamond\geq$ but Deputy Assistant Commissioner Starkey and Mr Inkling's doctors haven't: his frequent, reckless use of the funfair labyrinth.

A criminal trial is therefore completely out of the question. All we can achieve is a trial of the facts. Strict legal guidelines dictate that in a trial of the facts we can bark but not bite, and were even a bite possible it would be toothless. The court can neither deliver a verdict nor hand down a sentence, all it can do is make a hospital order (superfluous, given the circumstances), a supervision order, or an order for the defendant's absolute discharge. Piffling stuff in which the role of the jury is so negligible it might as well not exist.

The fact that Dr Anon, our one-man jury, has actually ceased to exist is therefore, to be brutally frank, of no consequence. Except to his loved ones. If he has any. I say we leave him where he is while we wind up the proceedings. He won't be any deader in an hour than he is now. And we've only got an hour at most because Tiffany will want to get the caff ready for the breakfast crowd, and from what you've said, Mr Honeyman, there's quite a bit of tidying up to be done in the corridor before she and her staff arrive.

Stick that half-eaten croque in front of him, and a cold cup of coffee. The customers will assume he's a night-shift worker who's nodded off over breakfast. It happens all the time in London caffs and I suspect in the provinces too: night-shift workers napping over their breakfast, a small percentage of whom will turn out not to be napping but dead. Morbid fatties with a sedentary lifestyle are the most susceptible. They tend to eat almost nothing but fry-ups and have arteries like over-stuffed sausages. Dr Anon fits the profile to a T; I'm surprised he lived as long as he did. Tiffany will know how to get him off the premises without upsetting her other customers. She's so adept at corpse removal they won't even notice it happening.

HONEYMAN: A valuable skill to have in the catering trade, given what you've just said.

~~~: Indeed. Her father and two of her uncles are undertakers, so discretion runs in the family. They glide into rooms

and glide out unremarked, as if on well-oiled castors, carrying their burden of responsibility with them. Tiffany learned how to do that even before she'd reached puberty, though her slightness of build precluded heavy lifting. Not so now. Years of gym work and systematic steroid abuse have built her up to the Charlene Atlas she is today. Even someone as large and dead weight as Dr Anon won't pose much of a problem.

But enough of that. Let's get cracking!

Closing Session

~~~: Before I launch into my summing-up, heart in mouth, like a bobsleigher tackling the Cresta Run on a glorified tea-tray, or for added thrills an actual tea-tray, do you have anything further to contribute by way of evidence?

HONEYMAN: [...]

TAYLOR: [...]

~~~: Not even you, Miss Mouthy? Don't look so offended; mouthy is what you are. Your friends call you that behind your back, as well you know.

STENOGRAPHER: You're no friend of mine.

~~~: I'll take that as a no. Good. Because I warn you, once I get going you'll have less chance of stopping me than you would an earthquake. The lateness of the hour is against us, and the prospect of Mr Inkling dying before we've had a chance to weigh up all the evidence is worrying. Not that we really need to, but let's do it anyway, for the sake of thoroughness. Also, Tiffany could arrive at any moment. She likes to get an early start, on the steroids if nothing else.

Tiffany's 16-week drug regimen
prior to a show
as noted in her workout diary:

1-8: *D-Bulk*, 50mg every day

1-10: *Testosterone Enanthate*, 750mg a week

1-10: *IQ*, 800mg a week

1-10: *Truckulence* E, 600mg a week

8-16: Start taking *Impulsis T3* at 25mcg ED and increase as required

10-16: *Testosterone Propionate* EOD 100mg

10-16: *Ramcarb Acetate* EOD 100mg

10-16: *Mega-ME Propionate* EOD 100g

10-16: *Wintroll* or *Avuncular* ED 50mg [sometimes both]

12-16: *Halotestin*, start at 20mg ED and increase by 10mg every week.

N.B.

If rampant paranoia
unprovoked rage and
apocalyptic visions
find you crouched down
in a corner of the basement
with no knowledge of how you got there
in near-total darkness
hyperventilating
carving knife in hand
dripping with blood
[as has happened once or twice before]
don't take any chances, Tiff
cut back on the *Halotestin*.

So, all in all, we have no option but to race against time, McCreedy Byrne and PTR be damned.

HONEYMAN: Isn't that rather dangerous? I mean in terms of general disorientation and producing ... how did you describe it?

STENOGRAPHER: Wait a sec, it's in here somewhere. Needle in a ... Can't see the wood for the whatnot. Okay, I think I've ... Unless I'm mistaken, this is what you're after: 'eccentric or perverse verdicts'.

HONEYMAN: Thank you.

~~~: Didn't you hear what I said at the end of the previous session, Mr Honeyman? A trial of the facts won't, actually can't, reach a verdict, perverse or otherwise. And as for disorientation ...

HONEYMAN: What about it?

~~~: In an ideal world – which unfortunately this one isn't, not yet, we're working on it – that's how courtrooms are meant to be: disorientating. Or, more accurately, unsettling. The accused mustn't be allowed to get too comfortable, to relax fully, because that's when the most plausible lies are hatched. Same goes for the witnesses, liars to a man.

STENOGRAPHER: And woman.

~~~: You said it, sister. But you're right, of course: no-one in a court of law, man, woman or child, will ever tell the truth, the whole truth and nothing but the truth. Humankind is incapable of it. Civilization was built on a foundation of lies. Be that as it may, we should be proud of our achievements.

HONEYMAN: You're saying we lie all the time, but when we're feeling comfortable in any given situation –

~~~: Relaxed is a better way of putting it.

HONEYMAN: Okay, relaxed. So when we're relaxed, the lies we concoct are somehow more plausible, is that it?

~~~: And the more thoroughly relaxed we are, the more plausible and elaborate the lie.

HONEYMAN: That's an astonishing claim!

~~~: Moreover we lie to ourselves. Constantly. From the moment we learn to speak. Your claim to be astonished is a lie, though I suspect you'll deny it. You may not even be aware of it.

HONEYMAN: So there's no truth to be had in this world?

~~~: None whatsoever. Truth, by which I mean absolute truth rather than endless wayward riffs on it, is as elusive as the Loch Ness monster and the philosopher's stone. That's something you came close to acknowledging in one of our earlier sessions.

HONEYMAN: Did I?

~~~: If I may remind you …

HONEYMAN: Please do.

~~~: You said you were concerned about the information Mr Inkling provided about his adoptive father, Rex Cribbage – whether it was accurate and unbiased.

HONEYMAN: Well, yes. I said that. Something like that. But I don't recall the exact words.

STENOGRAPHER: Shall I?

~~~: No need, I have it verbatim: 'the simple truth is that truth is elusive and often, despite our best efforts, nowhere to be found.' Ring a bell?

HONEYMAN: That does sound vaguely familiar. But often is not, by any stretch of the imagination, absolute, now is it?

~~~: If you're determined to be a niggledy hair-splitter, Mr Honeyman, be a good fellow and split hairs elsewhere. Often is ninety-seven per cent absolute, perhaps ninety-eight, and although percentages can be rounded up or down as one sees fit, we optimists, the yayers, always round up. And don't try to tell me you're a nayer, I simply won't have it.

HONEYMAN: Well ...

~~~: Even that tiresomely self-obsessed and chronically weepy

Every article of clothing
in his wardrobe made
of blotting paper
the better to
to soak up the tears.

son of yours, Jasper, is surprisingly a yayer, an ecstatic one, born again, halleluiahing like crazy, especially now he knows he'll soon be entering the Witness Protection Scheme.

HONEYMAN: Oh no he won't!

~~~: I think you'll find –

HONEYMAN: He won't, because there's absolutely no need for it. Not if Mr Inkling dies. Which he will. And soon, according to what's been said. Certainly before the end of the night, which, if that faint halo round the chimneypots and along the ridge tiles is anything to go by, is now or nowabouts. Listen – can't you hear what's happening out there? You'd have to be stone deaf not to. A cacophony of birdsong. Dawn is breaking. It's time for the vampires to slink back to their soil-strewn coffins and for Mr Inkling to breathe his last, to everyone's relief. Even Jasper, a sensitive soul with an easily crumpled heart will, I'm sure, feel it's probably for the best.

~~~: Too late, unfortunately.

HONEYMAN: What's that supposed to mean?

~~~: You've signed the WPS documents. All of you. It's legally binding and there's no quit clause. I'm afraid, Mr Honeyman, you have no choice but to submit to the warm, protective embrace of the WPS. It's for your own good. And look on the bright side: with Mr Inkling dead your family's lives will no longer be in jeopardy. You won't have need of the invisibility screen or armed WPS officers. And if that isn't sufficient cause for celebration, here's the clincher: today's the day the WPS in-house focus group will meet to brainstorm a new name for you.

HONEYMAN: So soon?

~~~: By lunchtime at the latest. Their collective brain is massive and they don't hang about.

HONEYMAN: Will I get a say in the matter?

~~~: From what I gather, no. But new name allocations are dealt with sympathetically and sensibly. You won't, for example, be given a passport, driving licence, bank and credit cards, etc. in the name of Abdul al-Alhambra or suchlike, especially if you're to be relocated, however temporarily, to a house in England's post-industrial heartland (i.e. wasteland) on a sink estate inhabited solely by whey-faced chippy racists with a bank of recessive genes who'd view you with rabid hostility, skin colour notwithstanding. You'd be scraping excrement off the

welcome mat and phoning a glazier to replace brick-shattered windows on a daily basis, twice daily at weekends and on bank holidays when your tormentors would have more time to get together, drink themselves stupid and engage in random acts of mob violence.

Trust me, the focus group will choose something much more appropriate than that. It is, after all, their area of expertise.

HONEYMAN: But I already know what I want to be called.

~~~: That's as may be, but it's irrelevant.

HONEYMAN: I want to be called Gerald Musgrave.

~~~: Of course you do. I don't blame you. Although Honeyman is the perfect name for a minor '70s porn star – as you once were, despite protestations to the contrary – it's not much good for anything else. Also, you look to me more of a Gerald than a Paul. But why Musgrave?

HONEYMAN: It's a trustworthy name. You could get away with murder with a name like that. Butter wouldn't melt, etc. Better still, *if you wrote about true crime, the solving of*, and your name was Gerald Musgrave, most readers would find themselves agreeing wholeheartedly with your conclusions, however outlandish those conclusions might seem at first or even second glance.

For instance, do you want to know who Jack the Ripper was and why he did what he did? Of course you do! Well, Gerald Musgrave knows the A-Z, stem to stern, Heaven to Hell, of everything Ripperwise and Ripperish. He's a meticulous researcher of primary material, including the cache of important documents recently unearthed in, of all places, Bangalore, to which no other Ripper scholar has had access. Buy his new book – 'the most rigorous investigation ever conducted into the Ripper killings,' according to the understated, almost coy cover blurb – and he'll give you the works. Top Ripperologists say it's the definitive text, the one they and the general reader have long been waiting for, and according to one of the world's leading Ripper experts, Hiram Graves, writing in *Ripping Times: The International Journal of Ripperology*, 'Musgrave seems to have managed to do what no other Ripper scholar has done and no-one thought possible: convince everyone, even the most hardened sceptics, myself included, of the perpetrator's true identity'.

~~~: Everyone?

HONEYMAN: Yes, apart from the descendants of the person named. But they're stunned and in denial and who can blame them. Hundreds of hours on the therapist's couch will be needed to restore their lost equilibrium.

Even Patricia Cornwell has declared herself fully in agreement with Musgrave's startling conclusion and has arranged not just for her own Ripper books to be withdrawn and pulped but for purchasers worldwide to be reimbursed in full and paid a small fee in lieu of time lost to reading that could have been spent more productively on other things, such as catching up on one's zzzzzs or fluff-mining one's navel.

The descendants of Frederick George Abberline, Inspector First-Class of the London Metropolitan Police, who was sent from Scotland Yard to Whitechapel to coordinate the hunt for the killer, say it's time to uncork the champers and pour it down the drain – the bottle of Billecart-Salmon Brut Réserve 1890, passed down through five generations, father to son, and now a vinegary sludge, that Frederick purchased to celebrate the capture of the Ripper and never got to drink.

Also, the descendants, if any there are, of Mary Ann Nichols, Annie Chapman, Elizabeth Stride, Catherine Eddowes and Mary Jane Kelly, can finally put familial sleaze behind them and get on with their lives. Closure, in common parlance.

Take my word for it, Gerald Musgrave is the perfect name for a true crime writer. The top spot on the *New York Times* best seller list (non-fiction) would soon be his, from which it would take a literary titan with a case of dynamite to unseat him.

~~~: Is there such a man?

STENOGRAPHER: *Or woman!*

~~~: Ah yes. Deadlier than the male, according to Bulldog Drummond. A man's man, Drummond, if ever there was one, and perhaps a woman's man too. I really wouldn't know.

HONEYMAN: No-one likely to use a case of dynamite – certainly not a whole case in one fell Fawkesian swoop, not to my knowledge. Nor weaponry of any kind. And since the death of Norman Mailer, the pugilist writer has become, as a species, all but extinct, though the vicious left hook of Joyce Carol Oates has been noted by Mike Tyson and elicited murmurs of approval from the cornermen at her local gym. But she's an atomweight, if that, a mere slip of a girl; she'd never be allowed to enter the ring with a cruiserweight like Gerald Musgrave, not officially. Although, when the World Boxing Association's back is turned, as often it is, illegal fights take place, often bare knuckle, in Irish bars and English pubs the length and breadth of North America.

And the great John L Sullivan, the so-called Boston Strong Boy, speaking to Tyson from beyond the grave, said that in his opinion Oates was so nimble, quick and extraordinarily thin that in a certain light she'd be hard to see, never mind hit, and if Don King didn't have rocks for brains he'd sign her up in a flash.

World, take heed! – Sullivan, seven years a champ in gloves under Marquess of Queensberry rules and another seven as a bare-knuckle brawler, knows his alliums.

~~~: And did he?

HONEYMAN: Who?

~~~: King, of course.

HONEYMAN: What about him?

~~~: Sign her up.

HONEYMAN: She demurred. Said she was too busy with her writing – two or three books on the go, two more recently published that she needed to promote.

But look, this is pure speculation; none of it has happened, nor is it likely to, unless the focus group can be persuaded to let me become the man I really ought to be – Gerald Musgrave.

~~~: Which may well come to pass. The odds appear to be heavily stacked against it, but stranger things have happened. Is there something you wish to add, Mr Δ≈ΔΔΔ°◇≥?

TAYLOR: Only that in February 1918, when Sullivan was due to be buried, the ground was frozen so hard that dynamite had to be used to blast out a grave.

HONEYMAN: Is that a fact?

TAYLOR: A fact, though perhaps not entirely true.

HONEYMAN: The difference being?

TAYLOR: If a fact is repeated often enough over many decades by a great many people, especially so-called authority figures, historians and the like, it becomes true by default.

~~~: Which brings me back to what I was saying a few moments ago. Truth doesn't exist except as an unattainable ideal.

HONEYMAN: Yet facts do.

~~~: Well, facts are facts, aren't they? – impossible to deny, unreliable though they are. As we've nothing better to go on, they'll just have to do. So ... let me sum up the facts about Mr Inkling that have been revealed to this court.

STENOGRAPHER: And not before time.

~~~: Dial it down, Miss Stenographer. Better still, turn it off. Your sotto voce comments are like the trumpetings of a distraught elephant, a cow whose calf is stuck fast in a trap.

STENOGRAPHER: [...]

⊖

~~~: James Julius Inkling, known to all and sundry in the overlapping worlds of business and light entertainment as
Jimmy Inkling, and within the upper echelons of crime
syndicates on five of the seven continents as Jimmy Jewels, is, so we've been told, reliably I hope, at death's door.
The door itself is unexceptional, of a kind sold in major
DIY outlets at the budget end of the market: white PVCu,
cottage style, a small pane of privacy glass at, if you're of
average height, eye level.

By the door, waiting to gain entry, stands a queue of
corpses. Or not-quite corpses. No-one knows whether
they're dead enough to qualify as such, though the outcome
isn't in doubt. Shoulders slumped, head down, they wait in
single file. No-one speaks or even so much as glances at his
neighbour. They look as miserable as sin, which, given the
circumstances, is only to be expected. Even the laughing
policeman would find little to chuckle about.

During rush hour, when there's a huge spike in road
fatalities, the queue snakes all the way down the garden
path and onto the pavement.

When planes crash and trains wreck, the queue gets
longer still.

HONEYMAN: PVCu – you're sure about that? No pearly gates?

~~~: Apparently not. I can only tell you what I've been told.

HONEYMAN: None of the fabled appurtenances of orthodox
Christianity?

~~~: Neither Christianity nor any other religion, however
obscure.

This, according to my informant, is what happens:

A face appears at the door's rectangular window, a
smudge of a face that only the walking corpse at the head
of the queue can make out.

HONEYMAN: Saint Peter?

~~~: Extremely unlikely, don't you think, given what I've just said. Please pay attention, Mr Honeyman.

The doorman wears a grubby boiler suit, goose-shit-green in colour. That's the most distinctive thing about him. His facial features are so vague that no accurate description is possible. He admits one person at a time then quickly shuts the door, presumably to prevent the rest of the queue from discovering what awaits them. Whereupon the queue shuffles forward, filling the space the previous corpse occupied.

Sometimes, to compound the misery, a hard rain falls, ice-cold regardless of the season. No-one has an umbrella to shelter under, not even those who were carrying one when they were struck by lightning, the metal ribcage of the umbrella having drawn the lightning bolt away from a nearby stand of trees. Bad luck, eh? Or to put it another way, lucky trees.

TAYLOR: Are you sure about this? I can't imagine Mr Inkling tolerating conditions such as those you've described.

~~~: It's not a matter of choice, Mr Δ≈ΔΔΔ°◇≥.

TAYLOR: I mean, he never queues for anything. Hasn't done so for decades. Especially not in the rain, getting soaked to the skin, while waiting to use the tradesmen's entrance – which this unassuming portal obviously is. There's no way he would allow himself to be treated so shabbily. Trust me, I know what I'm on about. He'd elbow his way to the front of the queue, pound on the little window with his fist until the doorman appeared, then demand to know the whereabouts of the grand entrance, the one with the marble columns and extra-wide double-height doors, one of which a commission-aire in top hat, white gloves and crimson three-quarter-length jacket with black velvet collar, the jacket adorned with more swags of gold braid than an admiral of the fleet, will open in timely fashion, saying 'Good evening,

Mr Inkling, sir' in a deferential tone of voice, 'how nice to see you again,' touching a forefinger lightly to the brim of his hat.

If I know Jimmy as well as I think I do, he'll have impossibly high expectations of privilege and luxury in death, no different from the expectations he had when he was alive.

~~~: Never backward at going forward is Jimmy Inkling. One has to admire his chutzpah.

HONEYMAN: No! One does not! It's a typically vulgar display of his misguided and, what's the word? – unwarranted. Yes, his unwarranted sense of superiority and entitlement.

TAYLOR: But in his defence, he's a big tipper. And by big I mean huge. Doormen's faces light up when they see Jimmy coming. Same goes for concierges and porters, parking valets, receptionists, bell hops and lift attendants. Someone even wrote a novelty song about it,

That someone
according to Srinivasa Ramanujan
[or someone claiming to speak for him]
is Mr Inkling
himself
though the lyrics are credited
to a certain
Coalhouse Porter
[aka Kevin Pevsner]
a former employee of Mr Inkling
and by all accounts
a passable Sinatra clone
often to be found singing
'The Lady is a Tramp'
at minor celebrity weddings
and on ships
cruising the Caribbean
and whose voice and junkie
veins will wear out
long before
the rest of him.

which has, as its refrain, 'Tips, tips, tips all round/Mr Inkling's come to town,' to the tune of a Christmas jingle.

Maitre-d's and waiters, too, receive his largesse, but only if the service they provide meets with his approval. That doesn't happen very often, especially when it comes to waiters. No matter how hard they try, waiters always seem to get one or two things badly wrong.

HONEYMAN: That's because nearly all of them are actors, silently rehearsing their lines, going over them again and again until the words lose all meaning and they start to feel dizzy and disorientated. They just can't help themselves. And while all this is going on they're taking, somewhat distractedly, the customer's order and trying to mask their inner turmoil. No wonder they make mistakes. — That's what Arkady says, and I'm inclined to take his word for it. Having spent some thirty years in the hospitality industry he knows its myriad pressure points and weaknesses. One of the key policies at our St Peter Port restaurant will be never to hire an actor to wait tables.

STENOGRAPHER: What about equal opportunities?

HONEYMAN: No actor, however good, can equal a good waiter, not even one whose mantelpiece is groaning with Oscars. Have you ever seen actors trying to act the part of waiters? Lamentable. Waiters find actors playing waiters unconvincing, woefully so. Even waiters who actually are actors, or claim they are, find them laughably bad.

STENOGRAPHER: That's not what I meant. The Equality Act 2010 prohibits discrimination in employment on the grounds of —

HONEYMAN: Even the likes of Meryl Streep would fail, despite her vitamin-enriched brand of thespianism and her three, so far, Oscars.

TAYLOR: Hang on ... unless I'm mistaken, and I'm pretty sure I'm not, didn't she do some waitressing at a hotel in her home town, Bernardsville, NJ, during the early 1970s, and perhaps more of the same while studying at Yale, prior to getting her big break?

~~~: I think perhaps we should –

HONEYMAN: But one has to ask: how good was she at waiting tables? It's telling that she has, to my knowledge, never been offered a role as a waitress, either in film or on the boards, despite her much-touted experience in catering and customer service.

TAYLOR: Perhaps she failed the auditions, unlikely though that sounds. But it's been said – admittedly by Miss Streep herself, and never corroborated – that she could work eight tables at a time, and that she never jotted down a single order, she committed it all to memory.

HONEYMAN: Utter tosh! The kitchen needs to know what to cook, and the cashier has to prepare the bill. An order ticket is required, a slip, a chit, some kind of written record. If Miss Streep did what you said she did she'd be a total liability. — But it might explain why she threw herself wholeheartedly into acting rather than try to forge a career in hotel management, the goal aspired to by most waitresses who aren't aspiring actresses, though very few succeed in either discipline.

TAYLOR: Okay, but –

~~~: Gentlemen, stop right there. We're veering off topic and time is running out. That goes for you, too, Miss Stenographer. I can see you're dying to stick your oar in where it's not wanted.

STENOGRAPHER: Can I just say –

~~~: No, you can't.

STENOGRAPHER: – that –

~~~: No-no-no. No means no. No. Absolutely not.

STENOGRAPHER: But I just –

~~~: I don't care. No-one does, so don't waste your breath. If you so much as mouth another syllable, I swear by the once boiling caldera under Arthur's Seat –

STENOGRAPHER: It's entirely relevant, so I won't shut up. Perhaps you should do the honours. We've heard more from you than all the witnesses put together and nearly everything you've said has been unhelpful, antagonistic or just plain stupid. Frankly I've had just about enough of it.

What you need to know, whether you like it or not, is that while Miss Streep was memorising the orders for each of the tables in her section, she was making quick character sketches of the customers on her order pad. At home she copied the drawings into A4 or A3 sketch books and worked them up for hours on end, late into the night, adding lots of fine detail. Apparently there are hundreds of them.

~~~: Sketch books?

STENOGRAPHER: Don't be silly. If she filled hundreds of sketch books there'd be thousands of drawings. Many thousands. No waitress at however busy a restaurant could handle that many customers in a single summer season, not even if she was servicing eight tables per shift, seven days a week, and probably, as waitresses are obliged to do from time to time, filling in for another waitress, someone unreliable who the boss, a typical man, had kept on the payroll for, well, extra-marital reasons. It happens.

~~~: How do you know all this?

STENOGRAPHER: Pipe down and I'll tell you.

~~~: How dare you speak to me like that!

STENOGRAPHER: Shush. Close your mouth. Breathe through your nose.

~~~: [...]

STENOGRAPHER: Ah, silence. How lovely. And you flare your nostrils just like a horse. I don't think I've seen anyone do that before, not even an equestrian.

HONEYMAN: It's because he's a god – so he says.

STENOGRAPHER: Delusions of grandeur, on top of all his other mental health problems. A Napoleon complex, also known as shortarse syndrome.

~~~: Mark my words, Miss Stenographer, the minute this trial is over I'll be contacting the British Institute of Verbatim Reporters and lodging a strongly worded complaint. Your breaches of protocol have been inexcusable. Not to mention the insolence.

STENOGRAPHER: Suit yourself, it's no skin off my nose. I'm sure they'll recognise your complaint for what it is: frivolous and vexatious. Much like you. Vexatious, in particular. But let's press on, since we're all keen to get this ordeal over with as quickly as possible. — The sketch books —

~~~: I still don't see the relevance, assuming there is any.

STENOGRAPHER: — had been placed in storage and all but forgotten while Miss Streep concentrated on her acting career. Her husband, the sculptor Don Gummer, discovered them in 2014 and was wowed. Justifiably wowed. My friend Esmeralda says Streep's drawings are almost as good as Raphael's; perhaps even better in certain respects. And she should know, she has a top honours degree in art history and works in the shop at the National Portrait Gallery.

Six months ago, one of her snooty curator colleagues told her, and inadvertently me, because I happened to be standing right behind her, the curator, pulling faces to try to make Esme laugh — she has such a mad laugh, like a kookaburra — that plans to mount a blockbuster show of Streep's QUOTE utterly swoonworthy drawings UNQUOTE were well underway. The gallery's publicity machine was, she said, gearing up to send the news worldwide.

HONEYMAN: Really? I'm on the gallery's mailing list and I've heard nothing about a Streep exhibition.

STENOGRAPHER: It's been delayed. Deadline slippage. All too common in the art world. Everything has to be finessed to everyone's satisfaction, and that includes lawyers, who never seem to be satisfied, not even with the colossal fees they rack up by the hour.

She also said the drawings are, in the main, of British diners, including quite a few famous faces, more than you'd expect given that Bernardsville is, apparently, a deathly dull upper-middle-income backwater.

That's what Esme was told by her curator colleague, who spent a fortnight in the town doing Streep-related research. More of a junket, really. All she discovered was the reason why Streep drew a high percentage of Brits: because, according to one of Streep's fellow waitresses (now a hotel manager but also the local am-dram queen), she was fascinated by their characterful and sometimes incomprehensible accents.

~~~: No surprise there, then.

STENOGRAPHER: And among their number was a drawing of ... go on, guess who ...

HONEYMAN: [...]

~~~: [...]

TAYLOR: [...]

STENOGRAPHER: Surely you can hazard a guess.

HONEYMAN: Okay, though I can't see what purpose this serves. Early '70s, you say? Hmm.

> Julie Andrews?
> Stirling Moss?
> Princess Margaret?
> George Best?
> Engelbert Humperdinck?
> Les Kellett?
> Tommy Cooper?
> Quentin Crisp?

You have quite the poker face, Miss Stenographer. If I chance upon the name of the person you're thinking of, please say so, otherwise I'd never know.

> Freddie Laker?
> Joyce Grenfell?
> Arthur Scargill?

Mary Whitehouse?

Joseph Kagan?

Basil Brush?

Maggie Smith?

Beryl Bainbridge?

Henry Cooper?

Any of the aforementioned or anyone associated with them? A hint or a clue would be most welcome.

Germaine Greer? – no, scratch that, she's an Aussie.

Bertrand Russell, perhaps? – no, he was dead by then.

Muriel Spark?

Bob Monkhouse?

Shirley Williams?

I can't think of anyone else. My mind's a blank.

TAYLOR: How about the man who was Private Widdle: Charles Hawtrey?

STENOGRAPHER: Clunkers galore. I should have guessed that would be the case. Let me put you out of your misery. Mr Inkling, that's who. Yes, Mr Inkling. So now you see why I'm telling you this. It had been thought that his first trip Stateside wasn't undertaken until 2012 when he was briefly a spokesperson for ... Oxfam, wasn't it? As mentioned by Mr Honeyman.

HONEYMAN: Uh-uh, not me. Dr Anon.

~~~: And UNICEF.

STENOGRAPHER: No matter. There he was – Mr Inkling, I mean – dining in the company of three hatchet-faced American gentlemen of Italian descent

Representatives
of the Gambino
Genovese and Profaci families
according to the FBI.

and all Miss Streep could recall of their conversation was that it was conducted in urgent, often aggressive whispers, more hisses than whispers at times, accompanied by lots of finger-jabbing and table-slapping, and it appeared to be entirely about waste management.

She said they seemed extremely tense, checking the door and glancing at a table to one side of them, at which three heavyset men with slicked-back hair sat bolt upright, looking even more tense, each of them glowering at their tablemates and saying nothing.

Apparently, in the foreword to the exhibition catalogue, Miss Streep relates how each of the men at the second table kept a hand half in, half out of his inside jacket pocket, as though suffering from heartburn and reaching for a pack of antacid. That might also explain why they ordered three espressos but didn't actually drink them, though they left a sizeable tip.

She drew the men at both tables, but discreetly, from behind her workstation, as it was obvious that what they wanted was to be left well alone.

Esme reckons that, when the show opens, the Inkling drawing will capture the imagination of pundits and public alike. Having seen a photocopy of it, I'm inclined to agree. It has a brooding quality and a weirdly sinister vibe. Very atmospheric. Highly dramatic. More Rembrandt than Raphael. She says the poster is bound to top the shop's best seller list. 'It'll knock the recent one of Kate Middleton, which makes her look older than she actually is and a bit waxworky, into second place. You wait and see.'

~~~: I'm sure we will. But in the meantime we have to draw these proceedings to a close, and soon, otherwise all the work we've done during this long, wearisome night will come to naught.

HONEYMAN: Aw, who cares. Let's toddle off home and forget all about it.

~~~: Toddle? *Toddle?* Are my hearing aids malfunctioning or has someone put something in the water?

HONEYMAN: *Someone's put something in the water?*

~~~: That's not what I said.

HONEYMAN: No, but come to think of it, it's entirely plausible. More likely than not, in fact. Mr Inkling has a history of doing such things – slipping a mickey into your drink while you're in the gent's.

~~~: You've misconstrued what I said.

HONEYMAN: After all, he was an enthusiastic early adopter of LSD-25. And the break-in at Powick Hospital's short-lived LSD Unit, in which the pharmacy was stripped of all its supplies of the drug – the largest quantity stored in any one place in the UK, larger even than the stock held at Porton Down – was rumoured to be the handiwork of Inkling's criminal associates.

TAYLOR: When was that?

HONEYMAN: Mid-'60s. Nineteen-sixty-four, I think. According to a leaked memo from MI5 to the recently elected PM, Harold Wilson, the drug was unlikely to end up being sold in the usual dens of iniquity, nightclubs and the like. The use to which it would probably be put was far more sinister: mass medication. Like they do with fluoride nowadays.

TAYLOR: Now I remember … the Queen Mary Reservoir story.

~~~: What on earth are you two on about?

HONEYMAN: The theory, mooted in, I think, *London Life*, a year or two after the theft, that the reservoir in question, near Shepperton – or some other reservoir in England, perhaps the one supplying Birmingham – could quite easily be spiked with LSD by terrorists, activists, pranksters or social scientists from one of the more left-leaning polytechnics (as nearly all of them were in those days). Or perhaps the KGB. Anyway, a group, cell, agency or individual intent, for reasons nefarious, or perhaps just out of idle curiosity, on dosing the tap-water-drinking inhabitants of Surrey or Birmingham with a powerful hallucinogenic drug.

TAYLOR: It wouldn't work, of course.

~~~: No?

TAYLOR: Chlorine renders the drug psychoactively inert. Not only that, because the Shepperton reservoir is so huge, the quantity of LSD needed to effectively dose everyone in Surrey would have to be astronomically large. At the mid-'60s rate of production it would take something like two hundred years to make enough of it, even if Sandoz ramped up production to the exclusion of all other product lines. On top of which, LSD doesn't dilute easily.

~~~: But you're saying Mr Inkling uses it.

TAYLOR: Not personally. Not any more.

~~~: On other people, I mean.

TAYLOR: Strictly small-scale. One, two or a few individuals at a time. No more than a handful. Introducing it to his victims via, for example, the filtration system that upmarket caffs such as this one have.

~~~: Well, competition among caffs in this part of London is fierce, and coffee enthusiasts have become spoiled for choice in the last decade or so. Tiffany tells me that filtered water with a guaranteed neutral pH of 7 gives her caff a slight edge over her competitors – four others in this street alone, one artisanal, the other three chain caffs of lower aspiration and quality. But needs must. Whatever brings the customers in and keeps them coming.

There is, so I've heard, a café in Dalston, next door to a church, that uses nothing but holy water in its beverages. Congregationalists flock to it after Mass, despite the fulminations of the priest. They've even been known to sneak a holy water espresso into the confessional booth, to steady their nerves while confessing to a variety of sins, often of a sexual nature. Talking filth to a priest gets some people hot under the collar and some priests enjoy it perhaps more than they should.

TAYLOR: And it's not hard to achieve – spiking a caff's water supply, I mean – once you've gained access to the premises. Wasn't there a technician working on the filtration system yesterday afternoon, completely unsupervised, while the witnesses, myself and Mr Honeyman included, were in the storeroom, naked, answering irrelevant, impertinent and intimate questions while wired up to a polygraph machine? Why we were obliged to do that, I have no idea.

HONEYMAN: Presumably to keep us on edge, as uncomfortable as possible, so we wouldn't be able to hatch plausible lies. Am I right, Mr Squiggle?

~~~: Bingo! But don't call me Squiggle.

HONEYMAN: So the whole thing was a set-up, a squalid *pièce de théâtre?*

~~~: There wasn't any film in the camera, if that's what you mean – not that anyone uses film any more, it's all digital nowadays. And the so-called polygraph machine was a prop borrowed from Pinewood Studios. Actors courtesy of the Tower Bridge Players. Amateurs they may be, but they were very convincing, weren't they? During their staged argument I thought the cameraman *actually would* hit the director rather than just threaten to, as indicated in the script. But the bad blood between them is always in danger of boiling over. Apparently, someone slept with someone else's boyfriend. Ugly.

TAYLOR: But this technician ... It would've been relatively easy for him –

STENOGRAPHER: Her.

TAYLOR: Yes, very observant of you, Miss Stenographer, her, but a rather androgynous her ... to have contaminated the post-filter feed without anyone noticing. And she could just as easily have spiked the water cooler in the staff room.

~~~: So if the witnesses drank coffee, etc. – which they did, at the end of our first session – that had been spiked with LSD –

TAYLOR: Ah, but bear in mind that it isn't just chlorine that renders the drug psychoactively inert. Coffee and tea do that too.

HONEYMAN: Okay. But we've all been drinking water, haven't we? Lots of it. Criminal trials, like glass blowing and deep pit coal mining, are incredibly thirsty work.

~~~: Are you suggesting, Mr $\Delta \approx \Delta\Delta\Delta°\diamond\geq$, that some of the evidence we've heard could be unreliable?

TAYLOR: Most if not all of it, I'd say. Easily overturned on appeal.

HONEYMAN: And do dead men usually mount appeals?

TAYLOR: If anyone could, Jimmy would. I'm sure his legal team has been prepped for just such an eventuality.

~~~: Look ... hang on. Surely you can't be serious about this water contamination malarkey. The water-filtration technician probably, in fact almost certainly, wasn't one of Mr Inkling's operatives, and lacing the caff's water supply with LSD is no more likely to have happened than Mr Inkling coming here several weeks or months ago to place chewing gum over the peephole in that door over there. Even less likely. How could Mr Inkling possibly have known we'd be convening a trial of the facts on a specific day at this precise location? We've heard screeds of evidence directly linking him to a significant number of major crimes, including the most heinous crime of all, murder, but now you're saying that the evidence we've heard cannot be relied upon because we've all been hallucinating without realising it? Surely not.

TAYLOR: Unfortunately, yes, though the drug in question may not be LSD and we may not be hallucinating. Who's to say? Mr Inkling's pharmacological knowledge and interests are extensive. But even the outside possibility of it having happened casts a pall over these proceedings.

HONEYMAN: Ah well. Easy come easy go.

~~~: Mr Honeyman! That comment is ... I don't know what to

say. You've floored me. Shocked me to the core. And to think I thought I was the unshockable type, calm under fire, cool as a refrigerator. It's outrageous. You've jarred my sensibilities, rattled my brain like a walnut loose in its shell, whipped the rug out from under my feet and sold it to a passing gypsy for a wilted sprig of heather. How can you be so blasé about something so important? *Of the utmost importance!* Murder should never be treated lightly or dismissed out of hand. Nor should manslaughter. Nor accidental death through negligence, such as that of the cleaner in the so-called funfair labyrinth. And what about the unexplained disappearances of a goodly number of Mr Inkling's employees, enemies and, occasionally, friends? Such friends as he has. Had, I mean. What about the unfortunates whose senses have been deranged, perhaps permanently, their wits scattered like puffball spores to the four winds? Should we just shrug our shoulders and go our merry way, skipping along and smelling the roses as though nothing untoward has happened? Mr Inkling is, by anyone's standard, and as Dr Anon described him, a fiend. We owe it not just to his victims but to society itself to ensure that justice is done, even if, in the absence of both a verdict and a sentence, all we can administer is –

HONEYMAN: Yes, yes. Don't run through all that again. We know ... A heartfelt sigh and a tut of disapproval. Piddling stuff. We're not even allowed to give him a thorough ticking off, never mind a slap on the wrist. Instead it's, 'Oh, Jimmy, you naughty, naughty boy, what have you done now! *Murder?*' Cue excessive handwringing. 'That's *really* not nice. Please don't do it again.'

And, of course, from now on he won't, because soon he'll be dead, bringing his reign of terror to an end, and with it your bullying. You ought to be ashamed of yourself, dishing out insults willy-nilly, making threats, and for what? Nothing. Because of your incompetence this trial has been a complete waste of time. Is that a fair evaluation, Mr Taylor?

TAYLOR: Ah. Yes. Well now. I probably wouldn't put it in quite those terms. But occasionally one has to speak truth to power, no matter how uncomfortable it makes one feel. So ... I'm bound to say that unhappily, reluctantly, I, umm, agree. Broadly speaking. I mean, if you think about it for a moment, things haven't gone terribly well, have they? I hope, Mr ~~~, as a fellow god and friend, not a close friend but, you know, birds of a feather and all that, I hope you'll take my criticism squarely on the chin.

HONEYMAN: What's the betting he's got a glass jaw, eh? Joyce Carol Oates would have him flat on the canvas and counted out within the first ten seconds of the opening round, artful slugger that she is.

TAYLOR: I'll take your word for it. I've never encountered Miss Oates, either on the page or in the flesh, though perhaps in the latter instance I wouldn't have noticed, not if she's as slight as John L Sullivan says. So I can't really say how good a pugilist she is. What I can say, Mr ~~~, is that as a judge you soon found yourself a long way out of your depth, didn't you? Caught in a rip tide. Drowning, not waving. In fact, the trial has been, well ... the gloves are off and I don't think there's any way to soften the blow –

HONEYMAN: Nor should there be! Hit him where it hurts! Give him the old one-two-smackeroo, right in the kisser!

TAYLOR: – a total disaster from start to finish. Absolutely total.

HONEYMAN: He's staggering. Weak at the knees. The fight's gone out of him, you can see it in his eyes. Yes, down he goes: timberrrrr!

~~~: But ... but we're not finished.

HONEYMAN: We: no. You: yes. I'd advise you to step down with as much dignity as you can muster and walk away with head held high, eyes moist and upper lip atremble under that ridiculously prissy waxed moustache you're wearing.

More
Hercule Poirot
than
Salvador Dali.
A glue job
lest appearances
deceive.
Courtesy
of the
Tower Bridge Players
costume
department.

You tried, you failed. Suck it up. We've all crashed and burned at one time or other. The road to Hell is, as the cliché-mongers say, paved with good intentions. Or in Jimmy Inkling's case, gold. But let's try to salvage what we can from this debacle. If we can persuade Miss Stenographer to do the summing up, I'm sure she'll supply in spades the gravitas you sorely lack. She seems to have her head screwed on tight and the facts, such as they are, at her fingertips. Stand down, Mr Squiggle, no-one will think any the worse of you for doing so, that's impossible. But if you try to cling on, let me be clear: I'll stamp on your fingers until they're bloodied pulp, don't think I won't.

~~~: Mr Δ≈ΔΔΔ°◇≥ ...?

TAYLOR: I'm afraid Mr Honeyman is right. It's probably for the best, under the circumstances.

HONEYMAN: So, Miss Stenographer, would you be willing to step up to the crease? By which I don't mean to imply that you're a cricketer with a high batting average in the lesbian league.

Almost as many notches
carved into
the handle
of a bat
as on the bedpost.

~~~: Lesbian league? What's that all about?

HONEYMAN: Typical. Just typical. That you need to ask such a question perfectly illustrates how out of touch you are with contemporary idioms and social mores, and therefore how unfit you are to sit in judgment of anything more challenging than a rock-paper-scissors competition.

For your information, the term 'lesbian league' is how women's cricket is referred to in private and occasionally, unguardedly, in public by politically incorrect sports commentators, as well as in the Long Room Bar at Lord's. The bar's habitués – not all of them, by any means, but a significant number thereof, and men, needless to say, especially those from a public school background of fagging, crumpets and hot buttered buggery – assume that most female cricketers, especially the less giggly, less girly ones who sport no-nonsense hairstyles and occasionally wear trousers and sensible shoes, are lesbians, and those who aren't pretend they are, to fit in.

Of course, that may not always be the case. Not in your case, anyway, Miss Stenographer, though I'm aware that things as they are are rarely what they seem. The world is full of surprises, many of which are unpleasant. I hope you're not one of them.

TAYLOR: Are you sure you've got the right sport, Mr Honeyman? Don't you mean hockey?

HONEYMAN: Same difference, as Mr Squiggle said a while back, about something else, I've forgotten what – and, to be frank, it doesn't really matter. To quote from one of the great stars of the Grand Ole Opry, a performer whose name is on the tip of my tongue and likely to remain there until no longer needed: Got my wires badly crossed/but that ol' appliance keeps a-hummin'.

STENOGRAPHER: [...]

TAYLOR: [...]

HONEYMAN: Not country and western fans? Songs around the campfire after a hard day's wrangling? I thought everyone liked that kind of thing. How about you, Mr Squiggle? Well, I'll be ... where's the old fool gone? Not hiding under a table or behind the counter, is he? *Paging Mr Squiggle! Where are you, Mr Squiggle? Reveal yourself or I'll set the bloodhounds on you. And by bloodhounds I mean dobermans, huge dogs with great slavering jaws and teeth like six-inch nails. Can you hear me, Mr Squiggle? Dobermans. Man-eaters. Judges their favourite food, especially discredited ones. Come out, come out wherever you are!*

TAYLOR: You'll have to shout a bit louder than that. He's in the kitchen, sulking. Actually, he may have left the building; I though I heard the alley door slam.

HONEYMAN: Left? That's much too passive a verb. Flounce is more like it, snake-eyed quitter that he is. Flouncing out – that's his style. A busted flush. A poltroon of the first order. Whatever his mode of exit, he's left us in the lurch.

TAYLOR: But isn't that a good thing? Him standing down, I mean. As he's ... what's the phrase? ... manifestly unfit to perform the duties of his office.

HONEYMAN: That's really not the point. There's such a thing as integrity, and, as we city cowpokes say in our typically urbane way, he plumb don't got none, do he?

⊖

STENOGRAPHER: Okay. To bring down the curtain on this wretched affair, and for personal reasons, I'll do as you suggest. So ... James Julius Inkling is at death's door.

Good. On that point at least we're all agreed. Let's hope he crosses the threshold without a murmur or a backward glance because if, God forbid, he rallies and discovers that this trial has taken place, we'll have to join the Honeymans in the Witness Protection Scheme. That or wash down a lifetime supply of paracetamol with a bottle of scotch. And if that isn't your tipple of choice for a self-annihilation party, take a peek in the storeroom. There, in one of the floor cupboards, behind multipacks of dispenser serviettes, you'll find gin, half a case of wine and a magnum of champagne. Unless, of course, the theatre group playing the part of a camera crew stole them, which they probably did, given that they were on day release from HMP Wandsworth under the lax supervision of their drama teacher

Once a jobbing actor
but
despite aspirations
pretentions and
ego aplenty
no Lear or Hamlet he.
Nowhere near.
Zero gravitas
that's why.
He's best remembered
among those in the know
for playing a talking mushroom
on children's television
constantly fluffing his lines
and tripping over things
[including things that weren't there]
occasioning gales of laughter
among the under-fives
and head-in-hands groans
from his peers.

who, come to think of it, was reeling around for most of

the afternoon, drunk as a skunk and twice as whiffy. Substantially increased rates of rehabilitation through the performing arts? Don't make me laugh. They'd've had the gold teeth out of your head if they thought they could get away with it.

TAYLOR: How did you know that? I mean, about the Tower Bridge Players being prisoners on day release.

STENOGRAPHER: Mr ~~~ forewarned us. Me and Mr Usher, that is. Told us to keep our valuables close at hand and don't tell anyone. Said he'd dock our wages if we gave the game away. Not only that, but –

HONEYMAN: Wait wait wait! Scroll back a bit ... Something you mentioned a moment ago requires unpacking. Personal reasons? What did you mean by that?

STENOGRAPHER: I'm Derek Noone's granddaughter ...

HONEYMAN: [...]

TAYLOR: [...]

STENOGRAPHER: ... and according to Stenographer family lore, in which I believe implicitly, Mr Inkling had him killed.

HONEYMAN: That's impossible. Inconceivable. It goes against everything I know about Mr Noone, *absolutely everything*. I've done the research, which, let me remind you, was praised for its meticulousness and accuracy by Deputy Assistant Commissioner Starkey, which is why I was inducted, though press-ganged is perhaps more accurate, into the WPS.

As I discovered, not without some difficulty, Derek Noone had a morbid fear of women. And not just women, the female sex in general. He wouldn't have anything to do with them. Wouldn't even, as a child, pat his uncle Teddy's ultra-friendly dog, a bullmastiff dam by the name of Lulu whose kennel name was Ladybug Rampton-Bassetlaw Splendiferous. That's how deep my research went, down down down into the depths of Derek Noone's twisted psyche, where monsters scream and thrash around in the dark and the air reeks of lactated milk and menstrual blood.

And that's why what you're saying is inconceivable. He simply couldn't have had a daughter, never mind a grand-daughter.

STENOGRAPHER: Oh yes he could, and did. I'm she, the grand-daughter in question, whether you like it or not. I may never have met him but I know all about him, which is obviously more than you can say as you don't seem to know hardly anything of what I know.

HONEYMAN: Then shouldn't you have recused yourself? There seems to be a clear conflict of interest, and your state-ment that 'according to Stenographer family lore, in which I believe implicitly, Mr Inkling had him killed' shows, if I may say so, a distinct and worrying lack of impartiality.

STENOGRAPHER: Recusals are for judges only, not stenographers.

HONEYMAN: Not even a stenographer standing in for an indis-posed judge? Or one, such as Mr Squiggle, who has been ousted?

STENOGRAPHER: It's never happened before. Not to my knowl-edge. If it makes you feel any happier, I swear my sum-ming up will be based exclusively on evidence the court has heard – by which I mean reliable evidence, precious little of it though there is. Personal feelings will be set aside and bias scrupulously avoided. That's something you wouldn't have got from Mr ~~~, no matter how strenuous his assertions of impartiality. Take, for exam-ple, what he told Dr Anon:

Mr Inkling is, he said (I'm paraphrasing a bit), *a good friend of mine, a very good friend, from whom I've received favours galore.*

Damned out of his own mouth. And if that didn't set alarm bells ringing, the account he then gave of his pal-cum-benefactor was of such honeyed sycophancy I'm surprised it didn't instantly rot his teeth down to blackened stumps or pitch Dr Anon into a diabetic coma.

TAYLOR: Perhaps that's what finally did for him. Dr Anon, I mean.

HONEYMAN: It would be prudent to wait for the autopsy report rather than jump to conclusions based on mere supposition. But you're probably right.

STENOGRAPHER: Mr Inkling was, said Mr ~~~, 'a sweetie, versatile, a quick thinker, a game changer'. Those, in my humble opinion, are the words of a brown-noser, a lizard-tongued lickspittle.

HONEYMAN: A toady in the hole, you might say.

TAYLOR: Although, to be fair, he also said some pretty harsh things about Mr Inkling during the course of the trial.

HONEYMAN: Ah, but did he really mean those things or was he playing Devil's advocate?

STENOGRAPHER: Or was he trying to level the playing field, having regretted giving what can only be described as a ringing endorsement? We'll probably never know. But with recusal in mind, let's be clear on where we stand vis-à-vis the murder –

HONEYMAN: *Alleged* murder, Miss Stenographer.

STENOGRAPHER: Alleged? Oh no. Put the weasel word back in its cage, Mr H. My grandfather, Derek Noone, was murdered. No doubt about it. And the man who murdered him, personally or by proxy, was his longtime friend and business partner, Jimmy Jewels.

HONEYMAN: You may, of course, think that, but –

STENOGRAPHER: Let's call a spade a spade, eh? The spade that is, so I've heard, Mr Inkling's weapon of choice. A proper skull-splitter if applied correctly.

TAYLOR: I don't know where you get your info from, but I'm impressed, it's top drawer. He joked that both his golf swing and spade swing were similar in that they had to be practised regularly to keep his shoulders flexible and aim true. He practised on pumpkins and other large squashes into which the faces of his enemies had been carved by a Turner Prize nominee he kept on retainer. Split them right down the middle with a single mighty blow. Whumph! Accurate to within three millimetres of dead centre and invariably plumb-line vertical. Were pumpkin cleavage to be introduced as an olympic sport, he'd be a shoo-in for gold.

To be honest, his golf game wasn't in the same league. I mean, how could it be? A typical score being 110 or thereabouts. But he cheated, often blatantly, to compensate for his lack of skill, hoping that his opponent would call him out and an argument or a scuffle would ensue. Always relished a ruck did Mr Inkling. It was his way of letting off steam and testing loyalty. He played golf only with underworld associates he suspected were skimming off his margin or cutting deals behind his back. He wanted to see whether they'd turn a blind eye to his cheating. Those that did – the cravens, so-called – were despised by Mr Inkling but kept on the payroll. Their uppityness wasn't deemed a significant threat and their greed could easily be kept in check. The others, the ones who accused him of cheating, were given a thorough going over, physically and financially, one they weren't likely to forget in a hurry, even after the wounds had healed and the scars began to fade. Several of them skipped town and melted into the greater criminal underworld, their oyster. One or two simply disappeared, mysteriously, never to be seen or heard from again.

> Shooting the rapids
> on a leaf and
> a twig
> the fate
> of many a luckless
> earwig.

‒ Kafka juvenilia
[allegedly]
said to have been spirited away
by person
or persons unknown
from Max Brod's
extensive archive in Tel Aviv
while his secretary
Esther Hoffe
was powdering her nose.

HONEYMAN: How do you know all this, Mr Taylor?

TAYLOR: Saw it with my own two eyes, and on more than one occasion. As I said earlier, Mr Inkling's bonehead operatives frequently dragged me out of bed at Vale Hall and drove me up to London, usually to The Marbles or Canary Wharf, sometimes still wearing a sleep mask and clad in nothing but jimjams, to satisfy his desperate need for company in the wee small hours.

And sometimes the wee small hours were neither wee nor small. Often enough, too often for my liking, I was held captive, deprived of sleep, living for days on end as Mr Inkling did on a diet of whisky and amphetamines. Had the authorities discovered what was going on, he would have faced charges of kidnapping and serious illegal detention. Only in Kyrgyzstan would such things be considered trivial.

HONEYMAN: What's so special about Kyrgyzstan? In that regard, I mean.

TAYLOR: I thought everyone knew. You don't? ... You really don't?

HONEYMAN: I assure you I don't.

STENOGRAPHER: Me neither.

TAYLOR: Okay then, I'll enlighten you. If, in the wilds of Kyrgyzstan (and even occasionally in urban areas such as Bishkek), a man kidnaps a woman to take her as his bride, the law against kidnapping is rarely enforced.

Offering a small bribe to a petty official is usually all it takes to smooth things over. Admittedly that scenario wouldn't strictly apply to me and Mr Inkling, even if we were living in Kyrgyzstan. I don't think I've ever been suitable bride material, nor, if I can help it, am I ever likely to be. Especially after having been kidnapped. As I soon discovered, being kidnapped made me crotchety.

HONEYMAN: More crotchety than usual?

TAYLOR: I'm not usually crotchety, Mr Honeyman. Far from it. Mr Inkling just rubbed me up the wrong way.

HONEYMAN: No offense meant. Let me rephrase that. More than averagely crotchety, taking, let's say, Mr Squiggle as the median?

TAYLOR: I'm not sure he's an appropriate median – or, for that matter, medium – but yes, much more. You wouldn't believe how much. Let's face it, who wouldn't be? Not that Mr Inkling cared a damn. He wanted me to shadow him at all times, going wherever he went, including, on occasion, the bathroom, and if I didn't like it, so what! If he took a nap – which, most afternoons, he did, because he rarely slept at night – I had to sit on a hard chair by his daybed and force myself to stay awake, matchsticks propping up my eyelids, pen poised, just in case he mumbled something important in his sleep.

That was before I broke my coccyx, of course; after which, hard chairs were a no-no without the intervention of a doughnut cushion, and even then the pain of sitting for any length of time would almost certainly have kept me wide awake.

I also had strict instructions to log Mr Inkling's snores, their duration and volume, I've no idea why. Perhaps for no other reason than to prove I'd remained vigilant. But mostly I faked the log and it didn't seem to matter. I mean really, why would it?

And while he was awake I was expected to match him

drink for drink, from breakfast to bedtime. That's something he insisted on, even though his capacity for alcohol was huge and mine of pipsqueak proportions.

By the way, it's worth noting that I rarely saw him hungover, though my own fierce hangovers may have blinded me to his suffering. I was, in fact, on one occasion, actually blinded, literally, after we'd both consumed wood alcohol topped up with what he said was an 'artisanal brujo brew', something called ayahuasca, a bitter concoction we had trouble keeping down. That was in a yurt deep in Epping Forest – the yurt I think I mentioned earlier, where the CCTV camera followed me.

Initially, because Mr Inkling was in an absolutely foul mood, I thought I was going to be killed and my body dumped in a shallow grave. Why otherwise had he brought along his favourite spade, the one his enemies said he slept with, the so-called 'iron wife'. But no, we were there, he said, of necessity, to undergo a purge. Purged of what and for why, I had no idea. He didn't explain and I didn't ask. But I certainly wasn't going to dig my own grave, bugger that for a lark, even if he said pretty please.

Anyway, within a few minutes of taking the ayahuasca we began to suffer horribly from dyspepsia and the squits. Then, without warning, my eyesight went, which scared the living daylights out of me. That's when the hallucinations kicked in. Bad hallucinations. Truly terrifying. Let me tell you, there are things far worse than death and this was one of them. After what seemed like an hour or more, the screaming – me mostly, though Mr Inkling probably did his fair share – stopped, simply because we were too exhausted to continue. The rest of our time in the yurt was spent writhing around, sweating, groaning piteously and filling our moleskin breeks with blasts of watery shit.

Next morning, back at Canary Wharf, my sight began

to return. Nothing but hazy black and white shapes at first. But I can't even begin to tell you how relieved I was.

We sat at one end of the long boardroom table and pushed a full English breakfast around on our plates until it began to congeal. Neither of us felt able to eat, we were still too fragile. Nor did we have much to say, which is just as well; our throats were painfully raw, voices hoarse and whispery from all that screaming.

Anyway, that's when he said – rasped, croaked – that now we'd been cleansed of our demons and were, as it were, on the same page, I was to be the Boswell to his Johnson. (Not, by the way, a euphemism for a sexual act.) My task, he explained, would be to write down everything he said and did, so posterity would know what kind of man he was. You would have thought that was something he'd want to avoid at all cost, but human foibles never cease to amaze me, vanity above all else. At such times I thank God I'm a god.

What I gathered was that, with immediate effect, I was to be given access to every nook and cranny of his life, including the deepest, darkest, cobwebby corners where things had gone to die. Those were places I didn't really want to look, or didn't want to be seen to be looking, not if it gave him the slightest satisfaction. But I didn't dare say no to his proposal – which wasn't really a proposal, more an order he expected to be obeyed unquestioningly. What choice did I have? It was either that or face the firing squad.

HONEYMAN: An actual firing squad?

TAYLOR: Just a figure of speech, though I wouldn't put it past him. — But no, on second thoughts, a firing squad is too ostentatious. Discretion is his watchword and he's cautious to a fault, which is why he's managed to evade the forces of law and order for so long. So a triggerman, a button man, just one. But then again, shooting can be a noisy, messy business compared to Ingo Peck and the eels. Yes, that's probably how I'd end my days: slaughtered by Peck and turned into eel fodder. But if Mr Inkling were to condemn me to death, I'd rather be shot than fed to the eels, they and their keeper give me the creeps.

HONEYMAN: But you'd be dead by the time the eels got to you.

TAYLOR: That's not the point. Anyway, as I was saying, my role as a two-bit Boswell was a fait accompli. No point grumbling; best just get on with it.

We began our collaboration the very next day. Using a spy mirror, I observed how he chaired a meeting in the boardroom at Canary Wharf – which, needless to say, was bugged. I was locked in an adjoining room that was disguised as a broom cupboard and told to listen carefully and take notes. Mr Inkling explained beforehand that he often prefaced meetings with a few casual remarks about gardening, all the while honing the lateral edges of his spade to razor sharpness with a whetstone – and that's precisely what he did. He spoke, as if in a casual manner, of his enthusiasm for turning the sod and dead-heading faded blooms. Said he kept the soil well fertilized with large quantities of blood and bone, of which he had a limitless supply.

Because of a fawning feature in *House & Garden*, everyone knew there was a large, private rooftop terrace immediately overhead – or rather an interconnecting series of tiered terraces, pyramidal in shape, several storeys high, stocked with rare and exotic plants and tended by horticulturalists moonlighting from Kew. Comparisons had been made with the fabled Hanging Gardens of Babylon, which Mr Inkling modestly pooh-poohed.

But many of his business associates also knew he had absolutely no interest in the garden the horticulturalists had created for him, citing year-round allergic rhinitis (though he seemed remarkably untroubled by it when we were yurting and hallucinating deep in Epping Forest; and according to entries in his desk diary he enjoyed many a rhinitis-free hour on the golf course).

His coded remarks about blood, bone and dead-heading were, however, easily deciphered by everyone in the room, and the atmosphere was, to say the least, tense. By which I mean electric. No-one could bring themselves to look at the spade, its cutting edges glinting in the spotlight that Mr Inkling had trained on it. As he spoke, he turned the spade head this way and that, admiring his handiwork.

The minute I got home I burned the notes in the barbeque pit and urinated on the ashes. It was, I admit, an act of childish rebellion, little more than a tantrum. But it made me feel good about myself, or at least a bit better. The peculiar thing was, Mr Inkling never asked to see what I'd written.

HONEYMAN: Just as well, really. But one wonders why a notorious control freak such as he should be so lackadaisical. It seems completely out of character.

TAYLOR: Quite. One can only assume –

STENOGRAPHER: Gentlemen, I'm sorry to interrupt.

TAYLOR: – given the circumstances –

HONEYMAN: So you should be. Mr Taylor's narrative is fast approaching maximum speed, and he has such a full head of steam you can almost see it coming out of his ears.

TAYLOR: – that –

HONEYMAN: He's stoked, in other words. Now's not the time to damp down the firebox and slam on the brakes.

TAYLOR: – that he thought I was broken in spirit, subservient, unable to stand up to him. Fat lot he knew.

STENOGRAPHER: Actually, just to set the record straight, Mr Honeyman, you were the one who first interrupted him, not me. But let's move on. The situation is as it is and this is how I see it. It's too late for Mr Taylor's spade-related testimony to be included in the body of evidence. And as for my grandfather's murder, which we were discussing just a moment ago, that wasn't even hinted at during the proceedings, therefore it too can have no bearing on or relevance to my summing up. Are we agreed?

HONEYMAN: I'm no legal expert, far from it. During the last decade I've barely glanced at the Prosecution of Offences Act 1985, not since Jasper was taken to court for shoplifting, though for a while it took precedence over the books on my nightstand. Jasper confessed, in all, to thirty-seven offences: an anguished cry for help if ever there was one. Why else would he try to steal items so ludicrously hard to conceal about his person: sofa cushions, an ironing board, a flat-pack shelving unit.

As for criminal procedure, I know very little about it, though I wasn't about to say so to that nincompoop Mr Squiggle. — What's your opinion, Mr Taylor? This is tricky terrain we find ourselves in, all brambles, quagmire and unexploded ordnance. Should we forge ahead, boldly, with God on our side?

TAYLOR: With or without, time will trundle on regardless, steamrollering everything in its path. Reality, as perceived, is so depressingly linear. One yearns for the temporal folds and parallel universes that science fiction writers and theoretical physicists escape into, somewhere we could hide without risk of being found and dragged back kicking and screaming to face the music (if there's music to be faced, which there nearly always is).

Miss Stenographer's summing up will, one hopes, if nothing else, soothe our shattered nerves and provide suitable distraction while Mr Inkling's miserable life ebbs away. Assuming that he isn't dead already. Not that a summing up is necessary given that our jury, Dr Anon, having undertaken an earlier crossing with Charon, is oblivious to everything we say or do.

HONEYMAN: As a psychic medium in regular communication with the dead, Mr Squiggle would probably say otherwise.

STENOGRAPHER: Fuck's sake, *who cares!* Let the poor deluded numpty say whatever he likes. He's toast. Burnt toast, at that. In a living hell of his own making, flames licking all around him.

HONEYMAN: Then perhaps, if a summing up is no longer required, perhaps you'd be kind enough to tell us why you think Derek Noone is your grandfather.

STENOGRAPHER: My mother told me.

HONEYMAN: Good. No, strike that. Excellent. As solid a piece of hearsay as one could wish for. Incontrovertible. Yet at the same time woefully inadequate. Would you care to put flesh on the bones? Perhaps offer some evidence to bolster your claim, if indeed you have any?

STENOGRAPHER: Don't be such a snarky-puss, Mr Honeyman. Every last bit of what I'm about to tell you can be corroborated. But, as you're well aware, we don't have time to seek corroboration, so you'll just have to take my word for it.

HONEYMAN: Mr Taylor, pass the salt. I suspect I'll be needing a large pinch or two. Actually, make that a sack.

STENOGRAPHER: Have you finished? Christ almighty, I do hope so. You're being extremely tiresome, which seems to be your default setting. Look, here's how it is ... My maternal grandfather, bless him, couldn't make, as it were, 'healthy wrigglies', so –

HONEYMAN: What, precisely, do you mean by 'healthy wrigglies'?

STENOGRAPHER: I think you know perfectly well what I mean.

HONEYMAN: For clarification.

STENOGRAPHER: Do you carry on like this at home? Your poor wife must be incredibly long-suffering. If I have to keep stopping to explain the bleedin' obvious we'll never reach the point where I actually get to tell you why I'm telling you this. Please, just ... if you'd *shut the fuck up*, just for one moment, and let me continue ...

HONEYMAN: [...]

STENOGRAPHER: So ... with Grandpa's permission, my grandmother visited a fertility clinic on Great Marlborough Street, one of the first of its kind to be licensed in the UK. That was in late March or April 1966. Four decades later it became possible to obtain key donor info that had previously been withheld, so Mum requested further details of her biological father, the man she'd always referred to, among those in the know – close family only, needless to say – as Mr Spunky.

What she received from the HFEA (Human Fertilisation & Embryology Authority) was unexpected: the full monty, i.e. an unredacted file. Probably sent that way in error, but who's complaining?

Gran's donor had registered at the clinic under the name Derek Mannazzu, and his last known address was a street in Ajaccio, Corsica. But he wasn't Corsican, or not entirely, despite the surname. He was described as pale-skinned, forty years old (he was actually forty-eight), six foot two, twelve stone three pounds, of slim build, with regular features, a full, dark head of hair and soulful (yes, soulful, I kid you not) brown eyes. Marital status: single. No children. Religion: none (though 'none' had been crossed out, and someone, in a different shade of ink, had written 'Christian').

TAYLOR: Ah yes, in those days religious affiliation was conferred at birth and stayed with you forever, like it or not.

STENOGRAPHER: The doctor who carried out the medical check gave Mannazzu a clean bill of health. Most importantly, there was no evidence of venereal disease. The box in which a goodwill message could be left for a child potentially conceived from the donor's sperm – i.e. wrigglies – was empty.

His name seemed strangely familiar, though Gran couldn't think why. But Mum recognised it immediately. I wonder, she said, whether that's Deke Mannazzu, you know, *the* Deke Mannazzu, aka The Great Mannazzu –

HONEYMAN: Never heard of him.

STENOGRAPHER: – the magician who shot up the showbiz ladder to dizzy heights (I later discovered that on the very day he donated the sperm that impregnated Gran he'd been booked to do a spot on *Sunday Night at the London Palladium* – not as the headliner, admittedly, but third on the bill, below the inestimable Dora Bryan and the now all-but-forgotten Mary Kaye Trio), before performing the most surprising trick of his career: he sacked his agent, cancelled his engagements and disappeared, all within a few short hours and without the slightest warning.

When, a few days later, a policeman called round at Mannazzu's Soho flat, the door was on the latch, as if he'd just stepped out for a moment. There was a half-eaten meal on the table, lights on in the kitchen and hallway, ciggies and matches in a jacket pocket, the jacket draped over the arm of a chair, the chair facing the gas fire (which was, according to the unusually thorough Missing Persons report, burbling away at its lowest setting – Miser Rate). The newspapers couldn't get enough of it, and speculation as to Mannazzu's whereabouts was rife. A silly rumour was floated in the press, and taken up by a mad gaggle of conspiracy theorists, that he'd been kidnapped by members of the Magic Circle hell-bent on learning the secrets of his unique box of tricks.

Knowledge of which
has been lost.
None of Mannazzu's
performances were filmed
and he left no written
record

<pre>
                    other than
                    a notebook
                    containing
               what was assumed to be
            depending on the commentator
             coded stagecraft information
                avant-garde poetry
                  or gibberish.
</pre>

According to the rumour, he'd died accidentally under torture or had, after telling his kidnappers all they needed to know, been killed in a ritualistic manner and his remains disposed of. But most of his showbiz colleagues knew he suffered terribly from agoraphobia, and that even playing larger venues

<pre>
            Between which he was transported
   in a specially adapted wardrobe-style steamer trunk
               into which as many of the
                  comforts of home
                    as possible
                  had been crammed:
       a well-padded armchair with a built-in commode
                  adventure novels
              a battery-powered reading lamp
       a fold-down shelf that could be used as a table
                   food and drink
                    soft pillows
               and an eiderdown duvet.
                  Also a ventilation
                   flap [Mannazzu
                 was a chain smoker].
</pre>

caused him considerable stress, so it was assumed he'd had some kind of breakdown.

TAYLOR: Perhaps all he wanted was a bit of peace and quiet. Away from the limelight. In a whitewashed house with small windows, the shutters permanently closed against oppressively dazzling sunlight. Hence Corsica.

STENOGRAPHER: That's exactly what Mum thought. She wrote him a letter, hoping he still lived in Ajaccio. A long shot but worth a try. Months passed. Nada. That's when she decided to check out Rue du Cardinal Fesch in person, to see who lived there.

She assumed there'd be a nameplate by the building's main door. And so there was: Hotel Bonaparte. A plaque above the threshold claimed that Napoleon stayed there in 1799, though the Bonaparte in question was probably his quarrelsome brother Lucien. But Napoleon's house was just round the corner, so, who knows, perhaps he popped into the hotel bar for a quick bro-bro catch-up and a glass of watered-down Burgundy wine, half and half, the way he liked it. Not much of a drinker was Napoleon. Apparently he was a stingy tipper too; abstemious in all things.

Of course the hotel wasn't called Bonaparte in those days, it was the Pasquino Corso. Not that it matters. The guest registers, which had recently been digitised all the way back to the 19th century, failed to cough up a Mannazzu. Nor, according to the propriétaire – an expat Brit from Ashby-de-la-Zouch who could hardly have been more helpful (I think he fancied Mum) – was Mannazzu a former member of staff.

In the meantime I'd been searching online and found a link to a blog, *The Deke Mannazzu Appreciation Society*.

TAYLOR: Forgive me for interrupting, and perhaps I'm being a bit slow, but … what's all this got to do with your alleged grandfather's alleged murder?

STENOGRAPHER: Hang on a sec, I'm getting to it.

HONEYMAN: Perhaps, instead of, as you say, getting to it, we should just pack up and go home. Mr Inkling is probably dead by now. What say you, Mr Taylor?

TAYLOR: How can one be sure? The gulf between life and death is vast and unfathomable.

STENOGRAPHER: Although the blog was dormant –

HONEYMAN: As is true by now of Mr Inkling, I hope.

STENOGRAPHER: – it contained a potted biography of Deke Mannazzu, aka The Great Mannazzu. And guess what? His real name was –

HONEYMAN: Noone. *Derek-bloody-Noone!* It was glaringly obvious what you were leading up to. You'd make a terrible comedienne: your premise wasn't sufficiently robust, the build-up was lacking in tension and suspense, and as for your timing – pah! – your timing was off. I mean badly. It, as they say nowadays, sucked ass, mega ass, more ass than a triceratops, contender for the fattest-assed dinosaur of them all. Consequently the punchline fell flat. Not much of a joke, really, was it? I assume it was a joke, you surely can't have been serious. — But enough's enough. While the going's good let's, to paraphrase the bard, hie we hither. Tiffany will be here at any moment. I'll scribble an apologetic note about the broken door and Dr Anon and leave a wad of cash to cover 'removal' expenses and repairs. According to Mr Squiggle she'll know what to do for the best. To be frank, she could probably get away with dumping Dr Anon in the back alley, behind the bins, for someone else to find. I mean, most of his clothes look like Oxfam relics, don't you think? Decades out of date and just plain shabby rather than shabby-chic. A bit grubby, too. And he could have done with a haircut several weeks ago. Not to mention those rogue eyebrows and the thickets growing out of his ears. Remove all identification and *voila!* he's a rough sleeper, familyless, friendless, someone who has fallen on hard times and slipped through the social care net, which as everyone knows has holes in it so large a shantungosaurus giganteus could pass through. But that's up to Tiffany. Let's mosey along – a Usain Bolt kind of moseying. Bed beckons. I swear, if I yawn any harder I'll disarticulate my jaw and turn my head inside out.

TAYLOR: I'm afraid I still don't understand. Why would Mr Inkling want to kill Mr Noone?

HONEYMAN: Please don't encourage her, Mr Taylor. We're in more than enough trouble as it is, even though our conduct has been beyond reproach. We were summoned here under false pretences to perform what we thought was our civic duty, but it was a total sham, or perhaps a scam, though it's hard to say what kind of scam and who the perpetrator might be. Then again, who else could it be but –

STENOGRAPHER: Mr Inkling –

HONEYMAN: Brava, Miss Stenographer! You took the words right out of my mouth.

STENOGRAPHER: – wanted –

HONEYMAN: Say no more! I know perfectly well what he wanted. I mean, now I come to think of it, it's blindingly obvious, isn't it? He wanted to get us to reveal how much we know about him, the incriminating stuff; and what better way to do it than by staging a mock trial, evidence given under oath, the so-called truth, whole truth and nothing but, which more often than not turns out, as we've established, to be *anything but.*

　　Even as we speak, Deputy Assistant Commissioner Starkey will be standing ('at ease, Starkey, at ease') by Mr Inkling's BUPA bedside, popping grapes into his mouth, slave-to-Roman-emperor style, and giving him the good news. And if not there they'll be settled in at Mr Inkling's penthouse, hugger-mugger, thick as thieves, clinking shot glasses and sipping a celebratory single malt, a Talisker from Skye, one of Mr Inkling's favourites, while monitoring our proceedings and drawing up a hit list.

　　Yes, of the two scenarios that's the most plausible.

　　And Mr Squiggle will have joined them, of course. He had to have been in on the conspiracy; they couldn't have hoped to pull this off without him. All that gushing praise he came out with that later he regretted and tried to squelch. But the squelching rang hollow compared to the praise.

What can we deduce from this but that we've been fed a pack of lies? Despite the Deputy Assistant Commissioner's claim that Mr Inkling is about to, as they say, kick the bucket – cannot, in fact, fail to kick the bucket, and with immediate effect – it's unlikely that he's come down with so much as a sniffle, never mind been hospitalised. I suspect he's remarkably fit and well, as always, and given what we know of his methods he'll have made plans to eliminate us, one by one, the minute we go our separate ways.

Perhaps we're already dying, even though the symptoms are, as yet, so mild they're barely noticeable – a slight twinge, an ill-defined ache, a feeling of disquiet that admits of no known source.

It's possible we've been poisoned: a slow-acting poison that one of his operatives – the woman technician who was here yesterday, or someone (perhaps, I wouldn't put it past him, Mr Inkling himself) disguised as a woman in the garb of a technician – slipped into the water supply; a poison derived from something piscean, puffer fish venom or suchlike, that in the process of killing us induces creeping paranoia bolstered by hallucinations that bend reality subtly out of shape; a poison that goes about its business in such an insidious manner (as, no mere coincidence, does Mr Inkling) we probably won't know what's happening until it's happened, by which time it'll be too late to do a damn thing about it.

STENOGRAPHER: For heaven's sake, Mr Honeyman, that's not what I'm on about. If you'd just let me explain ...

HONEYMAN: [...]

STENOGRAPHER: What Mr Inkling wanted to do was kill Derek Noone, and in a fit of volcanic rage that's precisely what he did.

[304]

HONEYMAN: So you keep saying. Except for the rage bit – that's new. Suspiciously new. You're making it up as you go along, aren't you?

TAYLOR: Look here ... I'm afraid I still don't understand why –

STENOGRAPHER: Because it's the truth.

TAYLOR: That's not what I meant. Why on earth would Mr Inkling want to kill Mr Noone? Weren't they best pals from way back when?

STENOGRAPHER: Because of the ReproSolutions scandal, that's why. Or near-scandal. A scandal narrowly averted.

TAYLOR: Come again?

STENOGRAPHER: Didn't I mention it earlier? ReproSolutions – the name of the fertility clinic Gran visited. On the second floor of the building in Great Marlborough Street that also housed Mr Inkling's headquarters, which, at the time, was the jewel in the crown of his burgeoning property empire. The offices on the other floors were leased to various seemingly innocuous and unrelated businesses, in all of which he was either the majority shareholder or sole trader. That's what I found out from Companies House.

It seems that when The Great Mannazzu's career became untenable because of his crippling agoraphobia, he started to spend more and more time at HQ, training the high-quality pickpockets and purse snatchers of which Oxford Street, Piccadilly and the mainline train stations can never get enough. Eventually he began to sleep at HQ rather than face the ordeal of making his way home, even though he lived only a few streets away, off Golden Square. That's when the police found his flat abandoned and declared him a missing person.

Mr Inkling didn't know that's what was happening. Not at first, anyway. He just assumed his business partner was a stickler, conscientious to a fault: first in of a morning, last out at night. Noone had always been painstaking in his work, dotting the eyes and crossing the teas, making sure everything was as it should be, even if he had to burn the midnight oil to achieve it.

I suspect – from what I've been told by several Inkling ex-employees, all of whom wished to remain anonymous (as would you were you in their shoes), and by joining the dots between one apparently disparate fact and the next, like the stars that make up Orion the Hunter or the Plough – that from 1966 until the day he died Derek Noone never once ventured outdoors, not even to nip down the road, hugging the facades of the buildings like a crab edging along the foot of a cliff, to the nearest pub, the Shakespeares Head, for a swift half and twenty, more likely sixty, Benson & Hedges.

The other thing Mr Inkling didn't know was what transpired after office hours when Noone was alone in the building. Because he had keys to every lock in ReproSolutions (the freezer vault, filing cabinets and desk drawers included), Noone could, if he so wished, venture onto the premises and avail himself of the 'facilities' – girlie mags and the like.

Also known as:
tit mags
porn mags
jazz mags
stiffy mags
jerk mags
skin mags
stroke mags
spurt mags
spatter mags
and
sticky pages.
Generically:
wank fodder.
Herewith

terms used
throughout Greater London
during that grim epoch
to describe the models
in magazines
such as those
mentioned above:
jism Janes
jack-off Jennies
hot shooters
prick magnets
dick dollies
and
log enlargers.
Let's face it
those weren't
particularly
enlightened times.

Despite his fear and loathing of all things female, Derek Noone was by inclination heterosexual – although, as you said earlier, Mr Honeyman, a deeply, perhaps uniquely disturbed one.

Once he'd made that day's 'donation', he labelled it and stored it in the freezer. Then he completed the mandatory HFEA donor form. At first he used variations on his own details, then, a month or two later, he started using those of his dead male relatives, then showbiz acquaintances (Harry Worth, Kenneth Williams, Billy Dainty, Danny La Rue, et al.), then the names of characters in books he'd recently read (Holden Caulfield, Joe Gargery, Eustace Chisholm, Nero Wolfe, et al.), and finally, after several years, when his donations had topped the five hundred mark and he was desperate for attributions, he plucked names at random from newspapers and the London phone book. Each completed form he filed neatly among similar paperwork. At the end of every session he locked the filing cabinet and tidied up, removing all trace of his activities (soiled tissues, stray pubic hairs, etc.). When the ReproSolutions staff arrived the following morning, everything was, or seemed to be, exactly as they'd left it.

There was no reason for anyone to suspect that Noone was doing what he was doing. In fact, his nocturnal activities – more accurately: emissions – probably wouldn't have come to light were it not for a telephone tip-off Mr Inkling received, which probably went something like this …

HONEYMAN: Telephone call? Probably?

STENOGRAPHER: Speculation in accordance with how things were done in those days, Mr Honeyman. Joining the dots. Poetic license, if you prefer, and even if you don't. Hear me out. — An inspector, so said an informant, would be popping into ReproSolutions after lunch, unannounced, to check for HFEA compliance. A formality. No need to worry. Mr Inkling immediately hurried downstairs to check the ReproSolutions paperwork, to satisfy himself that everything was in order. It was. Commendably neat and tidy. Nothing skimped or out of place. But that, of course, wasn't the problem, as he recognised almost immediately.

For whatever reason, Noone had made little or no effort to cover his tracks. Nearly all of the spurious donor info, year upon year of it, had been entered by hand rather than typewritten, and the penmanship was unmistakably his. Worse still, it was a matter of record that from the thousands of donations he'd made under his own and various assumed names, one hundred and sixty-two children had been born, many of whom, once they reached adulthood, would become curious as to who their progenitor was.

Mr Inkling must have been stunned. The implications were huge. No, not just huge: catastrophic. Fending the claimants off at ReproSolutions, via the HFEA, would, to say the least, become a major headache in years to come, especially when many of them found out what Mr Inkling already knew: that, like Derek Noone, they were probably suffering from a rare genetic disorder. Inevitably some grubby little ambulance-chaser from the litigation specialists Weasel, Weasel and Weasel would get involved and a class action suit would follow.

Because ReproSolutions was wholly liable, and the business was registered in his name, Mr Inkling would be taken to court and ruined. Compensation payouts would run to the tens of millions. But that wasn't the worst of it. Confidence in him would falter and perhaps fail entirely. His sterling reputation in the City of London, something hard won, that money can't buy –

HONEYMAN: Don't count on it.

STENOGRAPHER: – would be dragged through the mud and/or ripped to shreds, whichever you prefer.

HONEYMAN: Let's have both. Nothing is too good for Mr Inkling.

TAYLOR: This genetic disorder …

STENOGRAPHER: Lynch Syndrome. Hereditary nonpolyposis colorectal cancer, known to its friends – assuming it has any, which is unlikely – as HNPCC. It can also cause breast and prostate cancer, though there's a much greater risk of developing gastric cancer, ovarian cancer, small bowel cancer, pancreatic cancer, ureter and renal pelvis cancers, kidney cancer, bile duct cancer, as well as skin tumours (sebaceous adenomas) and brain tumours.

Apart from hair
nails and teeth
there's a cancer assigned to every
part of the human body.
Even
[though rare]
the heart.

According to Srinivasa Ramanujan
[or someone
claiming to speak for him]
the principal cause of
that cancer
is love.
This dour and cynical
pronouncement
most untypical of Ramanujan
may be
attributable
to a poor translation
from Tamil
to English.
Or misrepresentation.
Or aggravated by a discomforting
physical complaint:
the hydrocele testis
from which he suffered
that resulted in an enlarged scrotum
and caused soreness and
inconvenience
[and perhaps nervous impotence]
during lovemaking
in the early years
of his married life.
As regards the hydrocele
although surgery was successful
Ramanujan died without issue.

My mother wasn't a carrier of the faulty gene and neither am I. But because Mr Noone was, there's every reason to believe his agoraphobia and increasingly aberrant behaviour were symptoms of an undiagnosed brain tumour.

Brain tumours and colon cancer ran in the Noone family, rarely skipping a generation. Few of his close relatives survived long enough to celebrate their sixtieth birthday, and those who did did so from a hospice bed or wired up to life support. Imagine singing Happy Birthday to the ponderous beep-beep-beep of a heart monitor. Not much cause for celebration there. No wonder they were such an unremittingly dour lot. That's also probably why Noone never smiled, not even in Great Mannazzu head shots. It was assumed that he was embarrassed by his tombstone teeth, but, let's face it, he didn't really have much to smile about. At the time of his murder he was fifty-eight years old. The last few grains of sand were about to run through the hourglass. If Mr Inkling had waited just a year or two more, rather than flying off the handle and taking matters – and 'iron wife'? – into his own hands, nature would have taken its course and solved the Noone problem for him.

But anyway, when Mr Inkling realised what had been going on, he whisked the paperwork off to a print workshop near Waterloo and a note was pinned to the ReproSolutions office door: *Sorry – closed today due to staff illness*. It proved to be a particularly severe illness; no-one who worked there was heard from again.

HONEYMAN: Surely you're not suggesting they were, umm … despatched by Mr Inkling, are you? Either personally or at his behest?

STENOGRAPHER: They disappeared. That's all I know. I haven't a clue what became of them and speculation is, I'm sure you'll agree, a complete waste of time. Valuable time. So let's stick to the facts, such as they are.

What I learned from an anonymous source is that within a matter of days an entirely new set of ReproSolutions paperwork had been created by a team of master forgers. That's what the inspector saw and signed off on his return to Great Marlborough Street.

HONEYMAN: And the original documents, what became of them?

STENOGRAPHER: They're at home in a suitcase under the spare bed.

HONEYMAN: *They're what ...!*

STENOGRAPHER: Under the bed in the boxroom that's next to the airing cupboard at the top of the stairs. In a battered old brown leather suitcase with one broken clasp. At home – i.e. the place where, according to the electoral roll, I formally reside with my new partner, Gareth, a tall, unathletic web designer. The suitcase is tightly bound with blue nylon twine, wrapped widthways not twice but thrice and knotted in a double carrick bend, something I learned at Girl Guides. I thought I'd made that abundantly clear. The details were implied in the outline phrase: 'They're at home in a suitcase under the bed'. Perhaps you weren't listening carefully enough, something you're prone to.

HONEYMAN: We're all dead on our feet, what do you expect?

TAYLOR: Dead men walking, you might say.

STENOGRAPHER: Ahem.

TAYLOR: Apologies, Miss Stenographer. I didn't mean to suggest that, although a female of the species, which you most certainly are, and, if I may say so, a particularly fine specimen of such, you weren't to be counted among our number.

HONEYMAN: I sincerely hope not, though. Dead men walking, I mean. Not if Mr Inkling himself is dead.

TAYLOR: That's a pretty big if.

HONEYMAN: It's the *if not* I'm more worried about.

TAYLOR: But how ... it seems inconceivable ... how did you manage to get hold of the ReproSolutions documents?

STENOGRAPHER: 'Easy peasy fart and sneezy', as Mr Usher put it. I was, I admit, as surprised as you are. Using information I received from a chancer my mother knew – an old boyfriend of hers (I think; she wouldn't be drawn), the anonymous source I mentioned earlier – I found the workshop in question without difficulty. It was situated on the edge of an industrial estate bordering a railway line. The estate was and still is owned by a subsidiary of a subsidiary of Inkling Inc. but has long since fallen into ruin. I snipped through the perimeter fence with wire cutters and easily pulled the mesh apart. Then I tackled the workshop door, which was warped and spongy with rot and posed even less of a challenge. I could have broken in with a toothpick, but I opted to use the tools I'd brought with me: a lump hammer and a cold chisel. Two light girlish taps in the right place was all it took.

It was obvious that no-one had entered the workshop for a very long time. Decades rather than years. Everything was covered in a thick layer of dust, the special kind of dust you find on or near railway lines: large, heavy flakes, greasy, black, like dystopian snow. The workshop was stacked almost ceiling high with ancient office equipment and broken furniture, and right at the back, in the darkest corner, we –

TAYLOR: We?

STENOGRAPHER: – Gareth and I –

TAYLOR: Ah.

STENOGRAPHER: – came across a dozen filing cabinets, some bare metal, some clad in cheap wood veneer, all but one unlocked. The locked cabinet had its face to the wall, as though ashamed. We shuffled it round, levered it open, and *hey presto!* there they were, the ReproSolutions papers. Mum's old boyfriend (I'm pretty sure that's what he was from the way she talked about him) said he'd been told to burn them but never got round to it and didn't think it would matter. His ignorance was bliss. I offered him a couple of ponies –

HONEYMAN: Horses of a small breed, below fifteen hands?

STENOGRAPHER: – fifty quid – and told him to keep schtum, for the good of his health. Not a threat, just a bit of friendly advice. Schtum, he said, he was happy to keep, since he was feeling a bit poorly anyway.

HONEYMAN: *Dear mother of god!* – I've just realised what you were up to. A do or die operation, with die being the most likely outcome. *You were going to blackmail him, weren't you? Mr Inkling! Of all people!* You'd threaten to go to the press or the police with the ReproSolutions paperwork unless he agreed to buy it from you, one Derek Noone donation at a time: a steady drip drip drip of cash into your bank account, swelling the coffers, setting you and Garth –

STENOGRAPHER: Gareth.

HONEYMAN: Yes. Gareth. Setting you and Gareth up for life in, as they say, the lap of luxury. Well it's too late for that, Missy, your criminal plan has been scuppered. With Mr Inkling gone there's no-one to blackmail.

TAYLOR: Assuming he's actually gone …

HONEYMAN: Of course he's gone!

STENOGRAPHER: That's not what you said a moment ago.

HONEYMAN: I was erring on the side of caution, as one must with Mr Inkling. But he's gone, dead, he just *is* – I can feel it in my bones.

TAYLOR: Then why prevaricate? Let's go home and get some well-earned rest. It's been a long, gruelling night and, not to put too fine a point on it, an absolute fucking nightmare from start to finish. If indeed it has finished. And isn't that Tiffany I hear pottering about in the kitchen? We'd better get going. She'll be absolutely livid when she sees the state we've left the place in.

STENOGRAPHER: But what if Mr Inkling is still alive, then what?

HONEYMAN: Then, my dear, we're utterly fucked.

STENOGRAPHER: And if he's dead?

HONEYMAN: We're still fucked. Time will take care of that.

TAYLOR: To think that Mr Squiggle, as you call him, had you pegged as a yayer.

HONEYMAN: Well, it just goes to show how wrong he was, as most of us are, most of the time. But he in particular, despite his claim to be a god.

TAYLOR: We're not always terribly strong on omniscience, we gods, despite our reputation –

HONEYMAN: So it would seem.

TAYLOR: – but I did have the foresight, during the last recess, to remove all the cash from Dr Anon's wallet. Banknotes only. There's enough to recompense Tiffany, splash out on a full English breakfast for three at Snowies, and provide cabs to take us home – or, in your case, Mr Honeyman, the Athenaeum. So let's, you know …

HONEYMAN: I know. Do you know, Miss Stenographer?

STENOGRAPHER: I do.

HONEYMAN: I bet you say that to all the boys.

Also available from grand**IOTA**

WILD METRICS
Ken Edwards

1970s London: short-life communal living, the beginnings of the alt-poetry scene, not forgetting sex, drugs and rock'n'roll. Forty years on: where have the wild metrics of those days taken us?

This prose extravaganza dives into the inscrutable forking paths of memory, questions what poetry is, and concludes that the author cannot know what he is doing. Among the cast of characters are a Rock Star who has become a national treasure, a bunch of poets and writers, some now legends, and assorted other misfits and malcontents. Some names have been changed.

"The impact is similar to some serial music, cumulative and entrancing. The reader is drawn into the artifice and drama of speech acts. There is sometimes a sense of inevitability to the conclusion, a sort of rounded closure, as if the text were on a loop. Other endings are much less predictable."
– DAVID CADDY, on Ken Edwards' *a book with no name*

978-1-874400-74-5 244pp   £10

Production of this book has been made possible with the help of the following individuals and organisations who subscribed in advance:

Peter Bamfield
Peter Barry
Christopher Beckett
Andrew Brewerton
Ian Brinton
Jasper Brinton
Lee Ann Brown
Peter Brown
Mark Callan
Claire Crowther
Elaine Edwards
Gareth Farmer
Allen Fisher
James Flannery
Jim Goar
Paul A Green
Charles Hadfield
John Hall
Andrew Hamilton
Robert Hampson
Randolph Healy
Peter Hodgkiss
Rob Holloway
Anthony Howell
Peter Hughes
Richard Makin
Michael Mann
JCC Mays
Ian McMillan
David Miller
English Dept, Princeton University
Lou Rowan
Aidan Semmens
Valerie Soar
Keith Tuma
Visual Associations
Alastair Wilson
Anonymous x 5

www.grandiota.co.uk